Tejano

Master of the Wild, Book 3

J. Bradley Van Tighem

Dedication

To my loving father, who was always there for me.

Jean "Jack" Van Tighem

Acknowledgments

This story has been two-year endeavor with numerous contributions from friends and family. Any contribution, however large or small, was invaluable in helping me to complete this work. My heartfelt thanks goes out especially to these individuals:

A big thanks to the folks at NaNoWriMo, who provide a wonderful forum for creating early manuscripts and supporting authors. Most of *Tejano* was written in two November sessions of NaNoWriMo.

My illustrator, Kip Ayers, for his excellent depiction of Ramon Connelly, which became the cover. Thanks for working quickly and professionally.

My editor, David Gatewood, for many painstaking hours turning my creative chicken scratches into a readable manuscript, leaving no "t" uncrossed or "i" undotted.

My writing group: Amber-Rose Reed, Kerry Granshaw, Nathan Jackson, and Brandan Merrick. The story, the characters, the words are infinitely more interesting, believable, and entertaining thanks to your invaluable contributions.

And finally, special thanks to my wife, Lyn, and my sons, Jason and Aaron, for their unending love and support of my writing endeavors.

Contents

Glossary

aaa-hey: Comanche victory cry: *I claim it!*

ahpu: father

big-headed lizard: collared lizard or mountain boomer

bird-killer: short-winged hawk (accipiter) (also known as Cooper's hawk, goshawk, sharp-shinned hawk)

haa: yes

Lipan: an Apache band

Mescolero: an Apache band

nami: little sister

namunewapi: important person

Navoonah: Apache (the Enemy); what Comanches call Apaches

Nokoni: a Comanche band (the Wanderers)

Noomah: the Comanche (the People); what they call themselves

Northerner (*norteño*): the Comanche (from Apache or Mexican perspective)

nupetsu: wife

old man-beast: grizzly bear

paraibo: peace leader

Penateka: a Comanche band (the Honey Eaters)

pole-drag: travois (wooden frame pulled by a horse or dog to carry supplies)

puha: spiritual power

running bird: roadrunner

samohpu: brother

shimaa: mother

taiboo: white-skinned soldier or person

tekwuniwapi: young warrior

ura: thank you

waha-nanisu: two-spirit

wolf hawk: Harris's hawk

The Early 1800s. Unsettled Texas.

Dama de Medina

It was fear that put food on Ramon Connelly's table and fear that put pesos in his pocket. For years, the residents of San Antonio lived in fear of attacks by *indios*. It was the Lipan Apaches who rained fear on them when he was young, but then the *norteños* came, the Comanches. He wasn't sure where the name "Comanche" had come from, but he knew it was an *indio* word for "enemy," and these Comanches were the enemy of the people he was paid to protect—people of mixed skin colors and cultures from the Mexican province of Tejas. *Tejanos.*

"Ramon, the Dama de Medina should be just over that hill," said Miguel Romero, nodding. Miguel was a tall, trim man in his early twenties, and the son of Eduardo Romero, one of the wealthiest men in San Antonio. Eduardo was also Ramon's employer, and regularly put pesos in Ramon's pocket. The standard rate for a hired hand was a peso per day, which included a hearty meal when the job was finished. Ramon's salary was usually double that.

Ramon nodded an acknowledgment, but did not look over at Miguel. His eyes were fixed on the grassy savanna ahead of them, dedicating extra attention to the small clumps of juniper and oak where men on horses could easily hide.

A chain of mules was tied to Miguel's horse. Riding behind them was Luis Cabrillo, one of Ramon's closest friends, also a popular hired hand for dangerous jobs. With his heavy build, Luis would easily lose a foot race with young girls, but he was as skilled as any *vaquero* on a horse, and better

1

than most with a gun. He wore a long, horseshoe mustache, and the rest of his face had not been recently shaven either. His parents were Isleños, like Ramon's mother, settlers from the Canary Islands; they had now been residents of San Antonio for more than twenty years, the entirety of Luis's life. His Isleño bloodlines conferred on him an elevated status, above the mestizos, mulattos, and *indios* of Bexar County, with San Antonio as its seat.

The three men—Ramon, Miguel, and Luis—were dressed like *vaqueros,* Mexican cowboys. Miguel and Luis wore the more traditional sombrero with a tall crown and a floppy brim, while Ramon's sombrero had a lower crown and a straight, flat brim—a *bolero.* All of them wore leather chaps, *chapareras,* and leather half-boots, *botas,* to protect their legs from the harsh landscape, which bred aggressive plants with prickly teeth that could bore through a man's skin like it was hot tallow.

"This place makes me nervous, Ramon," said Miguel. "Let's not waste any time loading up these *mulos* when we arrive at the *rancho.*"

Their job was to pick up several sacks of pecans and maize from the Dama de Medina, a *rancho* owned by the Francisco family, and deliver them to Eduardo Romero's store in San Antonio. Of all Romero's suppliers, this *rancho* was the farthest from the protection of the Presidio, which was located in the heart of town. Like most properties around San Antonio, the Dama de Medina was bordered on one side by the Rio Medina, which was a half a mile west of the three men, a landmark to keep them on course.

The men and their mules arrived at the top of a grassy hill overlooking the Franciscos' farmland. Groves of pecan trees surrounded recently harvested maize fields. Three adobe dwellings stood near the river on the western end of the property, large enough to house more than one family each. A plume of smoke rose from the largest one. Several roughly built *jacals*—one-room huts made from mud and mesquite—were also spread about the land, used as shelters for hired men or food storage.

The *rancho* was bustling with activity. Several men were loading sacks of maize onto an ox-pulled cart. Children were running and playing outside.

Two women were gathering water from a well.

As the three men neared the houses, the children stopped playing and waved at them. An older gentleman, dressed neatly in a red and black tailored outfit, approached them.

"*Buenos días*, Señor Connelly, you are right on time," said Don Carlos Francisco, the *patron* of the Dama de Medina. He was a heavyset man in his mid-fifties, with receding gray hair and a neatly trimmed gray beard. His voice was loud and deep, as would be expected from a man of his size.

"*Buenos días*, Don Carlos," said Ramon, waving and then dismounting. "It is much easier to travel before the Bexar heat is upon you."

Don Carlos directed one of the younger boys to take the men's horses, while another boy grabbed the chain of mules.

"May I take your *caballo*, señor?" one of the boys said to Ramon. "What is its name?"

"*Su nombre es Cavador*," replied Ramon. The name meant "Digger," because the horse loved to dig in the soil. Cavador was a light bay gelding with a long streak of white on his nose.

The boy laughed. "We used to have a dog with that name, señor. He was a funny dog who loved to dig up *mi madre's* flowers." He led the horse away.

"Don Eduardo is smart to hire Bexar's best men-at-arms to guard his investment," said Don Carlos as he shook Ramon's hand, then Luis's. Looking over his shoulder, he shouted to one of the woman near the well, "Leta, bring our guests some *agua*. They must be very thirsty." To Miguel he said, "I expect your family is well, Miguel?"

"*Sí*, Don Carlos. The store is prospering. My father bought another *rancho* this year, and our surplus bins of maize are filling up more and more each day."

"*Muy bien*, Miguel." Don Carlos led them toward the largest of the adobe houses. "Come inside, *mis amigos*. Leta has a pot of beans on the fire. You can relax while my men load the *mulos*."

"*Gracias*," said Ramon.

The four men washed their hands in the pot of water outside the door, then entered the large adobe lodge, which was divided into at least three rooms, from what Ramon could see. The entry led to a dining room with a large wooden table and several chairs. The cooking fire was located at the far end of the room.

A little girl joined them from one of the other rooms and spoke to Ramon. "May I take your hat, Señor Ramon?" She was very dark-skinned with long black hair, neatly combed, and she wore a long white dress with blue trim. Ramon guessed she was about seven years of age.

"*Gracias…*" Ramon had met her once before, but forgot her name.

"That is my youngest daughter, Rosarita," said Don Carlos. He touched the girl's head gently and smiled.

"*Gracias*, Rosarita," Ramon said, handing his hat to her.

Rosarita gathered the hats of all the men and hung them on a small wooden rack in the corner of the room. She placed cups, plates, and spoons on the table in front of each of them and then set a small basket filled with tortillas at the center of the table. When she was finished, she walked over to the cooking pot and stirred it gently.

"It will be a great relief to know my harvest is safe in Eduardo's store," Don Carlos said in a more serious tone. "I always hire extra men to help guard the *Dama* this time of year, because I know the *norteños* are watching. They want the sacks of maize and pecans for their winter stores."

"Have you had problems with them?" asked Ramon, wanting to know everything about any *indio* attacks in the area since his last visit a few months ago.

"No, it has been fairly quiet, Señor Connelly," said Don Carlos, while Leta served them water. "We have very few horses, and they want our crops only after they are bundled up in sacks. They kill some of our cattle every so often, but that is a small price to pay for our safety. We don't have enough men to guard the *ganado* every hour of every day."

"When did you last see them?" asked Luis, biting off a small piece of his tortilla, not waiting for their host to bless the meal.

"About a week ago, I saw a group of *indios* on the other side of the *rio*. They looked like *norteños*. Their faces and horses were painted in many colors." Don Carlos wiped away some of the water that had dripped down his chin. "They watched us for a short time, then rode away."

"How many of them, Don Carlos?" asked Luis, his voice a little more serious.

Ramon understood his friend's concern. On their trip from San Antonio, they had been no more than three men and seven empty mules. Nothing an *indio* would want. But the trip back to San Antonio would be much more dangerous, as they would be carrying the maize and pecans, and they would be unable to move quickly while escorting seven loaded pack animals.

"There were five or six *indios*," said Don Carlos. "They rode off almost as quickly as they came."

"Will any of your men come with us to San Antonio?" Don Eduardo would sometimes pay Don Carlos's hired men—any who cared to join them—to return with the party to San Antonio, but Ramon didn't know if that had been arranged for this trip. He was hoping for at least two more men.

"*Sí*, four of them will be joining you." Don Carlos smiled and nodded.

Ramon was relieved to hear that. "*Muy bien*," he said. "You can't have enough good men in *indio* country."

Leta took Ramon's wooden bowl, but before she could serve him he said, "Nothing for me, señora, *por favor*. I need a sharp mind on the trail. *Muchas gracias*." Ramon never ate a good-sized meal until after the job was done for the day.

She put Ramon's bowl away and proceeded to serve Luis and Miguel, then Don Carlos.

The patron of the Dama de Medina then led the blessing for the meal. "Let us pray to our Lord Jesus Christ, and to the Blessed Virgin Mother, not only for this meal, but to keep the men safe on the road to San Antonio."

Skirmish

The bright noon sun scorched the air as Ramon Connelly and his company—seven riders and seven loaded mules—began their long, dangerous journey back to San Antonio. Each man's provisions were checked before leaving the Dama de Medina: weapons, water, trail food. Ramon spoke with each of them about what was expected of them. He repeated over and over, "stay together," no matter what happened.

"These are the slowest *mulos* I have ever seen, Ramon," said Luis, watching the mules walk.

"*Sí*, Luis. We should have brought two or three more," said Ramon. He signaled for Luis to ride to the back of the mule chain. The *vaquero* leader removed his hat, combed his long, dark brown hair back away from his eyes, and then put his hat back on, tightening the chin string.

Ramon led the company, and Luis watched their backs. The other men were dispersed on either side of the mules. The pace was slow as they traversed the grassy hills around the Rio Medina, which was in plain sight on their right when it wasn't hidden by cypress trees. Whenever possible, Ramon liked to stay on high ground. He did not want to be blindsided, and fighting on high ground had benefits. He would take any advantage he could get from his surroundings—mud, wind, a sloping terrain—anything that could slow the speedy *norteño* war ponies.

All was quiet except for the clopping of hooves and the rush of the river. The men were silent, tense—too nervous even for casual conservation. The faint whiff of a Mexican cigar faded in and out of Ramon's senses as he rode back to check on his men. He noticed one of the hired men from the Dama de Medina was sipping on mescal. Ramon smelled the alcohol on his breath when he rode past. *This is how he deals with his fear.*

The line of horses and mules descended to flat prairie. Patches of oak and juniper dotted the landscape ahead of them, but mostly it was wide-open golden grassland, dried by the summer heat and lack of rain. A screeching red-tailed hawk circled high overhead in a cloudless, azure sky.

If we can reach Camino de los Tejas, *we will be safer*, Ramon thought. The soldiers patrolled that road, and their presence was a deterrent for *indio* attacks, though Ramon wondered how effective soldiers were against hard-fighting *norteños*. These soldiers earned a salary of three hundred pesos per year, regardless of what work they did, and they were typically enlisted for ten years. Ramon felt it made them lazy and unwilling to face danger, unless Colonel Esteban Tejada himself was present to command them. In his absence, their response was unpredictable.

Ramon's hopes for a quiet trip were dashed by Luis's whistle—a loud, high-pitched sound that Luis made by curling his lips and blowing hard. Ramon signaled the company to halt, then rode back to speak with Luis.

"Up there on the hill, Ramon," said Luis, pointing back at the hill that they had just come from. "They must be following us."

Indeed, on the hill, looking down at them, were several *indio* horsemen. They were too far away to see clearly, but Ramon could see the silhouettes of their shields and feather-tipped lances. Two of the riders wore headdresses. *norteños.*

"They're watching us, waiting for *terreno* that favors them." Ramon spit out a sunflower shell. *This flat grassland is perfect for their attack.*

Ramon turned his horse to face his men. "*Hombres*, it is time to earn your *dinero*." He looked at the fearful faces of his men as he cantered back and forth on Cavador. "Do not waste your *balas*. Shoot when you know you have the target in range. Do not try to shoot through their shields. Target their horses or their backs when they turn. Load quickly. A man with an unloaded gun is a dead man, and if I know that, then those horse *indios* sure as hell know it too. Stay together and make damn sure we have loaded weapons ready. Move toward those oak trees ahead. If we can get there, we'll have some cover."

The green-eyed leader then turned his attention to Miguel. "You lead the *mulos*. I'll need you to handle them when the fighting starts. Keep them behind us so they won't be easy targets." Ramon had promised Miguel's father that he would try to keep him away from the fighting.

"*Sí*, Ramon," said Miguel, grabbing the lead of the foremost mule.

Ramon circled back toward Luis to keep a close eye on the invaders. Ramon continued to scan the landscape around them in case other groups of *indios* were watching them. In his experience, the *norteños* stayed together in one fast-moving, ferocious pack.

The still air was shaken by the familiar, terrifying sound of war: the *norteño* war cries. *Now it starts.* Ramon watched as the *indio* riders launched their mounts downhill, spreading out into a line of attackers. "Ready your weapons! Miguel, move the *mulos* back!"

The war ponies quickly reached a full gallop. They were painted in a collage of many colors: white, black, and varying shades of brown. Their riders rode effortlessly, with bows or lances raised, screaming their bloodthirsty cries as their horses ate up ground, churning through dust and grass.

Ramon pulled the long gun from the scabbard on his saddle, a single-shot rifle, saving his two belted pistols and his *escopeta*, also tucked in his saddle, for close range. *Four shots.* He knew he must save his shots because his men wouldn't. *Empty guns will mean the death of us all.*

All the other men, except Luis and Miguel, had dismounted and were aiming their long guns. Some had rifles, and others, muskets. None of them could shoot from horseback like he or Luis could.

"Wait! Wait!" Ramon yelled, knowing the *norteños* were not yet in range of their weapons.

The *norteños* weaved their mounts toward them, separated by at least two or three horse lengths. Ramon could see their black-painted faces behind their large, circular, feather-adorned shields. Two of the riders toward the center of the line were bigger than the others, much bigger than the average *norteño,* who was short and stocky. One of them was shouting commands. Surely he must be the leader, Ramon thought. He heard the twang of bowstrings, then arrows whistled toward them. All fell short.

Three successive shots from the long guns filled the air with deafening sound and blinding smoke, but none of the *indios* fell. The startled horses of Ramon's men grunted and scrambled for footing. The mules tried to run away, but Miguel held them together.

"Reload!" Ramon yelled at the men who had fired.

The *indios* loosed more arrows. This time one of them struck—hitting a man who was reloading. He screamed out in pain, grabbing at the arrow protruding from his shoulder, and fell to the ground.

There were two more blasts, including one from Luis, and one of the *norteño* horses collapsed to the ground, casting off its rider. The fallen *norteño* gained his footing and started to run away.

"I got this one!" yelled one of Ramon's men. He dropped his rifle, mounted, and grabbed his pistol.

Ramon moved Cavador away from the suffocating smoke to see where this man was going. "Stay with us!" he yelled, but the *vaquero* hastened away in pursuit, even after discharging his weapon.

Ramon had a clear shot at the retreating *norteño,* so he stopped his horse and fired. His *bala* struck the *indio* in the back, knocking him to the ground. A moment later, he heard three quick shots from a bow, followed by the screams of the headstrong *vaquero* as he tumbled from his horse.

The *norteño* riders turned their horses around, except for one of the larger riders—the one who did not command them. He rode toward the fallen *indio,* reached down and pulled his injured companion up onto his horse with one swipe of his powerful arm, then rode back toward the rest of the war party. When he rejoined them, one of the other *norteños* took the wounded *indio* from him.

The big warrior looked back at Ramon's men and yelled out words in his people's language. Then he charged them again—alone.

When he was in long gun range, Ramon's two remaining men fired at him, but both of them missed the fast-moving target, who dodged like a sidewinder. The warrior shot an arrow that whizzed past Ramon's head and struck one of the mules behind him in the mid-section. Ramon was stunned by the speed and power of the arrow; it moved as if shot from a cannon instead of a bow.

Again the *norteño* reached down from his mount, but this time it was to pull the injured *vaquero* up onto his horse. The *indio* screamed and waved a large steel knife in the air with his right hand while holding the half-dead man with his left. He stripped the man's scalp off with one stroke of his gleaming weapon—then he swept his knife across the *vaquero's* throat and threw him to the ground, still riding at nearly full speed. His horse's neck was now covered with the *vaquero's* blood.

The warrior stopped his horse to look back at them, screaming "Ah-hey" and yelling something that sounded like "Ess-a-tay." *He is claiming the kill by yelling his name.*

Ramon felt powerless to help the *vaquero* or to fight this *norteño* warrior. His rifle was exhausted, and he didn't want to risk charging after this frightening *indio*. *Stay with the men.*

Then the *indio* galloped back to his war party, waving the bloody scalp. They welcomed him with victory cheers:

"Ess-a-tay!"

"Ess-a-tay!"

"Ess-a-tay!"

The *norteños* rode in circles around the big man, and then the leader directed them all back toward the hill from which they had come.

The gun smoke around Ramon's men drifted away.

"Is it over, Señor Ramon?" said one of the *vaqueros*. The moaning of the injured *vaquero*—the one who had taken an arrow to his shoulder—and the screams of the wounded mule made it difficult to hear.

"I don't know," Ramon shouted. "But make sure your weapons are loaded." The *norteños* seemed satisfied with their victory, he thought, at least for the moment. *Perhaps they wanted only scalps.*

Quickly, he reloaded his rifle, making sure to clean out the muzzle well. Then he rode over to the fallen mule, dismounted, and pulled out his pistol. "It isn't going to make it." He shot the mule in the head, silencing it. "Cut it free, Miguel, and leave it for the savages." The *norteños* were still watching them from the top of the hill.

"The sacks of maize also?"

"*Sí*, Miguel. Let it slow them down. It's too much of a burden for us now." Ramon hoped that leaving the maize would appease the *indios. Better to lose a few sacks of food then any more lives.*

Ramon walked over to the injured *vaquero.* Luis was trying to comfort the wounded man, but pain and fear had a relentless grip on him.

"Señor Ramon, don't let them take my scalp! Don't let them torture me!" yelled the frightened man, the right side of his chest stained with blood.

"*Como te llamas?*" said Ramon, looking down at the man. They had been introduced back at the Dama de Medina, but Ramon did not have a good memory for names.

"Manuel Fernandes, señor," said the man, sweat dripping down his brow.

"Manuel, I won't let that happen. That is a promise. *Comprendes?*"

"*Sí*, señor."

"I bet your shoulder burns like the fires of hell."

"*Sí*, señor. It does."

"Well, the flames are going to get even hotter in a moment, but I promise you they will die down after that. *Comprendes?*"

"*Sí*, señor. I will do what you ask."

Ramon removed one of the man's gloves. "Bite on this and close your eyes."

The man did as Ramon asked—and Ramon twisted and pulled the arrow out as quickly as he could. The man screamed through the glove until at last Ramon had removed the bloody arrow from his shoulder.

"Luis, wrap his shoulder," Ramon said, tossing the arrow away, then standing up. "Manuel, you should wear a *chaleco* next time—it would have protected you." *Chalecos* were thick leather vests that many *vaqueros* wore for added protection. They weren't strong enough to stop a *bala* from a gun, but they could stop most arrows. Ramon usually wore his underneath his *sarape*. "We will take you to the Presidio. The doctors will help you get better. *Bien?*"

"*Bien*, Señor Ramon, *bien. Gracias.*"

"Was the man who died your *amigo*, Manuel?"

"*Sí,* his name was Alberto. He was a good man."

It was too late to tell Alberto that he should have stayed with the men. He had paid for this mistake with his life. Perhaps Manuel would learn from his friend's fatal error, but Ramon wouldn't talk to him about it now. The smoke and the heat of battle needed to settle first.

"Your *amigo*, Alberto, was a brave *hombre,* Manuel. I will make sure he is buried properly, with Padre Padilla's blessings."

"*Gracias*, Señor Ramon."

Ramon mounted his warhorse and looked over at the *norteños* again.

Luis rode up to him. "Ramon, that was the scariest *indio* I have ever seen. Holy Madre! His arrows were like *balas* and he had the strength of ten men!"

Luis was always prone to extremes with his words, but this time Ramon could not disagree with his Isleño friend. "I know, Luis. Let's get out of this *infierno.*"

Don Eduardo

"Doña Maria, the stew was *delicioso,* as always." Ramon smiled and stood up from the handsome dining room table in Don Eduardo's residence. The room glowed with the light of a dozen candles, many of them burning around a small altar adorned with a statue of the Blessed Virgin Mary. Several of Doña Maria's wildflower paintings hung on the stone walls.

Don Eduardo Romero's *casa* was like a palace. It had a dining room, two bedrooms, a living room, a large outdoor patio, and an adjoining store where he conducted his business. Ramon believed it was one of the sturdiest structures in San Antonio, as well as the largest residential dwelling. The house had been constructed entirely in adobe by Ramon's father, who was a stonemason trained in his native Ireland. Ramon's father had died seven years ago, and since then, Ramon had been living in Don Eduardo's former residence, an adjacent single-room dwelling.

"Did you get enough, Ramon?" asked the mistress of the house.

Ramon smiled. "If I eat any more I will burst like a tick."

Doña Maria laughed, the kind of loud, boisterous laugh that fills a house. "I'll leave you two *hombres* to talk." She was a proud woman with a pleasant, motherly disposition. And there was nothing quiet about her footsteps, which resonated from the wooden floor below her short, sturdy frame.

"Let's talk on the patio, Ramon." Don Eduardo wiped his mouth with a cloth napkin and motioned for Ramon to follow.

Don Eduardo was a handsome man in his late fifties, tall and slender.

His straight black hair was streaked with gray, and his forehead receded slightly. San Antonio residents knew him as a big-hearted man of notable generosity and a well-respected man of business. He had brought his family's wealth with him from New Spain and had invested it wisely in land acquisition, money lending, and the mercantile business. His store was now the largest and most successful in the territory.

The two men stepped out onto the patio. Several chairs around a small table that held two lit candles and a small wooden box full of cigars. Ramon saw trees silhouetted by the moon and heard the rippling waters of San Pedro Creek. Don Eduardo sat to Ramon's right, with the table between them, like they had dozens of times before.

"Would you like some wine, Ramon? Padre Padilla's finest reserve…" Don Eduardo prided himself on always have the best wine his money could buy, and as he was the wealthiest man in San Antonio, his money could buy quite a lot.

"*Sí*, Don Eduardo. *Por favor.*"

Don Eduardo poured wine from a Pueblan jug into two pewter cups, then offered one to Ramon.

"*Gracias.*"

"To good health and a long life," Don Eduardo toasted, raising his cup to Ramon's. His voice was deep, but it had a softness to it.

Ramon drank a sip of the red wine and felt it warm his body, a welcome feeling on a chilly fall evening.

Don Eduardo placed his cup on the table, grabbed a cigar, and lit it with one of the candles, sucking air in and out of his mouth several times. Finally, he exhaled a cloud of smoke. "What happened out there?" It was Don Eduardo's habit not to ask about the details of a dangerous encounter until he was alone with Ramon, typically with a drink in one hand and a cigar in the other.

"We were about three or four leagues south of the Dama de Medina when we saw them. About twelve *norteños*." Ramon pulled a white, clay-tipped pipe from his pocket—the same long-stemmed, church-warden pipe his father had brought over from Ireland. He dipped its chamber in a small sack of tobacco and tamped the tobacco down with his finger.

"You knew they were *norteños*?"

"They rode painted ponies, carried large war shields, and had black war paint on their faces. There was no doubt left when I saw them ride. No other *indio* rides a horse like a *norteño,* not even close. They were born and raised on *caballos.*" Ramon lifted the candle to light his pipe and took several puffs until the tobacco glowed red.

"Have you seen these *norteños* before?" Don Eduardo always seemed to hunger for every detail that Ramon could feed him. Ramon believed that much of his business success was due to his talent for listening and his knack for making interesting conversation.

"I don't know for sure. Two of them I am certain I have not seen. They were large, powerful-looking *hombres,* not the typical short and stocky *norteños.* But riding a horse, any *norteño* looks fearsome." Ramon took a puff from his pipe and exhaled.

Don Eduardo leaned over to Ramon, his face glowing in the candlelight. "Did the two men ride as well as the others?"

"As well as, if not even better. One of them was the leader. He was barking out commands. The other one killed Alberto and the *mulo* too. His arrows had no bend to them. They were fast, as if launched from *a canon,* and they buzzed like a swarm of hornets. He yelled, 'Esatai,' which I believe was his name."

"You did not take a shot at him?"

"No. I wounded one of their men with my rifle, but this Esatai did not ride in range of my *pistoles.* He rode like the wind and picked up his fallen brother with one hand, lifting him up to his mount, all in full stride." Ramon puffed again and let the smoke simmer in his mouth and lungs before exhaling. "I am worried, Don Eduardo."

"Worried about this Esatai?"

"I am worried for our village, for our people. The *norteños* are getting stronger, bolder, and fiercer. I felt helpless, powerless against these men today. I thought I was going to die. We were lucky that only one *hombre* was lost, and only one *mulo.* They have killed my father, my uncle's *familia,* and your *hermano*. How many of our people will die tomorrow and the next day? I dream of a day when San Antonians can travel from one *rancho* to the next without fear of *indios*. But I fear this dream will not happen in my lifetime, or perhaps ever."

"You shouldn't worry about this, Ramon. More soldiers will come from New Spain to help you fight these *indios*. You will see. We have brought peace and religion to many of the *indios* already." Don Eduardo waved his lit cigar as if conducting his words. "Look at the Lipanos. They were once our deadly enemy, but now they live peacefully in our missions. The *norteños* will also find peace with us and find salvation in our Lord, Jesus Christ. It has been this way for hundreds of years, and it will happen this way for them. You will see."

Ramon wished he had the same faith as Don Eduardo—that he could trust that things would work out peacefully with the *norteños*. But these savages were not like the Lipanos, the Tonkawas, the Karankawans. The way they used weapons and rode horses was far more advanced than these other tribes. And from reports he had heard, they were reaching settlements farther and farther south on their tireless mounts.

"Ramon, perhaps you should give up your life as San Antonio's protector. Find a good woman, buy some land, start a family. With those piercing green Irish eyes, and your light skin, you can have any woman in San Antonio as your wife. Maritza has taken an interest in you. I see the way she watches you. She is blossoming into a gorgeous young woman, and she comes from a prosperous Isleño family. You two would make a handsome couple." Don Eduardo returned the cigar to his mouth and nodded his head, as if hoping to coax Ramon into agreeing with him.

"I'm not ready for that, Don Eduardo. You know that. Maritza is much too young for me. I am twenty-two and she is only sixteen." Ramon was happy to talk about a more cheerful topic. Maritza was one of the most attractive señoritas in San Antonio, but to him she was still just a girl. And he knew in his heart, he wasn't ready to commit himself to marriage, or to settling down, for that matter.

"Suit yourself, *mi amigo*. But if Maritza is the apple of your eye, I wouldn't wait too long to take her hand."

Ramon smiled, but didn't reply. His pipe was finished now, so he tapped the chamber on the ground to empty the tobacco remnants, then set his pipe back in his pocket. He took a few more sips of wine. "I should retire for the night, Don Eduardo. Thank you for the fine wine and conversation."

"*De nada*, Ramon. I will enjoy another cigar and gaze at the stars for a while."

Ramon stood up to walk away, but Don Eduardo called to him. "Ramon. One thing I almost forgot to mention."

"*Que es eso?*"

"A white gentleman came to my store today. His name was Nigel Thompson. I believe he was from England, and he mentioned something about Nacogdoches. It was hard to understand his *español*. Anyway, he was looking for someone to repair his *pistole*. I told him you are the only *armero* in San Antonio, so he left it with me. It's an interesting weapon. I will show it to you in the morning. *Buenos noches, mi amigo*." Then Don Eduardo waved goodbye from his chair.

"*Buenos noches*, Don Eduardo. I am anxious to see this *pistole*."

Called By Thunder

Many Wolves sat atop a wide plateau, engulfed by a clear blue sky, waiting for the falling sun to paint the world in reds and oranges. It was through these colors that Many Wolves felt the Great Spirit's embrace, like a favorite blanket, and it was through the breeze that he felt the Great Spirit's life-giving breath. His mind floated from one memory to the next, like a butterfly touching blossoms in a field of wildflowers. Memories of people who had blessed his life, some more faintly than others, but still he tried to visit each one. And the last flower in the meadow was always his friend, his life-brother, Ten Arrows.

"*Ahpu?*"

"*Haa*, Taimah." Many Wolves opened his eyes, releasing the memory of his old friend. He sat cross-legged with his black wolf, Noche, at his side.

"Are you praying to the Great Spirit?"

"*Haa.* I'm asking the Great Spirit to help me remember my friends and family who have left this world for the next."

"I don't know anyone like that."

Many Wolves looked at his daughter. She was approaching her fifteenth summer. Everything about her was a reflection of his wife, Nina. Her long, dark hair and coppery skin were just like her mother's, a sharp contrast to his noticeably lighter hair and skin. The only part of her that wasn't Lipan was her father's green eyes.

"Because you are still young, Taimah. I pray to the Great Spirit that you will not have to remember your friends and family in prayers, because they

18

will still be with you in this world."

Laying next to Taimah was her wolf, Colmillo, the Sharp-Toothed One. Unlike Noche, who was almost entirely black, Colmillo was a mix of many colors: white, black, red, and brown. Many Wolves and Malone had rescued the two wolves from a French trapper when they were pups. The trapper had killed the other wolves in the pack, and their skins hung at his camp. Many Wolves had tried to barter with the trapper for the two caged wolf pups, but the trapper refused and threatened to kill him with his long gun instead. Before he could fire his weapon, Malone silenced him with two arrows.

"*Ahpu*, was your name always Many Wolves?" Taimah asked. She used Northerner words with him, but used mostly Lipan words with her mother.

"No, Wildflower. My white-skinned parents had a name for me, but I don't remember it. My Lipan parents called me Hollow Leg until my name was changed by the medicine man in our village."

"Why did he name you Many Wolves?"

"He saw me in a vision, riding with wolves. He wanted me to have a strong name to protect me. Just like I wanted you to have a strong name."

"Tell me again how I got my name."

Many Wolves smiled. It was probably the hundredth time he had told her this story. Noche rolled over on his back, begging Many Wolves to rub his furry chest, which Many Wolves did as he spoke. "The pain was strong in your mother's body, so we knew you would be coming into the world soon. Her pain lingered for most of the day, but still you did not come. I had never seen a childbirth before, but luckily Malone had experienced it once long ago with his child. He said prayers and gave your mother medicine herbs, while I tried to comfort her with words. She was in so much pain, I felt helpless to calm her. I remember it was a very hot, summer day, but as the shadows stretched toward the end of the day, clouds began to creep in, replacing the blue with gray, replacing the still heat with wind and rain. Then suddenly, *boom boom boom*, the thunder erupted from the sky. Your mother must have sensed that the Great Spirit was calling—calling you—so she pushed with all the strength she had left.

And moments later, you came into the world. Malone said that you were called by thunder, so we named you Taimah."

"Isn't it more of a boy's name?" She looked at her father with the curious eyes of a much younger child.

"Girls can have strong names too. The Great Spirit wanted you to have it."

The two of them sat silently while the reddened sunlight slowly chased the blue away. Many Wolves played with Noche by pretending his hand was a spider walking all over the wolf. Noche loved the game. Again and again the wolf tried to bite the spider, but Many Wolves always pulled it away before the needle-sharp teeth could clamp down on his hand.

"Look at those birds." Taimah pointed at the sky ahead of them. "They herd together like buffalo and then fly as one. One fast-moving herd across the sky."

"They're a flock, not a herd."

"I know that! Why do they do that, *Ahpu*?"

"Do you see that other bird? It's bigger than them, and it's chasing them," said Many Wolves, pointing.

"Is it a hawk or a falcon?"

"A small falcon. Most hawks don't hunt birds in the open sky like that. The smaller birds stay close together so they can protect themselves from the predator."

"How long will they keep doing this?"

Many Wolves loved Taimah's inquisitive nature. She was always full of questions. *All children must be.* He had probably been the same way when he was young, but for a large part of his childhood, there had been no one there to answer his questions—so he had had to find his own answers. But as long as he was in this world, Taimah would not have to find her own answers.

"Until the falcon tires out or catches one of them," he said. "You see how tired our birds get when they hunt. After two or three chases, they need to rest."

"I know. If we didn't hunt with birds, I would think that birds could fly forever and never grow tired." She stroked Colmillo's head.

"I used to think the same thing about horses, until I started to ride them. Understanding when animals need rest will keep them healthy. You don't want to push them when they're tired."

Many Wolves stood up and stretched his back. Their camp was a short walk away, and it was getting dark. "We should get back, Wildflower. Your mother is probably waiting for us to eat."

"Rabbit again?" said Taimah, a hint of dissatisfaction in her voice. Their three wolf hawks had caught three rabbits earlier in the day.

"I thought you liked rabbit?"

"It depends on how *Shimaa* cooks it," said Taimah, standing up. The top of her head barely reached his nose.

Many Wolves laughed. "Someday, you will have to hunt for your food and cook it yourself. You won't be so picky then."

He whistled, and the three wolf hawks, who had been resting on the rocks, rose into the air and followed them home.

A Willing Mind

Many Wolves and Taimah arrived at their home just before dark. Home was wherever their camp was, always within an easy walk of the Rio Pecos, but also always changing to find fresh new places to hunt. And though it was just a camp, Many Wolves thought of it as his village. There were two tipis, one for Many Wolves and his family, the other for Malone and his wife, Topusana.

Ninakabaru, Malone, and Topusana were sitting around the cooking fire when Many Wolves and Taimah arrived. "Someday, one of you will cook the meat and I'll watch the sunset," said Nina in a sarcastic tone.

Many Wolves greeted her with a kiss on the top of the head. "You know you don't like my cooking. I know you'd rather do it yourself." He hung his quiver by their lodge and drank some water from his water pouch.

"We already ate," she replied. "I don't like overcooked meat."

A rabbit carcass was heating on a low flame for Many Wolves and Taimah. Overcooked or not, it didn't matter to Many Wolves, as long as it filled his stomach. And he didn't need to eat as much as he used to. Nina removed the cooked rabbit from the fire and cut off a back leg for each of them.

"You salted it already?" Many Wolves asked as he sat down in front of the fire. Taimah sat down next to her mother.

"Yes, dearest *shika*," Nina said.

"Thank you, dearest wife." He shot a playful glance back at her.

Nina's cooking was much more creative than his. She knew where to gather many different kinds of seeds, roots, and bark to enhance her cooking, and from experience, she knew which ones would mix well together. She also only shared her cooking secrets with Taimah and Topusana, saying it was a "secret between women."

Many Wolves and Taimah ate the tasty rabbit meat while the two wolves watched with keen interest from a short distance away, waiting for their own last meal of the day. The three birds sat in the cottonwood trees that surrounded the camp, preparing to roost for the night, their appetites satisfied. Like the birds and the wolves, Malone and Topusana observed the eating ritual quietly.

"Malone, when will you teach me to hunt buffalo?" Taimah asked after swallowing a mouthful of meat.

"Is your arrow strong enough to pierce a thick buffalo skin?" asked Malone in his usual feathery tone.

Like the mountains, Malone had not aged a day since Many Wolves had met him. The only indications of Malone's age were a few wrinkles around his eyes and the sporadic grays that now sprouted from his long, straight black hair—grays that were usually plucked soon after they appeared. Though Many Wolves was the much younger man, Malone could still beat him in a foot race and an arm wrestling contest, and racing Malone on a horse was like trying to race the wind.

"Can you draw a man's bow?" Many Wolves added, remembering what his father, Red Arrow, had once said to him.

"I'm as tall as *Shimaa* and can ride better than *Ahpu*," Taimah argued in a bragging tone.

"This is true, Taimah. But to hunt buffalo, you must be able to kill it quickly, with one or two arrows. A weak arrow will bring suffering, and not death, to the animal," said the Northerner, Malone.

Secretly, Many Wolves had already discussed with Malone when the right time would be for Taimah to hunt buffalo. Hunting buffalo was the first step toward manhood in the Northerner tradition. They both agreed that Taimah could handle a horse well enough, but was she strong enough to kill a large animal? How would she react in the face of danger? But the time to kill the buffalo they would need for their winter store was quickly approaching, and Malone was spending more and more time each day trying to locate a herd that was close to their camp. If Malone believed she was ready, then that would be enough for Many Wolves.

"Taimah, when Malone finds the herd, we will decide if you are ready," said Many Wolves, at last.

Many Wolves and Taimah finished off the rest of their meal and tossed what was left to the wolves, who devoured it in a heartbeat and then started their nightly cleaning ritual, licking the fur on their legs and their paws.

"I'm tired," said Taimah, yawning.

"We were up early this morning with the birds," said Many Wolves.

Taimah was usually the first one up in the morning and the first one to sleep at night. She stood up and hugged her mother, then dragged her feet into their lodge.

"Peaceful dreams, Wildflower," said Many Wolves, his usual words before she slept. Though she shared his bloodlines, she did not share the nightmares he had had as a child. He was thankful that the Great Spirit protected her dream world.

Colmillo followed her, settled just outside the door, and resumed his cleaning ritual once more.

It was not long before Nina followed her to the lodge. "Don't count all the stars tonight, you two."

"Good night, sweet *nupetsu*," said Many Wolves, watching her go.

"I'm tired too," said Topusana. "I'll leave you two to your man talk." She kissed Malone and walked away into the darkness.

Malone went to his lodge and returned with arrow-making supplies. He made arrows for all of them, which kept him busy most nights. He often worked into the deepest part of the night, sacrificing sleep he didn't seem to need. With Malone, the wolves, and the horses nearby, their little village was well-guarded during the night.

"You still think she is ready to hunt buffalo, Malone?" said Many Wolves, the ever-cautious father, seeking further confirmation from the friend he most trusted on matters of hunting.

"*Haa.* She keeps asking about it, which tells me that she is ready. If she was too fearful, she wouldn't want to talk about it." Malone paused to tighten some sinew with his teeth. "I will let her use my second horse, who does not fear the buffalo. The horse will help to keep her safe."

"But is she good enough with the bow?"

"She is accurate enough, but it might take several shots to make the kill. I can help her with that." Malone used his teeth again to tie the sinew. "Will you be riding with us?"

"No, no, no." Many Wolves chuckled. "I don't want to fall again like I did two winters ago. It takes too many moons to heal my aging body, my friend."

"So, the daughter is willing, but the father is not." Malone smiled and continued with his work.

Flintlock Revolver

The mission bells woke Ramon at sunrise and hurled him into his day. San Antonians were slaves to their bells: bells for waking, bells for praying, bells for eating. It was the Franciscans' way of bringing order to the *indios*, and Ramon had been raised with the bells of the Mission de San Juan Capistrano.

And so his bell-driven morning routine began. He drew water from the well, washed himself with soap, combed his hair, and shaved, leaving only a neatly trimmed mustache and goatee. He kept the goatee at about six inches in length, braided and beaded with jade and turquoise.

He opened up the *Holy Bible,* one of the two books by his blanket, and read several passages, picking up where he had left off the previous day. Reading it served two purposes for him: learning lessons on how to lead a holy, Catholic life, and keeping the English language fresh in his mind. Since the death of his father, he had barely spoken English at all. The residents of San Antonio mostly spoke Spanish.

His single-room home was modest compared to Don Eduardo's residence. It was decorated with two chairs, a small table, a blanket to sleep on, a small mirror, and several candles. Next to his blanket were always two books: *The Holy Bible* and *Gulliver's Travels,* both brought over by his father from Ireland. In the far corner of the room were three baskets full of pistols, muskets, and rifles, as well as extra gun parts that Ramon had accumulated over the years. His working guns were loaded on a wooden rack against the wall. Don Eduardo jokingly referred to Ramon's house as "The Armory."

When he finished reading, Ramon left his house and walked an easy stone's throw to the "Romero Palace," where he normally went for breakfast.

"*Buenos días*, Doña Maria," he said, entering the dining room.

Doña Maria, dressed in her cooking apron, was sweeping the floor. "*Buenos días*, Ramon. You are here earlier than usual."

"I want to go to the store early today."

"Eduardo told me about the white man's *pistole*. He said you would be excited."

"*Sí*. I am. You know how I love to take new things apart and put them back together again." He sat down at the table after hanging his hat on a rack.

Doña Maria smiled. "Corn mush, *bien*?"

"*Sí, por favor*."

"With peppers?"

Ramon expected she knew the answer before it was spoken. "Of course. Is there any other way to eat corn mush?" He preferred spicy to sweet foods.

"Most people like it with sugar or honey, but not you. Your father never understood why you spoiled good corn mush with peppers."

"He used to scold me for it, but I guess one day he just gave up. One of the few things he was not strict about."

"Your father was much stricter with you than most *español* fathers. He would be very proud of the man you have become," said Doña Maria, with a slight quiver in her voice. "Here you go." She set down the bowl of corn mush and cut him some fresh peppers to add to it.

"*Gracias*."

It was delicious, as always. *The perfect meal to start the day.*

* * *

When Ramon arrived at the store, he found Don Eduardo waiting on a customer.

"Ramon, you are just in time. Can you help load a sack of maize for Señor Perez?"

"*Sí*, Don Eduardo. Right away." Ramon was often asked to help in the store, especially when Don Eduardo's sons were not around. It was part of his "arrangement" with the Romeros, which entitled him to live where he did without paying rent.

He lifted a sack of maize from the back corner of the store and carried it outside, securing it to Señor Perez's mule.

"*Gracias*, Ramon," said Señor Perez. "I'm sure I will see you at Mass *el Domingo*."

"Of course, Señor Perez. I wouldn't miss it." Ramon believed it was a sin against God and the Catholic Church to miss Sunday Mass, a belief passed down to him from his father and the Franciscans at his mission. He missed his religious obligation only when he was away from San Antonio, and that seemed to happen a lot more now that his father was gone.

Señor Perez waved goodbye and walked away leading his mule. Ramon went back inside.

"Let me get that package for you, Ramon," said Don Eduardo. He left the room and returned shortly carrying a small wooden box, which he set on a table. "Señor Thompson says it doesn't work at all anymore."

Ramon inspected it. On the top of the box was a drawing of a pistol and some words in English.

"What does it say, Ramon?" asked Don Eduardo.

"It says 'Flintlock Revolver' and 'E. H. Collier, London.' This Collier must be the gun's maker."

Ramon opened the box and found a partially assembled, well-worn pistol inside. He recognized several familiar parts: the handle, the hammer, the barrel. But one part was strange to him: a cylinder with five chambers in it. "It looks like this gun can carry extra *balas*." The only other gun he'd seen like it was called a pepperbox, which shot more than one lead ball at a time through six barrels, but it was very unreliable and dangerous to use.

"Señor Delacruz never had a gun like this?"

"No, this is new… and different." Señor Delacruz had taught Ramon everything he knew about gunsmithing when Ramon was a teenager, because as a boy he had shown great interest in tinkering with mechanical things. For the longest time, Señor Delacruz was the only gunsmith in San Antonio, until he packed up his family and returned to New Spain, fearing *indio* attacks. After that, Ramon instantly became the local gun expert, and he mostly served the soldiers of the Presidio.

"It looks like there are special tools here for fixing it, a mold for making lead balls, and some instructions." Ramon was fascinated by the pistol; it presented a new challenge for him. "Let me take this to *mi casa* and see if I can fix it. It could use a good cleaning, too."

"It's all yours. Señor Thompson wants it ready to go in three days."

"I'll have it ready in three hours," said Ramon.

* * *

Back at his *casa*, Ramon removed all the pieces from the wooden box and spread them out on the table, which also served as a workbench. Then, one by one, he removed pieces from the pistol and placed them so they were in the same relative location on the table as they were on the gun. He counted twelve pieces once the gun was fully disassembled, more than any of the single-shot pistols he normally worked on.

The parts were made from high-quality steel, and the same name, "E. H. Collier," was etched on the side of the breech. The hammer had a mainspring that powered it—it looked like a hairpin, but thicker—and Ramon saw that it was broken. *The thinnest piece is always the weakest.*

He looked through the barrel of spare parts for a mainspring that matched the broken one, but none of them fit correctly. Most of them were too big. He tried filing down one of the mainsprings to make it fit, but his tools were better suited for cleaning metal, not shaping it. *Pedro Ortega, the town blacksmith, could make it fit.*

Ramon gathered up all the gun parts, including some of his spares, and headed out toward the downtown area of San Antonio. Most of the businesses were located in the missions. Pedro Ortega's shop was located in the Mission de San Jose.

Ramon walked briskly along the vacant road until he reached the walls of Mission de San Jose. The mission grounds were bustling with activity. The women were busy weaving, grinding maize, or making soap and candles from tallow, the animal fat from cattle. The girls of the village were supervising the younger children while the women worked. And the men and boys were working together at their various trades: building or mending houses, making furniture, or working with the pigs, cattle, sheep, goats, and horses. One or two of the men played guitar, because the Franciscans always wanted music in the village, just as they always included it in their church ceremonies.

Ramon walked toward the sign that read, "Pedro & Sons, Blackmiths."

"*Hola,* Pedro," Ramon said as he walked through the door of the large, single-room establishment made from adobe and wood.

"*Buenos días,* Ramon. *Que pasa?*" Pedro said from behind the counter. He was a man in his late forties, and his cheerful voice was loud as always.

"I need you to make a *pistole* mainspring for me."

On the wall behind Pedro were tools of every shape and size: hammers, tongs, chisels. In one corner of the room was a forge, and in another corner, an anvil. "Let me see what you have," Pedro said.

Ramon took all the parts out of the bag and laid them on the counter. "This is the broken mainspring. I need one like this that fits under the hammer. If you don't have it, maybe you can file down one of these other mainsprings I have brought?."

Pedro put his spectacles on and examined the parts. "*Muy facil,* Ramon, *muy facil.* Give me *un momento.*"

The blacksmith turned to his tool wall and grabbed a metal file. He selected one of Ramon's mainsprings and filed it carefully, comparing it repeatedly with the broken one. After several minutes, he held a newly formed thin strip of metal. "How does that look, Ramon?"

"*Muy bien.* Let's see if it fits." Ramon took the spring and carefully snapped it into the trigger assembly. "*Perfecto!*"

Pedro laughed out loud, a broad smile across his face. "You came to the right man for the job!"

"Well, as my father used to say: Most jobs are easy with the right tool."

"Your *padre* was right, Ramon. The right tool and the right *hombre* to use the tool!"

"*Gracias*, Pedro. Can I ask you to make four more springs just like this one?"

"*Sí,* Ramon. It would be my pleasure."

"*Gracias.* What can I barter for your services?"

"*Nada.* I'm sure there will be a day when I need your services. *Correcto?*"

Ramon laughed. "*Muy bien.* I'll take the main trigger piece and leave the rest with you. I have a *pistole* to resurrect from the dead."

"*Adios,* Ramon."

"*Adios.*"

Ramon walked back to his house, excited to see if the pistol would work.

A large oak tree shaded his house, so the noonday heat did not warm up his room uncomfortably. He usually left the door open, so the air could circulate. It was very difficult to do delicate work like this on extremely hot days, but the hottest part of summer had recently passed, and now a fall chill cooled the air.

Sitting at his workbench again, he assembled the various parts of the trigger first, then connected the breech with the handle. The last two pieces he attached were the six-chamber cylinder and the barrel. Everything seemed to fit back in the proper place.

First, Ramon wanted to test the weapon without any balls or firing powder. He spun the cylinder around and noticed that it clicked into place when the chamber and barrel were properly aligned. Each of the chambers was tested this way. Then he repeated this exercise again, but this time firing the trigger with each chamber. Again everything seemed to be in working order.

Ramon removed the cylinder cover, which protected the load, and searched a small bag of lead *balas.* Most of his lead balls were too large for this weapon because they were made for the military pistols that most men in San Antonio used. However, he found some smaller balls, around .30 caliber in size, and discovered they fit into the chamber. After loading a single chamber with measured powder—a little less than usual, since this was a smaller caliber pistol—he added wadding and a lead ball, then sealed the chamber with the cover.

Behind his house was a wooden target mounted on an old oak trunk. He stood about ten yards away from it. The Romeros and other neighbors were used to booming gunshots from behind his house; he practiced his shooting often, in addition to testing the weapons he was repairing.

After he had primed the flash pan with more powder, the pistol was ready to go. He aimed and fired the weapon; it flashed and kicked out smoke. Though Ramon missed the target, he saw dirt kick up from behind it, and was pleased that the pistol had fired without any problems.

Now, the real test: to see what happened with more than one chamber loaded.

Ramon loaded all the chambers this time, covered them, then primed the pan when he was outside and ready to fire. He shot the pistol again, not concerned about hitting the target accurately. Then he turned the cylinder, re-primed, and fired again. He repeated this four more times, until all the chambers were empty. *This is an excellent weapon.* As compared to a single-shot weapon, rotating the chamber was much quicker than having to reload the muzzle every time, and all the powder measuring could be done ahead of time.

One bala as fast as a norteño's arrow.

Nigel Thompson

Once the pistol was tested to his liking, Ramon took it apart again and began cleaning it. He scraped off corroded areas and smoothed some of the rougher edges of the metal surface. He lubricated all the moving parts. Finally, he polished it so it looked barely used.

"Hello?" said a voice from outside—a voice speaking not Spanish, but English. "Hello?"

Ramon got up and walked outside.

A tall, thin man dressed in a tailored linen suit and wearing a top hat awaited. His knickers were tan, and his white stockings rode up to his knees. "Good day," he said. "You must be Mr. Connelly? Mr. Ramon Connelly. The gun smithy." His voice was high-pitched, and his accent was much like Ramon's father's.

Ramon stumbled with his thoughts, realizing he needed to speak English, not Spanish. "I am. And you must be Señor… uh… Mr. Thompson."

"Quite right. Dr. Nigel Thompson, to be exact." The man tipped his hat and wiggled his well-groomed mustache. His face was a creamy white color with blushed red cheeks, and his curly brown hair was cut short. He offered his hand, and Ramon shook it. He did not have the strong grip of a man who labored with his hands, Ramon thought.

"There's certainly Connelly in your eyes, and a bit of it in your tongue as well—but the rest of you is indeed Ramon," said Dr. Thompson, smiling.

"My father was Irish and my mother was Spanish, born in the Canary Islands, if you must know."

"It's blooming good to hear you speak the Queen's English."

It was hard not to think of his father when he spoke. "My father made sure I spoke it. I'm out of practice though, so I hope I don't butcher it too badly."

"Well, let me cut straight through the butter, Mr. Connelly. I heard the familiar blast of my sidearm and fancied an update on your progress."

"Come on in, Dr. Thompson. I'll show it to you."

Ramon led the Englishman through the door and offered him a chair by his workbench. Dr. Thompson removed his hat and performed a rudimentary inspection of the place. "You have a blooming armory here, Mr. Connelly."

Ramon laughed. "That's exactly what Don Eduardo calls it. Can I offer you some water? I don't have much else to offer."

"Water would be splendid. I'm as parched as a fish on desert sand."

Ramon placed two cups on the table and poured water into them from a clay pitcher.

Dr. Thompson drank several gulps and then exhaled, seemingly refreshed. "I see you've put quite a shine on ol' Betsy," he said, looking down at his pistol on the table.

"Betsy?"

Dr. Thompson smiled. "My sidearm. That's her name, Betsy. We've spent a lot of time together, Betsy and me, in the service of Her Majesty's Armed Forces. I wasn't much of a soldier, Mr. Connelly, but I served Her Majesty well as a field doctor. You could say that medicine is my specialty." He picked up the pistol and examined it closely, turning it in every direction. "Betsy was always at my side like a faithful dog during my tour in India."

"Where did you get Betsy, if you don't mind me asking?" said Ramon, curious to know where this unusual pistol had come from, and more importantly, if there was a way he could get one for himself.

"She's military issue, Mr. Connelly, and from what I gathered from some of the higher-ranking chaps, a bit experimental. But that was several years back, when I was still in Her Majesty's service." Dr. Thompson pulled open the cylinder and inspected the chambers. "I fancy she's in working order now?"

"It's in working order, Dr. Thompson. May I have it for a moment?" Ramon took the pistol from the doctor and dismantled it. He showed Dr. Thompson where he had cleaned the metal and lubricated the moving parts. Then he showed him the new spring that Pedro had made. "This spring was broken. That's why the pistol wouldn't fire. Pedro, our town blacksmith, made this to fit your pistol. I'm having him make some extras for you in case it breaks again. Shall I powder her up?"

"Let's give her a go, Mr. Connelly."

Ramon reassembled the pistol, then loaded up all of the cylinders with lead and powder. "I have a target out back." He stood up and led Dr. Thompson outside. "When you're ready, I'll prime the pan for you."

"All right, let's have a go."

Ramon poured a small amount of powder on the pan. Dr. Thompson raised the pistol and aimed at the target, his eyes squinting and hands trembling a bit. It took a while before he finally shot the weapon. With all that time spent aiming, Ramon had expected the shot to hit the middle of the target, but it didn't even graze it.

Dr. Thompson rotated the cylinder carefully and then cocked the hammer back, motioning to Ramon that he was ready for another try. Ramon primed the pan, and Dr. Thompson took another deliberate shot, again missing the target altogether.

"As I told you, I was never much of a blooming soldier," said Dr. Thompson, embarrassed, his already red cheeks turning redder. "Let's see what you can do with her, Mr. Connelly. I fancy you can do a bit better."

Ramon took the pistol, cocked and primed it, then waited for Dr. Thompson to back away from him. He took four consecutive shots in less than a minute, spraying wood from the target three times. With his priming powder hung around his neck by a leather strap, it took him only about ten seconds to prepare for each shot. *I feel like I'm getting faster with this pistol.*

Dr. Thompson seemed impressed. "Well done, Mr. Connelly, you're a blooming ace of a shot!"

"Thank you kindly, Dr. Thompson. I've had quite a bit of practice in my lifetime," said Ramon, handing the pistol back to its owner. He led Dr. Thompson back inside. "So, you're happy with it then, I take it?"

"Indeed. Mr. Romero and I agreed on a price of two pesos for the repair. I must say, that's extremely good value, Mr. Connelly."

In Ramon's mind, that was too much, but he knew that Don Eduardo always raised prices for customers from outside San Antonio.

"Dr. Thompson, before we settle our deal, I'd like to ask you something, sir."

"You wish to haggle a better price?"

Ramon smiled. "No, sir. That price is more than fair for my trouble." He paused, feeling a little nervous. "I'd like to know if you'd be interested in selling it?" For a man whose primary business was fighting *indios*, such a weapon would be priceless, Ramon thought.

The question seemed to catch Dr. Thompson by surprise. "I don't know, Mr. Connelly," he said, sounding uncertain. "Betsy is more than just a weapon to me. We've been through a blooming lot together. I'd have to take it into consideration. Did you have a specific offer in mind?"

"Don Eduardo tells me you have two sons," Ramon said. "How many firearms does your family own?"

"I only have this sidearm and musket from my military service."

"I can offer several muskets and pistols for that flintlock revolver, sir. The more firepower you have, the safer you'll be against the *indios* out there."

Dr. Thompson thought about that for a moment. "I should purchase more, then?"

"You should. At least one musket and one pistol for each of your family members, I'd say. You can buy what stock Don Eduardo has, but after that, you'll need to purchase directly from me. I could give you a much better price if it were a trade for your revolver. Just think about it. We can settle up later. And I should mention to you that any weapon you purchase from me comes with free repairs for the life of it."

"I will take it under consideration, Mr. Connelly, but I'll say that it will be blooming hard parting with my Betsy. Good day to you, sir."

Dr. Thompson grabbed his hat and his pistol, then left.

Up With the Sun

"Up with the sun, *Ahpu*, up with the sun!"

Many Wolves fell out of his dream. The lingering vision of it blew away like dust from his memory. He yawned and stretched, fighting the crisp morning air and the dying darkness.

"You promised we could hunt early today," said Taimah, leaning down toward him as he sat on his sleeping robe. Next to him, Nina grumbled about being disturbed so early.

Many Wolves's tired body was telling him that it would be nice to sleep a little longer, but he had a promise to keep, and now that Taimah was awake, the loudest wolf hawk he had ever known was also roused, squawking in harmony with his daughter.

"Chachara is ready to go," said his daughter.

"Chachara is always ready to go," said Many Wolves, still fighting to wake up. Chachara was the female wolf hawk's full name; it meant "One Who Chatters." Each of their three birds had been taken from a different nest at a different time. Many Wolves had tried to pick the bird that was the largest and healthiest from each nest, and Chachara happened to be the largest... and the loudest.

Noche woke up also, stretching his front legs out as far as they would go, as if they were being pulled by invisible rope. When the wolf was limber enough, he chased Chachara up to a higher perch. Many Wolves didn't know why Noche always chased Chachara and not the other two hawks; perhaps he was also annoyed by her. The bird always kept a safe distance away from the black wolf, and always seemed ready to evade his mock attacks.

Many Wolves packed some dried rabbit meat and his water pouch on his chestnut horse, Castano, then offered his mount a prickly pear, which was a favorite treat in fall when they could be harvested from the bear cactus. He always removed the spines of the fruit by rolling it in sand before offering it to his riding companion.

The two wolf brothers, Noche and Colmillo, howled with excitement.

"Quiet, you two!" said Many Wolves.

The wolves stopped for a moment, but like the rays of dawn sun creeping over the hills, their excitement was impossible to contain.

The pack leader put on his usual hunting clothes: his deerskin leggings and moccasins, and a thick leather hunting vest and headband to protect his shoulders and head from the bird's sharp claws. Away from the river, there were very few trees for the birds to perch on, so they used their pack leader instead. Taimah usually only had one bird with her, on her fist-perch. She wore a skirt and half-shirt made of rabbit fur, a rabbit skin wrap around her head, and deerskin boots that covered the lower half of her legs.

Many Wolves mounted Castano and signaled with the bone whistle for the wolves and birds to follow. When he held out his left hand, which was covered by a fist-perch, Flecha, the small male hawk, flew to him. Taimah, atop one of Malone's painted mounts, whistled with just her mouth, and Chachara flew to her hand. The third hawk, a female like Chachara, was named Espera, "the One Who Waits." She landed behind Many Wolves, on his riding pad.

"You lazy beggars," said Many Wolves. He knew they were resting up for the hunt. They were treated better than the holiest of holy men. *Maybe I should build them a sweat lodge someday*, he thought, then chuckled to himself.

He turned to Taimah. "There's a small ravine south east of here that we haven't hunted yet."

"I'll follow, *Ahpu*."

Many Wolves glanced over at Malone's lodge and wondered why

Malone had not shown an interest in hunting with birds; his knowledge of nature and animals was extensive. But whenever Many Wolves had invited him, he had politely declined, saying he preferred to hunt with his bow, in the traditional Noomah way. So Many Wolves had eventually given up asking him.

Taimah, on the other hand, never declined an invitation. Perhaps it was in her blood, or perhaps she did it to please her father. Many Wolves believed it was a little of both. And she also loved to hunt with Malone. Her father was pleased that she opened her mind and dove headfirst into both hunting methods. *When I am gone, she will need all these survival tools.*

Many Wolves and Taimah arrived at the top of the ravine, looking down on a dried-out creek. The floor of the ravine was blanketed in brush, mostly sage and mesquite, with some cactus mixed in. *A haven of cover for hiding rabbits.*

"One of us can flush them out down there and the other can wait up here with the birds," said Many Wolves. Usually the pack walked in a line on flat ground, shoulder-to-shoulder, covering a wide swath when they searched for prey, but Many Wolves wanted to give the birds more height to start from.

"I'll flush," said Taimah, "with the wolves."

Many Wolves nodded in agreement, then put the whistle in his mouth. He kept it tied to a strand of sinew wrapped around his neck.

"Chachara will probably want to stay with me," said Taimah, holding the chittering female wolf hawk on her left fist. Colmillo followed her down the slope. "Come, Noche," she said, then whistled.

When Taimah reached the bottom of the slope, Many Wolves watched her take a piece of fresh rabbit skin from her saddlebag and hold it down for the wolves to smell, just as he had taught her. After each wolf had sniffed at the skin, she returned it to her bag. The wolves then moved slowly forward. Chachara was quiet, bobbing her head up and down in anticipation.

Atop the small ridge, Many Wolves lined his horse up just behind Taimah's. He planned to follow Taimah and the wolves. Flecha watched the brush just ahead of the wolves with an outstretched neck. Espera was perched on Many Wolves's head, but he barely felt the tips of her claws on his scalp. Luckily for him, birds were not heavy at all, mostly feathers and hollow bones.

The sun was fully exposed now, but the air was still cool. Taimah watched from horseback as the wolves, one on either side of her, smelled the earth for living scents. Their pace was cautious and deliberate. Taimah had the patience of a spider that waits and waits and waits until finally a fly wanders into its sticky web. This was the greatest hunting skill Many Wolves had taught her.

"Stop if you hear anything that sounds like a rattle," yelled Many Wolves, not wanting any animal or person to go through the pain he had suffered from the fangs of a rattlesnake. Usually the wolves found any snakes first and warned the pack with barking and whining, but it was always wise to be cautious.

"I know, I know," Taimah said, shaking her head.

One thing that Many Wolves had learned as a parent was that children needed to be told things over and over and over again before those things would finally settle in their mind—like hundreds of lightning flashes that scorch the barren air until one eventually strikes a tree, leaving a permanent imprint.

Finally, from the brush ahead of them, a burst of movement. A jackrabbit.

"Go!" yelled Taimah.

Flecha sprung from Many Wolves's hand, followed closely by Chachara. Espera took her familiar spot at the back of the winged pursuers, gaining height with every beat of her wings. Flecha's wings chewed through the air at a rapid pace, closing the distance to the jackrabbit with every beat. Cutting and weaving just above the brush, Flecha mimicked every twist, every turn, of the swift rabbit, then lunged forward, claws drawn, and caught the back of the animal with one talon, knocking it off balance for a moment.

The rabbit spun away from its first attacker, but lost speed. Now Chachara swooped in. The bigger, stronger bird struck the rabbit with both claws extended, and predator and prey tumbled through the dirt and brush. Chachara regained her balance, talons still locked onto the screaming jackrabbit's head and neck. Espera joined the fracas, pouncing on the exposed rear of the kicking prey, trying to control its powerful back legs.

Many Wolves yelled to Taimah, who was closer to the struggle, "You take it!"

She jumped off her horse, yelling to the wolves, "Down!"

Noche and Colmillo crouched and waited at a distance that wouldn't frighten the birds.

Taimah ran over to the screeching rabbit, bent down, and grabbed its back legs with both hands. Once she had control, she reached into her hunting bag, which was tied around her waist. She searched it for several moments and then yelled to her father, "I don't have my knife. You'll have to kill it!"

Many Wolves rode over to her and jumped down. "No. This is your hunt. What would you do if I wasn't here?" This was a good test of her skill in a crucial moment. He wanted her to work through it, to work through the pressure.

"Try to break its neck?" she asked, breathing hard. The screams of the rabbit were a call to urgency.

"You remember how I showed you? Use your legs!" said her teacher.

Taimah stood up and placed her right foot behind the rabbit's neck. "Like this?" The rabbit's legs struggled to break free of her two-handed grip.

"*Haa*, but don't put too much weight on it. Just enough so the head doesn't move when you pull the legs."

"I hate this part of the hunt!"

Many Wolves smiled and murmured to himself, "It's not pleasant."

Taimah stretched the rabbit's legs back quickly, and the screaming stopped. "I heard it snap!"

"See, you are strong enough to do it that way," said Many Wolves, breathing easier knowing that the frenzied moment had passed.

Taimah closed her eyes for a moment and then looked up at her father. "So, now I do the trade?" Her voice was more relaxed.

"Did the Great Spirit hear from you?" Many Wolves hoped that she had remembered to thank the Great Spirit for this gift.

"*Haa, Ahpu*, I said the 'Life for Life' prayer to the Great Spirit."

"Good. It's important that the animal does not suffer, and even more important that you thank the Great Spirit for the animal's life. If you are ungrateful, then the spirit of the animal you killed will be lost forever, instead of being born into new life." *Like the lightning, these lessons need to be repeated over and over.* "Now, do the trade. The birds are waiting."

"But I need a knife."

"You should not leave camp without it," her father scolded.

"I know, I know."

Many Wolves handed her his steel hunting knife, a gift from Malone, and she cut open a cavity in the rabbit's chest, then reached in to find the blood organs.

The two female birds still clutched the kill, watching her every move with curious, tilted stares. Chachara's head was almost close enough to touch the knife. Taimah offered her the liver, and the hungry bird snapped it up greedily. The girl fed the bird the other organs this same way, and while the bird was distracted, she cut off the rabbit's front leg.

She grabbed a bandanna from her hunting bag, unrolled it, then persuaded the two birds to shift their position so she could cover the body. She offered Chachara the severed front leg, and the bird quickly jumped onto her fist-perch for the treat, ignoring her kill. This was the "trade" that Many Wolves spoke of.

Many Wolves called Espera to his fist-perch for a small morsel of rabbit meat, then carefully removed the bandanna and dead rabbit out of the birds' sight, placing it in his hunting bag. "Your trade was perfect, Taimah. Do you remember why we do the trade?"

"Because we never want to steal from the birds. It's their rabbit. It's their kill."

"*Haa*, Wildflower, and we don't want them gorging themselves until

43

the hunt is over. Hunger motivates them to work hard."

Many Wolves tossed a small piece of meat to Flecha for his efforts. "The Arrow" was the smallest of the three and reminded Many Wolves of the brave Chiquito, the little bird with the big heart. It wasn't often that Flecha missed an attack like this. He was the quickest of them, and usually the first bird to make contact with the fleeing prey. Like Chiquito, he was more confident and successful hunting rabbits than squirrels, which could fight back.

The wolves lay down in the dirt next to rest of the pack. Besides finding prey, they were the guardians of the hunt, watching for any danger that might be attracted to all the commotion: coyotes, mountain lions, bears. The sounds and smells of death carried far on the wind.

"Are you ready to go again?" said Many Wolves, climbing back on his horse, then calling Flecha back to his fist.

"*Haa*," said Taimah. "*Shimaa* wants us to bring home more than we can eat today. She wants to dry some meat for winter."

"Let's not disappoint her, then." Many Wolves smiled.

Many Wolves's Village

Many Wolves and Taimah arrived back at the camp around mid-afternoon after a long day of hunting.

"How did it go?" asked Nina, who was grinding some nuts in a stone bowl. Topusana was sitting next to her, sewing rabbit skins together.

"The Great Spirit blessed us with five jackrabbits," said Taimah, holding one of them up after she got down from her horse, her white teeth shining on her dark, dusty face.

Many Wolves was pleased to hear her acknowledge the Great Spirit. He drank some water, washed his face, and sat down next to Nina at the fire pit.

"Good. Now that your man's work is done, you can help me out." Nina glared at her daughter.

"Right now, *Shimaa*?" Taimah complained with a sigh.

"Take a little break first. I have some pine nuts and blackberries here if you're hungry. Then we need to get started on skinning those rabbits. Malone is gone for the day looking for buffalo signs, so you can't practice your riding and shooting with him."

Skinning the rabbits and squirrels after the hunt was one job Many Wolves did not miss. Before Nina and Topusana lived in his village, and while Taimah was young, he had done most of the skinning himself—but now he had three women in his village to do this "woman's work." He was thankful for the extra time to rest. His body tired more easily, now that he was older, and it seemed it always suffered some ailment: a pain in his

45

shoulder or ankle, a bruise on his leg, a sore back. He never remembered these little nagging pains when he was young. They followed him around like biting flies. Perhaps it was part of growing old.

He also found greater joy in watching other people do things instead of doing them himself. He was happy to let Taimah work the flush and the kill today. Almost as much as watching the birds hunt, he enjoyed watching the interactions between the birds and the wolves. He found it challenging to try to figure out what they were thinking, and see if he could predict their behavior. Noche chasing Chachara was always predictable, but other behaviors in the pack were not. And not having to command the wolves on the flush or cut open the carcass after the kill enabled him to step back and observe. Perhaps this too was part of growing old and gaining wisdom.

Taimah found the pouch of blackberries and poured some in a clay bowl, then found herself an open spot around the crowded fire pit, which was lit only with embers, no flames. She attacked the bowl as if it were her first meal in many sun-ups, while Colmillo lay beside her.

Many Wolves motioned to her that he wanted a blackberry, so she tossed one to him from across the fire pit. He plucked it from the air and dropped it in his mouth. "Some blackberry water would taste good right now." He was hoping there was some made already.

"Go make it yourself," said Nina, her hands bloodied from a rabbit carcass. "We are busy."

"I'm the leader of this village and I have to make my own drink?" Many Wolves spoke with a joking tone on his tongue, expecting to get a reaction from his wife.

"The self-appointed leader who does nothing but sit around the fire pit, lost in his thoughts," snapped Nina, pulling the guts from the chest of the dead rabbit. "I'll save these guts for you, *namunewapi*, so you can bury them away from our camp."

Taimah and Topusana glanced at each other and smiled.

"See, you call me *namunewapi*, so I must be an important person in this village."

"I don't know the word for 'important fool' in the Northerner language, or else I would have used it." The crease in Nina's lips was as straight as an arrow.

Many Wolves laughed. He had laid the snare and caught the witty remark he was hoping for, but he was in a good mood and wanted to set more snares. "Perhaps, sweet *nupetsu*, we should spend some time in our lodge and you can decide if I'm a leader or a fool." Many Wolves looked over at Taimah, and she rolled her eyes.

"You and your crazy talk, old fool," said Nina, in mock anger. "You're like a male dog with his red thing sticking out, a Red He-Dog. That's what I should call you from now on."

"It's a strong name. I would enjoy living up to that name," said Many Wolves, with a smile. "Topusana, do you think Red He-Dog is a good name for me?"

Topusana looked up from her sewing and smiled. "I'm not jumping into this."

Many Wolves laughed again.

"Topusana, I have a question for you," said Taimah.

Many Wolves suspected that Taimah wanted to discuss other things. He couldn't blame her. Though Taimah had seen them couple many times, she seemed uneasy talking about it.

"What is it, Taimah?" Topusana stopped her work and looked at Taimah.

"How did you and Malone meet?"

"I've told you this before."

"I want to hear it again," insisted Taimah. "I'm tired of this He-Dog talk."

Topusana shrugged. "We met when Malone and your father came to Crooked Eagle's village. I was married to another man then. My husband's brother was Ten Arrows." Topusana used the name of the deceased because they had agreed that his soul was safely rooted in the next world. "My husband died of the white man's fever three winters ago. Many Penatekas from our village died from this fever."

"It was an evil spirit punishing the village," added Many Wolves.

"Punishing them for what?" asked Taimah.

"For making friends with the white men from the east." Many Wolves sincerely believed it was a curse of some kind.

"Malone believed it was a fever brought to the village by a sick captive," said Topusana, with vigor. "No one really knows who is right, but it was a terrible sickness, and many people died, including my husband."

"It sounds horrible." Taimah's earlier smiles were lost, buried in sadness.

"It *was* horrible. The medicine men and women tried everything to help these sick people, but they died so quickly, sometimes in less than a few sleeps. Fortunately, Malone and your father lived away from our village."

"I'm sorry. I forgot about the sad part of this story," said Taimah, looking down in shame.

"Sadness is like a snake bite or the sting of a bee. It hurts, but sometimes it cannot be avoided, and facing it will make you stronger," said Many Wolves, remembering his near-death experience with the rattlesnake's poison.

"That is the saddest part of the story, Taimah. The rest is happier," said Topusana in a reassuring tone.

"Good," said Taimah, the smile returning to her face.

"After my husband died, Malone came to my village and helped with the burial. He helped with my sadness, too. My husband was the last of my family. I lived with the medicine woman, Cooks Out The Marrow, for a time. Until finally Malone asked Crooked Eagle to release me from my mourning. Malone wanted to bring me here to your father's village."

"You see, sweet *nupetsu*, who the leader of our village is?" said Many Wolves, laying another snare for his wife.

"Quiet, fool!" barked Nina.

The whole group laughed this time.

"So that's how it happened, Taimah," said Topusana, chuckling at Nina's remark.

"Are you Malone's first wife?" It sometimes seemed to Many Wolves that Taimah had a question for every star in the sky.

"No," said Many Wolves in a serious voice, before Topusana could speak. "Malone had a wife and daughter a long time ago, when he lived in Laughing Crow's village. They were killed when the Pawnee attacked his village. He mourned many winters for them."

Topusana's arrival at their village had been one of the happiest moments Many Wolves could remember. Not only had it brought a mountain of happiness to Malone, but Many Wolves was very fond of her as well. Malone always said that she was a "feast for the eyes," and Many Wolves did not disagree. Many Wolves spent a lot of time with her alone, talking about Ten Arrows. There was so much he wanted to know about him. It helped to keep the fire of his friend's memory burning brightly.

"I'll make you some blackberry water, *Ahpu*, if I can have some too," offered Taimah, at last.

"You better make some for everybody, Taimah," said Nina, "or your father will really think he's the leader of this village."

* * *

It was late in the afternoon when Noche uttered a low, rumbling growl, and Many Wolves heard the beating hooves of a horse. But Noche's growls did not intensify; instead they quickly turned to tail wags as Malone rode up to the camp.

He dismounted and said, "I've located the buffalo herd. The scavenger birds led me to it."

"Where is it?" asked Many Wolves, who was alone at the camp with the birds and Noche. Nina and Topusana were out gathering nuts and berries, while Taimah was a short distance away, grooming her horse.

"North along the river. We should be able to set up a base camp close enough to them by sunset if we pack now. We can cross the river at Three Trees Crossing. It's shallow enough for the horses to walk across easily." Malone reached behind him and pulled out three dead prairie dogs from his hunting bag. "I killed these on the other side of the river. We can cook them up before we leave." He tossed the carcasses on the ground next to the fire pit, drawing immediate interest from the three birds and Noche.

"No, these aren't for you, beggars," said Many Wolves. To Malone he said, "I'll start cooking them up. The women are west of here. They'll have the tipis packed and ready long before the sun has fallen." He stood up and shouted to Taimah, "Taimah, come help me with these prairie dogs!"

"*Haa.* I'll be there in a moment, *Ahpu.* I'm almost done here."

By the time Malone had returned from watering his horse, Many Wolves and Taimah had finished skinning the prairie dogs. Taimah raised a new fire from the embers of the previous one and hung the carcasses over the low-burning flames on cooking sticks.

Cattle Drive

Ramon woke before the mission bells, knowing he had to get an early start. Luis had informed him the previous day that a large cattle drive was leaving San Antonio before sunrise. *Patrons* from several *ranchos*, including Don Carlos from the Dama de Medina, had agreed to work together to drive as many head of cattle as they could to the annual Saltillo Festival, hoping to improve their profits. The good news was that Colonel Tejada was bringing along a small company of soldiers to help protect the round-up from *banditos* and *indios*. This was a huge load off Ramon's mind, knowing he wouldn't be depended on for the group's protection. His duties were mostly as a *vaquero* and not a protector.

Ramon skipped his morning routine of shaving and reading, and grabbed the supplies he had prepared the night before, including his two pistols, rifle, and *escopeta*.

As he was leaving his room, he noticed something on the table in the waning darkness. It was a wooden box—the wooden box with Dr. Thompson's revolver. *Is it broken again?*

Next to it was a handwritten note:

> *Ramon, I offered the Englishman a deal he could not pass up. Use it well,* mi amigo.
>
> *Regards, Don Eduardo*

"I'll be damned," Ramon said to himself.

He hurriedly removed the pistol from the box and loaded the five empty chambers. Once ready, he tucked the revolver under his belt and then placed as many of the smaller lead balls as he could find into a pocket in his leather vest. *I will have nine shots now, and not just four.*

The light of morning was dawning as he packed his provisions on Cavador. He heard another horse coming and a quiet whistle. *Luis.*

"*Buenos días*, Ramon. We need to get going," said Luis, stopping his horse.

"*Hola, Luis.* I just need to load some food and *agua*."

Ramon filled his leather canteen with water left in his pitcher, then snatched his leather satchel loaded with dried tortillas, pecans, and *charqui* jerky. He loaded his supplies on his horse, draped his black *sarape* over his shoulders, strapped on his hat, and mounted.

"*Vamonos*, Luis!"

Ramon urged his horse forward, Luis whistled a command, and the two men galloped west toward the meeting place just outside the Presidio.

* * *

When they arrived, about thirty men were already gathered. Most were soldiers in their military uniforms—blue coats and white trousers; the remainder were *vaqueros*.

"Ramon! Luis!" A man in his early forties on horseback signaled for them to come over.

"*Buenos días*, Don Tomas," said Ramon, while Luis just nodded.

Don Tomas de Leon was the *patron* of the Rancho de La Parra, one of the biggest *ranchos* in San Antonio, and the primary organizer of the round-up, along with Don Carlos Francisco, the *patron* of the Dama de Medina. He was a well-dressed man, wearing matching burgundy trousers and waistcoat. He was average-sized, in good physical condition, and his graying beard made him look older than he really was.

"Ramon, we have driven *ganado* before to Saltillo," he said, "and this round-up will be no different. The wild cattle are sparse, but we will find as many unbranded animals as we can and bring them into the herd. We will drive them south along the Camino en Medio. Colonel Tejada will patrol the route for us. We hope to reach Saltillo with at least a hundred head in less than a week's time, covering over a hundred leagues. We have to keep them moving though. We have twelve days before the festival ends, and I don't want to arrive there on the last day."

"*Sí*, Don Tomas. You will need me to add some meat to the fire?" Ramon usually helped out the drive by providing the men with fresh game.

"Of course, Ramon. *Gracias*! Whatever you can add to the pot at the end of the day will be most welcome. Most of my men are much better with a rope than a gun. Colonel Tejada's men will also hunt for us."

Just then, Colonel Tejada rode up to them. He was impeccably dressed, as always, in the uniform of an officer of the Mexican Army. The chest of his dark blue waistcoat was decorated with several medals and golden shoulder straps. His hat was a blue bicorne with a large yellow plume hanging from it, a decoration possessed by no other officers or infantry.

"*Buenos días*, Don Tomas and Ramon," said Colonel Tejeda in a low, booming voice. If a toad could talk, thought Ramon, his voice would sound like Colonel Tejada's.

Don Tomas and Ramon nodded respectfully.

"My men are ready when you are, Don Tomas," said Colonel Tejada. He turned to Ramon and Luis. "If we run into *indios*, Ramon and Luis, you will hear our trumpeter sound the alarm. We may need your help, since you are experienced *indio* fighters, more so than most of my men."

"*Sí*, Colonel Tejada," said Ramon, and Luis nodded his acceptance. "May I offer some advice, Colonel?"

"What is it?"

"The *indios* will want our horses."

"More than the *ganado*?"

"*Sí*. Without our horses, we are helpless against them. We must guard our horses at all times."

"I will keep that in mind, Ramon," said Colonel Tejada. And he rode off to meet his troops.

"Let's go. The herd is waiting at the trailhead," said Don Tomas, signaling the other *vaqueros* to follow him.

When they reached the herd, Ramon, Luis, and the other *vaqueros* fell into position around the cattle. The herd was a mixture of old and young, cows and bulls, ranging in color from red and white to all shades of brown. The bulls, and many of the cows had large, curvy horns that could be a serious danger to any rider near them. They were hearty livestock who could easily live off the barren plant life in South Tejas.

A distant shout from Don Tomas signaled the start of the drive. Immediately, whistles and shouts rang out from the *vaqueros*, and dust kicked up from the earth-shaking hooves of cattle and horses. The orange sun peeked over the horizon to Ramon's left, guiding them southward.

So began Ramon's day as a working *vaquero*.

The men spread out around the perimeter of the herd. Ramon removed his *sarape* and held it in his right hand. It would be used like a whip for threatening the cattle. He and Luis were stationed as flankers, near the rear of the herd, a familiar spot for them. Any cattle that strayed were their responsibility. A shout or a whistle and a waving *sarape* were usually enough motivation to urge the straggler back into the group.

For Ramon, herding cattle was enjoyable work. He had performed it for over a decade, and it was second nature to him now; it brought his mind peace. No heavy thoughts or worries, just reacting to the herd, keeping the stragglers from straying too far. The physical work made his body feel strong, and it was good for Cavador as well. Not having to look for *indios* also took a load off his mind. He didn't know how much experience Colonel Tejada had with *indios*, especially *norteños*, but at least the soldiers would be the first line of defense, rather than him and Luis. And once they crossed the Rio Bravo into Coahuila, they would be leaving *norteño* territory, Comancheria, and *indio* attacks would be less of a threat.

They reached their first major river crossing, the Rio San Miguel, at midday. Colonel Tejada and half his troops crossed first, so they could guard the southern river bank, while the *vaqueros* contained the herd. The river was low, the water barely covering the boots of the riders. as was to be expected in late summer and early fall when there was very little snowmelt or rain to fill its width. When the soldiers reached the other side, they allowed their mounts to drink for several moments before coercing them back to service.

Then shouts from Don Tomas and other riders in the front of the herd stirred the lumbering cattle toward the river. Some of the animals drank, but most were frightened by the river and did not want to linger long in the flowing waters.

A few refused to enter the water altogether. Ramon approached an old, stubborn bull. He whistled and waved his *sarape*, trying to get the resisting beast to move. *Keep calm and don't frighten it.* Preventing panic in the herd was the primary aim of every good *vaquero*, in addition to keeping the animals safe. After many attempts, Ramon finally prodded the bull in the direction of the rest of the herd. It followed them into the river. "That's it, old *toro.*"

Ramon was thankful that the river was low enough to cross easily. As his horse entered the river, his mind flashed back to a time when he was a seven-year-old boy and stepped into the Rio San Antonio. He had lost his footing and fell into deeper water, where he could not feel the bottom. He struggled to stay above water with every gasping breath. His father rescued him before the current could carry him away, but that overwhelming feeling of helplessness was one of the most vivid memories from his childhood. *There was a devil in the deep water.* Though the Rio San Miguel was shallow and safe, Roman felt a small sense of relief when he reached the other side.

It was not long after the crossing that a brilliant red desert sunset signaled the end of the day for the cattle drive. Both men and animals were ready for rest and a meal. Several fire pits were started after clearing away the dried grass, and mesquite was gathered to create the flames for cooking.

The landscape was flat, and it was difficult to see past the engulfing foliage. The land was dappled with mesquite, creosote, and cactus. The bats and nighthawks were beginning to sweep the air for insects while chirping locusts filled the sky with sound. After over twelve hours of rumbling hooves, Ramon welcomed the quiet. He removed the red bandanna from around his nose and mouth and breathed in the dust-free air.

"Señor Connelly. I see you got a *pecari* for my stewing pot." It was Jorge, a man in his early thirties, who was the main cook for the *vaqueros*. He usually rode ahead of the herd in his cart, which was full of food and cooking supplies.

Ramon had shot a wild pig, a *pecari*, at the end of the day, after spotting a herd of around fifteen of them from the trail. He had not spent a lot of time hunting; rather, he had simply waited for easy game to present itself. Wild pigs were common and easy kills. They were much easier to kill than deer or rabbits, because they didn't flee as easily or quickly. Usually one of the herd did not run and stood as the group's protector, which had made an easy target for Ramon's rifle. If he had not found pigs, or deer or rabbits, armadillos were everywhere, and they were even easier targets than the wild pigs.

"*Sí,* Jorge. Go ahead and take it."

Jorge unstrapped the dead pig from the back of Ramon's horse and took it away. "*Gracias,* Ramon." He waved with the pig slung over his shoulders.

Ramon restrained his horse with a rawhide hobble so Cavador could graze, but would not easily run away if frightened. Then he stroked the horse's nose gently and spoke softly while Cavador nickered back at him. He wanted his horse to remain in his sight and within earshot. *An unguarded horse is always the first to be taken.*

Ramon had never had a mount stolen from him, and he had every intention of keeping it that way. Though the soldiers would be watching the horses in shifts, that was not enough for Ramon, not when there were *norteños* around. In his estimation, they could steal a man's *sarape* right off his back as he slept. But it wasn't *sarapes* that were their precious livelihood, the *dinero* of their culture—it was horses.

"You want any *frijoles* with *puerco*, Ramon?" asked Luis a while later, pointing at Ramon with a bowl in his hand.

"No, *gracias,*" said the green-eyed *vaquero*. The aroma of mesquite-cooked pork and beans permeated the night air. Ramon was hungry, tempted by the offer, but beans were heavy on the stomach and brought deep sleep. He wanted one ear and one eye peeled for danger around him. There would be safer opportunities for meals when they were south of the Rio Bravo.

Ramon relaxed near the fire, letting the heat from the flames fight off the chill in the air. His blanket was rolled up behind him as a backrest, and he rested his left arm on his bent left knee. His pistols and rifle rested at his side within easy reach. He pulled some *charqui* from his pocket and bit off a chunk of the salted meat. This and a dried tortilla would be his meal for the night.

Luis lumbered over and sat to his right, a steaming bowl in his hand. "These are tasty *frijoles*. They taste better the farther you get from home, *mi amigo*." His lips smacked together as he chewed, and he moaned contently, like a dog having his belly rubbed.

A howl echoed in the distance, and Luis froze. "Coyote?"

Ramon nodded his head. *Yes, I think so.* Ramon knew that the *indios* used animal sounds to signal each other. He was surprised the other men around him did not pause to listen. *Are they not concerned about indios?* Instead, they carried on talking loudly and laughing. Some were playing cards, and others were playing dice.

When he had finished eating the hard jerky, the Irish *vaquero* pulled his church-warden pipe out of his pocket and packed it with tobacco. He sucked in the flame from a small stick he took from the fire. He did this several times, until at last the tobacco embers burnt freely. Ramon breathed in a mouthful of the smoke, held it in for a few seconds, then slowly sent it back out of his mouth and nose. This was the moment he thought of during the day, a reward for himself, especially when his body was rife with fatigue.

"Is that a new *pistole*, Ramon?"

"*Sí*. It's the one I told you about. The Englishman's *pistole*," said Ramon, removing the weapon from his holster.

Luis set his bowl down and took the pistol, inspecting it. "The barrel is much thinner than your other *pistole*."

"The *balas* are much smaller, Luis, around thirty caliber. But there are five of them loaded and ready, and not just one, when they are needed." Ramon took the revolving *pistole* back from Luis and spun the cylinder around slowly.

"A forty caliber *bala* will drop a man dead," said Luis. "I don't know about the *balas* in that *pistole*. I'm not sure that's a chance I would take, Ramon."

Sí, but if you miss with your one-shot pistol, then you are the dead man, thought Ramon. But he held his tongue. He didn't want to argue with Luis, especially since he didn't really know how this *pistole* would shoot in a real fight. He had hopes that the revolver would shine against fast-charging *indios*.

He put the pistol back in his belt, then returned to nursing his church-warden. Luis returned to shoveling more beans into his gut.

"Will you play some cards tonight, or should I give up asking?" asked Luis, licking the sauce from his bowl.

"No, Luis, I don't think so. But you can keep asking. Maybe someday I'll change my mind."

"Is it because of your mother's *hermano* or because you worry about *indios*?"

"Both, Luis. Both."

When Ramon was ten, his mother's brother Guillermo had stumbled home one night drunk and with a *bala* in his stomach. He had been shot over a "stupid *juegos de cartas*," his mother had said. She was a nurse at the Presidio and said there was nothing she could do to comfort him. He died later that night. She must have said "stupid *juegos de cartas*" at least a hundred times that night, and for many days after that. She told Ramon to stay away from the dice and card games, especially if there was money and liquor involved, or he too would end up a bloody *cadaver* like Guillermo.

"I worry for you, *mi amigo*," said Luis. "You keep to yourself. You keep all your worries bottled up inside, as tight as the leather stretched over a drum. You should spend some time with the men, get to know them over a friendly game. Share a drink and a smoke."

Ramon exhaled a puff of smoke. "I have what friends I need."

"You have me and maybe Don Eduardo, *amigo*, and that's about it," said Luis, setting his empty bowl down on the ground.

Luis was right, Ramon thought. *I am a loner.* As far back as he could remember, he had been "the boy with the *gringo* skin and green eyes." Only he and his father in all of San Antonio had ever looked this way. Then his father died, and it was just him. In his home, in his village, Ramon had never felt like he really belonged. He was an outsider.

"Well, I'm going to play some cards. You stay here and make sure the fire doesn't run away," Luis joked.

Ramon smiled. Luis was not like his Uncle Guillermo. He enjoyed games, but he was not a careless drinker, especially when he was away from the security of the town. Luis always stayed sober in case Ramon needed him.

The coyote howled again. This time several more joined in. Ramon was fairly sure these were really coyotes, but he wasn't going to let the sounds lull him to sleep. He kept one eye on Cavador and the other eye on the fire, making sure it didn't run away.

Faith

Colonel Tejada's loud voice, and not the usual mission bells, woke Ramon the following morning. He sensed there was no alarm, just a commander rousing his men as part of their morning routine. Ramon glanced over at Cavador, who was grazing peacefully about twenty yards away. Once the coyotes had settled down for the night, it was only Luis's snoring that had challenged the chorus of night insects. Ramon was relieved that there had been no incidents in the early morning hours, when he had finally succumbed to his fatigue.

"Wake up, Luis," said Ramon, kicking the large, snoring man in the side of the leg. Luis was not one to be up with the chickens.

Ramon and Luis had slept near the other *vaqueros*, while Colonel Tejada and his men were a short distance away—a gathering of men, horses, and cattle surrounded in endless chaparral. Dew glistened on the edges of the mesquite, soon to be burned away by the hot desert sun.

The big *vaquero* just moaned and rolled over. "*Sí sí sí. Un momento.*"

Ramon left Luis to drain his bladder. He splashed some cold water on his face to help wake himself up, then washed himself with his bandanna. When he returned, he found Don Tomas sipping from a cup.

"*Buenos días*, Ramon. There is a pot of hot cider on the cooking fire over by Jorge's wagon," said Don Tomas. "Looks like I might have to pour Luis's cup down his pants to wake him up!"

Ramon chuckled. "He'll be ready when we need to ride. That cider smells good." He took his own cup over to the fire, poured himself some steaming cider, and took a sip. In the cool air of dawn, it felt good going down.

"Señor Connelly, there is fresh corn bread also, if you like," said the outfit's cook, offering a piece to him.

"*Gracias*, Jorge." Ramon smiled and accepted.

Colonel Tejada walked over and filled a cup from the pot.

"No signs of *indios*, Colonel?" asked Ramon.

"All quiet. Nothing reported from any of my patrols." Colonel Tejada sipped from his cup.

"*Muy bien.* Hopefully we will have good fortune on our side. Though it seems like there are more *indio* attacks every year." Ramon took a bite of cornbread.

"People think there are more attacks, Connelly, though under my command there have been less. The attack on San Saba last year is not easily forgotten by the people of San Antonio. We have brought many of the Lipanos into the missions. We will save their lives and their souls through Jesus Christ. Only the *norteños* resist us now, and their time will come to give themselves up to us and to God."

The colonel shared the same faith as Don Eduardo. Ramon thought that faith worked for people who believed in God—but what about other people, others who did not know God? Ramon believed it was like the parable in the Bible about the sower and the seed. Some seed fell on fertile ground and flourished, while other seed fell on rocky ground and withered. It seemed like believing in God was black and white like this. Either you accepted Him, or you didn't. Perhaps *indios* had their own god. *Who's to say their god is any better or worse than ours?*

"Do you believe this, Connelly?" said Colonel Tejada, drawing him from his thoughts.

"Do I believe what?"

"That the *norteños* will eventually give themselves up to us."

Ramon couldn't imagine *norteños*, with their superb fighting skills, suddenly walking into a mission, laying down their weapons, and giving themselves up to the Spanish and some strange god. "I believe they will fight until their last warrior cannot stand. And that it will probably not happen in my lifetime."

"You have little faith in God and in our people."

"I have faith in God and many other things, Colonel, just not faith that the *norteños* will lay down like tame dogs for us." Ramon finished his cooled cider in two large gulps, washing down the cornbread.

"You do not have the same faith in God that your father did."

Look where his faith got him, Colonel, Ramon thought. *Where was God when the norteño arrows pierced his chest? And where was God when my mother died of the fever?* Before his father died, Ramon had believed that anything was possible with enough prayers and a strong, unyielding belief in God. Now he was doubtful. What he took from the Bible and from Mass was still a sketch of how he should live his life, but only a sketch. He took what he felt he needed for his personal beliefs, and left the rest to the church and its servants.

"I guess I do not have the same faith as my father, sir," admitted Ramon. "*Adios,* Colonel, I need to get ready to ride," he said. And he walked away.

Deep Water

Two days later, the herd reached the tumultuous Rio Bravo, the boundary between the Spanish provinces of Coahuila and Tejas, and most importantly to Ramon, the southernmost boundary of Comancheria. To this point, Ramon hadn't seen any *indios*. Colonel Tejada reported that only one band was spotted, and his soldiers couldn't tell if they were *norteños*.

Once they were south of the Rio Bravo, the greater concern would be for cattle rustlers. And to Ramon, they were preferable. They only wanted to steal a few heads of cattle, not horses, and unlike the *norteños*, their encounters were typically nonviolent, acts of thievery. Handling these sporadic, *bandito* gangs was well within the capability of Colonel Tejada's company.

But first, they had to cross the big river—and a late-afternoon storm was rolling in at a brisk pace.

"Let's get this herd to the other side before the storm makes the river impassable," yelled the trail leader, Don Tomas, above the gusting wind.

The strong jolts of air were sporadic, but Ramon knew they would become more and more frequent. A light drizzle fell on the *serapes* of the men, who rode with heightened urgency now. The more experienced riders rode at the front of the herd. Many were mestizos—men with mixed Spanish and *indio* bloodlines—who had grown up on horseback. They were poor men, laborers, but they were also brave men who would not hesitate to risk their lives for their cattle or their horses.

"Keep them moving!" shouted Don Tomas.

The riders guided the lead steer into the big river, far upstream from where they expected the cattle to end up on the other side. They shouted at the cattle and at each other.

When a third of the herd was in the river, the first thunder rumbled through the sky. The cattle panicked, both in and out of the water. The men in the river fired shots from their pistols to try to scare the cattle back into formation. Ramon, still on land, rode hard to cut off several cattle who bolted from the herd. A shot from his pistol sent them back toward the mass of animals. He heard Luis yelling and whistling on the other side of the herd, trying to control them.

Then the rain began to pour down, turning the earth to mud. The cattle still moved in the right general direction, but only because of the efforts of the herders. The wind gusted and flashes of lightning lit up the dark, cloud-filled sky. With every flash, there was another runner, and with every rumble, there was more panic, from both horses and cattle. Ramon felt the pressure building up in his head, the fear strangling his mind. He tried to focus on the job at hand, to keep his mind occupied, but it was difficult.

Cavador stumbled as he stepped into the river, sending a jolt through Ramon's body, but both rider and horse recovered. *I have to stay on Cavador.* The wind blew Ramon's hat off his head, and he would have lost it if not for the chin strap that held it against his neck. But now his unprotected face felt the full force of the pelting rain, and he couldn't see anything. He felt all alone in the swelling river with only a dozen cattle in view. *Keep these cattle together. Get to the other side.* The water was rising with every step forward.

Another peal of thunder sent one animal into a frenzy of bellowing cries and thrashing horns. Ramon grabbed his rope and lassoed the long, curvy horns of the terrified beast, then signaled Cavador to pull back. The flailing rope was like a writhing snake, pulling them into deeper water. *Stay away from the horns.*

Both animals, horse and steer, were swimming now, paddling with their front hooves to stay afloat. Cavador's back was arched downward, and he grunted with labored breaths. Ramon held on, but he could feel his grip on the swollen reins slipping. *I have to stay on Cavador.*

Ramon let out more rope to ease the tension on his horse. *We need footing, Cavador. Swim to the other side.* He tried to steer Cavador straight toward the north bank of the river at an angle away from the steer's movement, letting out more rope as needed.

Then lightning crashed in front of them, sharp and bright. Cavador screamed and reared, crashing sideways into the water. Ramon was thrown off, and immediately went under.

His childhood nightmare came back to him. Lost in a dark world with no air. Floating like a bee in a honey jar. No sound at all. He was sinking down, down into nothingness.

Finally he felt the river bottom under his feet. He kicked his body upward, reached the surface, and sucked in a mouthful of life-giving air. His heart was fluttering wildly.

But again he sank, despite his efforts to keep himself afloat with his arms. Again he kicked off the bottom. *It's getting deeper.* Reaching the surface again, he yelled for help and tried to swallow more air before falling again. He felt his body weakening and his mind giving in.

I can't do this. I can't breathe. It's getting deeper.

As he sank for a third time, he felt something rub his arm. *A rope.* He grabbed it with both hands and felt tugging on the other end. It was like he was being lassoed—for once he was the bull and not the *vaquero. Just hang on.*

The rope dragged him like a dead fish on a line, until at last he reached the bank. He coughed several times and spit the water from his lungs. *I'm alive.*

He heard muffled voices. Then his ears cleared, and so did the voices. All the sounds of his world returned to him: the rain, the wind, the shouting men, the screaming cattle, and a familiar voice.

"Ramon, are you all right? Ramon!"

"Luis?" said Ramon, wheezing for air.

"*Sí, sí, sí*! It's your *amigo*, Luis! Ramon, are you all right?"

"I think so."

"*Lo siento,* Ramon. I'm sorry. I should have been watching you."

Ramon coughed out some more water. "It's fine, Luis. I'm fine. Is Cavador okay?"

"*Sí,* Cavador is on the shore. And we pulled in that big old bull too!"

Ramon breathed a sigh of relief. "*Muy bien,* Luis. *Muy bien.*"

"What happened, Ramon? Why didn't you swim?"

"I fell off Cavador and I panicked. I don't know how to swim, Luis. Every since I was a boy, I have been afraid of deep water like this."

"I didn't know, *mi amigo.*"

"I know. I never told you."

I never told anyone.

First Kill

Many Wolves's village was up with the sun. They had settled along the east side of the Rio Pecos. Malone and the women rode out ahead to scout the herd of buffalo, while Many Wolves remained behind. He had taken the birds out at first light to hunt. After numerous distractions from prairie dogs—which quickly disappeared into their burrows whenever a bird got close—the birds had finally caught a jackrabbit. Many Wolves split the kill among them and gave the rest to Noche. He wanted them fed early so they wouldn't be a distraction during the buffalo hunt later.

With full crops, the birds remained perched in trees around the makeshift camp as Many Wolves rode off with Noche to find the rest of the village. Malone had promised to wait for him before starting the hunt.

Tracking four horses and a wolf would not have been easy in tall grass, but Many Wolves didn't need to follow the hoofprints; he simply rode out toward the circling scavenger birds, knowing the buffalo and his family would be there. As he drew closer, the overpowering, pungent scent of the herd crept over the hills like a pervasive fog, blocking all other scents. Noche, however, was not easily fooled. The wolf barked to signal his leader that he had found the trail to the rest of the riders and Colmillo.

"All right Noche, you are the lead tracker," said Many Wolves. "Your brother has left signs in the tall grass that only you can find."

After following the black wolf for some time, Many Wolves sighted his family at the top of the hill. Noche ran ahead to greet his brother.

"*Ahpu*, I've seen turtles move faster in the mud," Taimah called down to him as he climbed. Malone had painted her face red in preparation for the hunt, and she was riding one of Malone's horses, a brown and white gelding with buffalo-hunting experience.

Many Wolves was startled by her appearance. He had never seen her face painted like this before. Malone had also painted his own face and the faces of the two horses to protect them in the hunt. Nina and Topusana were there, too. A pole-drag was tied to each of their horses for hauling the buffalo parts back to camp. They would watch the hunt from a safe distance and join the rest of the hunting party after the kill.

When Many Wolves reached the top of the hill, the huge herd appeared before him. The herd seemed relaxed, not alarmed by their presence. Most were actively grazing, while others rested. Cows tended to their moaning calves, and bulls guarded the outside of the herd, grunting and snorting at any challengers. Still other animals were wallowing in the dirt, trying to rid themselves of annoying insects.

Many Wolves thought to ask Taimah if she was ready, but he knew what her answer was already. He could see it in her excited eyes. He was probably more nervous than she was, but he was comforted knowing that Malone would be with her stride for stride.

"Will you ride with us, Many Wolves?" asked Malone.

"I'll follow," Many Wolves replied, "but I'll stay out of your way. I don't want to miss this." He wasn't as confident on his horse as Taimah. The memory of a past fall during a buffalo hunt ate away at his confidence like a hungry caterpillar chewing on a leaf.

Malone shifted his mount to face Taimah. "We'll attack the herd with the wind in our face. Otherwise they will smell our scent before they see us. The older bulls will signal the cows and calves to move away from us. I'll find a young bull on the edge of the herd and separate it. When you see my signal, I want you to charge from the right side of the animal. Aim just behind the shoulder, where the animals draw their breaths. You want your arrow point to pierce its air-sack, which will slow the animal. Feather Dog will pull you to the right after you shoot, to avoid the sweeping horns or the animal's fall."

"Should I keep extra arrows ready in my left hand?" asked Taimah, pulling a stone-tipped arrow from the quiver on her back. Malone always used stone arrows for buffalo hunting because they cut deeper into the animal than iron-tipped arrows.

"No. Pull them from your quiver one at a time and shoot. You will need the extra strength in each shot to penetrate the thick hide and bone. It's the force of the arrow, not the speed of the release, that is most important."

Taimah nodded.

"Are you ready, Daughter of Thunder?" said Malone, his eyes locked on hers.

"Yes, Malone. I'm ready," she said, a nervous smile on her face.

"Follow me, then, and stay back when I reach the herd," said Malone, spinning his black and white horse around to face the buffalos. He held several arrows and his bow with his left hand, and a quiver was slung over his right shoulder. He was shirtless, wearing only a breechcloth, leggings, and moccasins. A single eagle feather hung cocked to one side from his scalp-lock.

Malone approached the herd cautiously at first. Taimah followed him, but maintained a gap between them. Many Wolves stayed close behind her.

Then Malone launched into a gallop, shouting. The once-calm herd erupted into a thunderstorm of pounding hooves. Many Wolves lost sight of Malone, who was swallowed up by the swarm of beasts. Blades of grass flew into Many Wolves's eyes, and dust choked the air around him, but he kept Taimah in his sight.

Then Malone reappeared ahead of them, screaming and waving his bow at a bull on his right. He drove it away from the rumbling herd, away from the dust, then signaled to Taimah with a shout and a wave of his arm.

Taimah charged, quickly catching up to the animal, and approached it from the other side. With one hand on her bow and the other hand on the bowstring, she balanced herself at full stride on the horse—a skill granted only to Northerners, Many Wolves believed. She drew her bow and unleashed an arrow from three horse lengths away. The arrow hit the buffalo, but barely cut through the thick skin. Taimah and her mount pulled right, avoiding the menacing horns, and she pinched a new arrow from her quiver.

"Closer! Get closer!" yelled Malone, still guiding the animal from its left side.

Taimah charged again at the animal. This time she got closer. But as she nocked her arrow, it slipped from her grasp and fell to the ground. She commanded her mount with a shout to draw even closer to the target, and as it did, she loaded another arrow—and loosed it. This arrow dug into the animal, but it was high, above the shoulder. The animal bucked to the right, and she quickly turned to avoid it.

"Too high, Taimah!" Many Wolves yelled from several horse lengths behind.

Malone somehow kept the animal's attention, still yelling and waving at it, despite its efforts to try to return to the safety of its herd. *It must be tiring.* Taimah reloaded again and charged hard at the animal. Many Wolves heard the twang of her bowstring and the scream of the buffalo as the arrow cut into its side. The beast stumbled, but it did not fall. Regaining its balance, it slowed to a stop, moaning in pain, its breath labored.

Many Wolves stopped his horse, as did Malone, while Taimah circled back for another shot. But before she could release it, the animal stumbled again, and fell to the ground.

Malone cheered. "Yee-ah, Taimah!"

Many Wolves shouted too. So much pride welled up inside him that it was difficult to breathe, and the water in his eyes made it difficult to see.

All the tension in Taimah's face was drained away, replaced by a smile that stretched from ear to ear, as she rode back to meet them in front of the fallen beast. She dismounted to watch the buffalo live out what was left of its life, her three arrows protruding from its side—her kill.

The animal lay on its side. It moaned for several heartbeats, straining for air, straining for life—then, finally, it breathed its final breath.

The prairie around them was silent; the rest of the herd had dispersed. All that remained was the settling dust and the single buffalo lying on the ground.

"Do I say a prayer now, *Ahpu?*"

"You can give thanks to the Great Spirit when your bury the heart, Taimah," answered Malone, "and ask Him to call more buffalo spirits to our world to replace the one that was lost."

She nodded respectfully to her teacher.

She was blessed, Many Wolves thought, to have a skilled warrior and hunter to teach her. What Many Wolves had seen her do today... they were achievements far beyond what he could ever do—and they were what he always dreamed for her. She was not born with Northerner bloodlines, but there was Northerner in her heart and in her spirit. And Malone nurtured this spirit as if she were his own child.

Many Wolves walked over to her and embraced her. "You are a son and a daughter to all of us, Wildflower. We are proud of everything that you are and everything that you can do." He was moved by a swirling emotion as he looked into her eyes. "Today you are a warrior of our village."

Nina and Topusana had now joined them as well, with their pole-drags. "I am very proud of you too, Little Flower," said Nina, hugging Taimah as soon as Many Wolves released her. "You will be a warrior who does woman's work too."

"Yes, *Shimaa*," said Taimah, smiling at her mother.

Topusana also hugged her. "I've never seen a Penateka woman hunt like that. It is a special gift you have, Taimah."

"Look, Taimah," said Malone, pointing at her prize. "Three arrows, and none of them are broken. That is a good sign. You will enjoy many successful hunts."

"But it took me four arrows to kill it, Malone."

"One arrow killed it. This one," he said, pointing at the arrow that dug deepest into the buffalo. "The other ones were just practice." Malone laughed. "I want to hear about each of these arrows when you dance tonight around the ceremonial fire."

Malone drew his knife and cut into the gut of the large animal. Reaching into the cavity, he extracted the buffalo's liver and presented it to Taimah. "This is for you, Daughter of Thunder."

Taimah took a big bite from the bloody organ and smiled. "It's so tender and warm. It melts like snow in my mouth."

"It's all yours. You don't have to share it with anyone," said Malone.

"It's for the hunters to enjoy," said Topusana. Nina and Many Wolves agreed.

Taimah took several more bites, then offered it to Malone. Between the two of them, they ate the whole liver quickly. Taimah shared a couple of small pieces with the two wolves as well.

"You should take the heart out now, Taimah, then Topusana and Nina will start stripping the hide from the carcass," said Malone. "Many Wolves and I will help with the bigger cuts."

As the women worked, the quiet was broken by the distant boom of a French long gun. Then two more shots followed the first.

"We are not alone hunting the buffalo," said Malone, listening for more sound.

After a silent pause lasting several heartbeats, more shots rang out. The sound was like short blasts of thunder, and it continued for quite a while.

"Who do you think it is, Malone?" asked Many Wolves. "French trappers?"

"The Raccoon-Eyes use the French guns. So do the Kiowa," said Malone. "After we pack this meat on the pole-drags, I should ride out to see who it is. The Penateka will want to know who is hunting on their lands."

Hollow Men

With everyone in the village helping, the buffalo was skinned, butchered, and packed on the pole-drags with sunlight still remaining in the day. Nothing from the kill was left behind, aside from the heart that Taimah buried. Topusana and Nina pulled the remains of the carcass with their two horses, and the hunting party walked single-file westward toward the Rio Pecos and the temporary camp that was set up there. The two wolves scouted ahead of the group, stopping often to pull sounds and smells from the meandering breeze that blew at them from the river. The three birds joined the party as well and circling around them, occasionally landing on one of the pole-drags to rest.

When the group reached the tree-lined banks of the Rio Pecos, Malone dropped back alongside Many Wolves. "I should scout those gun hunters before darkness comes. Come with me, Many Wolves. We will stretch the horses and be back before the sun falls."

"Can we leave them here?" said Many Wolves. He always felt safer on the other side of the river, where the buffalo, and the men who hunted them, rarely roamed.

"They will be safe," said Malone. "These are Penateka lands, and we have their protection. The trees will keep them covered. Taimah and Colmillo will guard the camp. Let's go."

Many Wolves saw that Malone was anxious to leave and that he wanted his company. If he'd had any of the white lion's paw flower left, he could scout the gun hunters with a mind-journey with Flecha. But that wasn't a possibility now, and besides, he was sure that Malone wanted to see with his own eyes.

Many Wolves pulled his horse up alongside Nina's. "Malone wants to scout those hunters we heard earlier. I am going with him. We'll be back before dark." Then Many Wolves turned to Taimah. "You and Colmillo will guard the camp. We'll be back soon."

"You will back for my buffalo dance?"

"*Haa*, Wildflower."

Many Wolves swung his horse around and whistled for Noche to follow him. "Try to keep up, Noche," he said. Then he commanded his horse to follow Malone, and they rode north toward the commotion they had heard earlier.

They traveled along the river at a steady gallop. Malone kept looking back to make sure Noche was keeping up with them and not tiring. The horses were used to running long distances, but the wolf was used to shorter sprints. From time to time, they stopped so Noche could catch his breath and drink some water.

"We are almost there," said Malone, breathing briskly.

How does he know? Many Wolves looked around and spotted a strand of smoke reaching its hand out to the sky. His body was tired, but he felt strong, exhilarated. He didn't spend nearly as much time on the back of a horse as Malone and Taimah did. *I will be sore tomorrow.*

"Are you ready to ride again?" Malone asked, then took a drink from his water pouch.

"I'm ready if Noche is ready." Riding with Malone was like riding with a ghost who never tired. It hardly mattered that Malone had many more winters in his bones.

They started off again. And before long, Many Wolves spotted a swarm of scavenger birds circling near the smoke trail. They approached a small slope, and Malone signaled with his hand to slow down.

As they crested the rise, they got their first glimpse of the carnage—and their first whiff of the rotting flesh. Many Wolves counted ten buffalo carcasses, and he expected there were more out of his eye's reach. All of them had been skinned and left to decay. Vultures, crows, and ravens had already started in on their feast, while other birds scampered on the ground around the carcasses, waiting their turn. Several coyotes also prowled the landscape, stealing an occasional bite here and there, keeping an eye out for larger predators.

Malone shot a grim look at Many Wolves. "The hunters are probably still here somewhere. They take the skins and leave the rest for the scavengers. These are not Raccoon-Eyes or Kiowas, but hollow men with poisoned minds. White men."

A faraway gunshot echoed in the silence, and distant laughter followed. Noche shuddered. Many Wolves felt his heart race like bee's wings, and a shiver shot through his body like the sudden strike of a coiled snake.

"Let's go," said Malone. "I want to see these hollow men for myself."

"We should be careful. We don't know how many of them are there."

"I will try to stay hidden until we know their numbers." Malone urged Many Wolves to follow him at a trot.

To Many Wolves, the stench of rotting flesh brought back vivid, unpleasant memories of the village that Laughing Crow had burned long ago. The village of the loving people who raised Many Wolves. It was mindless slaughter back then, as it was here. Mindless slaughter by mindless men. Like Malone said: *hollow men.*

Many Wolves followed Malone, weaving around one horrific abomination after another. So much food wasted. Sinew to make bows—wasted. Bones for tools—wasted. Bladders to make water bags—wasted. Who were these people who didn't need fresh meat or bows or tools? Many Wolves felt anger burning away the chill of the air. He needed comfort, and he found it in his quiver, a bow, and a nocked arrow. Malone had already prepared himself with his own weapon.

Malone motioned for Many Wolves to stop. In the distance raged a bonfire, and beyond it, Many Wolves spotted three men and a boy. He watched silently with Malone, undetected. One of the men aimed a long gun at a carcass near him and fired, leaving a puffy cloud of smoke around him. Many Wolves looked over at the man's target and saw a crow, now injured and flopping on the ground. The man with the gun cheered, and the other two with him laughed. There was already a dead crow on the ground near the injured one. *They killed that one too.* Many Wolves's mind flashed back to his wolf hawk Cazador's death from Laughing Crow's arrow. The memory angered him even more.

He was close enough to see that the men were white-skinned like him, and all of them had hairy faces like the French trapper Malone had once killed. They were all fully clothed and all wore head coverings. "Are they French trappers, Malone?"

Noche growled, a drawn-out rumble in his throat.

"Easy, Noche. Stay, Noche," commanded Many Wolves, looking down at the wolf.

"I don't know," said Malone. "They are white men of some kind. French trappers or the white men from the east, Mare-cans. I am told that far to the east, there are Mare-can villages as far as the eye can see. They are coming for our land to make more villages."

"Why do they kill the buffalo if they want to make villages here?" This was the first time that Malone had spoken of these white men, these Mare-cans. White-skinned men who were different from the French trappers and the French men who traded goods to the Northerners.

"They don't need the parts of the buffalo to make villages. They get what they need for their villages from the east. They trade the buffalo hides to those villages to get what they need."

Many Wolves still had many questions. "How long have they been here?"

"They have just started to come. Each new moon brings more white men to take the land and kill the buffalo," said Malone above Noche's steady growl.

"Why do the Northerners let them stay here?"

"The white men are coming from all directions, like wolves surrounding a buffalo. The Penatekas and Nokonis can fight off one or two of the wolves, but the others will attack the unguarded flesh. Others bulls from the herd must help: the Raccoon-Eyes, the Pawnee, the Kiowa. They must all protect the herd. *We* must help protect the herd."

"What can we do? There are only two of us," said Many Wolves, fearing what Malone was going to say next.

"I will show you what we can do," said Malone, his eyes glaring with hatred. "Stay here, Many Wolves. Stay out of sight."

Malone urged his horse forward and rode out toward the hairy-faced hunters. He screamed a war cry as he raced toward them, his bow and several arrows grasped firmly in his left hand. The men spotted him and quickly ran for their long guns. The boy ran away to hide. Malone pulled up and started taunting them with his prancing black and white pony, keeping his distance from their long guns. The three men looked frantic as they loaded their weapons.

Malone's horse continued prancing from side to side as if Malone was waiting for some signal to attack. He taunted them with his words as if trying to draw their fire. Many Wolves prayed to himself when he saw the men aiming their weapons. But Malone held his pose and his distance, seemingly unafraid.

Two of the weapons blasted almost precisely at the same time. Many Wolves's heart jumped from his chest, but Malone was still alive, still barking at his attackers. And apparently this was the signal Malone had been waiting for. He charged to a full sprint, straight at them, weaving left and right like a swift bird dodging invisible trees. The third man, surrounded by a cloud of smoke from the other two guns, fired at Malone, but the Northerner did not fall or even flinch.

Malone drew his bow, and Many Wolves heard three quick twangs. Two of the men fell. The last man started to run, but Malone rolled straight at him and shot an arrow through his back, sending him face down into the earth. Before the smoke from their weapons had even floated away, Malone had sent all three men to the ground, badly injured and screaming for their lives.

Malone dismounted, and at the same time, Noche bolted toward him.

"Noche!" yelled Many Wolves, but the wolf did not slow. Many Wolves set his horse into motion and followed the black wolf.

Malone walked over to the first man, knife drawn, and swiftly brought an end to his life by slashing his throat. A second sweep of his knife popped the man's scalp off in a heartbeat. The enraged Northerner repeated the same killing stroke with the second man, then stripped his scalp as well. But it was Noche who ended the third man's life. He tore the man's throat apart, swinging him back and forth like a child's doll.

"Noche, come!" called Many Wolves, jumping off his horse. The wolf released his victim and returned to his leader, his ears pulled back and his tail hung low.

"Where did the boy go?" said Malone, his hands bloodied by his deeds. He placed the two scalps in his hunting bag.

"He's hiding over there behind the hoop-drag," said Many Wolves. A hoop-drag was a pole-drag with hoops on either side that allowed it to roll. It was pulled by two horses. The white men used it for hauling their supplies.

"I see him."

"You're not going to hurt him, are you?"

"No. Unless he tries to hurt me first."

Malone traded weapons again, placing his knife back in his leg sheath and drawing his bow and a few arrows from the quiver on his back. Many Wolves followed him, with Noche on his leader's heel.

Malone approached the hoop-drag cautiously. The boy could be heard whimpering underneath a blanket on top of the wooden supply carrier. Carefully, Malone flipped the blanket away and found the boy curled up, no weapons in his hands.

"Bring one of their horses," said Malone.

Many Wolves walked over to the other side of the hoop-drag. He untied a horse and walked it over to Malone.

Malone signaled several times with his hand for the boy to come to him. "Come. Come."

Reluctantly, the teary-faced boy got up and jumped to the ground. He looked at Malone briefly, but then his eyes locked on Many Wolves. The boy mumbled some words that Many Wolves didn't understand.

The boy was about the same age that Many Wolves had been when he left his village. Many Wolves recalled the horrible dreams he had of his white-skinned parents dying. *Are any of these dead men his father? Will he have the same nightmares?* He felt a strange bond, and a deep-rooted sympathy toward the blue-eyed boy who shared his skin color. He smiled at the boy, but like a stone thrown into a lake, the smile was not returned.

Malone took the lead of the horse and offered it to the boy. "Take it and go! We will not harm you. Take it!" His voice was firm and convincing.

The boy took the lead, then mounted the horse.

What will he eat? How will he hunt? "Wait," said Many Wolves to Malone.

Many Wolves walked over to the bodies of the dead men. He grabbed one of the long guns that was lying on the ground, then grabbed a bag of the metal balls from one of the bodies. From another body he took what looked like a food bag, then he walked back and handed them to Malone. "He will need these."

"To fire the French gun, he'll need the magic black powder as well," said Malone. "Grab the horn from that body and bring it here." When Many Wolves had done so, Malone stashed all the supplies in the horse's riding bag and handed the long gun to the boy. Then he shouted and slapped the horse's leg, releasing the lead.

The boy looked back at Many Wolves one last time and rode off.

Malone untied the other three horses and released them. "The Penatekas will find them." Then he looked around the camp. "If there's anything you want, take it now. I will burn the rest, except for the bodies. The scavenger birds won't need to travel far to find their eyes."

The Silver Lion

It was late afternoon on a warm day as Ramon and Luis rode slowly on the main road through Saltillo, keeping their horses at a slow walk to avoid the throngs of people. Their contract with Don Tomas and Don Francisco had been met in full, and like many of the people here, they each had a pocket full of pesos.

Each year Saltillo hosted a festival that attracted visitors from all over New Spain, from as far north as Santa Fe and as far south as Mexico City. The streets were packed with merchants selling everything from boots to hats, tobacco to wheat, gunpowder to mining supplies. The eating and drinking establishments were bustling with activity. Screaming children ran through the streets, and music filled the air.

It was Ramon's third trip to the capitol of Coahuila. It was easily the largest city he had visited, and a stark contrast to the quiet, subdued town of San Antonio. After seven days on the cattle trail, he was ready to relax, eat, and drink at one of his favorite places.

"Are you heading to the Silver Lion, Ramon?"

"*Sí*, Luis."

The Silver Lion was a little more expensive than some of the other local establishments, but Ramon didn't mind paying a premium to avoid the noise and packed crowds.

Luis laughed. "You are a man who likes his *paz y tranquilidad* and is willing to pay for it. I am looking for a good card game and the cheapest *mezcal* in town."

Unlike most of the working class *campesinos*, Ramon was willing to part with silver *reals* and not just *cuartillos*. After a few drinks, he looked forward to a good meal and modest accommodations, where he could enjoy a warm bath and a smoke. One night of luxury was worth a few silver pieces.

The two men arrived at Ramon's destination, the Silver Lion Cantina.

"*Adios*, Ramon. See you *manana*," said Luis.

"*Adios*, Luis. I will treat you to a *grande* meal before we leave tomorrow, to thank you for pulling me out of the *rio*."

"*Gracias*, Ramon. I look forward to it."

"It's the least I can do to thank you, *amigo*."

Luis tipped his hat and rode off.

Ramon entered the large stone building with vines crawling over its walls. Several men stood at the bar to his left, and others sat at the tables to his right. The decorative chairs and tables were hand-carved of walnut, and the bar was glazed mahogany. The décor was stylish and meticulously cared for.

Many of the patrons paused to glance at Ramon as he entered the cantina, but then they returned to their conversations and drinks. There was a card game in the corner, but it seemed gentlemanly, tame enough. Ramon found an empty table in the opposite corner, past the bar, and next to another table with a lone patron. He removed his *escopeta* shoulder holster and set it on the ground next to him, then sat with his back to the wall, so he had a good view of the place.

An older, well-dressed man in his fifties, with silver hair and a thick mustache of the same color, approached him with a serving tray. A white linen cloth was slung over his arm. "*Buenos tardes*, señor. Welcome to the Leon de Plata. My name is Amadeo. How may I serve you?" The man's voice was soft, subdued. Ramon remembered the old *patron* from previous visits. *Amadeo.* His posture was perfectly straight, he was always gracious, and his service always excellent.

"Are you serving chile mead today, Amadeo?" Chile mead was a sweet and spicy, mildly alcoholic drink. It was one of Ramon's favorites, and this establishment served some of the best in New Spain.

"*Sí*, señor. An excellent choice," said Amadeo, nodding respectfully.

He left for only a minute, returning with a pewter mug. "My son, Julio, made this batch himself. I hope you enjoy it."

"*Gracias*." Ramon took a small sip of the peppery mead and let the spicy liquor roll around on his tongue for a bit. "*Esta delicioso*." He pulled out a four-real coin from his pocket and placed it on the tray. "This will cover three rounds?" Ramon knew his offer was overly generous.

"*Sí*, señor. *Muy bien*! I'll keep your *jarra* full of Julio's brew. *Gracias*." The old server bowed his head and walked away.

Ramon looked around the cantina. The walls were decorated with paintings of female flamenco dancers. *The old man has good taste.* The room was filled with the sounds of laughter and relaxation. Ramon took another sip of the delicious mead and sat back, taking it all in.

"Señor, I share your love for the chile mead," said the man seated at the table next to him.

Ramon smiled and raised his drink as a salute, but did not say anything.

"Julio makes the best chile mead in Saltillo, señor!" said the man, laughing and flashing his white teeth. "There's a touch of lime in it—can you taste it?"

"*Sí*," Ramon replied.

"I am Francisco del Castilla y Salazar, señor. But most call me Paco. What is your name?"

"Ramon Connelly."

"*Salut*, Señor Connelly. It's rare to see a man with green eyes. Your Spanish is too good for an Americano. Where are you from?" Paco was on the heavy side and wore a graying beard and mustache. Ramon guessed the man was in his late forties.

"San Antonio de Bexar."

"Ah, *sí*. You have an Irish father and a Spanish mother, am I right, Señor Connelly?"

"*Sí*."

"Let me guess again, señor. You are one of the *vaqueros* who drove the *ganado* down from San Antonio?"

"*Sí*," said Ramon, taking another sip of his mead, trying to enjoy it. It tasted better with silence.

"You are a fighting *vaquero*, I see. Two *pistoles* and an *escopeta*. I don't see many *vaqueros* packing that much gunpowder."

"Tejas is a dangerous place."

"*Sí*. Speaking of danger—see the big *hombre* who just walked in?" Paco spoke with a hushed voice, and Ramon noticed heads turn toward the cantina's entrance. "That's Pancho Jimenez. Most men call him 'Pancho the Pig' or just 'El Porcino.' Trouble follows him around Saltillo like a starving dog. I wouldn't look him in the eye."

From the looks of it, Ramon's hopes for a peaceful afternoon were long gone.

El Porcino

The loud talking and laughter ceased. Ramon saw that all eyes were glued to El Porcino. He was tall and heavy, built like a bull; his legs were like the trunks of oak trees. His beard was black with gray streaks. His white shirt dangled outside of his black pants, and the spurs on his boots clinked as he walked along the polished stone floor.

"*Buenos tardes, patrons* of the Leon de Plata!" His booming voice easily filled the place.

He was accompanied by three men. They looked dirty, shabby, and unkempt, like him, but none approached his size. Two of them stayed at the door, like guards, and the third stood next to him. All of them had pistols, and the taller one of the two at the door had an *escopeta* strapped on his back.

"This is a special day for Pancho Jimenez! Do you know what day it is?" He looked around the place like he was giving a sermon. "No one knows? I am disappointed, *mis amigos*. I am hurt." Pancho shook his head in disappointment. "This is the day that Pancho Jimenez was born! It is a happy day for me, and I want it to be a happy day for you too."

Pancho began to pace along the bar as he spoke. "I would like us to have some drinks together, *mis amigos*, to celebrate my day of birth. Now, isn't it a tradition on birthdays for a man's friends to buy him drinks?" He spun around, pointing at everyone in the bar. "You are my friends, and it is my birthday, right?"

Then he shifted his voice to imitate a softer-spoken man. "Pancho, I think we should buy you drinks today—and your friends too!"

He returned to his normal, loud voice. "Great idea, my friend. How should we do this?"

Again he spoke in a soft falsetto. "We should have a little collection and have everybody donate a few of their silver coins, Pancho."

"*Perfecto, mi amigo*! I'm glad you are here to speak for everybody. It can be like Sunday Mass where we pass a collection basket around and everyone gives a little bit of their spare silver for Pancho. It will make you all feel so much better to give, just like at Sunday Mass."

A man at one of the tables near the door stood up and tried to run out, but the two men at the door grabbed him.

"Now, *amigo*," said Pancho, walking over to the man. "We can do this peacefully or violently." Pancho swung his right fist at the man, knocking him down, then picked him up by the shirt and threw him at an empty table as easily as most men throw a blanket.

The man was dazed. He wiped the blood from his nose and crawled back to his chair.

Pancho whispered something to the thin man who was following him around. Then he turned back to the cantina. "Here's what we will do *amigos*," he said calmly as if nothing had happened. "Tito and I will walk around, and you will put your spare silver in his hat. Imagine the hat is a collection basket, eh? It's very simple, and no one else has to get hurt. *Comprendes?*"

Pancho and Tito started at a table where four men were playing cards. The hulking man grabbed the coins that were in the middle of the table and tossed them into the sombrero. "You see how easy that is, *amigos*? Just pretend that Pancho had a full house and won the hand!"

The two men went from table to table collecting silver. When they came to the table where the man with the bloodied nose sat, Pancho grabbed him by the shirt and said through gritted teeth, "You, *amigo*, will empty your pockets into the hat. That is the penalty for your insolence!"

The man reached into his pocket, his hand trembling, and dumped a handful of silver into the hat.

"*Gracias.* Now that wasn't so bad, huh?" El Porcino laughed loudly. Tito echoed him like a giggling hand puppet.

After extorting coin from several more tables and the men who sat at the bar, Pancho arrived at Paco's table. "Now, here is a familiar face. My good friend Paco Salazar. You didn't know it was my birthday?"

"Here, take my *donación,* you greedy pig!" Paco slammed two coins on the table. The pleasant, easygoing manner that Ramon had seen in Paco was gone.

"Paco, Paco, Paco. No kindness for a *compadre?* I'm disappointed! Only two *reals?* I expect double that from you, *hermano.*" Pancho's right hand hovered over his *pistole.*

"If you ask me to pay more, *Porcino,* I'll put a *bala* in your fat belly!"

Ramon saw that Paco's pistole was drawn under the table.

Pancho flung Paco's mead in his face, then flipped the table on him. Paco's *pistole* blasted errantly into the ceiling. Pancho then lifted up the table and slammed it on Paco several times shouting, "This is how you treat your friends, Paco! You are a weak, pathetic little *cucaracha!* I should kill you now, but I don't want to spoil my *fiesta!*"

Paco was curled up on the floor, moaning. Blood was dripping from his face. More coins had fallen out of his pocket, so Ernesto gathered them up and added them to the collection.

"A little bonus, Tito, for our troubles," said Pancho.

This Pancho is just another bully, Ramon thought, *picking on older and weaker men like Paco.* Ramon had seen his share of bullies before. As the only *gringo* boy in San Antonio, he had been a target for the bigger, stronger, older *español* boys. He had never backed down, because it wasn't tolerated. His father used to say: "Fighting is in our blood, lad. No son of mine is gonna back down."

Now, under his large round table, Ramon held his loaded *escopeta* in his left hand and his revolver in his right. He was ready to defend himself— again.

Pancho faced him. El Porcino's fierce black eyes looked like lifeless beads. The man's stench assaulted Ramon's senses. His brow was covered in sweat, and his breathing was labored from exertion.

"So now, the last man. The *gringo*. Will you put some coin in the hat, or do I need to beat it out of you too?"

Ramon looked around. He set his revolver in his lap as he calmly took another sip of his mead. Pancho's guards still stood by the door. *I have three guns ready and two men to kill, before they come.*

"I don't have any coins for you... *amigo*," said Ramon, in a low, even voice.

Pancho roared with laughter. Tito joined in, holding the collection hat.

"You come into the Leon de Plata with no silver, *amigo*." Pancho laughed some more. Then he stopped laughing. "You think I am a fool?"

Ramon took another gulp of his mead, then poured what little that was left on the floor. *I don't want him throwing this in my face.* Then he returned his left hand to his weapon. His eyes were locked on El Porcino's face, but he could see the man's gun hand from the corner of his eye. Ramon wasn't concerned about Tito; he was a follower, not a leader.

"I don't think you are a fool, Pancho. You've collected a tidy little sum already at your little 'Mass.' I just don't think you need my *donación*." Ramon laughed to himself.

"What is so funny, *gringo*?" Pancho's eyes were glittering with rage.

"Your life, Pancho, will travel full circle. You were born... and then you died. All on the same day."

Pancho gritted his teeth and reached for his pistol, but as he did, Ramon flipped the table up at him. The Pig's pistol fired into the ground. Ramon stood up and blasted the big man in the chest with his *escopeta*, knocking him off his feet. With his other hand, he shot Tito in the gut with his revolver. Tito's weapon fired into the ceiling as he fell backward.

Ramon ducked behind the table, hiding also behind the veil of smoke, as the two men at the door charged toward him with their pistols drawn. Each fired at him, but the table blocked the *balas*, spitting wood into the air.

The Irish *vaquero* dropped his *escopeta*, pulled out his second *pistole*, and shot the closest man in the chest. That was a miscalculation, since it was the other man who had a loaded *escopeta* still. This other man blasted his weapon at Ramon, but the powder exploded in his face and sent him screaming to the ground with his hands over his eyes.

That was lucky.

Only the man with the *escopeta* and Pancho were still moving, but both were in severe pain. Ramon bent down over Pancho and cocked the hammer to ready his next shot.

"Ramon, look out!" shouted Paco.

Ramon looked up and saw, too late, that the man with the misfiring *escopeta* was charging at him with a knife. Ramon had no time to dodge or fire.

With a loud blast from Ramon's left, the man dropped. Smoke rose from Paco's *pistole*.

Lucky again.

"*Gracias*, Paco."

Paco smiled at him with bloodshot eyes and a bleeding mouth.

Ramon walked over to Pancho, who was lying on his back, groaning. *The bigger the man, the harder it is to get back up.* It had always seemed that way to Ramon when he was growing up.

"I will see you in hell, *gringo*!" yelled Pancho, looking up at him and coughing up blood. Blood had already soaked through his shirt, and it stained his teeth. Life was slipping from his eyes.

Ramon looked down, along the top of his gun barrel, at the fading eyes of the pathetic wretch of a man. "The Mass is ended, *El Porcino*." He cocked the hammer of his pistol, paused for a moment of silence, and took a deep breath.

Then he squeezed the trigger.

"Go in peace."

Investigacíon

The buzz of chatter started right after the final gunshot in the Silver Lion, and it spread out onto the dusty streets of Saltillo. Within minutes, a crowd was outside spreading information from person to person about the gunfight, like a trail of ants that had just discovered a dead grasshopper. Ramon and several other men in the bar dragged the four dead bodies out into the street.

One of the men said to him, "The coffin maker will be busy tonight."

Ramon glanced at the man, but didn't reply. *The coffin maker will need to make an extra large box for El Porcino.*

Ramon re-entered the cantina, picked up the coin-filled hat from the ground, and handed it to Amadeo. "Make sure your customers get their *dinero* back." Then he reached into his pocket for some pesos. "And take this—it will help pay for the clean-up and broken tables."

Amadeo accepted the hat full of coins, but politely declined to take Ramon's offering. "Señor, you have done a great service today for the people of Saltillo. I cannot accept that."

Ramon spoke loudly to the patrons in the cantina. "A round of drinks on the house, *amigos*." He winked at Amadeo, then handed him the pesos. This time the cantina owner accepted.

Suddenly, a commotion broke out in the street. Soldiers entered the bar with a high-ranking military man, a captain or colonel, leading them.

"That is *Capitán* Esperanza. He is the head of Saltillo's militia," whispered Paco, who was standing next to Ramon.

J. BRADLEY VAN TIGHEM

"Who is responsible for killing these men?" asked the captain, bellowing with authority. Captain Esperanza was a middle-aged man with speckles of gray in his hair and mustache. His uniform was neat and trimmed to fit the contours of his slim body.

"It was Ramon and me," said Paco, motioning to Ramon. "We were defending ourselves, *capitán*. We did nothing wrong."

"I see four *cadavers* in the street who won't be able to share their side of the story, Paco," said Captain Esperanza in a serious tone. "I will need to commence a full *investigación* into these matters. To begin, I will need to take your weapons, Paco, and the *gringo's* too. Take them off, *por favor,* and set them on the bar." The captain looked them over from head to toe. "That includes any concealed weapons."

"I will get these back?" Ramon asked. He was worried about never seeing the rare revolver again.

"*Sí,* if you are innocent. If not, you won't be needing them anymore." The captain's voice was firm.

Ramon hated the idea of relinquishing his weapons in a strange place, but there was no other choice. He removed the pistols from his belt and placed them on the bar, then did the same with his shoulder scabbard. Finally, he unstrapped the leg sheath, which held his knife, and set it on the bar as well. Paco did the same with his own weapons.

One of the soldiers searched the two men, then nodded to the captain that there was nothing else.

"Tie their hands," the captain ordered.

One of the soldiers approached Ramon. "Put your hands behind your back." Ramon obeyed, and the soldier tied his hands tightly with rope. Another soldier did the same with Paco.

"Follow me," said the captain.

The soldiers surrounded Ramon and Paco as Captain Esperanza led them through the crowded streets. Ramon did not feel like a criminal, since most of the people were smiling at him.

"He's the *gringo* who killed El Porcino," said one to another.

"Bless you!" yelled a woman.

"*Gracias!*" shouted several men.

Ramon did not know how justice was served in Saltillo. In San Antonio, fines were levied, lashes were given, and the most severe crimes were met with a firing squad. It also seemed that the stiffness of the penalty was often governed by your social and ethnic status. Mestizos were more likely to be given lashes, while an Isleño lawbreaker was treated more leniently. Most crimes in San Antonio never made it to a courtroom.

They arrived at a stone building with bars on the windows. *The Saltillo Jailhouse.* Ramon had seen it several times from the street, but had never been inside. Until now.

The door opened onto a big room, sparsely furnished with a large wooden table, a few chairs, and a couple of trunks. The walls were decorated with nothing but a couple of candleholders and the bloodstains from past beatings. On the right side of the room were two empty jail cells, enclosed by iron bars. A stone wall divided the two cells from each other, and each had a barred window at the back.

A soldier with a ring of metal keys—the jailor, Ramon assumed—opened one of the cells. The jailor was young-looking, perhaps only in his late teens, and was probably one of the lowest-ranking men in the militia. His uniform was shabby, perhaps from leftover military surplus, Ramon thought.

The soldiers pushed Paco and Ramon into the cell. The stench of excrement hung the air, and the walls were decorated with carved words and sketches from previous inmates. The only furnishing were a wooden bench, a stool, and a small hole in the corner for human waste. The jailor locked the cell on his way out.

"*Amigos,*" said the captain, "I will be back as soon as my *investigación* is complete." He then left the jailhouse, his soldiers close behind, leaving Ramon and Paco with the jailor.

Ramon sat down on the stool and Paco on the bench.

"How long will the *investigación* take, Paco?"

"I don't know, Señor Connelly. I've never been in jail. But if I were to guess, I would say anywhere from two days to two weeks. The *soldados* are in no hurry to gather information."

"What happens after that?"

"If we are innocent, then we leave. If not, then your penalty depends on who you know in Saltillo. Politicians and wealthy *haciendos* never spend time here. If you are their enemy, *amigo*, or the enemy of the military, you will stay here awhile. For serious crimes, like murder or robbery, you will face a firing squad."

Paco took off his sombrero and untied the bandanna from around his neck. As he looked at Ramon, his smile looked amiss. "But we have one *problemo*, Señor Connelly. It is a very big *problemo*."

"What's that, Paco?"

"The man you killed, Pancho Jimenez, has an older *hermano*. His name is Roberto. He is a big man like Pancho."

"Why is he a problem?"

"He is a sergeant in the militia, a very influential man in Saltillo. He will want you to face a firing squad for killing his brother. He will insist that anything less will not be justice."

The Buffalo Dance

When Malone and Many Wolves arrived back at the village camp after sunset, Colmillo greeted them with a wagging tail and a wet tongue for Noche's face. Many Wolves smelled dead buffalo, the pleasant scent of a successful hunt.

The women sat alone in the darkness like ghostly silhouettes, with only a small fire for light. A buffalo hide hung on a crude wooden rack beside them. An empty rack was beside it; Many Wolves assumed it had been adorned by strips of buffalo meat during the hot part of the day.

"You said you'd be back before dark," snapped Nina. The two women rose to greet them. "I heard several gunshots. I was worried."

Many Wolves dismounted and hugged her with one arm, holding the horse's lead with the other. He held her for several moments, pressing her fire-warmed cheek against his own. Taimah came out of the shadows and wrapped her arms around her father, then she took the two horses away to drink.

"What happened?" said Topusana, freeing herself from Malone's embrace.

"We found the men with the guns. White-skinned men with hairy faces," said Malone, grimly. "They were killing buffalo. More buffalo than they needed to kill. They won't be killing anything anymore."

Nina pulled back from Many Wolves. "You killed them?" she said with a tone of displeasure and worry.

"*Haa*," said Malone.

"Are they going to track us now?" said Nina, crossing her arms and looking at the men for an answer.

"There were three of them, and they're all dead," said Many Wolves. "A boy was with them too. We let him go. I don't think they will be following us."

"The boy will die out there alone," said Topusana, concerned.

"He has a horse, food, and a long gun," said Malone. "If he rides east, he will find his people, unless the Penateka or Kiowa find him first. His blood will be on their hands, not mine."

"All this killing scares me. Do you want to be hunted again?" Nina asked, looking at Many Wolves. "You've spent your whole life running from men who wanted to kill you."

"I would rather die from a white man's hunting party than starve to death because there are no buffalo to hunt," Malone said angrily. He started throwing buffalo dung on the fire to grow the flames. "But I would not have killed these men if I knew it would endanger us."

Malone's temperament was usually gentle, kind, and soft as a feather. Even back when they fought Thorn Bird's men, long ago, Malone had not shown this much anger. But these buffalo killers had thrown dung on his hidden rage. Many Wolves believed there was something about these strange white men, these Mare-cans from the east, that scared his friend.

Taimah returned to the camp. Many Wolves was glad she hadn't heard this conversation.

"Enough of this sad talk; we have a special ceremony to prepare for," said Malone, looking at Taimah. In the blink of an eye he had turned back into the feather-voiced man that Many Wolves knew so well.

"The buffalo dance?" asked Taimah with bulging, excited eyes.

"*Haa*, the buffalo dance." Malone smiled and performed a mock dance in front of her.

"I don't know how to dance a buffalo dance," said Taimah.

"I will show you what to do—how it was taught to me in my Nokoni village long ago." Malone put his arm on Taimah's shoulder, then looked into her eyes. "We had all kinds of dances. Victory dances. Scalp dances. Buffalo dances. All these dances tell stories. You will tell us *your* story. Your spirit will guide you through it."

"What do I wear?"

"Put on your best deerskin outfit. The one with the beads and shells," said Malone. "Then meet me in my lodge. Topusana and I will prepare the rest of your ceremonial clothing."

Taimah left to get dressed, and Malone went to the river to wash up. Then he and Topusana disappeared into his lodge, leaving Nina and Many Wolves to sit alone by the now vigorous fire.

"You must be hungry," said Nina. "Let me fix you some meat from your daughter's kill." She left briefly and returned with two skewers of buffalo meat and a pot of water. Using two sticks like pincers, she lifted two red-hot cooking stones from the fire and placed them in the pot to make the water boil.

Buffalo meat was a welcome change from their normal diet of smaller animals. And after a hunt like this, there would be plenty of buffalo meat for everyone to eat for days. Just as it was time for the bear and many other animals to fatten up and prepare for another lean winter, so it was time for Many Wolves's village to do the same.

"Did you kill the men or did Malone?" asked Nina, keeping an eye on the pot.

"It was Malone. He wanted me to stay back."

Nina seemed satisfied with that. She placed the skewers in the boiling water to cook the meat.

"It was strange looking at that boy." Many Wolves pictured the boy in his head. "He had my skin, and he had blue eyes. He stared at me. I kept thinking to myself: Is that what I looked like as a boy?"

"Did you talk to him?"

"He didn't understand us, and we couldn't understand his words," said Many Wolves. He paused. "I felt sorry for him. I wondered if one of the men was his father. If so, he had to watch his father die like my white-skinned father. He will have my childhood nightmares."

"Those people are our enemy now. You can't worry about them. They would have killed you if you hadn't killed them first."

"Is it strange that my enemies are white like me, Nina?"

"It's what's in a man's heart that makes him your enemy, not his skin color," said Nina, huddling closer to him. "Look at Malone. He is your closest friend, but his skin is the same color as men who are your greatest enemies."

Nina was right. Then again, all the people he knew, friends and enemies alike, had dark skin. It was hard to imagine that other people existed in the world, but Malone said that more white men were coming from the east. What would these white men think of a man with the same skin color? *Will I be just as much an enemy to them?* He remembered what Walking Free said to him long ago: that his skin color would allow him to make friends with white people. *Is that true?*

"I am pleased that Malone is teaching our daughter the traditions of his people," said Nina, holding Many Wolves's hand. "She may someday marry a Northerner and live in a Northerner village. She will know their language and their traditions. She will be accepted quickly."

Many Wolves tried to imagine Taimah in another village. "She will want to hunt with the men and not do woman's work. I have never seen a woman ride in a Nokoni or Penateka war party." *I will have to ask Malone about this.* "Compared to a man, all she lacks is strength. She has proven today that she is brave." Many Wolves's words were woven with pride.

"It was amazing what she did," said Nina, squeezing his hand. "I knew she could ride and shoot a bow, but she was fearless. I don't think she knew how dangerous it was."

"She had you to worry for her," said Many Wolves, smiling at his wife.

Nina smiled, but then pulled it back. "Sometimes I worry that she isn't scared enough."

"It is a gift, Nina. We can teach her to ride, to shoot a bow, to hunt with birds, but it is very difficult to teach someone not to fear. Fear is a disease in the mind. Only the mind can cure it."

Nina squeezed his hand again and then moved to check the pot. She picked one of the two arm-long skewers of buffalo meat and handed it to her husband, then sat next to him again.

"*Ura,* my *nupetsu,*" said Many Wolves, using the Northerner word for "thank you." The meat was too hot to eat, so he took another sip of the blackberry water that Nina had brought him earlier.

"I wonder what they are doing in there?" said Nina. "Topusana worked on making a headdress the whole time you were gone."

Many Wolves had never seen a buffalo dance before. Ten Arrows used to sing and dance by himself around the fire, but it was never a formal ceremony, and Many Wolves had never seen Malone dance at all. Perhaps a white-skinned man wasn't enough of an audience for this kind of celebration, or perhaps he did it only in private. Many Wolves agreed with his wife that Malone teaching Taimah the traditions of his people was valuable for her future, and Many Wolves was sure that it was just as valuable to Malone's spirit.

When the meat was cool enough to eat, he took several big bites. As he ate, he saw Noche staring at him. Every time he looked at the wolf, that long bushy tail wagged. *Little beggar.* Many Wolves gave in to the wolf's pleading eyes and tossed the final piece of meat to his companion.

Witnessing the handout, Colmillo walked over and lay down next to his wolf brother.

"Not you too," said Many Wolves. Nina handed him the second skewer and then took the pot away from the fire. Many Wolves looked at Colmillo. "You'll have to wait, beggar wolf."

"Watching you eat is one of their favorite ceremonies," said Nina.

"It's time to be quiet," said Topusana from behind them. She sat down next to Nina.

Many Wolves quickly ate the rest of the meat off the skewer and gave a generous piece to each of the wolves. After eating his scrap of meat, Noche ambled over and lay next to Many Wolves, nudging his master's hand with his nose to initiate the petting ceremony.

The air was still. The crackling bonfire, with it's sharp, flaming teeth and hot spitting embers, fought off the chill. Silhouettes of the three sleeping birds glowed in the trees around the camp, their heads buried deep in their feathers, deep in their bird dreams, oblivious to the world.

A slow drumbeat rose from the quiet of night. Malone approached from his lodge, striking his hand on his war shield. He was dressed in his finest deerskin, his face decorated in bright reds and yellows, and his head adorned with a single eagle feather. He chanted and danced toward the fire, raising his knees high and swaying with the drumbeats. The drumming stopped for a moment, then Malone reached into a pouch at his side and threw dust into the fire. The flames popped and spat more embers into the dark sky.

"Antler dust to waken the spirits," whispered Topusana.

Many Wolves nodded, remembering the time Ten Arrows used antler dust to make the flames talk and dance.

Malone danced and chanted, circling around the fire, raising his head to the sky, and casting more of the antler dust into the fire as he passed each of the four directions.

"Daughter of Thunder, the spirits are ready!" he chanted in a low voice, after his full circle was complete, still beating on his shield, softer and slower. Topusana shook a stick with many snake rattles tied to it, following her husband's beat and filling the air with a scratchy, rhythmic sound.

Taimah came out of Malone's tipi, dancing slowly, tracking the beat. She wore her beaded deerskin and moccasins. Her face was painted the colors of blood and fire, like Malone's. On her head was a buffalo headdress, like the ones worn by Nokoni warriors, and one of Malone's buffalo tooth necklaces hung around her neck. She held her bow in her left hand.

Her chanting followed Malone's, but hers was louder and higher-pitched like the song of a bird. As she danced past her parents, she glanced at them and smiled, then turned her head back toward the flames. Many Wolves had felt a shiver run through him seeing his daughter dressed like a warrior from his childhood nightmares, but Taimah's smile had quickly smothered the chill. She was a warrior now, a buffalo hunter, but still she was his child.

Taimah circled the fire, lifting one knee then the other, sometimes spinning. The beat was slow at first. Taimah danced with her hand over her eyes, looking around. *She's blocking the sun, searching the sky.* Once, twice, three times she circled the fire, still looking in the sky with her dance.

Then, pointing upward, she stopped and yelled, "Buffalo raven!" Again she circled the fire, paced by the slow beat of Malone's drum and Topusana's rattle. She stopped and crouched down, her bow hand following the beat, her other hand covering her eyes again. She looked left and right and left again. *Searching the land.* Again she stopped and pointed, shouting, "Yee-Ahh!" *I claim it.*

Malone beat the drum harder and faster, and Topusana followed his lead. Taimah danced faster and raised her knees higher, stomping on the ground. *The hooves of the horses. The hooves of the buffalo.* She held this frantic pace and circled the fire two, then three times, stomping hard, kicking up dust all around the fire. Then she raised her bow and shot a ghost arrow into the fire. The fire crackled with embers from Malone's antler dust. *The buffalo is hit.*

Taimah danced to another spot around the fire and shot her bow. Again the sparks flew from the bonfire. Her third shot did not cause the fire to crackle, but the fourth shot caused the biggest blast of them all. *The fourth arrow killed it.*

Taimah screamed in celebration, lifting her arms to the sky. Malone and Topusana slowed the beat down. Slower, slower, slower, until it stopped, and the dance was over.

They all cheered for the dancer. Many Wolves was bursting with pride, soaking in the sunshine of her accomplishment. This was a happier moment than any he could remember.

He wanted it to last.

Comanchero

Ramon understood now how Pancho Jimenez had terrorized the town of Saltillo for so long: he was protected by the law. No one would dare touch him. Though he was a vicious thug, it was his brother's brutal justice that everyone feared. Ramon's father had once said that "politicians wield the sharpest swords," and Ramon believed it. The politicians made the laws and the military enforced them, and together they were the coziest of bedfellows. It was difficult to separate one from the other in towns like San Antonio and Saltillo.

Ramon knew he was in a bad situation, but there was nothing he could do from his jail cell. This wasn't how he had planned his evening. At least Paco was a pleasant enough man, with a warm personality. Ramon could have done far worse for a cellmate. And Ramon had admired the way Paco didn't give in easily to the brute's demands. Most importantly, Paco had stood up for him in the Silver Lion, protecting a man who was practically a stranger to him.

Paco pulled a cigar from his pocket and walked over to the door of the cell. "Señor, can I get a light, *por favor?*"

The jailor grabbed a candle from the table and brought it over to Paco.

Paco puffed several times, then bowed his head. "*Muchos gracias*, señor." He returned to his seat on the bench.

Ramon was growing increasingly more fearful of what might happen. He needed to put his nerves to rest. Perhaps Paco could ease his mind.

"So, what's your story, Paco? What brings you to Saltillo?"

"Would you like a cigar, Señor Connelly?"

"*No gracias.*"

"I live on a *rancho* outside of Saltillo with my *familia*: my wife, my mother, and my brother. We have a few heads of *ganado*, a few goats, and a few horses. About half of the land is an apple orchard. It's a modest living, Señor Connelly, but we are happy."

"You have lived there all your life?"

"Originally it was my father's property, but when he died, Rodrigo and I returned to help my mother. That was about fifteen years ago."

"Rodrigo?"

"He's my *hermano*. Rodrigo Salazar was the most dangerous man in Tejas with his rifle, señor, until he lost his eye. I've never seen a man who could shoot like him. He had some special rifles that could shoot a great distance, and he was deadly accurate with them. Now his son Pablo owns the rifles and lives in Comanche lands. He is what most call a 'Comanchero.' He and the *mexicanos* that ride with him trade with the Comanches. He is still doing what Rodrigo and I did for many years."

"You were friends with Comanches?" Ramon's interest was piqued by talk of *norteños*. He wanted to know everything Paco knew about them, everything about his enemy. And the conversation was helping to distract Ramon from his troubles.

"*Sí, sí,* Señor Connelly. Very good *amigos*. We would buy Comanche goods and then sell them in Taos and Santa Fe. That was our living, until Rodrigo lost his eye."

"How did that happen?"

"It was horrible, señor. I will never forget it. Do you want to hear the whole story?"

"*Sí,* Paco. Every gruesome detail. There is nothing but time to kill in this place."

Paco smiled, took a puff from his cigar, and began his tale. "My men and I agreed to ride with the Nokoni Comanches. They were led back then by Señor Alcaudon. His Comanche name was Thorn Bird, and he was the greatest Comanche warrior I have ever seen. He was a mestizo, half

Comanche and half *mexicano*, and a very powerful warrior. I once saw him fight ten Comanches by himself, and he was the victor! But that is another story and one that I have told hundreds of times in the towns of Santa Fe and Taos."

"I'm sure you have." Ramon laughed. *Paco is a man of many words.* "You will have to tell me that story sometime as well."

"So, our band of *mexicanos* and Comanches numbered around twenty, and we were fighting just three men: two Comanches and a *gringo* named Many Wolves."

"A white-skinned *indio?*"

"*Sí.* He was raised by Lipanos after his parents were killed. Señor Alcaudon wanted to kill him for revenge. This Many Wolves killed Señor Alcaudon's father, Laughing Crow, who I did not know, but there are many stories about him as a great Comanche leader."

"The name Laughing Crow is familiar, Paco. His stories have passed through the lips of San Antonians as well. Go on."

Paco sucked on his cigar and then kicked out the smoke, filling the cell. "Well, we had our hands full with these three men. The two Comanches were as good as any Comanches I have seen with their horses and bows, and the *gringo* commanded a huge red wolf. It was this animal that ripped my brother's eye out. They were smart to attack Rodrigo first, because he would have shot them dead otherwise. After the wolf attacked, it was …" Paco paused, searching for the right word. "It was *pandemonium*. It was complete pandemonium, Señor Connelly. Arrows and *balas* were flying everywhere. Horses and men were screaming. I helped Rodrigo onto my horse; he was bleeding everywhere and in terrible pain. Then I rode away with him and his son, Pablonito. That's all I remember. But what I heard later was that this *gringo* killed Señor Alcaudon. To this day, I have no idea how this man could have killed a legendary Comanche warrior. He has some strange magic. They say he hunts with hawks and not with bow and arrow. I have not seen this, but I saw what that wolf did with my own eyes, so I know this magic is real."

"This Many Wolves killed both Laughing Crow and Señor Alcaudon?"

"*Sí*, señor."

"He is the enemy of the Comanches then?"

"I don't know. He is friends with them and he is enemies with them. In Tejas, your friends and enemies aren't always marked by the color of their skin."

"Many Wolves is still alive?"

"I don't know." Paco paused to exhale more smoke. "I will say this, Señor Connelly. He has the same green eyes as you."

The smoke in the air helped to filter out the pollution from the cell's latrine and made Ramon yearn for his own tobacco. He grabbed his pipe from his pocket and his pouch of tobacco, then packed the chamber. He was surprised that the soldier hadn't taken it away. He stood up and walked to the door of the cell. "Señor, I would like a flame, *por favor*."

Paco stood up also and walked over beside Ramon, a fresh cigar in his hand. "Make that two flames."

Again the jailor came over with a candle. "This is the last time, *amigos*. I am not supposed to talk to the prisoners."

Ramon nodded and Paco said, "*Gracias*. I will save my cigars. It might be a while before I can get any more."

The two men sat down again.

"Tell me more about the Comanches, Paco. What are they like? Can you speak their language?"

Paco smiled. "No, Señor Connelly, I cannot speak their language. I used hand signs to communicate with most of them, except for Señor Alcuadon. He spoke fluent *español* because his mother was a *mexicano*. That helped us to become friends. I discovered that they are like any other people trying to survive in a harsh and violent world. They want the land and the buffalo, and will fight to protect them. They get everything they need from the buffalo: food, shelter, clothing, tools, everything. But they only kill what they need. They have a respect for the land and the animals that I admire."

"But they are savages. Killers, Paco," said Ramon. "I have seen them take life and then celebrate it."

"If strange men tried to take San Antonio from you, Señor Connelly, you would fight to protect it, right? Well, to the Comanches, all of Comancheria is San Antonio to them. They are fighting to protect it."

What Paco was saying made some sense to Ramon, but it seemed to him that the *norteños* went far beyond just protecting their land. "They scalp and they torture, Paco. That is not defensive, it is savage."

Paco took a deep breath from his cigar, then exhaled, "The Comanches, like many *indios*, are a warrior culture. Taking scalps and torturing are their ways of showing bravery and proving they are stronger than their enemies. In Comanche culture, scalps taken are a measure of bravery, and horses owned, a measure of prestige."

"That's why they steal horses?"

"*Sí.* They want control of the land, the buffalo, and the horses. They know there is no one who can match them on a horse. It is a great advantage for them. Comanche children are sitting on a horse before they can walk. That's why they are the greatest riders, even better than *vaqueros.*"

Paco's words reminded Ramon of the horsemanship he had seen with this one *norteño*. "Paco, do you know of a Comanche named 'Esatai,' or something that sounds like that?"

"*Sí.* Esatai is Señor Alcaudon's son. I only knew him when he was a little *chico*. His *hermano* is Cold Raven, who is Laughing Crow's son. They share the same *madre*, a tall, strong-looking, attractive *mexicano* woman named Valencia. She believed that someday Cold Raven would be the leader of the Nokonis, and Esatai a great warrior like his father, Thorn Bird."

Ramon remembered that Esatai was a large man and wondered if the same was true for his father. "Was this Señor Alcaudon a large man?"

Paco laughed. "*Sí, sí, sí! Muy grande* and as strong as a *toro*! He was much bigger than the other Comanches, and I am told that his father, Laughing Crow, was also a large man."

Every bit of information about his enemy was priceless to a man who was paid to fight them, Ramon thought. It was Esatai and Cold Raven who had attacked his men. He was sure now.

The front door of the jail creaked open and a soldier entered with a tray of food.

"Your meals are here," said the jailor, taking two wooden plates with bowls on them from the tray. "*Sopa* and bread is what you get here, and you're lucky you get that.*" He slid the plates under the door, then went back to the table where his own meal was waiting.

Ramon cleaned his pipe by tapping it on the ground, then stashed it away. The light was fading, and the sun's heat would soon be gone. He had enjoyed his talk with Paco, but he worried now about what was going to happen to him—the man who had killed Pancho Jimenez. *How will Roberto Jimenez avenge his brother? Will he influence Captain Esperanza's investigation?* Ramon hoped there was justice in Saltillo. His life depended on it. *I will pray tonight for justice, but I need to eat now to keep my strength up.*

The Bullfight

A door slammed, waking Ramon in the dark of night. He sat up and pushed the hat from his face so he could see what was happening. The calm in his body was shattered by his thumping heartbeat.

"Soldier! Wake up! I have business here. Light the candles, *pronto!*" The voice was loud and gruff.

One at a time, candles were lit inside their holders. The flickering flame from the final candle revealed the silhouette of a man. A large man.

"Señor Connelly," said Paco in a hushed voice. "That is Roberto Jimenez."

"Bring the *gringo* to me, soldier!"

Perhaps this is my sentence, thought Ramon.

The door of the jail opened with a jingle of keys. The jailor had been replaced by a new one while Ramon slept, and the new jailor looked as young and inexperienced as his predecessor.

"Bind his hands!" Jimenez shouted.

If I run now, this man will have an excuse to kill me.

Ramon stood up, tossed his hat to Paco, and put his hands behind his back.

The jailor tightened the knot twice to satisfy himself that Ramon's hands were secure. Then he led Ramon outside the cell and locked the door on Paco.

"Bring him here. Put him in this chair." The big man kicked a chair toward them, and the jailor pressed Ramon down into it.

Jimenez removed his sombrero and tossed it to the jailor. Then he leaned over Ramon so close that Roman could feel his breath and smell the mescal on it. "Do you know who I am, *gringo*?"

"*El hermano*. El Porcino's brother," said Ramon, fighting to remain calm.

"That's right, you *hijo de puta*! Sergeant Roberto Jimenez of the Saltillo Militia. I am *el hermano* who makes the rules, while Pancho was the one who broke them. That is, until you put a *bala* in his head!" The sergeant took off his jacket and started to roll up his shirtsleeves. "You know, *gringo*, I never liked the nickname 'El Porcino.' My brother didn't seem to mind it—that was his choice. Let me ask you, Señor Connelly, what do you think of when you think of a pig?" Sergeant Jimenez's bearded face came closer again, glowing in the flickering candlelight. "Tell me, what word pops into your head?"

"Fat."

"*Muy bien, gringo.*"

Roberto's fist crashed into the left side of Ramon's face, knocking him off the chair. Pain surged through Ramon's body. The big man's fists were as hard as hooves, and the force was as potent as a mule's kick. Ramon felt blood trickling down the side of his mouth as the jailor pulled him back up and set him back in the chair.

"Tell me another word that you think of," said Sergeant Jimenez. His voice was calm and even.

Ramon tasted the blood in his mouth as he said, "Filthy."

"*Excelente!*"

Again a rock-hard fist slammed into Ramon's face, but on the right side this time, and not as hard. *His left hand is not as strong as his right.* Ramon's head crashed against the stony floor. He spit out the blood that was pooling in his mouth. He wanted to yell because of the pain, but he did not give in.

The jailor propped him back up in the chair.

"Any other words, Señor Connelly?" the big man asked.

"They root in their own *excrementos*."

"Well, that is more than one word, señor, but it's *bien. Muy bien.*" The sergeant laughed and then threw another punch with his right hand, knocking Ramon down for a third time.

Ramon heard The Pig's brother grunt on every punch. The powerful man was not holding anything back. Ramon was in pain and bloodied, but his mind was still clear. He was not a stranger to brawls, and he prided himself on how well he could take a punch. He remembered his father's words: "Take the punishment, lad, and then pummel them when they're weary and broken-spirited." *Save your strength, Ramon.*

"Stand him up," commanded his torturer.

The jailor helped Ramon to his feet. His legs were a little wobbly, but there was still strength left in them.

"Señor Connelly, have you ever been to a bullfight?" The sergeant stood face-to-face with him. Ramon estimated he was about two inches taller.

The Irish vaquero mumbled, "No."

The sergeant laughed, with the same bravado as his brother. "You *gringos* have no culture! There is no greater beauty in this world than a skilled *torrero* dancing toe to toe with an animal that can gore him to death with one swipe of its powerful horns!" Sergeant Jimenez danced on his toes, imitating a matador and humming a little tune to himself. "You are in a bullfight, Señor Connelly. Did you know that?" He laughed again. "But you are not the *torrero*, but the *toro!*" Now the big man bellowed with laughter.

"So, I guess that makes you the skilled *torrero*…" said Ramon in a low, raspy voice, spitting out more blood.

"No, no, señor. I am not the *torrero*. The *torrero* is the one who kills the bull. My role is the *picador* and the *banderilla*. Do you know what the *picador* does, Señor Connelly?"

"No. I told you I've never been to a bullfight." Ramon's left eye was swollen shut, and it was difficult to breathe out of his nose.

"The *picador* is a man on a horse who stabs the bull on the *morrillo* with a large lance. Not just once…" Sergeant Jimenez hit Ramon hard in the stomach on the right side while the jailor held Ramon up. "But twice…" He hit Ramon again, but on the left side, grunting loudly. "Or maybe three times…" He said this through gritted teeth, then punched Ramon a third time. "The back of a *toro's* neck is full of muscle, but it needs to be softened."

Ramon coughed up blood and breathed hard. His eyes watered, but he shook his head to send the tears away. *Don't show this man any weakness. Don't give him any satisfaction.*

"You are a brave *toro*, Señor Connelly. The crowd would love you! The braver the bull, the greater the fight! So, now that the bull is weakened and bleeding, it is the job of the *banderilla* to steal more strength from the bull." Sergeant Jimenez turned toward the jailor. "Rip his shirt off, soldier."

The young jailor tore off Ramon's shirt and threw it to the side.

Sergeant Jimenez grabbed Ramon by the neck and slammed his back against the wall, then drew a knife and waved it in Ramon's face while pinning him with a chokehold. "The *banderilla* uses two sharp sticks and digs them into the bull's shoulders."

The blade cut into Ramon's chest, just above the heart. Blood poured out of the burning wound. The sergeant switched the knife to his left hand while he held Ramon's neck with his right. The blade cut Ramon on the right in the same way. Ramon tried to kick his attacker, but the fat-legged man was too strong.

"Bravo, señor! Bravo!" Sergeant Jimenez cheered. "You are still standing! Put him back in the chair."

Ramon slumped in the chair, weakened by the beating and the blood loss. It was difficult to keep his head up, but he fought the urge to drop it. He didn't want to take his eyes off his tormenter. A wave of pain traveled through his body like wildfire. Most men probably would have blacked out by now, but not Ramon. In his youth, he had endured many beatings from gangs of older boys—though this was by far the worst.

"So now, Señor Connelly, the next part of the bullfight is the *tercio de muerte*," said The Pig's brother in a tranquil tone, enunciating his words very carefully. "It is the final part of the bullfight, and the most dramatic. It is the dance of death where the *torrero* shows his true skill as a bullfighter. When the dance is concluded, the *torrero* uses a sword called '*estoque*' to kill the bull. *Muy fantastico!*" Sergeant Jimenez kissed the tips of his fingers and saluted the sky. "But I told you, Señor Connelly, that I am not the *torrero* on this day. That is unfortunate, because I would enjoy it thoroughly. No, the *torrero* will be the firing squad, Señor Connelly. *Your* firing squad! I will ask Captain Esperanza if I can command the execution myself."

"Sergeant Jimenez?" Paco's voice came from behind Ramon.

"What, Paco?" the sergeant snapped, seemingly annoyed by the interruption.

"I have been to many bullfights, Sergeant Jimenez, and I've never seen one where the feet of the *toro* are bound with rope." Paco paused for a moment, then continued. "Isn't the fight more exciting if the *toro* has a sporting chance to fight back?"

Unbind my hands, Sergeant Jimenez. Ramon dropped his head and stared down at the floor, but he was listening carefully.

"So, you are saying that this bull here, this *gringo* bull, is not yet ready for the *torrero*? He needs more softening and blood loss? Is that what you are saying, Paco?"

"No, I am saying in the spirit of true bullfighting, Señor Connelly should have a chance to fight back. What I have witnessed here is not a fair fight. You have a *reputación*, Sergeant Jimenez. I'm not sure what I have seen here will help it any."

Paco is bold. I have nothing to lose. If I am to die anyway, let me die fighting.

Sergeant Jimenez lifted Ramon's head up and stared into his eyes. "You want a shot at me, *toro*, or have you had enough for now?" He let Ramon's head slip back down.

Ramon's body was racked with pain. His ribs were sore, probably cracked in several places. His eye was swollen half-shut. His nose felt like it was broken, and he had two large gashes on his chest. Despite all this, his mind was still clear, and he was ready to "scrap," as his father called it.

He looked up and nodded at his tormentor. *Yes.*

"Free his hands, jailor, and stay out of the way," shouted the sergeant.

Defend. These large pigs tire easily.

When his hands were freed, Ramon stood up, stretched his stiff arms, and raised his fists up to his chin, just like his father had taught him.

Sergeant Jimenez came at him with a right, and then a left—sweeping, roundhouse punches that tire a man quickly and leave him staggering after each one. Ramon deflected the blows with his arms, blocking his body, his fists in front of his face. *It will be much tougher to draw my blood now, Sergeant Jimenez.*

Ramon danced around the room. His legs were still wobbly, it was difficult to see with just one eye, and his injured nose forced him to breathe mostly through his mouth. But he felt invigorated now. *Keep your hands up and keep moving.*

Sergeant Jimenez grunted and charged him, pushing him up against the wall. He unleashed a flurry of angry punches at his adversary, to the body, to the head, and back to the body, but Ramon did not fall.

He is winded now.

Ramon pushed the sergeant back with a loud grunt, grabbed his shirt, and slung him against the wall. It was time to see if this big man could take a punch. He hit the bigger man, once and then twice, alternating hands, and felt the wind leave Roberto's bloated gut. The sergeant reeled in pain. Ramon hit him hard on the side of the head. The sergeant dropped to the floor with a loud thud, his body convulsing with pain.

He is done.

The Irish vaquero looked down on the big *mexicano*, who was helpless now, a quivering mess who barely seemed to know who or where he was. "Sometimes the bull wins in these fights, eh, Sergeant Jimenez?"

"Señor! Get back in your cell!"

Ramon turned around and stared into the barrel of the jailor's pistol. The young soldier unlocked the door of the jail cell and left it slightly open, then motioned with his head for Ramon to get in.

Ramon picked up his torn shirt and pulled the door open, closing it behind him. The jailor locked the door before setting his pistol back in his belt.

Sergeant Jimenez stumbled to his feet, swaying. "You will die for this,

Connelly." His words were slurred and hard to understand. "Your death sentence has been signed with blood." Then he left the jailhouse.

"Can you get us a wet cloth, soldier, to clean his wounds?" Paco asked as he helped Ramon back to his seat on the bench.

"*Sí, un momento*," said the jailor. He left and returned shortly with a wet cloth, handing it to Paco through the bars.

"*Gracias*," said Paco.

The cuts on Ramon's body and face stung as Paco cleaned them. Ramon's chest was still bleeding, but not as profusely as before. He took a mouthful of tepid water and spit out the mixture of blood and water. His body burned all over, but he'd had similar injuries before and knew they would completely heal in time.

Paco flashed a smile. "Indeed, Señor Connelly, the bull has won tonight."

The Papers

The throbbing in Ramon's face and body did not let him sleep for the rest of the night. Paco's mumbling was all he heard in the dark. He surmised that Paco was trying to charm some woman in his dreams into doing something unsavory. However, even Paco's muttered gibberish was strangely comforting in this grotesque place that stank of human excrement.

As Ramon rested on the floor of his jail cell, he wondered when Sergeant Jimenez would recover well enough to exact more revenge on him. The big man had proven to be a worthy adversary, and Ramon knew that their business wasn't finished. *He will be back when he comes to his senses.*

When the sun rose the next day, Ramon heard the clip-clop of horses' hooves approaching. He rose from the blanket the jailor had provided and sat on the bench, his back resting against the back wall of his cell. *Now there is even more blood on these walls. My blood.*

Colonel Tejada burst into the room, followed by two of his soldiers.

Is he here to sentence me?

The colonel walked over to the cell and inspected the prisoners. "What happened to you, Connelly?" he barked in a deep voice, then turned to the jailor.

"He was trying to escape, Colonel," answered the jailor, who stood up to salute the officer.

The colonel looked around the room. "There is a lot of blood here. On the chair. On the floor. On the wall. I can see blood seeping through Connelly's shirt. It seems to me it wasn't a simple capture."

"He fought with Sergeant Jimenez. That's where all the blood came from," said the jailor, standing at attention.

"It was not a fight, Colonel, it was a beating," said Paco, leaning against the cell door.

"I figured Jimenez would come here to administer his own justice," said the colonel, looking around and then turning again to the jailor. "Where is he now, soldier?"

"He left, sir, after we got the prisoner back in his cell."

"He left after Señor Connelly knocked him out. That is the truth, Colonel," said Paco.

Colonel Tejada laughed and pointed at Paco. "I believe this man, soldier. What is your name, prisoner?"

"Francisco del Castilla y Salazar. But you can call me Paco." Paco lifted his hat in greeting.

"Do you know why I believe Paco, soldier, and not you?" Colonel Tejada spoke to the jailor and pointed at Ramon. "Because Ramon Connelly has stone hands like his father. There is not a tougher man to fight in all of San Antonio. Sergeant Jimenez chose the wrong man to trade punches with."

"*Sí*, Colonel," said the jailor. "I saw if for myself, but you have caught me in a lie. I apologize for not telling you the truth."

"Soldier, it doesn't matter what happened. Don't worry, I won't report you this time." The colonel paused for a moment, a hint of a smile on his face.

"*Gracias*, Colonel. It won't happen again."

"I have the papers here for the immediate release of these two men," said the colonel, reaching into his shirt and drawing out a folded piece of paper. "You'll find that everything is in order." He handed it to the jailor.

Paco walked back to Ramon with a big smile, slapped him on the arm, and whispered, "You must have friends in high places, Señor Connelly."

The soldier glanced at the paper quickly and put it in his pocket. He grabbed his keys and unlocked the door. "You two are free to go."

Ramon breathed a sigh of relief. *I owe my life to the colonel.*

"*Gracias, amigo!*" Paco laughed.

"I'll grab their weapons, sir, and bring them outside," said the jailor.

Ramon stood up slowly, put his hat on, and walked outside with Paco, Colonel Tejada, and the colonel's two soldiers. It felt like every bone and muscle in his body ached.

"*Gracias,* Colonel," said Ramon. "How did you get the release papers so quickly?"

"Let me tell you a little secret, Connelly," said the colonel, walking with him and lowering his voice so the soldiers, trailing behind them, couldn't hear. "There are not many soldiers in Saltillo who can read."

"Ha ha ha! Very clever, Colonel!" Paco laughed and pointed his finger to his head as a gesture of cleverness.

Colonel Tejada let a rare smile appear on his face.

"Won't you get in trouble, Colonel, for the fake papers?" Ramon figured that Captain Esperanza would eventually discover the falsified documents and report it to his superiors.

"Not to worry, Connelly. Captain Esperanza and I are *compadres*. When I talked to him last night, he said that the *investigación* was going very much in your favor and that he only needed to speak with two more witnesses." The colonel took the lead of his horse from one of the soldiers. "All I have done here is expedite your release."

"I was very lucky you were here, Colonel," said Ramon, respectfully.

"Indeed you were, Connelly." The colonel resumed his stern demeanor as he turned to face his soldiers. "Men, make sure Connelly's wounds are bandaged. I don't want him dying on his way to San Antonio." Then he mounted his horse. "Ramon, I would not linger in Saltillo if I were you. You have made a very dangerous enemy. *Adios.*"

"*Adios,* Colonel," Ramon and Paco said at nearly the same time. And without another look back, Colonel Tejada rode away.

"Señor Connelly," said one of Colonel Tejada's soldiers. "I will find Luis in town and have him bring your horse to you."

"*Gracias.*" *I won't be able to treat Luis to that meal I promised*, Ramon thought.

Another soldier said, "Remove your shirt, señor, so I can bandage your wounds." The soldier wrapped both of Ramon's shoulders with bandages. He worked slowly and methodically, with the patience of a surgeon. First the right, and then the left, with Paco lending a hand when needed. Ramon's whole body ached, but he hoped the bandages would help speed up the healing.

When the soldier was done, the jailor, who had been watching the whole procedure, handed both Ramon and Paco their weapons. Before returning inside, he said, "*adios.*"

Ramon was relieved to see his weapons again, especially the revolver. He hadn't been sure if he would ever see them again, knowing that men like Roberto Jimenez were in charge here.

While they were strapping their weapons on, Luis arrived with Ramon's horse. "Are you all right, Ramon?" He quickly dismounted and handed Cavador's lead to Ramon, then looked over his face and winced. "You got beat up pretty bad."

"It was a very long night, Luis," said Ramon. "But my good friend Paco here helped me through it."

Paco smiled. "I must say my goodbyes, Señor Connelly. You must not stay here much longer. It was a great honor and privilege to spend the night in jail with you, *mi amigo*. I now have another great story to tell anyone who wants to hear it!" Paco's teeth shined in the early morning light. He hugged Ramon gingerly. "I don't want to make you bleed anymore, Señor Connelly."

Ramon grimaced and drew back a bit, but did not complain. After the men separated, he said, "Paco, you have led an interesting life. I hope someday you will come to San Antonio and share your stories with the people there, as my guest, of course."

"*Sí*, Señor Connelly. I will remember that. Paco does not forget these kinds of things!"

With some difficulty, Ramon climbed up on his horse and then tipped his hat to Paco. "*Adios, mi amigo.*"

"*Adios*, Señor Connelly," said Paco, bowing and removing his sombrero.

Paco is a good man, thought Ramon, *even if he is a little long-winded.*

The Road Home

Ramon and Luis rode out of Saltillo along the dusty road that headed north to San Antonio. They had a long journey ahead of them, and Ramon was in no condition to ride hard, but he was relieved to have the rear of his horse staring at the bustling capital of Coahuila. A man could find almost anything in a town like Saltillo, except for solitude and peace of mind. Perhaps it was a different town when the festival crowds weren't there, but then, for a man like him, there would be no reason to visit at any other time of year. This time, he felt lucky to leave Saltillo on the back of a horse, and not the back of a coffin maker's wagon.

"Luis, I'm sorry you missed that meal I promised you," said Ramon, looking over at his friend through the slit that was his swollen left eye.

"*No hay problema*. It's good we left when we did, or I would have lost all my *dinero*," said Luis, laughing under his breath.

That was one of the things Ramon liked about Luis—he always looked at the shiny side of every coin. No matter how dangerous, how terrible things were, he never lost his shine, his sense of humor. Ramon wished there were more men like him in the world.

"So, what happened, Ramon? In the Silver Lion?"

"Just another bully throwing his weight around."

"You killed the man who did all this to you?"

Ramon smiled. "No, it was the bully's *hermano* who did all this to me, while I was in jail."

"How many men did you kill?"

"*Tres.* Paco killed the fourth."

"That's a lot of dead men, though it sounds like you made a new *compadre*, Ramon. Not bad for a man who doesn't make many friends."

Ramon smiled—then grimaced as the horse jostled his sore ribs. At least the sun was finally high enough to warm his stiff bones, and the heat felt good on his back. He tried hard to avoid any unnecessary movement in the saddle, because the pain waited to greet him again. "It turns out Paco is a very interesting man, Luis. Behind that *grande* smile of his is one tough old *hombre*. He used to trade with *norteños*, you know."

"But there aren't many *norteños* in Saltillo?"

"*Muy correcto.* He used to live as a trader far north up the Rio Rojo."

"Ah, so he was a Comanchero?"

"*Sí.*" Ramon's mouth stung when he spoke, so he tried to avoid any unnecessary words.

"That sounds like a tough life, Ramon. Surviving in *norteño* country like that. You make enemies with one *norteño*, and the whole bunch of them will cut you up—then burn your remains like they did to those people in San Saba."

"*Sí.* Though Paco never had problems with them."

"You don't kill those who serve you well, I guess." Luis grabbed his leather flask of water and sucked down a gulp or two, then offered it to Ramon, who declined.

The landscape was sparse here. Oaks and mesquite poked up through the earth in scattered bunches. Rabbits scampered away when they got too close. An occasional deer watched them from a distance and armadillos ambled around, unperturbed by the presence of men. Vultures circled the skies looking for bones to clean, before disappearing into the horizon or behind a mesa. A coyote watched them from amid the thick chaparral, keeping a safe distance.

Ramon enjoyed the peacefulness. No stomping cattle or whistling men to break the calm. No dust to cloud his eyes and choke his breathing. No one to answer to. Just him and Luis in this vast, untamed desert landscape. Riding a horse was not rest, but it was restful, especially after the trials he had endured on the trail and in Saltillo.

"Luis, how was your card game? It sounds like it didn't go well."

Luis shook his head in disgust. "I couldn't get any cards to match up to save my life, *amigo*. No pairs. No cards of the same suit. No straights. Nothing." Luis stopped as if a new idea had popped into his head. "But you know what, *amigo*? I realized when you are losing your money, you are making friends. Everyone hates the winners. So it wasn't such a bad time after all. An expensive way to make friends, but not bad at all."

The shiny side of the coin.

"I'm glad you enjoyed yourself."

"I know one thing: I enjoyed myself much more than my *compadre* Ramon!" Luis laughed, and the horses started up again.

The men's horses cantered deeper into the dry wilderness, leaving all signs of the city far behind them. Ramon wanted to forget the dust, the smells, the sounds, and the sights of Saltillo. He was looking forward to his home in San Antonio, where there was one thing left to cleanse: his soul. Killing was the kind of sin his father had called a "mortaller," which was his way of saying a mortal sin. His father also said that "when you die, an unforgiven mortaller is like having poison on your soul." So one of the first things Ramon would do when he arrived in San Antonio was confess his sins to Father Padilla and eradicate the poison.

"Ramon, how did the new revolver do in the gunfight?"

"It was deadly, *mi amigo*. Deadly enough to put a hole in a pig's skull." At close range, the smaller *bala* didn't seem to make a difference, but the quick reload time might have saved his life—had Paco not saved it for him.

"*Muy bien*, Ramon. *Muy bien*," said Luis, reaching into one of his saddlebags. "Hey, you want any *charqui*?" Luis held out some jerky for Ramon.

"No, I can't chew anything right now. I'll be eating *sopa* for the next few days."

Luis chuckled. "*Muy bien*. I'll kill an armadillo for us before the sun turns in. Luis's special armadillo soup for my *buen amigo*!"

"Be careful out there—those 'dillos have some nasty claws," Ramon said, jokingly.

Luis laughed. "I'll try not to shoot my foot."

Ramon looked forward to Luis's special soup. He had eaten it many times before. Not many men carried cooking spices with them on the trail, but Luis did. But now Ramon had a question simmering in his mind, as he thought back to his confrontation with Roberto Jimenez. "Luis, have you been to many bullfights?"

"I have been to a couple. Why do you ask?"

"Does the *toro* ever win?"

"*Sí, mi amigo.* I've never seen it, but the best *toros* will sometimes win. And if they win, they get to retire and make little *toros* for the rest of their life! A very good life, I would say."

Ramon grinned.

The bull had won in Saltillo, too.

Father Padilla

After a few days on the road, Ramon arrived in San Antonio. He had said his goodbyes to Luis earlier, when his friend had taken a different road home to his *rancho* and his family.

Now, as he rode through San Antonio, a boy of about ten years old ran up and fell into step beside Ramon's horse. "Señor Ramon, what happened to your eye?" he asked.

"Just a little fight with a man in Saltillo," said Ramon, which was enough of the truth.

"It looks like it hurts a lot, señor."

Though he seemed familiar, Ramon didn't remember the boy's name. "It looks much worse than it is." Most of the swelling was gone, but Luis had joked that he looked like a man with an eye patch—a *bandito*.

"I hope it gets better, Señor Connelly. I need to head home now. *Adios.*"

"*Adios.*"

Ramon rode past the San Fernando Church. *I should see if Father Padilla is busy.* It was the largest and oldest building in San Antonio, with its two impressive bell towers that reached high into the sky. Though the church was over seventy years old, the white stone exterior was exquisitely decorated and had been detailed with skilled hands.

He dismounted and tied Cavador's lead to a post, then entered the church. Inside were high ceilings supported by huge columns and archways. Ramon estimated that it was large enough to seat at least three hundred people. Everything, from the altars to the pews, was clean and well cared for. Father Padilla was a stickler for neatness.

The only person in the church was a boy cleaning the pews.

"Have you seen Padre Padilla?" Ramon asked the boy.

"*Sí*, señor. He's in there." The boy pointed to a door at the back of the altar.

"*Gracias*," said Ramon. He knelt and made a sign of the cross as he passed the altar, then headed through the door. He knew the way; as a boy, he had been a server for Father Padilla, who had been the pastor of San Fernando Parish for as long as Ramon could remember.

He found Father Padilla sitting in a chair, polishing a chalice.

"*Buenos tardes*, Padre," said Ramon.

"Ah, Ramon! *Como estas?*" The elderly missionary removed his spectacles and looked up at Ramon. Father Padilla was a short man in his seventies, with a thick gray mustache and receding gray hair, which he combed back. He wore a brown robe, his daily vestments for missionary work, and old, well-worn sandals. Most of the missionaries were either Franciscan or Jesuit—Ramon could tell which was which by their robes— and Father Padilla was a Franciscan. "I see you were in another tussle," Father Padilla continued. "Not a lot changes from the boy to the man."

"*Sí*, Padre."

Father Padilla stood up and shook Ramon's hand in both of his own hands. "I haven't seen you in Mass lately."

"I was out of town, Padre, on a cattle drive."

"*Sí*, too many empty pews when the men are away," said Father Padilla. "What can I do for you today?"

"You had confessions yesterday?" Ramon knew that Father Padilla usually forgave the sins of the parish on Wednesdays.

"*Sí, correcto*."

"Is there any way I could confess my sins before next Wednesday?" *Six days is a long time to have a poisonous stain on your soul.*

"I have some time, Ramon, if you would like to do it now."

"*Sí*, padre."

Father Padilla smiled, grabbed his Bible, and put his arm around Ramon. "Come with me."

They walked to the confessional booth on the side of the church. One door was for the priest and the other for the penitent, the sinner. Ramon opened the penitent's door and entered the small, dark room. He knelt, facing the priest. A little window with a curtain separated him from Father Padilla.

"Go ahead, Ramon."

"Forgive me, Padre. I am here in your presence to ask God's forgiveness for my sins. My last confession was about three months ago." Ramon had memorized these words from his childhood.

"What sins would you like to bring before God today?"

"I killed three men about a week ago, and another man I hurt in a fight." Ramon was relieved to get that off his chest.

Father Padilla sighed, seemingly displeased, and paused for several moments before continuing. "Did you lie or steal anything from anyone? Were you unkind to anyone or treat them unfairly?"

"I was unkind to those men I killed and the one I injured, but besides that, I have tried to be fair to everyone. I don't think I stole anything or lied to anybody, Padre." Ramon tried to recall anything else that he thought could be a sin.

"Is there anyone who was weak and needed your protection that you did not protect?"

"No, Padre. Not that I can recall."

"Did you use the Lord's name in vain?" Father Padilla was very thorough with his confessions, much more so than the other missionaries at San Fernando.

"I might have a few times, *sí*."

"Did you look upon a woman in a lustful way?"

"No, Padre. I have been on the trail quite a bit," said Ramon. Then he remembered another sin he committed. "I have missed Sunday Mass several times, also."

"Is that all you want to bring before God today?"

"Please forgive me for any sins that I may have forgotten. I'm sure there were a few." Ramon always said this at the end of his confessional, in case he missed any.

"Please recite the Prayer of Contrition while I absolve your sins."

Ramon began saying the Prayer of Contrition; he had had learned it as a boy from Father Padilla. Meanwhile, Father Padilla said his own prayers, all of them in Latin. When Ramon was finished, he closed his eyes and listened to Father Padilla's words, though he didn't understand them. He felt a swell of goodness enter his body. It was the same feeling he got when he did a good deed or donated his time for charity.

"For your penance, I want you to say 'Our Prayer to the Holy Mother' ten times and then 'The Lord's Prayer' once."

"*Gracias*, Padre." This would be his penance until his next confession. He would say it not only after confession, but at every Mass as well.

"That is all, Ramon. Go in peace and try not to sin again."

Ramon stood up to leave the confessional, but then Father Padilla opened the curtain.

"Ramon, can we talk?"

"*Sí*, Padre." There was a little chair in the confessional, so Ramon sat down.

"It is much cooler and quieter here than outside," said the Father. He turned his head to face Ramon, a stern look on his face. "Ramon, did you have to kill these men or could you have avoided it? Our Lord Jesus Christ teaches us that we must turn our cheek in the face of violence."

Ramon felt a touch of the Catholic guilt he had struggled with as a boy. He had always felt that there was something he was doing wrong; he would analyze everything this way. As he had grown older, he had been able to shed some of that, but not all. "Padre, the Bible also says that we are the shepherd protecting the flock that cannot protect themselves. I chose to be the shepherd, instead of walking away from the injustice."

"Okay, Ramon. Just remember what your Prayer of Contrition says: to avoid occasions of sin. Though I do agree with what you say. Men are called to serve God in different ways, as missionaries, as builders like your father, as farmers, and as shepherds too. Your father was a very devout Catholic, Ramon. He never missed Sunday Mass, and he confessed his sins weekly. Your father and your father's *hermano* were a missionary's dream. I can still remember the day they arrived here from Ireland."

"Why were they a missionary's dream? Because they were religious men?"

"*Sí*, Ramon. Not just religious men, but devoted Catholics. All three of them: your father, his brother, and his brother's wife. It makes a missionary's life easier when there are other men to help lead the flock. Your father was a master stonemason. Our town needed a man like him to teach the *indios* and mestizos how to build. Not only did your father build much of what you see in San Antonio, but he taught the men to work with stone—and they will pass on what they learned to their children and grandchildren. And yet your father's greatest legacy was not building and teaching these men to build, but sharing his Catholic faith with them."

"What did my uncle do? What was he like?" Ramon's uncle and aunt had died before he was born, killed by *indios* like his father. If any man would remember them, it would be Father Padilla, since he was one of the oldest men in San Antonio and seemed to know everybody.

"He was older than your father, but you would never have known that, because your father was always more serious. Your uncle was lighthearted and more of a dreamer than his brother. He helped your father with masonry, but that wasn't his passion. He loved all kinds of animals: horses, goats, sheep, chickens, dogs. He had so many animals on his *rancho*. He was a good farmer, too. It was a very long time ago, when they died. It was tragic because they had a little boy. He was about four years old when they were taken by *indios*."

"The *indios* took the boy too?"

"*Sí*, Ramon. None of them were ever seen again. The *indios* are not kind to their prisoners. I don't want to think about what might have happened to them. I still pray for them to this day. I know they are all up in heaven together."

"It must have been hard on my father."

"Their loss took a little piece of his happiness, and I don't think he ever got it back. A *hermano* like that can never be replaced."

A moment of silence fell between the two men for several moments.

"I remember one other thing about your uncle that made me very fond of him," said Father Padilla with a far-off look on his candlelit face.

"What's that, Padre?"

"We shared a love for birds, he and I. He loved all kinds of birds, especially the hunting birds. It was his dream someday to catch a falcon and train it to hunt. He said it was a sport of kings in Europe. We used to talk about it all the time."

Training birds to hunt. The thought jarred Ramon's memory. Paco had talked about a man who had done that. It was the white man who had killed those two *norteños*. The man with the strange animal magic. *Many Wolves. Was this man his uncle?* No—his uncle would be fifty years old now, and this man had sounded much younger. Paco had also said this Many Wolves was raised by Apaches. *Was Many Wolves his uncle's son, then? The four-year-old?*

"Are you all right, Ramon? You became quiet all of a sudden."

"I'm fine, Padre. Do you remember anything else about my uncle's son?"

Father Padilla paused to think for a moment. "I remember his name was Aidan. I do not forget the names of the children I baptize, Ramon. He was a cute little boy with big green eyes. I thought it strange that he had green eyes, because his father's eyes were blue and his mother's brown. He had green eyes like your father, and like you, Ramon."

It was the exact same thing Paco had said.

All Saints' Day

The Feast of All Saints came less than a week after Ramon had cleansed his soul. It was a holy day of obligation, which meant all Catholics were required to attend Mass. It fell on a Wednesday this year, and Ramon faithfully attended Mass in the morning, fulfilling his obligation and keeping his soul clean, at least until his next transgression.

After the evening Mass, there was always a celebration within the walls of the Mission de San Juan Capistrano. The women of the town brought many different kinds of food for the feast. The savory aroma of simmering stew preyed on Ramon's senses as he walked through the plaza. Cloth-covered tables, lit with candles, were loaded with baskets and cooking pots filled with foods from the harvest: maize, squash, beans, and potatoes. The men brought wine, mead, ale, and cider to drink.

The air was filled with the sounds of singing children. They were dressed in their best church clothes, performing from a wooden stage facing the tables, singing songs they had rehearsed in school. A wooden platform for dancing was located between the stage and the dining tables. For as long as Ramon could remember, the celebrations in San Antonio had always centered around the church and its holy days.

"*Hola*, Luis," said Ramon as he walked by the table where Luis and his family, a wife and two daughters, were sitting.

"*Hola*, Ramon," said his friend, standing up to shake Ramon's hand.

"*Buenos noches*, Maria," said Ramon, tipping his hat.

"*Hola*, Ramon." Maria was a pretty woman with an infectious smile to match Luis's.

"Now…" Ramon put his hand to his chin. "Which one is Carmina and which one is little Gabriela…" He knew their names, but loved to pretend he didn't. "Carmina!" He pointed at Gabriela on purpose, then winked at Maria.

"No no no!" the two girls protested, then giggled.

"You never get it right, Señor Ramon," said Carmina, who was the oldest at eight years of age. Gabriela was only six.

"I'll get it right the next time. I promise!"

"You better give him a hug, *chicas*, or he will forget the next time," said Maria with a big smile.

The two girls bounced out of their seats and ran to embrace Ramon, their faces lit with joy.

"You're getting so big, you two," said Ramon, squeezing them. "Soon I won't recognize you at all."

Ramon enjoyed children, but he wasn't ready to have any of his own anytime soon. He believed it was too dangerous a world for children, but he admired people like Luis and Maria who focused so much of their energy and time on raising a family. After seeing the sacrifices they had made as parents, he had realized, without much difficulty or thought, that he wasn't ready to make those same sacrifices himself.

Ramon released them back to their seats. "Luis, I should go. Don Eduardo is waiting for me."

"Okay, Ramon. *Adios, mi amigo.*"

Ramon tipped his hat again to Luis's wife, and she bowed her head and smiled back at him. He made his way toward the table where Don Eduardo was sitting with his son, Miguel. On his way there, he greeted several men and women who were acquaintances of his, but did not stop to talk to any of them. A brief wave of his hand or tip of the hat was enough.

"Come on over, Ramon," said Don Eduardo, waving his arm.

Ramon shook both Don Eduardo and Miguel's hands before sitting across from them.

"Where is Doña Maria?"

"She is helping out with the cooking, but the truth is, she is probably bossing everyone around!" Don Eduardo and Miguel both laughed.

Ramon just nodded and smiled.

"They will be serving soon. You are just in time," said Don Eduardo, with a glass of wine in his hand. "Miguel, have one of the señoritas bring Ramon a *copa* of wine."

"*Sí, padre*," said Miguel. Then he rose from his seat and left them alone.

"Ramon, you have heard about this *americano* named Austin who is bringing more families into Tejas?" Don Eduardo had to speak loudly to be heard over the children's singing.

"*Sí*, Colonel Tejada mentioned it. He hoped it wouldn't be more work for his men."

The smoke from Don Eduardo's cigar rose up into the night sky. "This Austin has the governor's approval to sell land between the Rio Colorado and Rio Brazos, to *americano* families of Austin's choosing. I heard it from the governor himself yesterday."

"That is *norteño* land," said Ramon. "Have these people forgotten about what happened at San Saba?"

Don Eduardo took another puff of smoke. "The greedy *americano* cares only about the land and the money he can get from it. He has hired another *americano* named James McCord to protect the settlers from *indios*. Apparently, this *americano* has considerable military experience and is a proven *indio* fighter. Have you heard of him, Ramon?"

"No, but if he's an enemy of the *indios*, then he's already a friend of mine. I don't care if he's an *americano* or a *mexicano* or a mestizo." Ramon recalled what Paco had said about how it was hard to tell friends from enemies by the color of a man's skin.

When the children finished their final song, everyone stood up and cheered for them. They all bowed to the crowd in return, then exited the stage, led by Father Padilla and one of the missionary sisters who taught at the mission's school. The food servers then began delivering plates of food to hungry guests.

"I have heard that McCord's men have incurred losses already, to *indios*," said Don Eduardo. "It could have been the same *norteños* who attacked you. They say the *indios* leader is named Cold Raven."

"I have heard that name, Don Eduardo. A man I met in Saltillo, named Paco, spoke of a *norteño* with that name. In fact, this Cold Raven is the brother of Esatai, the *norteño* warrior I told you about before."

"Well, maybe this *americano* will do us all a favor and bury these *indios* once and for all."

"That would be a good thing, though we will be safe for now, with winter coming." Ramon could not recall an attack by *indios* in winter. It was possible, but unlikely. It was the safest season in San Antonio.

"Here comes our food, Ramon, and Miguel has your wine. Good timing!" Don Eduardo extinguished what was left of his cigar.

Miguel placed the wine in front of Ramon and then sat down. A señorita brought two steaming plates and set them in front of Ramon and Don Eduardo.

"*Delicioso!*" said Don Eduardo. "A good meal followed by dancing and musical entertainment. Bless the Lord for his holy days, Ramon!"

"*Gracias,*" said Ramon, bowing his head respectfully to the young serving girl.

As they ate, a small band of musicians— two with guitars, two with violins, and one with a trumpet—roved among the tables playing traditional Spanish music for the guests. They took requests from the crowd and graciously accepted any tips.

Ramon felt like a stuffed pig after two generous portions of rabbit stew, cooked to perfection with just the right amount of spicy chile peppers. He suspected it was Doña Maria's recipe, but he wasn't absolutely sure. Although some of the poorer families in San Antonio struggled to put meals on the table each day, there was always more than enough food for everyone at these church celebrations.

"I have heard that Maritza is going to sing a song later tonight," said Don Eduardo. "There is nothing that weakens an old man's knees like the beautiful voice of a young woman. Nothing, *mi amigo.*" A boyish grin spread across his face.

"Is that why Maritza wasn't serving food with the other señoritas?"

"*Sí,* perhaps, Ramon. Maritza isn't one to get her hands dirty. It will take her all day to make one candle, but Padre Padilla doesn't care as long as she is filling the plaza with her singing while she works."

They were right, both Don Eduardo and Father Padilla: Maritza had a beautiful voice and sang all the time. She always told Ramon that some day she would be a famous singer in Mexico City. Her desire to leave San Antonio was one of the things about Maritza that was unappealing to Ramon. Why anyone would want to leave the quaintness of San Antonio for the crowded city was beyond his understanding.

The mission bells rang, signaling that it was time for the younger children to retire for the night. Mothers and older sisters, mostly, gathered the children, who were largely unwilling to leave all the excitement. But eventually, after about thirty minutes of commotion, the plaza was quiet again. The musicians were setting up on the stage to play music for the adults to dance and listen to.

Once the music began, couples abandoned their tables and danced together on the wooden platform, propelled by the beat of the strumming guitars and a fluttering trumpet. Some tunes were for slower waltz or polka-style dances and others were quicker in tempo, beckoning the couples to dance *zapateado* style, with hard-stomping feet, clapping hands, and cheers from the dancers. Ramon was not much of a dancer himself, but he enjoyed watching the faces of San Antonio light up with excitement on the dance floor. Dancing allowed the people's spirits to soar into the night, and for the moment, to forget about the hard lives they lived each day.

Ramon spotted Maritza dancing on the platform several times and with different partners. She was hard to miss in her long, satin red dress, which was cinched tightly to her trim waist. *Maritza has many suitors.* She smiled and waved at him when she was close enough to see him. One side of him wanted to dance with her, but another, overpowering side held his body locked in his chair, fearing embarrassment. He had inherited his father's clumsiness on the dance floor, much to his mother's disappointment. Ramon remembered vividly his mother dancing with other men, a wide grin on her face, while his father watched, though he didn't seem to mind.

"You need to get over this fear of dancing, Ramon," said Miguel from across the table. "Maritza is watching you almost as much as she is watching her partner."

"I'd rather just watch her enjoy herself. I don't think she wants a clumsy partner. She is much too sophisticated to risk embarrassment," said Ramon.

"Well, then you wouldn't mind if I asked her to dance myself?"

"Not at all, Miguel."

When the song ended, Miguel offered his hand to Maritza for the next dance, and she smiled and accepted. Ramon pulled out his church-warden and lit it up with the table candle. The smoke relaxed him, continuing what the big meal and wine had begun.

Maritza was laughing and having a good time with Miguel, who was a skilled and lively dancer. The expression on his face while he dug his heels into the wood seemed very entertaining to her. She danced as well as the most experienced dancers, though her tall, lean body and her long, shining black hair still reflected her youth. Ramon sensed from everything she did that she was ready to leave her childhood far behind.

When the song was over, the band stopped. One of the guitarists, who was also the lead singer, announced to the crowd, "We will take a little break, señors and señoras. When we return, we will end our performance with a very special song for you."

"Whew!" Don Eduardo returned to the table, wiping the sweat from his brow with a bandanna. "Dancing is as tiring as riding a horse. I am not getting any younger, Ramon!"

"You looked like you were floating on feathers, Don Eduardo."

"*Gracias*, Ramon. You are too kind," said Don Eduardo, still trying to catch his breath.

"Maritza's performance is next, Ramon," said Miguel.

"*Sí*, Miguel. I see she is talking with the musicians now." Ramon kept an eye peeled on her as he puffed on his pipe.

The fiesta banter quieted down when the band's leader began to speak. "Our final song tonight is a traditional Spanish folk song called 'The

Winding Road of Tears.' We have played it many times without singing, but tonight, we have the beautiful voice of Maritza Castaneda to accompany us. I hope you enjoy it, *amigos*." He bowed and smiled.

The song began with the weeping strings of a violin and the delicately picked notes of a guitar. The sounds danced together like blades of grass in the wind. Music played like this—softly, emotionally—grabbed at Ramon's heart. He closed his eyes for a short time to let the music carry him away.

Then Maritza's sweet voice joined the duo of musicians. Not a note was out of place as her voice, laced with emotion, blended in perfectly with the stringed instruments. With experience seemingly beyond her years, she poured her soul into the vocal presentation. Then the rhythm slowed, her voice pitched lower, and a second guitar began strumming a Spanish beat. The couples dancing sensed the change in rhythm and swayed their hips to match the strums of the guitar.

To Ramon, Maritza's voice was the voice of an angel. She effortlessly reached the notes of the sad song with great precision, displaying what seemed to Ramon to be an almost endless vocal range. Her eyes were closed most of the time she sang, but when she opened them, she looked right at him, sending a bolt of emotion straight through his soul. Eventually, her voice was relieved by the husky, heroic blasts of a trumpet, which rose like an eagle circling high above them.

When the song ended, Maritza smiled and bowed to the rousing cheers of the crowd. Ramon stood and applauded with them. It was truly one of the most beautiful songs he had ever heard. The beauty and softness of San Antonio were a welcome contrast to the brutality and ugliness he had found in Saltillo.

Maritza

Ramon sat dazed by the performance; the aftertaste remained with him like an expensive wine.

Don Eduardo's voice shook him out of his trance. "I told you, Ramon. Nothing weakens a man's knees like the sweet voice of a beautiful woman."

"Indeed, that was *muy bonito*, Don Eduardo," said Ramon. He hadn't wanted the song to end. He kept replaying it in his mind, trying to grasp as much of it as his memory would hold, just like when he used to memorize prayers in school.

"Look, Ramon. Here she comes now," said Don Eduardo. He removed his hat as Maritza walked toward them. "*Magnifico*, Maritza! *Magnifico!*" Then he bowed and offered his opened hand to her.

She laid her hand on his, and he gently kissed it. "*Gracias*, Don Eduardo," she said. Then she turned to Ramon, her eyes reaching into his. "How did you like my song, Ramon?"

"It was *muy bonito*, Maritza. I enjoyed it tremendously." He didn't know if he was expected to kiss her hand also. He had never done that before with other women. Instead, he bowed his head and tried not to be awkward.

"Ramon and Maritza, we must leave you now," said Don Eduardo. "Doña Maria is signaling to me that she is ready to walk home, and Miguel must wake up early to open the store. Enjoy the rest of this evening. *Buenos noches.*" He bowed to them and winked at Ramon, then put his hat back on and walked away.

Miguel smiled at Ramon and tipped his hat to Maritza, then followed his father, leaving them alone.

"I was hoping you would ask me to dance, Ramon." Maritza's voice was sweet and innocent, with remnants of a child's voice still remaining in it. It was impossible to completely mask her young age.

"You know I don't like to dance. I would embarrass us both." That was mostly the truth, though a part of Ramon was afraid of Maritza's youthful charm.

"I don't understand how a man cannot dance when he can ride a horse as well as you." Some of the innocence in her voice was replaced by fire.

"I have had years of practice on a horse."

"You should practice your dancing too. Every gentleman in San Antonio knows how to dance, Ramon." The sweetness had returned to her voice. She twisted a strand of her long black hair with her right hand as she spoke.

Dancing does not put bread on my table.

Ramon felt pangs of nervousness. *She's too young.* He was trying to convince himself that she was wrong for him, but her delicate smile, the enticing scent of her perfume, and the shimmer of her shiny, gorgeous black hair melted those thoughts away, leaving him alone to fight his physical urges. Her physical beauty was crumbling the walls of his intellectual fortress. What man could resist the company of a beautiful señorita who seemed interested in him?

"Would you like to walk with me, Maritza? It's a clear night and not too cold yet," said Ramon, trembling inside, and not sure what else to say. "Unless you are still upset about the dancing, or it is too late in the night." Ramon offered her an escape, if she wanted it.

She smiled and gazed into his eyes. "It's not too late at all, Ramon." She offered her arm to him, and he took it.

The air was cool but not cold. The night sky was speckled with stars, and the landscape glowed from the light of a nearly full moon. They walked outside the mission walls toward the trickling waters of the Rio San Antonio. The path along the river was a popular spot for an evening walk.

Lovers and older couples were the most frequent visitors, but anyone seeking to enjoy the tranquil waters of the river found peace here.

"Have you been to Mexico City, Ramon?"

"No. It's a long journey and I have no reason to go there."

"I hear it is one of the greatest cities in the world. The best food. The best music and dancing. The best of everything is there," said Maritza, gazing into the night sky.

"Who told you that?" Ramon was skeptical.

"My grandmother said she was there once. She said it was a magical place. There are more people there than any other city in New Spain."

They were walking along the bank of the river now. The moon's reflection caressed the top of the rippling waters. A cool breeze teased Maritza's hair, forcing her to constantly brush it away from her eyes with her long fingers.

"*Mi padre* said that he would take me to Mexico City next year," she said. "I am almost seventeen, you know."

"That's a long and dangerous trip, Maritza. Much farther than Saltillo, where I have been."

"*Mi padre* says it is much safer to get there by ship, via the Gulf of Mexico. We have to save some money though. It is an expensive trip, but I can make some *dinero* singing with the *hombres* in the band."

"Why do you want to go there so badly?"

"I don't want to make soap and candles all my life, Ramon. There is a better life for me there. I know there is. Don Eduardo and Padre Padilla both believe I can be a singer in Mexico City. Do you think so, Ramon?"

"Your voice is very beautiful, Maritza." Ramon hadn't heard many other singers outside of San Antonio. Maritza's singing was certainly the best here, but Mexico City was a much bigger city, with many more singers.

Maritza squeezed his arm and smiled. "What was Saltillo like? Lots of music and dancing and people dressed in fancy clothes?"

Ramon didn't want to tell her what Saltillo was really like. Yes, there was music and dancing, but there was also a dangerous side, which he had experienced firsthand. It was no place for a sixteen-year-old girl with stars in her eyes. Perhaps Mexico City was a safer place, but he didn't know.

"*Sí,* there was music and dancing and lots of people. But I don't think Saltillo would be safe for a señorita like you."

"If I can go with a big, strong man like you, Señor Connelly, I would feel safe." Maritza ran her hands up his arm and squeezed his bicep.

Does she want me to go with her to Mexico City? Is that why she is interested in me? In a strange way, that made sense to him. But it would take a lot more than a pretty face to force him back into a crowded city like Saltillo. He could barely stand to visit there, let alone live there.

"I'm not going back to Saltillo any time soon." Ramon figured that by now there was a price on his head in Saltillo. A certain *torrero* and his friends would offer to pay it—or they would just do the job themselves.

"I'm feeling a chill, Ramon. Can you hold me close?"

The two of them stopped, and Ramon wrapped his arms around her. He felt his body against hers. She was warm, her body still girlishly slender. He rested his head on the top of hers. The fragrance from her hair made his face tingle. His heart was beating wildly, like a blacksmith's hammer, and her ear was pressed straight up against it. *I am like an excited boy.*

"You are so warm, Ramon. I feel so safe here. There is nothing that can harm me." She looked up at him. Her black eyes flew at him like a flock of a hundred crows. She raised up to him on her toes and touched her lips gently to his, for just a moment, then pulled them back to look at him. "Your eyes are like two sparkling emeralds. I could stare at them forever."

His mind was tied up in knots. It was difficult to think straight with all these feelings strangling his mind and body. *She's too young for me. I can't go to Mexico City with her. This isn't right.* But at a young age, Maritza already knew how to the use a woman's weapons. He was wounded, helpless. He touched her face and drew her mouth to his. He kissed her long and slow.

When the tender moment was over, she rested her head against his chest again. He saw a man standing in the distance, watching them. "Is that your father, Maritza?"

She turned her head around to look, then looked back at Ramon, a little embarrassed. "*Sí.* I have to go." She kissed him again quickly. "Will you walk with me again sometime, Señor Connelly?"

"*Sí.*" It was the easiest thing to say for the moment.

"*Buenos noches,*" she said, waving goodbye to him.

He just smiled and tipped his hat.

Without the warmth of her, he instantly felt the chill in the air.

Winter will be here soon.

The Warmth of Winter

"The storm will be here tonight," said Malone, talking loud over the whistling wind. "We'll need to help the women gather more mesquite and secure the lodges while there's still light."

Blankets of white spotted the foothills around the Gray Face camp, and still, more snow was coming. Malone, Taimah, and Many Wolves were now gathering the horses; Malone wanted them hobbled close to camp in case of thunder. A spooked horse could run forever, and in any direction. Many Wolves and Taimah were dressed in their winter deerskin outfits: shirts, leggings, and moccasins. Malone was shirtless, as always, but his legs and feet were covered in deerskin.

The Gray Face camp had been Many Wolves's winter home for as long as he could remember. It was close enough to the fall hunting spots, yet far enough south to avoid the freezing northern winds and treacherous blizzards, which were frequent occurrences north of the Rio Colorado. It also offered an abundance of rabbits and squirrels for the birds to hunt, and deer and elk for Malone. It was an ideal location.

"I can help once the horses are safe," said Many Wolves. "It's too windy to take the birds out anyway." He saw Taimah's disappointed reaction. They had hoped to get another hunt in before dark, but now they would have to wait until the storm was over. "I am sorry, Taimah. But that elk you killed early this morning will help feed all of us through this storm."

When they arrived back at the camp, the wind was still bending the trees, and it was getting colder and colder. A thick layer of clouds was rolling in. Nina and Topusana were still busy curing the elk meat.

"I'll get a raw piece and feed it to the birds," said Taimah, dismounting and handing her horse's lead to Many Wolves.

"Generous portions, Taimah," said Many Wolves as she was walking away. "They'll burn through it quickly in this cold weather." He remembered how Reina had died in the cold weather because he had made the mistake of not feeding her enough.

"Yes, *Ahpu*. I was going to do that," said Taimah.

"Topusana," said Malone from his horse, "will you be able to gather wood for the fire before it gets dark?"

"We're up to our neck in elk blood," Nina snapped. "You'll have to do it."

"I'll gather the wood," offered Many Wolves. "Let me attach the pole-drag to Castano." He dismounted and dragged the empty pole-drag over to his horse, then tied it tightly. "I'll gather as much wood as I can carry."

Malone nodded his thanks. "I'll tie down the horses and stake the lodges."

* * *

Many Wolves arrived back at the camp with a fully loaded pole-drag. Noche had followed him every step of the way. Many Wolves hoped that most of the wood he had gathered was dry enough to burn. In this regard, the Wind Wolf, the spirit who ruled the wind, had been his friend. The snow was patchy and melting, but by sunup tomorrow he expected the landscape to be painted softly in white, like down feathers.

Malone crawled out of Many Wolves's lodge to greet him. "I'll help you load those into the lodges."

The rest of the village, apart from the animals, was huddled up around a fire in Many Wolves's lodge. He smelled the elk meat roasting on the flames and looked forward to a feast and a night of storytelling.

Malone helped him to unload the wood, mostly mesquite and pine, into each of the lodges. Then they tied Castano with the other horses and returned to Many Wolves's lodge.

The heat of the lodge was a welcome comfort. The thick buffalo-hide walls of the tipi kept the freezing winds out and the fire's heat in, while the cold night sky sucked all the smoke out through a hole at the top. There was enough space inside for both families and the two wolves, as well as spare firewood, cooking tools, sleeping robes, weapons, and anything that needed to stay dry. The people of the village sat circled around the fire: the men sat cross-legged while the women tucked their legs to one side.

"Has everyone else eaten?" said Many Wolves, sitting down in his usual spot next to his wife. Nina was roasting a large piece of elk meat over the flames.

"*Haa*. You're the last," said Topusana, who sat across from him, next to Malone.

"The leader of a wolf pack is always the first to eat," said Many Wolves, holding his breath in anticipation of a snappy response from his wife.

Nina just rolled her eyes and shook her head.

"The Wind Wolf bit off your crooked tongue, my *nupetsu*," said Many Wolves, still trying to lure out a reaction.

"Malone, can you tie him up with the horses?" said Nina, at last, bringing smiles and laughter to their faces. The brightest and loudest was from her husband.

The wind whistled outside, and rain began to pelt the tipi walls.

"Malone, is this going to be a big storm?" said Taimah.

"*Haa*, Daughter of Thunder. But you're not afraid, are you?"

"No. I like these storms. You and *Ahpu* tell the best stories when the wind whistles and the thunder crashes."

Many Wolves remembered that feeling from his childhood as well. His grandfather had always had new stories to tell on stormy nights, as if he had been saving them for the occasion, and the wind and the thunder always seemed to make the stories come to life. Unfortunately, he couldn't remember many of his grandfather's stories; it was so long ago. Most of the time, he had to create new ones from his life experiences.

Nina served Many Wolves the cooked slab of elk she was preparing on a large piece of bark. The steamy aroma awoke his hunger. He took a small bite, because it was still very hot. "Delicious, my *nupetsu*," he said. He loved the herbs and spices she used in her cooking, especially the salt.

The heavy droplets of rain relented, but the wind continued to howl, shaking the walls of the lodge from time to time.

Taimah crawled over to the door of the lodge and peeked out. "It's snowing now."

"We'll be buried in here like prairie dogs," said Malone.

"As long as I'm a warm and dry prairie dog," said Nina.

Many Wolves had finished eating the first part of his meal and was hungry for more. Nina didn't even have to ask; she just started preparing another slice of elk meat for roasting.

"Malone, is there a story behind your name?" asked Taimah. "It is very unusual. It doesn't sound like any Northerner words I know."

Many Wolves was curious to know also. He couldn't remember if Malone had told him before.

"You're right, Daughter of Thunder. My name isn't from a Northerner word. It's a name from the white man's world," said Malone. The soft tones of his voice barely floated over the crackle of the fire and the whipping wind outside.

"Why would you have a white man's name?" asked Taimah, cocking her head slightly like the wolf hawks do when they study a morsel of food.

"I chose to bury my old Noomah name and take this white man's name. I still remember the man who had this name. He was one of the bravest I have seen."

"Who was he?"

"He was a captive that Laughing Crow captured and tortured," said Malone. "Laughing Crow and his men did terrible things to this man, trying to break his spirit, but the man did not beg or cry out for mercy. He died very bravely and with great dignity."

"Were you a boy?" asked Taimah.

"No, I had lived around thirty summers by that time. Laughing Crow had just become the leader of our village."

Many Wolves was suddenly very curious about this white man. He had always suspected that it was Laughing Crow who was in his childhood nightmares—Laughing Crow who was killing his parents in those awful dreams. This white man did not die so easily.

"Were there any other captives with this white man? Any women or children?" asked Many Wolves.

"I don't remember any other scalp dances from that raid, or any other captives."

Many Wolves sensed that Malone was uneasy talking about these memories.

"The man was alive when you brought him back?"

"*Haa*. He was pierced by an arrow in the chest, but he was very much alive."

Many Wolves was certain now that this man was not the man who had died over and over in his nightmares. Those dreams had been so vivid when he was a child. He didn't remember many of the details now, just fleeting memories, but one of them was a white man dying, and he had always believed the man was his father. "He must have been a very brave man, Malone, for you take his name," said Many Wolves at last, still wondering if his dreams could have shown him anything that wasn't the truth.

"*Haa*, he was, Many Wolves. It was long ago. I don't remember a lot of the details."

"So there is some white man in you, Malone. In your name. You're just like us!" Taimah grinned, clearly pleased with herself.

"You are right, Daughter of Thunder."

"*Ahpu*, do you have any more Gray Face stories?"

"None that you haven't heard hundreds of times already," said Many Wolves.

"When I sit on that ledge outside, I try to imagine what it would be like to face a bear like that. You must have been terrified, *Ahpu*."

"I was terrified when his claws were ripping through the tree trunk, trying to climb up to me. But once I realized Gray Face could not get to me, I grew less scared and more confident. When I looked down into his black, lifeless eyes, I saw his fear for the first time. I knew then, at that moment, that I had to kill him, that I could kill him. It was Gray Face that brought Ten Arrows to me. From that horrifying experience came a great friendship. The Great Spirit works in crooked ways. Remember that lesson, Wildflower, that grass is greener and stronger after a fire."

"Someday, maybe I'll have stories like that to tell," said Taimah, smiling at him.

"You've already told us a great story: your first buffalo hunt," said Nina, looking over at her daughter with pride.

"Have you killed buffalo before, *Ahpu*?"

"*Haa.* But not from a horse like you. I had to sneak up on it like a wolf and shoot it from a distance. I can't ride and shoot like a Northerner, like you and Malone can."

"Malone and I can teach you," said Taimah.

Many Wolves laughed. "I'll stick with what I know—hunting small animals with birds, not arrows."

While Many Wolves ate his second portion of elk, Topusana busied herself with sewing, and Malone was buried in his arrow-making. Taimah left momentarily and returned with the old *libro* that Walking Free had given to Many Wolves on his last day in the Lipan village. Many Wolves kept it buried in a leather pouch in the Gray Face camp. During the winter, Taimah enjoyed looking at the bird pictures, which were mostly faded after so many winters.

"I like this picture, *Ahpu*." Taimah showed him a picture of a falcon perched on a fist-perch. "But I like this one too. What is it?"

"It looks like a shield with a dog or wolf on it," said Many Wolves. It was the only picture in the *libro* with colors in it.

"I think it's a family symbol. I think white people and Mexicans mark their *libros* with those symbols like you mark your arrows," said Nina, glancing over at the *libro*.

"May I see it?" asked Malone, looking up from his work, his curiosity piqued.

"You've never seen it before?" Taimah asked.

"I've seen the *libro*, but not the pictures inside it," said Malone.

Taimah handed it to Malone. He stared at the pictures. "I've never seen a *libro* with so many pictures on the leaves. The Nokonis use the leaves to strengthen their war shields."

"Those leaves are called *paginas*," said Nina. "The Mexican women in my old village used to have *libros*. They said they contained stories about their Great Spirit."

"Where did you get this, Many Wolves?" asked Malone, looking straight into Many Wolves's eyes.

"The medicine man from my Lipan village gave it to me. He said that it belonged to my white-skinned parents. He said someday that it might help me to find them."

Malone returned to his arrow-making, saying nothing.

Part II

Lead Fingers

Wings

The sun's warmth was finally returning to the foothills around Many Wolves's village, bringing green grass and blossoming wildflowers. Birds filled the crisp air with song, and small animals scampered around the Gray Face camp, looking for food fresh from the earth.

Many Wolves was pleased to have another winter behind him. He had feared a storm that would come and bury everything, but it had never happened, not this winter. The village always dug its way out of every storm, and somehow Malone or Many Wolves found a lone deer or some wandering rabbits to supplement their food stores and carry them through the next heavy snowfall.

Many Wolves had especially worried about his birds. They were desert animals and not accustomed to cold climates. He knew from Reina's untimely winter death that small animals were fragile and couldn't survive long without food. When the winds blew hard or the snow blinded the birds' vision, they couldn't hunt and were solely dependent on the other village hunters for their survival.

Now that spring was here, the birds, like all the wild animals around them, were reborn into a seemingly new, unblemished world, a gift from Mother Earth. They were jumping from branch to branch like blue jays, squawking at Many Wolves and Taimah to take them hunting. Naturally Chachara was the most vocal of the group, which drove Noche to madness and incessant barking. *The quiet of winter is over.*

"Soon we should journey north to Three Trees Crossing," said Malone, preparing his horse for his morning ride, seeming unbothered by the noise. Topusana was out gathering roots, but Nina was there grinding nuts for their morning meal.

Many Wolves nodded, but he was still distracted by the noise. "Taimah, do you have some fresh meat with you?" he asked.

"*Haa, Ahpu.*"

"Feed that bird something." Many Wolves hoped that a satisfied Chachara would bring a little less noise to his camp.

Taimah slipped on her fist-perch and whistled for Chachara to fly to her. The bird immediately swooped down to her hand and gulped down a few hunks of red meat.

"Not too much. I want her sharp for the hunt," said Many Wolves, relishing the newly found silence from the female wolf hawk, which also calmed the black wolf. *There's nothing like fresh meat to muzzle a noisy bird.*

"She's a lot more content now," said Taimah.

"Wildflower, there is another journey that I need to make, and I want you to go with me," said Many Wolves, revealing a thought that had been slumbering in his head for several moons.

"What journey, *Ahpu?*"

"We need to find the white lion's paw flower."

"The medicine you use for your mind journeys?" Taimah's eyes lit up like stars.

"*Haa.* My flower medicine bag is empty, and I want to show you where the flower grows." One of the last times he had used the white flower medicine was when Rojo died. He had barely used it since, and what was left of his supply had long ago crumbled to dust. There were still plenty of peyote buttons in his medicine bag, the other ingredient for his mind-journey medicine, because they were easier to find in the desert. But the white lion's paw flower was a much greater challenge to harvest. He would have to remember the path he had taken with Ten Arrows to find it again.

"Will you show me how to use the medicine, *Ahpu?*" Taimah's eyes were full of excitement.

"*Haa*, in time. But we need to find the flower first," said Many Wolves.

"How long will this journey take?" asked Nina.

"We will be back before the new moon if we leave from Three Trees Crossing," said Many Wolves.

"That's a long time for a young girl to be away from her village." There was worry in Nina's voice.

"I'm not a young girl anymore, *Shimaa*, and *Ahpu* will be with me," protested Taimah.

"She needs to learn to survive outside our village, like I did when I was her age," Many Wolves said.

He sensed that his wife was unhappy with his decision, but for now, she remained silent. *There will be more talk later.*

"Taimah," said Many Wolves, "take the birds out to the spot we hunted yesterday. I'll meet you there in a moment." He wanted to speak with Nina alone, with Taimah away.

Taimah swung her arm upward. "Up, Chachara, up!" The bird flew to the branch. Taimah grabbed some things from the lodge and mounted her horse. Then she whistled for the birds to follow and rode away. Colmillo followed after them.

"She's not as strong as a boy would be at her age, Many Wolves," said Nina in a hushed voice. "It's a dangerous world away from our village— dangerous for you too."

"She is ready, Nina. She is not strong like a man, but she shoots and rides as well as one. She was beating me in horse races three summers ago, and she has already killed her first buffalo."

"It won't be you chasing her out there," said Nina, pointing to the world outside their camp, "and buffalo don't kill like men do. What will you do if white men find you or the Nokoni? Is Malone going with you?"

"Many Wolves is right," Malone said. He was now carving the shaft of an arrow. "She is a strong rider. She practices every day to get better. It is important that she finds this flower. Many Wolves will protect her, and I'll be here to protect you and Topusana. Her wings will not grow strong unless she flies from the nest."

Many Wolves felt the same fear as Nina. The fear of letting go of a child. The fear of releasing her into a dangerous world. He walked over to his wife and put his arm around her. "It's hard for me too—to see her leave our nest. I will be with her though. There are things she must learn outside our village."

"But she is a girl, not even a woman yet." Tears were welling up in Nina's eyes.

"She is just as much a son as a daughter to us, *nupetsu*. Malone and I have taught her everything that we would teach a son, and you have taught her as a daughter. Her village is not a traditional village. She needs to know how to do man's work as well as woman's work in our little village. I want her to know how to survive without any village at all."

Nina's emotions were not easily calmed. "She is not a man like you... or like you, Malone. Women don't live in the wilderness alone. They live in villages with a husband to provide for them and protect them." A tear rolled down her face as she spoke. "Isn't that what you want for her?"

"*Haa*, it is what I want too, but until that time, she must learn to take care of herself." Many Wolves looked into his wife's dark eyes and smiled.

"I am scared, dearest *shika*. I am scared for her, and for you."

"I know. I am scared too, *nupetsu*. Especially after seeing those hairy-faced white men," said Many Wolves, kissing her on the forehead. "But as Malone said, we must help to make her wings strong, and I need to show her where to find this special flower."

Another spring must not pass.

Matsokai

It took Many Wolves's village two sleeps to reach their spring camp at Three Trees Crossing. The northward journey was not difficult, since the Rio Pecos led them most of the way, and the weather was warm and clear. There was an abundance of edible fruits, plants, and roots to gather along the way, and small animals were plentiful, much to the birds' liking.

The camp was isolated from most human contact, because the buffalo herds did not roam that far west in the spring. And the green prairie lands were perfect for deer, antelope, and the occasional elk, which made this spot one of Malone's favorites. Rabbits were everywhere for the birds, and when they needed a new challenge or a change in routine, there were plenty of quail and prairie dogs to hunt.

Their first morning hunt at the new camp went well. The birds killed two jackrabbits and a prairie dog that had strayed too far from its burrow. Flecha was especially pleased with that kill, chasing off the other two birds like a ferocious wolverine protecting its kill from pesky scavengers. Many Wolves and Taimah were letting Flecha eat as much of it as he wanted, since it was the last kill of the day.

"I bet that prairie dog tastes as good to him as my buffalo did to me," said Taimah. She was sitting in the tall prairie grass, stroking Colmillo's fur and playing a fetching game with Chachara: throwing a morsel for her to fetch and then calling her back to the fist-perch with another morsel.

"There's always a better flavor when you know you killed it yourself," said Many Wolves. He was sitting with Noche, feeding Espera a rabbit leg on his fist-perch. It was one of his favorite parts of the hunt, especially since Chachara was preoccupied this time with Taimah's game.

"Can we leave tomorrow, *Ahpu*, for the flower journey?"

"Perhaps not tomorrow, but soon, Wildflower. There is no reason to wait. I don't want your *shimaa* to talk me out it." Many Wolves was pleased that she seemed as excited as him about the trip. "We will travel with few provisions. Just our weapons and our sleeping robes is all we will need."

"I've never been high in the mountains before. What's it like?"

"It's like climbing a hill that never ends. There's less grass and more trees, like pines and junipers, and rocks of every size. If you try to run, you get tired faster, and the sun is so close that you feel you can almost touch it."

"And there are more grizzlies too?"

"*Haa*, but we will have Colmillo and Noche with us. Most bears won't want to tangle with a pack of predators." Many Wolves was not only trying to calm her fears, but to convince himself that there was nothing to fear.

"And one of them a proven bear hunter," said Taimah, with pride.

Many Wolves laughed. "That was a long time ago, Wildflower." Many Wolves had never been attacked by a bear when he'd had Rojo with him. He hoped Noche and Colmillo would give them the same *puha*.

"Is it scary?" asked Taimah.

"Is what scary? Being in the mountains?"

"No, *Ahpu*. A mind-journey. Is it scary to fly so high in the sky? I get scared looking down from a tall rock."

"No, it isn't scary. It's hard to describe. You'll have to see for yourself."

Many Wolves had only told her about his mind-journeys with his birds, not with Rojo. He wasn't sure if he wanted her to know it was possible with a wolf. His mind-journeys with Rojo involved dangerous situations— scouting men who were his enemies with an intent to kill. Those were stories better left untold.

She also didn't know that he had killed Thorn Bird and Silent Weasel, or that Rojo had killed Laughing Crow. These were all men that she knew as Malone's people, from Malone's stories. He had asked his village to keep these killings a secret, until he felt it was the right time to tell her. When she asked if he had killed any men, he said "yes," but he did not give any names, and he said it was always to protect himself, which was truthful. The time was coming to tell her about these men, though—because sooner or later she would hear from someone outside of his village.

"Are you ready to go home?" he asked, standing up. Flecha had just finished off his prairie dog meal and was preening his feathers and cleaning every scrap of meat off his beak and toes.

Taimah nodded and stood. They called for their horses, who were grazing nearby, mounted them, and then directed them toward the Three Trees camp.

After a short ride, Many Wolves and Taimah arrived at the camp. Their friend Matsokai was there talking to Malone. The wolves sniffed the air and kept their distance from the Northerner, but they did not bark, or even growl, because he was not a complete stranger.

Matsokai was a Penateka scout and warrior who was over twenty-five winters of age. He had once been close friends with Stretches Like A Dog, Ten Arrows's brother. He and Malone became close friends after Stretches Like A Dog's death. They hunted together often, and Matsokai kept Malone informed about events in Crooked Eagle's village and throughout the Penatekas' homelands. Malone believed that Matsokai was like a spider who had his webs spread out all over the plains, gathering vital information for his people.

Many Wolves and Taimah dismounted and greeted Matsokai—Many Wolves by grasping his forearm and Taimah with a quick embrace. Taimah then took the two horses and led them away, leaving the men to talk alone.

"Matsokai says that spring has brought more white men to the plains," said Malone. His tone was serious, and Matsokai's smile quickly floated away.

"More buffalo hunters?" asked Many Wolves.

"No. White men with sticks and tents," Malone said. "Matsokai's village believes that these men are claiming the land around the Rio Colorado for their lodges. Once the tents are set up, they don't leave, and some of them have started to make white man's lodges."

Matsokai petted Noche, who had approached him. "These *taiboos* came when the summer moon roamed the night sky," he said. "We attacked them, killing their men and taking their women and children as captives. When the summer moon had passed and the leaves fell from the trees, the *taiboos* brought many men with guns to protect them. The man who leads them is called 'Lead Fingers' by the Noomah. He is the bravest of the hairy-faced warriors. He shoots five lead balls, one for each finger, before he has to reload his magic gun. He and his men have killed many of our warriors.

"The men who ride with Lead Fingers use *mestano* mounts, like the Noomah, and not the larger, slow-footed horses who tire easily and need the *taiboo's* grain for food. They pursue our warriors deep into Noomah lands, unlike any *taiboo* we have known before, because they have a Navoonah tracker named Little Sky to uncover our path."

Little Sky. It was a familiar name from Many Wolves's past. Little Sky's father, Big Sky, had helped to fight Laughing Crow. Little Sky was a friend—but now he had chosen new friends: the hairy-faced Mare-cans.

"I know this Lipan warrior, Little Sky," said Many Wolves. "He was my friend long ago, when Laughing Crow was my enemy."

"He is not your friend anymore, Many Wolves," said Matsokai. "The Penetaka drove his people south to the Rio Bravo, and now anyone who is an enemy of the Noomah is a friend to Little Sky's people."

My people are now my enemies. Many Wolves still considered the Lipans his people. They were Nina's people too, and Lipan blood flowed through his daughter. *When I raise my bow, how will I know who my enemy is?*

"I told Matsokai about the buffalo hunters we killed last fall." Malone looked at Many Wolves. "Matsokai has seen more white men coming to kill the buffalo in spring."

Matsokai spoke again. "Crooked Eagle believes that the white men outnumber the buffalo in villages far to the east, and that more and more of them will come to make their villages here. Crooked Eagle does not worry about his future because he is very old, but he worries about the future of our people. The Wichita and Kiowa share the same fear. Crooked Eagle has made peace with them to fight this common enemy."

"What about Cold Raven's village?" asked Malone.

Cold Raven was Laughing Crow's son, and was the leader of the Nokonis now, along with his brother Esatai, Thorn Bird's son. Many Wolves remembered Cold Raven and Esatai as Valencia's sons from Thorn Bird's village. They were just small boys then, but he could still picture Cold Raven's face at the end of his arrow shaft. That was the day he freed Nina from their village.

"There is still unrest between Crooked Eagle and Cold Raven," said Matsokai, looking at both of them now. "He will not easily forget Thorn Bird's war with you, Many Wolves, or that Penateka blood was spilled in that war. As long as Crooked Eagle still breathes, there will be no peace with Cold Raven's Nokonis."

"Thorn Bird made many enemies," added Malone. "He killed Gray Elk long ago, and as long as Gray Elk's scalp still hangs in Cold Raven's village, there will be no peace between their two Nokoni villages. Thorn Bird cut out the heart of his village, and now they are left to wither in the wind like the bones of a carcass that has been picked clean."

"Warriors like Cold Raven and Esatai do not wither away, Malone," said Matsokai. "They will take many lives before they lose theirs. Crooked Eagle may be wise to reconsider a friendship with their warriors." Many Wolves heard as much concern in Matsokai's tone as in his words.

"Matsokai, will you stay and enjoy a meal with us?" asked Many Wolves. "The birds killed two rabbits, and there's half a prairie dog left also."

"I have stayed here too long already, Many Wolves." Matsokai knelt down to say goodbye to Noche. "I've been living off the back of my horse and on pemmican for most of this moon. Crooked Eagle wants to know where the *taiboos* will walk before their feet touch the earth."

"We want to know where the white man walks as well, Matsokai," said Malone. "I will keep my eyes open on the western plains."

"*Ura*, my friend. Thanks as well to you, Many Wolves. May your animal spirits protect you." Matsokai mounted and rode off.

Many Wolves considered Matsokai's news. The Penatekas and Nokonis had been raiding the white villages and fighting the Lipans for many winters far to the south. In their ongoing war with the Lipans, Many Wolves could not choose one side over the other, because both the Penatekas and Lipans were his friends, so he and Malone had chosen to live in obscurity in a village far apart from either of these two warring peoples. Now the white man was bringing the war to them, and he worried that the peace he had enjoyed since Thorn Bird's death was vanishing. A cloud of war was falling over the prairie, and it would be difficult to see who his friends and enemies were through the blinding mist.

"What do we do, Malone?" he asked.

"You must travel with Taimah to get the mind-journey flower. Your mind-journeys are a weapon we can use in this war. You must ride west tomorrow with the rising sun at your back. There is no time to waste. I will keep this camp hidden and my eyes open. I will need to be the wolves of our village while you are away."

To the High Country

Taimah woke Many Wolves while the world was still dark and pleasantly quiet. Even Chachara was still asleep, so her usual ruckus didn't break the silence. Many Wolves's sleepy mind guided him through his morning routine. Familiar tasks were the best way to stretch his mind and body, to prepare it for the day. He needed his mind to be sharp, knowing that his travels would take him to strange places he hadn't visited since Taimah's birth. They had packed the horses the night before, to hasten the start of their adventure into the high country.

"Are you almost ready?" asked Taimah, whispering and with eyes eager to see new places. Colmillo was next to her, stretching his legs.

"*Haa*. I'd like to leave before that crazy bird wakes the rest of the camp," said Many Wolves.

"It's too late for that," said Nina, stretching and yawning from the sleeping robe she shared with her husband. "You two are not going to sneak out of here without saying goodbye."

Taimah met her mother at the entrance to their lodge, and they embraced. "We will be back soon, *Shimaa*."

"Be safe, and don't shoot anything with big teeth or arrows," said Nina, with tears in her eyes.

Taimah smiled.

"Goodbye, my *nupetsu*," said Many Wolves, hugging his wife. "Malone will take good care of you and Topusana."

"I wish Malone was taking care of you instead," said Nina. "Please be safe, and don't let my sleeping robe stay too cold, *namunewapi*."

Many Wolves smiled at her. They had enjoyed each other's warmth throughout the night, knowing they would soon be apart.

He roused Flecha with a piece of red meat from the previous day's hunt, luring him to his fist-perch, and he tossed a small piece on the ground away from Noche for Espera to eat. Taimah woke Chachara the same way. *A bird can't squawk and eat at the same time.* With a little food in their crops, Many Wolves and Taimah called the birds to follow them out of the camp.

Heading northward, Many Wolves and Taimah easily crossed the cool waters of the Rio Pecos, which were shallow at the Three Trees Crossing.

"They will enjoy the peace and quiet," said Many Wolves. "No howling wolves or chattering birds. I know if I were them, I'd enjoy a break from Chachara anyway. Too bad we couldn't leave her at the camp."

"*Ahpu*! You know I would miss her. And so would Espera and Flecha."

"Noche and I would not." Many Wolves grinned.

"I think you would. But maybe not Noche," Taimah conceded.

"I like the braids and beads in your hair, Wildflower," said Many Wolves. Taimah's hair was braided on both sides of her head, with beads woven into the strands of her dark brown hair. There were three braids on each side.

"*Shimaa* and Topusana helped me."

"You look like the wife of a Northerner headman."

Taimah smiled. "I'm glad you like them, *Ahpu*."

They continued north along the river. By the late afternoon, they had reached a steady slope upward that signaled the start of the high country. The grassland around them was spotted with manzanitas and oaks, mostly, with some pines and junipers mixed in. In another day they would be leaving the foothills, leaving the manzanitas and oaks far behind.

"Should we hunt the birds soon, *Ahpu*?" asked Taimah. "They've flown a long way today."

"They can wait a little longer."

The birds had been following them along all day, occasionally perching on a fist-perch or one the horse's riding pads. Many Wolves wanted to cover as much ground as he could during the day and then save a sliver of daylight to hunt the birds before dusk.

"What did Matsokai say, *Ahpu*? He didn't stay with us like he usually does."

"He said there were more white men coming to their lands." Many Wolves wanted to be truthful, but he also didn't want to expose too many grim details. He chose his words carefully.

"Like the hairy-faced men you and Malone killed?"

"How did you know about that?"

"Malone told me."

"*Haa*, Taimah. Matsokai was talking about the hairy-faced white men. He wanted us to keep our eyes open for more men like them."

"Are they coming to kill our buffalo?"

"*Haa*, and to take our land for their lodges."

"Don't they already have homes somewhere else?"

"Most of them live far to the east, where there are many villages. Perhaps they think that since there are no white man villages here, they can take the land."

"But the Northerners won't let them take the land, will they?"

"No, Wildflower. They won't." Many Wolves hoped it was as simple as that, but he had sensed the fear in Matsokai's voice, particularly when he had spoken of the white man named Lead Fingers. Perhaps if the Penetakas or Nokonis could kill this man, then the threat would be over, the same way it had been over after he killed Laughing Crow and Thorn Bird. *The next time I see Matsokai, we will celebrate the death of this man, Lead Fingers.* Many Wolves wanted to keep pleasant thoughts on his mind, so he convinced himself that this would eventually happen.

As they rode farther from their village, Many Wolves spotted a short-winged bird-killer hawk circling overhead. He thought of his short-lived friendship with Fiera, his bird-killer. He still remembered some of the chases she had with quail, and his brief mind-journey with her. She was a relentless hunter and pursuer, but her spirit was too wild to tame.

He imagined that many other animals were wild like this: mountain lions, grizzly bears, badgers. Animals that were used to living alone, not depending on others of their kind to survive, unlike dogs and wolves. Bird-killers, like mountain lions, were not meant to be tamed, while wolf hawks were as tame as village dogs. There were times he had seen bird-killers leave their meals half-eaten, as if the killing was foremost on their mind, not survival. In this regard, they reminded him of the mindless buffalo killers, the hollow men that Malone had killed. After his experience with Fiera, he had never again tried to tame a bird-killer.

"The sun is low now, Taimah. We should set our camp here and hunt the birds."

"*Haa, Ahpu.* I'm hungry too."

A River of Possibilities

"Ramon! Have a look at this," said Don Eduardo, handing him a poster. "I cannot read it because it is written in *inglés*. An *americano* handed it to me, but didn't say much because he didn't speak *español.*"

Ramon was sitting in his home, cleaning a *pistole* he had just fixed for one of Don Eduardo's customers. A vase filled with spring wildflowers, handpicked by Doña Maria, rested on his table, scenting the air with a sweet fragrance. The spring sun warmed the small dwelling and spilled its bright light from one end of the room to the other.

"What does it say, Ramon? I recognized the names of 'Austin' and 'McCord.' I told you about them last *noviembre.*"

Ramon looked it over. "It says that Stephen F. Austin is looking to hire men for the defense of Tejas against *indios* under the command of Captain James W. McCord of Tennessee. Then it says to meet at the Stone House in Nacogdoches on March 13 for *audicións.*"

"This *americano* McCord is a proven *indio* fighter and has won many fights with *norteños,*" said Don Eduardo, taking the poster back from Ramon.

"Why does he want men from San Antonio? Aren't his men *americanos?*" asked Ramon, motioning for Don Eduardo to sit in the other chair.

"Not all of them. Some of his men are *mexicanos,* and he uses Lipanos as trackers," said Don Eduardo. "I have heard that he and his men burned a *norteño* village last fall and killed their leader."

"Where was the village?" Ramon wanted to know if they killed *norteños* in their homeland.

"In the Llano Estacado," answered Don Eduardo. "A place where few white men have traveled."

Ramon had heard stories of the Llano Estacado. If the *indios* didn't kill you, starvation or thirst would. They said a man could lose his shadow on the Llano. For this man McCord to kill *norteños* there was an impressive accomplishment. He must know the lay of the land. *There is much I can learn from a man like him.*

"I would like to meet this *hombre* McCord." Ramon poured his guest a cup of water from the pitcher on the table.

"You want to join him in his fight with the *indios?*"

"I'll think about it, Don Eduardo. It sounds *muy peligroso,* but it would be a great service to the people of San Antonio to rid ourselves of this *indio* threat forever."

Don Eduardo smiled.

"Why are you smiling?" asked Ramon.

"I was thinking that you would be settling down with Maritza, *mi amigo.* There are whispers around town of a spring wedding for you two." Don Eduardo cast a sharpened glance at him.

Nothing escaped Don Eduardo's watchful eye. Ramon had spent a lot of time with Maritza and her family since their walk along the river on the Feast of All Saints. He had attended church celebrations and shared meals with her family. The two of them had become inseparable.

"I think everyone else has agreed on this arrangement except for me."

"Maritza is sweet and *muy bonito,* Ramon," said Don Eduardo with a devilish grin. "What is your hesitation?"

"She is so young, Don Eduardo, and she has dreams of living in Mexico City. San Antonio is my home." Ramon knew in his heart that Maritza would not be happy living in San Antonio. Her mind was firmly set on going to Mexico City to see how far her singing talent would carry her.

Don Eduardo took a drink of water, then set his cup down. He looked at Ramon very seriously. "Marry her, Ramon, and take her to Mexico City. Let her chase her dream. If she succeeds, you will be a wealthy man. If she does not, she will want to return to San Antonio. How can you lose?"

Ramon had never thought it through like this before. Leave it to Don Eduardo to analyze the situation from every angle. It was this kind of thinking that made Don Eduardo a successful businessman. However, Ramon still wasn't convinced he would be happy in Mexico City, even with the comforts of wealth. His dreams were here in San Antonio. His dreams were to make the town—this town that he loved, that his parents had loved—a safe and prosperous place to live. Money couldn't buy his dream.

"Now, before you say that Don Eduardo has been smoking too many cigars, also consider this. As my wedding gift to you and Maritza, I will pay for your trip to Mexico City. Now you really can't lose, *mi amigo*."

"Why would you do all this, Don Eduardo?" Ramon was flattered by such a generous offer, but he was also a little scared by it. The cost of traveling to Mexico City was his best excuse for not having to go there.

"Because I believe that this marriage is what your mother and father would have wanted," said Don Eduardo with compassion. "I don't think they would want you to end up in a unmarked grave buried deep in the Llano, *mi amigo*."

"How long have you been planning this?"

"Ever since I saw you two together at the Feast of All Saints," said Don Eduardo with a spark in his eye.

"Does anyone else know about this?"

Don Eduardo hesitated for a moment. "I've had a couple of very informal *discusions* with Maritza's *padre*, just to measure his response to the idea."

"And?" said Ramon, a little perturbed. He would have preferred it if Don Eduardo had come to *him* first with this plan, a plan that would change *his* life in almost every possible way.

"Well, Ramon, Maritza's *padre et madre* are very fond of you. You probably know that by now. He has told me in very casual terms that it is an idea he approves of."

At least that part wasn't a surprise to Ramon.

"So you see, Ramon, I have removed all the fallen trees from the river, so there is nothing to slow the path of the water."

But a fallen tree can also save a man from drowning.

Beauty

"Padre Padilla, that was another inspiring sermon today," said Ramon, shaking Father Padilla's hand.

Sunday Mass at San Fernando Church was over, and the people were greeting Father Padilla as they left. Ramon, along with the Castenedas and Romeros, was among the last to exit. On this occasion, Maritza was not with them, because she was singing with the church choir.

"*Gracias*, Ramon," said Father Padilla with a huge Sunday smile on his face. Sunday was the Father's favorite day of the week—when all the people came together from all around San Antonio for his morning Mass. The holy man was dressed in his traditional purple Lenten vestments.

Don Eduardo, who was behind Ramon, shook Father Padilla's hand next. "I enjoyed your homily, Padre. However, I don't think I'm as rich as the rich man in that story."

Father Padilla's sermon had elaborated on the day's gospel reading about Jesus and the rich man in the 'eye of the needle' story, where Jesus tells the rich man that it would be as easy for him to enter God's kingdom as for a camel to pass through the eye of a needle.

Father Padilla laughed. "Don Eduardo, I'm sure God will look favorably on your good deeds and your undying support of our parish."

"*Gracias*, Padre," said Don Eduardo with a hearty laugh. "It was a beautiful ceremony. Maritza's voice was the voice of an angel again today. There is scarcely an empty pew when she sings in the choir."

"Music is a very important part of our Mass. It is very uplifting for the

166

people's spirits. *Gracias* for your kind words."

Don Eduardo and Father Padilla were very close friends who depended on each other. Don Eduardo relied on Father Padilla's spiritual guidance, and the Father relied on Don Eduardo's financial support. On days like this, Ramon believed that Don Eduardo's *donación* was more generous than usual because of the guilt inspired by Father Padilla's sermon.

While Maritza's parents and Doña Maria were talking to Father Padilla, Maritza walked out of the church. She spotted Ramon and walked over to him and Don Eduardo. Her face was beaming with joy.

"Ah, Maritza! The singing angel!" Don Eduardo hugged her and kissed her gently on the cheek.

"You are much too kind, Don Eduardo," said Maritza, her dark eyes gleaming.

"As always, not a single note was out of place. *Perfecto*!" Don Eduardo kissed his fingers, then released the kiss to the sky.

"*Gracias*," Maritza said, meekly.

"I will leave you two to enjoy this gorgeous spring day," said Don Eduardo. He tipped his hat to Maritza and left them alone.

"I feel as high as a cloud, Ramon. Singing does that to me," said Maritza, raising her arms to the sky and twirling on her feet, "and then my emerald-eyed *hombre* is waiting to whisk me away to the river."

Ramon was a little uncomfortable with all this youthful exuberance, but he loved to see Maritza's beautiful smile. He held out his arm for her to take, and together they walked outside the walls of the mission toward the river, their usual routine on Sunday afternoons.

Maritza was wearing her Sunday attire, a long white cotton dress and a red, open-necked cotton blouse. Ramon was in his Sunday-best black waistcoat and pants, with a red sash. He wore a different black, flat-brimmed sombrero on church days, one that was not stained by trail dust or blood.

"Did you work at Don Muchaca's *rancho* again this week?" asked Maritza, looking up at him as they walked.

"*Sí.*"

"Catching more wild *mestanos?*"

"*Sí*, Maritza. We caught more wild *caballos* for Don Muchaca's *manada*."

Don Muchaca was a very successful horse rancher. At the start of the year, the governor of Spanish Tejas reduced the tax on wild-caught horses, so Don Muchaca hired more men, like Luis and Ramon, to capture horses for him, and then to help the *mesteneros* break the spirits of the newly caught mustangs. Men like Don Muchaca competed with the Northerners and Lipans for wild horses. Fortunately, there had not been any incidents with *indios* since Ramon had been employed by Don Muchaca two weeks ago.

"It sounds very dangerous, Ramon, and very exciting."

"*Sí*, but it's also very hard work. It's a long day for the men," said Ramon. He was so busy and tired from his work that he couldn't find the time to visit her during the week.

Listening to the rushing water of the Rio San Antonio, Ramon was thinking more and more about his recent conversation with Don Eduardo. He had been mulling over the idea of living in Mexico City, but he couldn't convince himself that he'd be happy there. *More noise and more people than Saltillo.* He would have the company of a beautiful señorita, but was that all he needed to find happiness?

"Ramon, what are you thinking about?"

"*Nada*, Maritza. I'm just enjoying the warm day."

"You can tell me. What are you thinking about? I can tell your mind is occupied."

"Maritza, would you be happy living in San Antonio?" Ramon kicked out the question that was preying on his mind.

Maritza didn't answer right away. As Ramon waited for her response, a heron waded slowly through the shallow river water looking for fish or frogs to stab with its long, spear-like beak.

At last, Maritza answered. "I don't know, Ramon. If I could sing for people, then I think I could be happy anywhere. But the only places to sing in San Antonio are the missions. There are many more places to sing in

Mexico City, I am sure." She paused for several moments, and then she spoke again, more excited than before. "Ramon, I heard my *madre* and *padre* talking the other night about Mexico City. I think they thought I was asleep. My *padre* was asking her about Mexico City because she had visited there once. I remember my *madre* said that there were thousands of people there and that you could buy anything from the shops."

Ramon was relieved that she hadn't heard anything about Don Eduardo's plan. If she knew about it, there would be no stopping the charge of her pleading dark eyes. They had a grasp on him, he knew, like a lasso around a stallion's neck. When she really wanted something, he usually gave in to them. Luckily, Mexico City was still a faraway dream to her, but he knew that Don Eduardo's plan would bring it closer to home—much closer to home.

"Is that the answer you wanted to hear, *mi corazon*?" Endearing nicknames like "*mi corazón*" and "*mi vida*" and "*mi amor*" were other weapons she used against him. They pierced his heart and his loins. *I need thicker skin.*

"I don't know if Mexico City is as magical as you think," Ramon said.

"I know that Saltillo was unpleasant for you, but everyone has told me that Mexico City is a much nicer place."

"Señorita Maritza! Señorita Maritza!"

Ramon looked behind him and saw a little girl running toward them carrying a handful of flowers. An older man and two boys were chasing after her.

"Señorita Maritza!"

Ramon and Maritza stopped to let the little girl catch up to them.

"Teresa, wait for us!" yelled the older man. He was falling behind the boys.

Ramon laughed. "You see, you are a celebrity here. You don't need to go to Mexico City." He did not know them by name, but their faces were familiar. He knew that they lived and worked with the other *indios* and mestizos around the mission, and he saw them at Sunday Mass every week.

The little girl stopped when she reached them. She was wearing a dirty, tattered white dress. She looked like she was a mix of *indio* and *español*, a mestizo. The boys, who were a bit older than her, looked like her brothers. The man was old enough to be their grandfather and was dressed in dirty, ragged clothes. He wore a red bandanna around his head.

"Señorita Maritza," the little girl said, breathing hard, "I wanted to give you these flowers." She paused to catch her breath. "You are *muy bonito* and your voice is so pretty!" She offered the handpicked offering to Maritza.

"*Gracias*," said Maritza, taking the flowers from the girl. She didn't even smell or look at them, and her smile seemed forced.

"I want to be a pretty singer too."

"Not everyone can sing, little *niña*," said Maritza. Her voice was suddenly cold.

"My name is Teresa," said the girl, a bright smile on her dirty face, her uncombed hair hanging down in her face. Despite her impoverished appearance, there was a glow about her and a sparkle in her eyes.

"Your singing is very beautiful, Señorita Maritza," said the old man in broken Spanish, panting. He looked like a full-blooded Lipano. Like the little girl, his eyes were sincere, and he seemed embarrassed to talk to Maritza. "I am sorry to bother you. She is too fast for me."

Maritza didn't say anything, a half-smile on her face.

"It's no bother at all," said Ramon, after waiting for Maritza's response that never came.

"Let's go, Teresa," the old man said, grabbing the girl's hand. "Sorry to bother you," he said again in earnest, bowing his head and thrusting his eyes quickly to the ground after glancing at Maritza. He raised his head back up and spoke to Ramon. "Sorry to bother you too, Señor Ramon."

"Goodbye, Señorita Maritza!" said the girl, smiling and waving as she and her family walked away.

Ramon tipped his hat and smiled at the girl. "*Adios,* Teresa."

The couple started to walk again, not arm-in-arm anymore.

"You weren't very nice to that little girl," said Ramon.

"She was a dirty little mestizo, Ramon. She thinks that *she* will be a singer?" Maritza laughed to herself, mocking the thought. "*Buena suerte!*"

Ramon knew that Maritza thought highly of herself and her talents; she was very confident. And she was also always kind to him. But he had seen her coldness surface with other girls, and with men who she deemed socially below her. Until now, however, he hadn't seen her act this way toward children.

"I thought you liked children? You are nice to your brother."

"He is not a mestizo or an *indio*, Ramon," said Maritza with a spiteful look on her face. She stopped walking and turned to him to speak. "And that old man… I almost fainted when I smelled him. Just because you are poor doesn't mean you can't be clean! Soap is easy to get from the mission." She carried the flowers at her side like they were of little value. "They kept staring at me. They had no manners!"

"They stared at you because you are beautiful to their eyes." Ramon was feeling more and more angry with every hateful word that cut through Maritza's lips. "They are complimenting you with their stares, Maritza, and you scowl and turn them away! All they wanted to do is say nice things to you and nice things about your singing."

"What are their compliments worth to me, Ramon? Nothing!" Her temper was starting to flare. "They are as worthless as these flowers they picked moments before they gave them to me."

She flung the flowers angrily into the river. "Their eyes made me feel cheap and dirty. Just because they brought those flowers didn't give them the right to stare at me! Don't you understand that?"

"No, I don't understand." He shot an angry look back at her. "There was nothing dirty, cheap, or disrespectful about them. If anything, they were cleaner, purer, more innocent than most people I know." The message, "blessed are the poor," was one of the most prevalent themes from the Bible, and Father Padilla preached about it often in his sermons. Ramon didn't understand why Maritza thought differently, or why it wasn't her belief, like it was for most Catholics. *Has she been too busy thinking about her next church song to listen to his sermons?*

"Why don't you understand?" she said, tears welling in her eyes.

"I do understand. I understand more than you know."

Tomorrow I will ride out to Nacogdoches to meet James McCord. There is nothing keeping me here.

Slowed By Pain

Many Wolves and Taimah were up again early the next day, though not before the chattering Chachara. The birds were stretching their wings and the wolves their legs, preparing for another day of travel. Many Wolves's body was sore from a long day of riding.

"You're moving slowly today, *Ahpu*."

"My body is not used to riding a horse all day long," said Many Wolves. "How are you feeling?"

"I'm a little tired, but not too sore."

"Well, you ride a lot more than your old *ahpu* does." The soreness in his body was all over, but it was most painful in his back. When he was younger, he could ride as much as he wanted without any soreness afterward, but it was different now that he was older. "Let's get going. I'll feel better once I start moving and the sun can warm my bones."

The trail they followed turned westward, away from the Rio Pecos, just as Many Wolves remembered from when he was tracking with Ten Arrows. The path led steadily along a hillside that sloped up to their left and dropped down to a flat meadow on their right. The warmth of the midday sun felt good on Many Wolves's body, but its healing power wasn't as potent as he'd expected. His back was still painfully sore, and it was not getting better, but worse. He slumped down as he rode, trying to escape the pain. It seemed to help some.

"That looks uncomfortable, *Ahpu*."

"It helps a little. I guess I'm not like other horsemen on the plains."

"Not ones who are still alive!" laughed Taimah.

"So I look like a corpse? Are there any buzzards circling yet?" Many Wolves had known what it was like to have buzzards circling around him when he was poisoned, but still he made a joke of it. *Was that a dream, or did buzzards really circle around me?* He couldn't remember for sure. Certainly the pain he felt then was far worse than now.

They followed the path until the sun disappeared, leaving them in shadows. Pines and junipers were the only trees now, and patches of nearly melted snow dotted the landscape, so Many Wolves knew they were in the high country.

"We should stop here for the night." It was sooner than Many Wolves would have liked, but he hoped lying down would help his back feel better. The wolves seemed tired also, their tongues dangling from their mouths like dead snakes in a running bird's mouth.

He moved slowly as he got off his horse and unpacked his sleeping robe and water pouch. Taimah took his sleeping robe from him, cleared out all the rocks from a flat patch of grass, and laid it out for him. Many Wolves, hunched like an old man, lumbered over to the sleeping robe and dropped his body onto it.

"Are you going to be all right, *Ahpu*? I'm worried."

"I just need to lie down, Wildflower, for a little while. You're going to have to hunt without me." His back was feeling a little better already.

"Let me make you some mint tea," said Taimah, getting out her fire-sticks and a drinking-shell. "That might help with the pain."

She left him and returned shortly after with some dried pine needles and branches. She dug out a small fire pit, placed the pine needles in it, and started twisting her fire-sticks. Before too long, Many Wolves saw smoke creeping from the fire nest; a small flame appeared soon after that. Taimah filled the drinking-shell with water, dropped some mint leaves in it, and rested it near the flames. "It will be ready soon, *Ahpu*."

"You better get going," said Many Wolves, feeling relaxed in his sleeping robe. Noche was lying next to him with his nose on his leader's leg, and Colmillo was curled up next to his wolf brother.

"I think the wolves are staying with you. I'll take the birds with me."

"I want you back before dark, even if you have nothing to show for it," said Many Wolves in a stern voice.

"*Haa, Ahpu.* I'm glad the wolves are staying with you."

"I'm glad Chachara is staying with you."

Taimah smiled back him and mounted her black horse, whom she had named Sombra. She whistled for the birds and rode away.

Watching her, Many Wolves couldn't help but see himself. *Is that what I looked like when I was her age?* He couldn't ride a horse nearly as well as that when he was fifteen winters old—or even now—but the three birds had jumped to his command the same way they did with her, motivated by their hunger. The only difference now was that the birds had two leaders and not just one. They responded equally well to either of them.

He remembered how the other wolves of the pack had looked up to Rojo and Noir, their leaders, when he had watched them long ago, in a meadow not far from where he was. That memory made him smile.

Soon after, Many Wolves was asleep.

Circling

Many Wolves felt the cold air rush past him. He was sailing high above the ground, looking at the world through a bird's eyes. Other birds were flying with him, circling, turning left, then straight, then left again. He saw vultures and crows, too, in the same circling formation, some higher and some lower than him. Looking behind him, he saw a wolf hawk.

"*Ahpu*, where are we going?"

It was Taimah's voice.

"Where are you, Wildflower?"

"I'm behind you. Chachara and I are behind you."

Many Wolves looked back again at the wolf hawk. It was Chachara, and she was looking right at him. *Taimah is with me. She is mind-journeying with me.*

"I don't know where we are going. We are circling, but I don't know why."

Fluffy white clouds drifted past them and through them as they floated in the blue sky. Currents of air dropped them down, then raised them back up again. He had forgotten how exhilarating it was to fly.

Suddenly, Taimah screamed. "*Ahpu*, something hit me! Something pierced my body. Where did it come from? I don't see anything, but something is causing this pain. It hurts, *Ahpu*. Help me! Please help me!"

"Taimah, where are you?" Many Wolves looked back, but Chachara wasn't there. Then he looked down and saw her flying downward in a tightening spiral.

"I'm not flying anymore, *Ahpu*! I'm not with Chachara. It hurts so much. I can taste the blood in my mouth now. I'm feeling weak, *Ahpu*."

His hawk tucked its wings and dove downward, then pulled into a tight circle, still descending. He could see the details of the earth again, trees and rocks and grass. *Something is down there. Something is lying in the grass.*

He dove down again. The cold air blasting through him was like an overpowering headwind.

And then he saw more clearly. *It's a body. It's Taimah's body!*

"Taimah!" he shouted in his loudest voice.

* * *

Many Wolves opened his eyes and sat up on his sleeping robe. *It was a dream.* He felt a rush of relief as he wiped the sweat from his eyes. It was early dawn, and his back was still very sore, but it felt better. *I've been sleeping all this time?*

Then he heard the wolves growling and Chachara squawking. Ahead of him, Colmillo and Noche were hunched in an attack pose, hackles raised. *What are they looking at?* The three birds were perched on rocks around the camp. But where was Taimah? She had left him to go hunting, he remembered. *The birds were with her.*

"Taimah!" he yelled again. But this time it was real and not a dream.

"Many Wolves!" a loud voice replied—but it wasn't Taimah's voice. It was the voice of a man. "Taimah is with us. Calm your wolves!"

The words were Northerner words. The voice sounded like Laughing Crow. *Laughing Crow is dead.*

Many Wolves stood up, grabbed his quiver, and took his bow and an arrow from it, then ran to the edge of the slope and looked down.

"Tell your wolves to stay back or we'll kill them!"

Eight Northerners sat on horses, and Taimah was with them on her own horse. Her hands and mouth were bound. From this distance it appeared as though she was unharmed, but she was too far away to know for sure.

Heat rushed to Many Wolves's head seeing her like that. *What are they going to do with her? What have I done, letting her hunt alone?*

"Colmillo, down! Noche, down!" Many Wolves commanded in a stern voice. "Easy! Stay back!" Many Wolves nocked his arrow.

The wolves settled some and held their growls in their throats, though Chachara kept on squawking.

"Who are you?" asked Many Wolves, looking down at them.

"I am Cold Raven of the Nokoni," the man said in loud voice, but not shouting.

Laughing Crow's son. He was not a boy like Many Wolves remembered, but a man, a large man like his father. *The other big warrior must be Esatai.* Esatai was holding the lead on Taimah's black horse. The two men, as well as the other Nokoni, were armed with bows, lances, and war shields.

"What have you done to her, Cold Raven?"

"She has not been harmed, Many Wolves. You will not find a cut or bruise on her. That is my promise," said Cold Raven. He held a bow and arrow in one hand and a shield in the other. The shield was adorned with a big, black bird—just like his father's. Cold Raven turned to Esatai and spoke more words, but Many Wolves couldn't hear them clearly.

Esatai drew his knife.

Many Wolves raised his bow and aimed it at Esatai, but the warrior cut Taimah's hands free and then slapped her horse hard, yelling a command to move.

They're releasing her!

Taimah rode quickly to her father. When she reached him, Many Wolves drew his knife and cut the rope from over her mouth. Her face was covered with dirt and tears, and her hands and face were burned from the ropes that had bound her.

"Are you all right, Taimah? Did they hurt you?"

Taimah's eyes were withdrawn and dazed. "I'm all right, *Ahpu.* I'm not hurt," she said in a somewhat sad, emotionless voice. Then she looked back at the Nokonis with fear in her eyes.

"She is unharmed, Many Wolves, like I promised," shouted Cold Raven. He returned the bow and arrow to the quiver on his back, then walked his black and white painted mount closer, motioning for his men to stay back.

Many Wolves was still doubtful, but the Nokoni was right—there were no bruises or cuts on Taimah's body that he could see. *Perhaps she is just scared.* His wolves were growling again, so Many Wolves calmed them with his words, but he kept his bow ready. *I will get one shot at Cold Raven before they kill me.*

"We still have her weapons here. I will trade them back to you, Many Wolves," said Cold Raven in a voice that was softer than before.

"What do you want from me?" asked Many Wolves, angered. "You capture my daughter by force, bind her hands and gag her mouth, and now you want a simple trade? Why didn't you find me last night when you found her?"

"It was dark when we found her. We needed to control her and the wolves. I didn't want to harm them or you. I am sorry for this unnecessary force, but as I said, she was not harmed. I just want a simple trade. I will bring the weapons to you, and we will make talk together. Just you and me," said Cold Raven. "Returning your daughter to you is my peace flag."

What does he want? If he wanted revenge, Taimah would be his captive, or dead. The wolves would be dead as well, and I would be bound to a horse.

"Her weapons don't mean anything to me. They can be remade. But I will talk to you," said Many Wolves. "If you wanted me dead, I would be dead already, or strung to the back of one of your horses."

"Tell your daughter to restrain the wolves, and I will send my men away."

Many Wolves motioned to Taimah. She dismounted slowly from her horse, not with her usual confidence and energy. She whistled and called the wolves by name, then led them to a spot a short distance away, on the same high ground as her father.

Then, with one wave of the Nokoni headman's hand, his riders rode farther down the slope before turning and stopping their mounts. They were farther away than Taimah, but still in sight of their leader.

Many Wolves walked back to his sleeping robe and waited.

Cold Raven dismounted and led his horse to where Castano was tied. He tied the leads of the horses together, unstrapped his quiver, and hung it on the side of his horse. Then he grabbed another quiver from his horse. "These are Taimah's weapons," he said. "I will set them here on the ground."

Many Wolves nodded and set his own weapon down next to his sleeping robe.

The Nokoni joined Many Wolves with a long pipe in his right hand and sat cross-legged on the other side of the fire pit. Many Wolves revived a small fire from the embers that were left from the previous night so there would be a flame for his pipe.

"Do you want anything to eat or drink?" Many Wolves asked.

"No. But I will smoke, so you know there is only truth in my words. Will you smoke with me, Many Wolves?"

"*Haa*," Many Wolves said. "But I don't have my own pipe."

"You can share mine."

Many Wolves watched with wary eyes as Cold Raven padded the bowl of his pipe with tobacco using the big, muscular hands of his father— warrior hands delicately preparing what was usually prepared by the feeble hands of an old medicine man. His shoulders were powerfully built, again like his father, though both Laughing Crow and Thorn Bird were larger than this man. His oiled black hair was straight, long, and parted in the middle like most Northerners. A single eagle feather dangled from his scalp-lock. There was no war paint on his face, and only one or two tattoos—this was unlike his father, whose body was covered with them.

Cold Raven lit the bone pipe, adorned with feathers and beads, with a twig from the fire pit, sucking in the flame several times before he was satisfied. Then he inhaled deeply and held the smoke for several moments before pushing it back out. He handed the pipe to Many Wolves, smoke still escaping from his mouth and nose, and smiled. "It is your turn now."

Many Wolves took the pipe and inhaled the smoke like he had done many times before with Ten Arrows and Malone. He felt the Truth Spirit stronger in him now. It was bad luck to cross the Truth Spirit with a lie.

Cold Raven began to speak with earnest eyes. "Do you remember the day I saw you through the shaft of your arrow? It is a moment that is burned in my memory. It could have been my last day in this world, but you spared my life. Your path of vengeance ended there and then. You chose life, not death. My father's path of vengeance ended with his death, as did the path of Esatai's father. They chose death, not life—and our village suffered dearly for it. It still does."

Many Wolves studied the son of the man from his nightmares. Cold Raven's hands, arms, and muscular body were his father's—but his voice and his eyes, strangely, were not. He remembered Laughing Crow's and Thorn Bird's voices all too well, and the one common tone in both was hate. A hate that started at the pit of the stomach and crawled through the whole body, poisoning the heart and sickening the mind. Caged like a vicious animal, the voice and the eyes released it into the world. But where was the hate in this man? Many Wolves hadn't detected even a sliver of it from Cold Raven's calm voice or honest eyes. *Is it a trick?*

The young Nokoni leader took another puff from his pipe. "Their paths of vengeance not only killed them, but like a violent dust storm, those paths slung sand in the faces of many others, and made many enemies: the Wichitas, Gray Elk's Nokonis, Crooked Eagle's Penatekas. You said long ago that my village was a 'village of hate,' and you were right. We don't have many friends. Our only friends are the *mexicanos* who trade with us. Now our children have more Mexican blood than Noomah blood. They grow up drinking the Mexican firewater, which makes them forget the traditions of my people. How do we protect ourselves with so few warriors?"

Cold Raven paused to pull out something from a waist pouch. It was a small lead ball. He held it out to Many Wolves between his fingers. "Do you know what this is?"

"It's a lead ball that the Mexicans use in their guns."

"*Haa*, Many Wolves. When a Mexican fires one of these balls, we can shoot twenty arrows before he can fire another. But now, with their new guns, we can only shoot one arrow before he fires again. The white men are bold with these new guns. They are so bold that they hunt *us* and attack *us*—in *our* villages. Last fall they killed our leader, Half Weasel, and my mother when they attacked our village. Ever since, we have been hiding like scared rabbits, fearing the hairy-faced, white-skinned hunters. I don't want to lose my people, Many Wolves. I don't want to lose my village."

Many Wolves remembered Half Weasel as Silent Weasel's son. He was one of the men, along with Thorn Bird, who had tormented him with a torture dance. And he remembered Cold Raven's mother: Valencia, the tall Mexican woman with much anger in her heart. Apart from Thorn Bird, these two had felt the most hate for him. Perhaps this was one reason why Cold Raven wanted to talk peace now.

Cold Raven passed the pipe to Many Wolves. It was Many Wolves's turn to smoke and speak. He took a puff from the pipe and let the Truth Spirit fill his lungs. "What do you want me to do to help your village?" He offered the pipe back to Cold Raven, but the Nokoni refused.

"Crooked Eagle's ears are deaf to my voice. I want you to be my voice in Crooked Eagle's council, my peace flag. He trusts you, and if he knows there is peace between us, he might consider an offer of peace to my village. Tell him I have no path of vengeance—that I'm trying to cover the trail of blood left by my father and Esatai's father. Tell him that I want my women to marry his warriors and my children to play with his children; and in exchange, my warriors will fight side by side with the Penateka in this war with the white man."

This plea for help caught Many Wolves by surprise. He had never expected there to be peace between him and Laughing Crow's village, but now it was being offered to him graciously by a man who looked like Laughing Crow. Part of him had to remain suspicious; after all, Cold Raven had captured Taimah in order to gain higher ground for this talk—and that tactic had put a stain on his character. But another part of him wanted to accept this offer of peace. It would be an enormous relief knowing that he had one less enemy in this hostile world. And it was an agreement Many Wolves knew he could easily keep; he had never attacked them before, only defended himself.

"Cold Raven, your words seem sincere and truthful. I don't like the bullying tactics you used to start these talks, but I'm trying to bury them deep in my mind. I accept your offer of peace with me and my village. However, I will need to speak with Malone about attending a council with Crooked Eagle. I am not sure how much influence I will have with the elder Penateka leader. Your peace with him is an agreement I cannot promise."

"All I ask is that you tell Crooked Eagle of our peace and of my wish to have peace with him. I don't expect anything more. Also, my peace is offered to Malone as well, but I will want to speak to him with smoke on my tongue as I have done with you."

"After I talk to Malone, how can I find you?"

"I will come to your camp at Three Trees Crossing. I will speak to Malone then also."

"You knew we had a camp there?"

"We have known for a very long time, Many Wolves." Cold Raven took his pipe from Many Wolves, stood up, and mounted his horse. "I will see you in four sleeps' time at Three Trees Crossing."

Then he waved and rode off.

Bright Eyes

Many Wolves and Taimah stood on the edge of the slope and watched Cold Raven ride away.

"Tell me what happened last night," said Many Wolves.

"I was on a kill, and they surprised me…" Taimah didn't offer any more detail.

"They surrounded you on their horses?"

"*Haa.*"

"Then what happened?"

"They tied my hands and gagged my mouth." She was looking down at the ground, only glancing up at him when she spoke.

"Did they tell you who they were?"

"*Haa.* Cold Raven did. Do I have to tell you all this?" She started to cry.

"No, Taimah, you don't have to tell me this now," Many Wolves said. He wrapped his arms around her.

She cried for a long time while he held her, and not another word was spoken. At those times when she fell off her horse or cut herself with a knife, she cried for only a short time, not like this. *She probably thought they were going to kill her.*

But he needed to know if she was just frightened, or if they had done something that she did not want to talk about. There were no signs of abuse on the bare skin that he could see. Nothing on her arms or legs or face. She didn't react when he touched her back, either. *She wasn't hurt outside—but she was damaged inside.*

Many Wolves felt responsible for her capture. *I should have gone with her.* But he hadn't expected to see men in the high country, especially Nokonis. Now he knew that they had eyes everywhere. They probably know where all his camps were, even the Gray Face camp, which he had kept secret for many winters.

There were so many questions in his head. *Why didn't they bring her back when they found her?* She could have shown them the way. *Was she tied up all night in the dark? Did they talk to her? Did they threaten to harm her just to scare her?* And the question that burned the most, that cut at his insides like a barbed arrow point: *Did they force her do something she didn't want to do?* If this was true, then there would be no peace with Cold Raven. *Let his village rot in this world and the next.*

"Let's take it easy today, Wildflower," said Many Wolves. "My back is better, but it can still use more rest." He walked her with him to the sleeping robes and placed the two robes together. "Here, sit here."

Taimah sat on her robe, and Colmillo instantly lay by her side.

"Are you hungry? Can I make you some mint tea?"

She shook her head and lay back on her sleeping robe, her left hand stroking Colmillo's head.

Many Wolves sat on his robe with a large rock behind him as a backrest. Noche strolled over to him and curled up on his right side. Taimah sat up and leaned against his shoulder. He kissed her on the forehead and put his arm around her. It had been a long time since she had wanted to curl up next to him like this. When she was young, they used to spend afternoons this way, in a quiet place overlooking a creek or a valley. They would sit and let nature come to them, small animals and birds mostly, and they would watch them together without speaking, just being together. Often they would play a game to see who would fall asleep first. When he fell asleep, she always woke him, her bright green eyes staring at him, saying, "*Ahpu*, you fell asleep. I win! I win!"

Somehow, Cold Raven had taken those bright eyes from him.

Nacogdoches

Ramon arrived in the small town of Nacogdoches—a town much smaller than San Antonio—at around mid-morning on March thirteenth, hoping to make the acquaintance of Captain James McCord. He had learned from Don Eduardo that Nacogdoches was the hub of commerce between the French to the east and the Spanish and *indios* to the west.

At the crossroads of Old San Antonio Road and La Calle de Norte was the largest dwelling in the town, the Stone House. It was a long, rectangular building made from adobe and walnut, spanning at least twelve horse-lengths, and tall enough for an upper and lower level. Toward the center of the structure, underneath an overhang, sat a man at a table. On the wall behind him was the same poster as the one Don Eduardo had presented to him. *This must be the place.*

Ramon tied his horse to a railing and walked over to the table. "Is this where I can meet this Captain McCord?" he asked, pointing at the poster and using his English words.

"Ya sign up here before you meet anyone," said the white man in a gruff voice. He had a bushy mustache and a shaggy beard and wore a high-crowned, brown hat on his head. There was a small stack of paper on either side of him and a quill pen in his right hand.

"I'd like to make his acquaintance before I sign anything," said Ramon politely.

The man groaned. "He's too busy. I reckon you'll meet him soon enough after you answer some questions here."

Ramon sighed. "All right. What questions have you got for me?"

The man took one of the papers from the stack to his left. "Surname?"

"Connelly."

"You're pretty dark-skinned to be Irish, boy." The man wrote the name on his paper. His writing was crooked and unrefined. "Given name?"

"Ramon."

"Age?"

"Twenty-two."

"Birthplace?"

"San Antonio."

"Well, I'll be damned," said the man, looking up, surprised. "A Tejano who can speak Anglish. Ain't many of those runnin' 'round. You got any next of kin, Tejano?"

"Not really."

"Anyone we should tell if ya get yourself kilt?"

Ramon thought about that. "Don Eduardo Romero of San Antonio."

"All right then." The man looked him over, taking note of his weapons. "A rifle, a shotgun, and two pistols. That about it for weapons? You gotta knife somewheres?"

Ramon rolled up his pant leg to show the man his knife sheath.

"Good."

"You gotta horse here somewheres?"

"The light bay gelding over there." Ramon pointed at Cavador.

"Little Sky! Check out the geldin' over there," yelled the man, turning his head as if talking to someone from behind him.

An *indio* walked out through the door, approached Cavador, and inspected the horse carefully. Little Sky felt the horse's leg and back muscles, looked over his hooves, and checked his nose and eyes. When he was finished, he nodded at the man at the table.

"The injun says you gotta good horse, so you won't need no loaner. We ain't in the biz'ness of givin' out loaners."

"As good a mount as you're going to find in Tejas," Ramon said with pride. "Why all these questions for me?"

"Cap'n Mac wants to know about the fellas he'll be ridin' with is all," said the man, looking up at Ramon. Then he handed him the quill pen. "Here, make your mark at the bottom there," he said, pointing at a spot on the paper.

Ramon printed his named as neatly as he could, though he was out of practice.

"Heck, you're the first fella who wrote somethin'. Most of 'em just make a squiggle or an 'x' or two. I take it you can read?"

"English and Spanish."

"That might be of some use to Cap'n Mac as well." The man made another note on his paper.

"I'm not signing up to do this, am I?" asked Ramon.

"Nah. Rangerin' is your choice, Tejano. We ain't draftin' ya like a soldier. We're payin' a dollar a day as your wage, and you supply your own horse and weapons. From the looks of it, you seem well set up in those areas."

"So, when do I meet Captain McCord?"

"At ten o'clock tomorra mornin' about a mile northwest of here. Cap'n Mac will want to see all the recruits and see if you can ride and shoot. You can't miss it, it's by an old barn out there."

"Thank you kindly, sir. What was your name again?"

"I'm Lieutenant Jack Akers, but most folks call me Possum Jack."

"Good to know you, sir. I'll see you at noon." Ramon tipped his hat.

"All right then."

Cornelius

Ramon woke up the next morning after sleeping under the stars just outside of town. He ate a light breakfast of tortillas and jerked meat, then began to clean his *pistoles*. When, thirty minutes later, he heard gunshots going off in town, he figured that was the ranger auditions. He quickly finished up with his second *pistole*, double-checking that the cylinder was properly set in the revolver, and tossed his saddle on Cavador.

He rode back to town following the directions that Possum Jack had given him, though the gunfire seemed to be all that he needed. The large, gruff man seemed like a decent enough fellow, he thought, but his manner of speaking would take a little getting used to. Ramon hadn't spoke much English since his father died, and his father's Irish accent was certainly different than this man's.

Ramon spotted the old barn that Possum Jack mentioned and saw about a dozen men gathered around an open field. Out in the middle of the field were two logs with wooden slabs sitting on them. *Targets.* There was also a canvas sunshade, held up by four poles, where Possum Jack and his *indio* partner were sitting next to a table. Ramon picketed his horse next to the others and then walked over to the two men.

"Name?" said Possum Jack.

"Ramon Connelly."

"I remember ya, Connelly," said Possum Jack, checking his name off a list. "Go stand over there with the other fellas. I'll call your name when we're ready for ya."

Ramon tipped the brim of his hat and walked over to where the other men were standing. All but one were white men, dressed in overalls, and the other was a *vaquero*. Some of the men wore animal skins for hats, from raccoons or wildcats, while others wore short-brimmed bowlers. One man was dressed neatly in a gray suit and was introducing himself to all the others. He seemed like the friendly sort. A couple of the other men were talking and laughing with each other, too, but most were alone like him.

Ramon wondered if one of these men was Captain James McCord.

He felt a hand on his shoulder and turned around to see the gray-suited man smiling at him. "Hello, I'm Cornelius Potts. Pleased to make your acquaintance." The man offered his hand in friendship.

"I'm Ramon Connelly," said Ramon, shaking the man's hand.

"An Irishman. You can't disguise an accent like that, and your surname certainly validates it, Mr. Connelly. Your first name tells me that a woman of Spanish descent brought you into this world." Cornelius had a very neat mustache, waxed at the tips, and a goatee. His skin was smooth, not hardened like most men who labored or worked outdoors.

"Yes, sir. My mother was an Isleño."

"Ah, from the Canary Islands. I've made the acquaintance of a few islanders in my time." Cornelius paused to stroke the tip of his mustache. "Where do you hail from, Mr. Connelly?"

"San Antonio."

"Of course. There's a healthy population of islanders in San Antonio."

"Where are you from?" asked Ramon. Potts's straight-laced, near-perfect English was definitely American, but he didn't know where from.

"Born and raised in Charles Town, South Carolina, sir."

"What do you do for Captain McCord?"

"Well, I'm not primarily a fighting man, Mr. Connelly, but more a man of science. My surveying services have been procured directly by Mr. Austin, who's funding this operation."

"Surveying? What is that exactly?"

"I read maps and do measurements, mostly. Mr. Austin has apportioned land grants to families of his choosing. I mark off the land and help get them settled here in Tejas, with the protection of fighting men such as yourself. *Habla español*, Señor Connelly?"

"*Sí.*"

"Splendid! A useful skill indeed. I only dabble myself, but I know that many of the natives from Tejas speak Spanish, including our tracker, Little Sky."

"Is Captain McCord here?"

"Well, as a matter of fact, he just arrived." Cornelius pointed over Ramon's shoulder. "See the man on the horse?"

Ramon turned around and looked. The man on the horse was dressed neatly, but not as formally as Cornelius, and he had a neatly trimmed mustache, but not a beard like most of the other men.

"I was expecting a bigger man," Ramon said.

"Don't let his diminutive size fool you," said Cornelius. "He rides a horse like the wind and can shoot the eye out of a snake from fifty yards…while he's on the horse. He's more than a match for the hard-riding Comanches and their deadly bows."

"That's why he's the captain," Ramon said to himself, though loud enough for Cornelius to hear.

"Precisely, Mr. Connelly."

"So, what are we going to do here?"

"Captain Mac is going to evaluate how well you handle a horse and a weapon, of course. He has neither the time nor patience to be training upstarts. This is a deadly undertaking. Just watch and listen, Mr. Connelly. Watch and listen."

Captain Mac

Captain Mac and Possum Jack rode over to the gathered men.

"Gather up!" yelled Possum Jack.

The men turned to face the two men on horses. By now, over thirty men had showed up for the audition. Ramon didn't recognize any of them, even the three or four *vaqueros* there.

"I'm Possum Jack. Y'all know me. This here is Cap'n James McCord." Jack pointed to his left, and the captain nodded his head briefly, but remained stoic. "First off, fightin' injuns is dangerous biz'ness. If the sight o' blood makes you soil your pants, then you best move on. You ain't gonna git rich here neither. Thirty dollars a month is the wage, and a handful o' you fellas ain't even gonna see that, 'cause you'll be pushin' up wildflowers somewhere on the prairie, if you git my meanin'. All of you got your own mounts and weapons or else I woulda sent you on your way. We ain't in the biz'ness o' givin' out loaners. We'll supply your food and reloads, but that's about it. Any questions so far?"

Possum Jack looked around at all of them, but there were no questions. Captain Mac was watching them like a hawk, sitting up straight with perfect posture.

"All right, them's the preliminaries, as Captain Mac likes to call 'em. The next thing we gots to know is whether or not you can shoot or ride a horse. If you can't, then yer no use to this rangerin' outfit. When I call your name, I want you to dismount, load your rifle or musket, and fire at them wooden targets out there from between those two markers. You got three

191

shots to show us somethin'. When you're finished there, we want you to mount up and ride as hard as ya can around that oak tree out there yonder and back. For your final test, we want you to mount up with your loaded pistol and ride hard past the target and shoot before you're ten yards to it. Again, you got three shots to show us somethin'. Any questions?"

"Yeah, I got one," said one of the men. "You want us reloadin' on our horses or on the ground?"

"On your horses," barked Captain Mac, speaking for the first time. His voice was higher-pitched and younger than Ramon was expecting.

"All right then. Let's git started," yelled Possum Jack. He and Captain McCord rode off to the side of the target area, then turned and waited.

Cornelius tugged on Ramon's leg and spoke in a low voice. "Ramon, make sure the Mexicans here know what to do. They probably didn't understand a lick of what Possum Jack said."

Ramon signaled each of the *vaqueros* to ride over to him, then he summarized Possum Jack's instructions for them.

"*Gracias*," a few of them said.

"Tom Wilkins!" shouted Possum Jack.

Wilkins grabbed his flintlock musket from his horse and jogged out toward the starting markers. He fired and missed the targets. Then he started to reload his weapon, measuring the powder from his horn carefully.

"We ain't got all god-damned day here, Wilkins!" yelled Possum Jack. "Part of the test is to see how fast you can load her up!"

Wilkins moved faster, then fired and missed again. But his third shot ended with a loud crackle as the lead ball splintered the target, knocking it down.

Then he mounted and galloped to the oak tree and back, while Possum Jack timed him with his stopwatch and wrote it down in a little book he had with him. Finally, Wilkins charged at the target three times with his pistol aimed at the target. He failed to hit any of them. That seemed like the hardest challenge.

Ramon watched as the other men performed these same trials. Some, like the *vaqueros*, were very adept at riding, but couldn't shoot accurately with their pistols or long guns. Others were the opposite: they had a somewhat steady hand with a gun, but couldn't ride that well. The best shooters hit the targets twice; one man did it with his *pistole* and another with his musket.

"Connelly!" yelled Possum Jack. "You're the last one!"

Ramon dismounted, grabbed his rifle, and ran to the starting point, between the markers.

His weapon was already loaded, so he aimed and fired. The *bala* kicked up dust just before the target. He reloaded the barrel with powder and a new ball, then carefully aimed, but his shot missed to the right of his target. Again he reloaded, and on the third shot, he heard a pop and saw the target fly off the log.

He ran back to his horse, returned his rifle to the leather scabbard in his saddle, and mounted. He rode up to the starting point and waited for Possum Jack's hand signal. When the big man's arm dropped, Ramon dug in with his spurs, and Cavador sprang from the starting line. The horse reached a full sprint in seconds, and Ramon kept his eye peeled on the oak tree ahead. As they reached the tree, he pulled back on the reins to slow Cavador down and turn him to the left. They curled around the tree, and Cavador dug into the earth again to build up speed. Ramon slowed his horse just past the finish line and pulled him to a stop. "Good boy, Cavador." The horse shook his head and snorted to catch his breath.

Ramon rested his horse for a few moments while he double-checked the cylinder in his revolver. While all the other riders had taken three passes with their *pistole* shots, he wanted to do just one, firing all three rounds with no reload time, to show what his weapon could do.

"Let's go, Connelly! We ain't gettin' any younger!" shouted Possum Jack. He didn't know that Ramon would need only one run at the targets.

Ramon locked his cylinder back in place and shoved the revolver in his belt. "Go, Cavador!"

The horse bolted from a standstill. The Irish *vaquero* eyed the target he wanted, the wooden target that was second from the left. When he was about twenty yards from it, he drew his weapon and fired once, then twice, then a third time in quick succession. None of the shots hit the mark, but dust flew up all around the target, so he knew he was close. Disappointed that he had missed, he pulled Cavador to a stop just past the log, and shoved the weapon in his belt.

"Connelly! Come with me," barked Captain McCord.

Ramon followed the captain and Possum Jack to the group of gathered men.

"Gentlemen," said Captain Mac. "You saw what Connelly did?"

"Yeah, he didn't hit shit!" shouted one man, followed by laughter from the others.

"Who said that?" asked the captain. "Show yourself."

"Jeffries," said the man as he stepped out from the crowd to face the captain.

"Well, Mr. Jeffries, you missed the lesson," said Captain McCord, glaring. "What you saw was a weapon that shot as fast as a Comanche bow. Consider this, Mr. Jeffries. You take one shot at a Comanche and he takes ten at you. Who do you think dies in that fight?"

"Well, sir, if I hits 'em, then he can't shoot no mo' arras."

"And if you don't hit him, Mr. Jeffries?"

"Well, I'm probably gonna be needin' a coffin, sir."

"That's right," said Captain Mac calmly. Then he looked around at the other faces. "The kind of shooting I saw today, gentlemen, would keep the coffin-maker busy for a fortnight. Now, I can't make you sharpshooters overnight, but I promise I will make you better shots. It *will* take practice, however—so much practice that your trigger fingers will turn blue."

Captain McCord took one of his pistols out his belt and held it up in the air, riding back and forth in front of the row of men. "Do any of you know what kind of gun this is?"

There was silence until Ramon spoke out. "It's a revolver, sir."

"That's right," said the captain. "More specifically, a Colt Patterson revolver. It is my personal belief, gentlemen, that this weapon here will win this war with the god-damned Comanches. Without it, there is no hope for us, because as Mr. Jeffries astutely pointed out, if we don't hit them, we're going to be needing a coffin."

"Well, Cap'n, that's a lotta big talk, sir," said Jeffries. "I ain't seen nothin' that that there revolver can do that I can't do with my pistol."

Captain McCord stared back at Jeffries. Ramon was expecting an outburst, but the captain didn't say a word.

Instead the captain returned his weapon to his waist belt and whirled his horse around toward the starting markers. His horse made a hard right when it reached the marker, then sprinted toward the target. In Ramon's estimation, the captain's horse was the fastest one he had seen that day. McCord drew both his pistols when he was about twenty yards out, and Ramon heard the pop of the weapon followed by a clack on the target in lightning-fast succession.

It all happened so fast, but Ramon thought he counted ten shots and saw seven of the targets fall from the log. It was the most amazing demonstration of marksmanship he had ever seen. And the other men were clearly as astonished as he was, trapped in a pool of silence.

Captain McCord rode back and took his place beside Possum Jack.

"We'll see y'all here tomorrow at the same time," said Possum Jack. "Except for," he looked over his little book, "McCormick, Ramirez, Gonzalez, and Smith. You four can go home."

Colt Revolver

Ramon was riding away from the audition when he heard Possum Jack yelling to him.

"Connelly! Cap'n Mac wants a word with ya!"

He turned Cavador around and rode back to where the trials were. Possum Jack, Captain Mac, and the *indio,* Little Sky, were sitting under the sunshade. Ramon picketed his horse and walked over to them.

"What is it, Captain McCord?"

"You showed some promise today, Connelly. I'll give you that. We might make a ranger out of you yet," said Captain Mac, taking a drink from a cup.

"Thank you, sir. I could have done better."

"Your shots were close enough, Connelly. If that piece of wood was a Comanche, you would have done some damage" Captain Mac betrayed a hint of a smile.

"Thank you, sir."

"So, where did you get that revolver?" asked the captain, glancing down at Ramon's belt.

Ramon pulled it out and handed it to the captain. "I got it from an English fella. He said it was made in England."

Captain McCord inspected the revolver for over a minute, turning it this way and that, opening and closing the chamber. "I wonder if Colt knows about this."

"Who's Colt?" asked Ramon.

"He designed and manufactured my revolvers, and he's a close friend of mine," said Captain Mac, still examining the weapon. "How do you prime it?"

"I use my fingers like this." Ramon motioned with his fingers.

Captain McCord took his revolver out and showed it to Ramon. "You see this thing here? It's a percussion cap. You don't need to prime this gun, and it's a lot more reliable when it's wet."

Ramon looked over Captain Mac's revolver. It was a beautiful weapon and seemed well constructed. The percussion cap was a big improvement. He wondered if he could make one for his weapon. He wished he could take the Colt Revolver home to take it apart, but it wasn't his.

"If your pistol ever needs a thorough cleaning, Captain Mac, I'd love to do it for you. I fix weapons in San Antonio for folks there."

"That's a generous offer, but I prefer to do it myself," said the captain. "You got Mexican blood in you, Connelly? You sure dress like a Mexican."

"Yes, sir, on my mother's side."

"Well, I don't think I'll be trusting my weapons to a Mexican any time soon. You're going to have to earn my trust." Captain Mac's eyes bored into him like spikes. "You're going to have to work twice as hard to gain my favor because of your mother, so keep that in mind."

"Yes, sir." This was nothing new for Ramon—being treated differently because of his skin color. All throughout his schooling years in San Antonio there had always been a Mexican kid who thought he was better. The only difference—back then, it was the lightness of his skin that drew their ire; now it was the darkness.

"Possum Jack tells me you speak Spanish too," said Captain Mac. "That will come in handy, because believe it or not a lot of Comanches out there speak Spanish. It's a helluva lot better than having to use that god-damned sign language."

It didn't surprise Ramon that *norteños* knew Spanish. Many of the *indios* and mestizos in San Antonio knew Spanish as well. The *norteños* probably learned the language from their captives.

"I'll help out when I can, sir. I can also help out with hunting game for the men, sir."

197

"I'll keep it in mind."

"Thank you, sir."

"So, rest up, Connelly. The hard work starts tomorrow," said Captain Mac. "And remember, you're going to have work twice as hard as most of those white boys out there. Get what I'm saying?"

"Yes, sir, I do."

* * *

Ramon was impressed by Captain McCord on the first day. He had never seen a man who could ride and shoot like the captain. And Ramon wondered what *he* could do with that Colt revolver; his revolver was inferior by quite a large margin. He wanted to get his hands on one of those Colts, but he'd have to figure out a way. Maybe, as the captain suggested, it would be through hard work with this rangering company. He could do that, he thought to himself.

I'll have to learn everything I can from this Captain Mac.

The Waiting Flower

Chachara woke Many Wolves early the next morning. It wasn't as jarring as usual, because he was already partly awake, with Taimah asleep in his arms. The night had passed slowly with very little sleep. He was thankful that Taimah had closed her eyes late in the night after a light meal of pemmican and mint tea. He wanted to let Taimah sleep more, but his commands were not enough to silence the screaming bird.

"We should try to find the flower today, *Ahpu*," she said, yawning and still lying with her head in his lap.

"How are you feeling, Wildflower?"

"I'm fine," was all she said.

"Riding will be good medicine for you," said Many Wolves. He hoped that riding would take her mind off whatever was troubling her, at least a little bit.

Taimah didn't answer. She stood up, removed the bandanna from around her head, pushed her hair out of her eyes, then tied it around her head again. "Chachara is making my head ache," she said.

She had rarely complained about the squawking bird before, but Many Wolves couldn't disagree with her. Chachara made his head ache all the time.

"We can hunt the birds where I found rabbits yesterday," she said, with no smile and some grogginess in her voice. "It's just off the trail ahead. That will keep her quiet."

"It always does."

Many Wolves rolled up both sleeping robes and tied them to the horses, then cleaned up their supplies. He put his fist-perch on his left hand, and Taimah did the same. They mounted and headed northwest, away from this sad place, though the sadness was still with them.

Farther ahead on the trail, the birds spotted a rabbit on the hillside. Aided by height, the three birds chased, and Flecha soon overpowered the dodging, bounding prey before it could reach the safety of its burrow. Many Wolves reached the captured animal and took its life quickly. *Life for life.* He divided the carcass among the three birds. Flecha received the richest reward for his efforts, but all three birds ate a generous portion, their meal for the day. Many Wolves stashed the remains of the kill in his hunting bag.

Taimah watched everything from the top of her horse without uttering a word.

Many Wolves remounted and shouted for the pack to follow him back up to the trail. His back felt much better now, perhaps because of the extra rest, or perhaps due to the unwanted distraction of the previous day. In any case, he almost felt like himself again, with only some soreness in his body. Which was good, because he now felt urgency to find the white lion's paw flower. He hoped it would lift Taimah's spirits.

As they ventured deeper into the high country, they were now climbing mountains rather than hills, and the smooth grassy slopes were replaced by jagged rock formations. The pines and junipers were more sparse, and the snow melt was heavier. The air worked their lungs harder and felt cooler, though the sun seemed closer.

Though Taimah still barely spoke, she seemed to enjoy the new scenery. She was alert and looking around constantly. Many Wolves saw infrequent glimpses of her old smile now and then, but even then, it wasn't the same ebullient spirit that he was accustomed to.

Dusk eventually pulled a blanket of darkness over them. Many Wolves built a larger fire than he usually did to chase away the crisp mountain air. He wasn't as concerned with unwanted human attention in such a remote place, especially since the Nokonis were no longer hunting him. The leftover rabbit from the earlier hunt was their meal for the night, though Taimah didn't eat much of it. At different times he asked her how she was doing, each time hoping to get more than a one- or two-word response, but nothing came of it. They sat silently all night, huddled next to fire.

Finally he said to her in a soft voice, "I think we'll find the flower tomorrow. We are very close now."

But all he heard from her was silence. Soon she was asleep in his arms.

He stared up at the stars. And in what he expected would be another sleepless night, he asked the Great Spirit for help.

Help me to reach out to her and pull out this sadness.

For now, all Many Wolves could do was wait. Wait like the blooming flower waits for a bee to come and spread life to another waiting flower. Bound by its roots to the earth, the flower waves its beautiful colors with the dancing winds to try to capture the insect's attention, but the bee may not come for many sleeps, or may not come at all.

A White Weasel in Winter

The next morning, Taimah didn't spring out of her sleeping robe with the first rays of sun like she so often had before. Many Wolves decided to let her sleep. He quietly called for the birds, and Noche, to follow him on foot. Rabbits would be scarce in this landscape, but rock squirrels were not. The trick was to catch them before they could reach the safety of their rocky villages.

Although Many Wolves left Taimah alone with Colmillo and the horses, he made sure that she stayed in his sight. *I won't make that mistake again.*

The terrain was stony and steep on his left, but on his right it was flat with a mixture of melted snow and vegetation—squirrel food. The birds made a few lazy passes at the reddish-brown animals that were much smaller than their tree-loving brothers, but ended up with empty claws and confused looks on their faces.

After a few more failed attempts, the birds seemed to figure out a better approach. They eyed the squirrels that were farther away from the rocks, grazing on the grassy side of the trail. Like a clever wolf pack, the two female birds positioned themselves on boulders while Flecha flew in a circular path around the squirrels, chasing them back toward the two waiting females. Many Wolves sat and watched them from his own outlook on a large boulder.

The birds' first attempt using this new plan ended in a near miss by Chachara. But on the second attempt, Espera caught a squirrel before it reached its hiding place. Her knife-sharp claws squeezed down on the squirrel's head, and she was able to kill it easily herself. Many Wolves helped by cutting open the squirrel's thick skin to help the bird get at the juicy red meat more quickly. He cut off small pieces of the dead squirrel for the other two birds, then saved the rest of the carcass for his hunting bag.

Before resuming the hunt, Many Wolves looked back at Taimah. She was still sleeping with the horses nearby and Colmillo alertly looking back at him.

The pack moved ahead and caught one more rock squirrel with the same flush-and-ambush tactic. But as they attempted to capture a third squirrel, Flecha pursued its prey into a rocky crevasse. He sat there for several moments looking into the burrow where the squirrel had disappeared, as if expecting it to reappear. Nothing came out that hole—but next to one of the rocks near it, Many Wolves found what he was looking for: the white lion's paw flower. Excited, he picked the flowers and put them in his medicine bag, then thanked the Great Spirit for helping him find them again.

Many Wolves looked around and realized the place did look familiar. The excitement of the rock squirrel hunt had distracted him from noticing the landmarks. He had been here before with Ten Arrows. It was the same place where Ten Arrows had killed the giant grizzly, the one that had left a scar on Many Wolves's leg. It seemed so long ago, though the scar was still clearly visible as a reminder of that frightening day.

Many Wolves called for Noche, then hurried back to tell Taimah.

"Wildflower, wake up," he whispered, leaning over her with one of the flowers in his hand.

She opened her eyes and said in a sleepy voice, "What is it, *Ahpu*?"

"Look!" he said, holding the flower up in front of her.

"You found it!" she said, with a smile he hadn't seen for over two sleeps.

"*Haa*, Wildflower. They're hidden around the rocks here. Do you want to help me gather them?" He hoped that this would finally cheer her up.

"*Haa*, *Ahpu*." Taimah crawled out of her sleeping robe and brushed her hair back, then drank some water.

"We can walk there. They'll be easier to find that way," he said.

Many Wolves packed up the sleeping robes and tied them to the horses. He handed Sombra's lead to Taimah, and they walked with the horses along the trail toward the spot where he'd found the flowers.

"They are hard to see. You need to look carefully around each rock. They are facing east so they can soak up the morning sun."

Taimah and Many Wolves walked slowly around the rocks, then tied the horses to a tree so they could pass more easily between the boulders. The birds and wolves followed them curiously. *They are hoping for some kind of an easy meal*, thought Many Wolves. If the little flowers had smelled like lion's paws instead of lion's paw flowers, the wolves would have been of some use in seeking them out. But when Many Wolves tried to put one of the flowers in front of Noche's nose, the wolf just gave him a puzzled look.

"Here are some!" said Taimah, holding a flower up.

"Put them in your medicine bag."

The morning sun, fully exposed above the trees, helped them to find more of the secretive plants. Even then, it took a while to find each new patch. Like a horned toad in a pit of sand or a white weasel in the dead of winter, they blended in well with their surroundings, hidden among the larger, more common wildflowers and patches of snow melt.

For the remainder of the morning they gathered as many of the mind-journey flowers as they could find. Taimah was in better spirits, but still it seemed like a piece of her happy self was missing. Many Wolves felt that at least she was mildly distracted by this new task.

"We have enough, Wildflower. I want you to try to remember this place. You will need to come here again, perhaps without me," said Many Wolves. "Do you see that rock formation up there?" Many Wolves looked up and pointed. "I call that the Rock of Feathers because it looks like three feathers sticking out of it. Do you see it?"

"Yes, *Ahpu*. It almost looks like fingers rising from a hand."

Many Wolves smiled. "You can name it Rock of Fingers if you want. Ten Arrows and I always called it the Rock of Feathers."

"Rock of Feathers. I'll try to remember that."

They returned to their horses, mounted, and headed back down the slope.

"When can I try the mind-journey medicine, *Ahpu*?"

"Soon, Wildflower. It looks like clouds will soon take away our clear sky. It might be too hard to see. Let's wait until we find Sky Lake, where I did my first mind-journey. The weather should be clear by then." Many Wolves had named it "Sky Lake" because it was the first lake that he had seen from the sky.

Silence fell between them after that, and the clopping of hooves was all he heard.

In a Cloud of Hate

Late afternoon clouds rolled in, blocking the sun and leaving them in a murky world of gray. Without the sun, the light breeze chilled Many Wolves's skin, making the hair rise on his arms. It didn't look like a storm, just gloomy weather, which was not uncommon in the high country.

Many Wolves and Taimah made their way toward the camp they had slept at the previous night. The gathering fog made Many Wolves feel thankful there was an animal path to follow. The cool mist enveloped his body, leaving droplets all over him. Every step they took carried them into deeper fog. He felt like he was moving through a cloud—as he had done in his mind-journeys.

He looked back often to make sure he could see his daughter. The wolves and birds stayed close to them as well. Flecha and Chachara sat on fist-perches, and Espera used Many Wolves's riding pad to perch on. *It must be difficult to fly with damp wings.*

"It's getting harder and harder to see, *Ahpu*. Should we stop and wait for it to pass?" Taimah said after a long period of silence.

"No. Just follow the trail. As long as we can see it, we won't get lost."

Then the wolves stopped ahead, ears up, growling.

Many Wolves commanded Castano to wait and signaled for Taimah to stop. He couldn't see anything through the fog, and he doubted the wolves could either, but they heard, and perhaps smelled, something.

From within the veil of mist to their left came a loud, bellowing groan.

Many Wolves knew what it was instantly. *Old Man-Beast. Grizzly.*

"What is it, *Ahpu*?"

"Grizzly," said Many Wolves in a hushed voice. "Stay on your horse and don't move. Get your bow ready."

Many Wolves's heart was pounding in his chest. He flung Flecha into the air and snatched his bow and an arrow from the quiver that was slung on his back. He remembered the pain he felt when the grizzly that Ten Arrows killed tore through the skin on his leg. He remembered the awful, life-threatening wounds on Ten Arrows's back from Gray Face. But the picture that froze in his mind was Gray Face's deathly black, pig eyes.

The wolves were barking now, and the groans and roars grew louder and closer. The horses snorted and shuffled nervously.

"Don't move, Taimah," whispered Many Wolves. "It's trying to figure out what we are. It must know there are two wolves here, and it probably smells us and smells our horses. It just wants a closer look."

"Do you see it?"

"No. But the sounds are getting closer." Many Wolves only heard the grizzly when the wolves stalled their barking and growled instead.

Then the wolves bolted toward the bear sounds. *They must see it.* They were snarling now. The bear wailed in agitation, though Many Wolves could not see it or the wolves. He tried to make out shapes in the fog, but nothing was there. The wolves were still growling and snarling, but the bear was quiet. *Is it leaving?*

Then, without warning, Taimah whistled for her horse to run. She charged into the fog.

"Taimah! No!" *What is she doing?* Many Wolves kicked his horse to a sprint after her.

He heard the thumping hooves of Taimah's horse and then the twang of her bow. The bear roared in anger. *She must have hit it.* Then two more twangs of her bow rose above the sound of the hoofbeats. The animal roared again. Many Wolves heard its huge footsteps and the wolves chasing it.

Taimah's horse screamed, perhaps terrified by what was chasing it, and then Many Words heard a thump and Taimah screaming out, "*Ahpu*, help!"

She's fallen.

Many Wolves dismounted, knowing he could shoot better from the ground, and ran toward the sound of her scream.

He spotted her just as the bear pounced on her. Taimah was lying on her stomach trying to protect her head, and the massive animal was clawing and biting. The wolves were snarling, barking, and nipping at its heels.

Draw its attention. Many Wolves raise his bow and fired into the bear's flank. The Man-Beast rose off of Taimah, turned to face its new attacker, and reared up on its hind legs, snarling with fangs bared. *That's it. I'm the one you want.*

Noche bit at the bear's rear leg, causing enough pain that the bear dropped to all four legs and snapped viciously at the wolf. The angry black wolf backed away in time. *The wolves are distracting it.*

He drew his bow again and fired at the bear, which was now turned to face the wolves. The arrow cut through the skin on the back of the bear's neck. It screamed and turned again to Many Wolves, as if sensing that he was now the greatest danger. The bear stared at him with its large, black menacing eyes. To Many Wolves, it was like looking into Gray Face's eyes again. He felt his body twitch in fear. The beast was only five or six horse-lengths away.

Then it charged at him, its eyes locked on his, through the shaft of his loaded arrow.

Many Wolves fired at its head, but the arrow missed and hit the bear's thick neck again. The big animal swerved, then stumbled and fell to the ground. That gave the wolves enough time to catch up. Colmillo lunged at the beast's throat before it could get up. The bear hollered again, a fearful scream, and then the scream faded into a subdued moan. Blood was pouring from its neck where Colmillo had torn it apart with his teeth. The grizzly moaned and gasped for breath—

Then it exhaled a final time, its life drained from its body.

Taimah! Horrified, Many Wolves ran over to Taimah. Her back was bloodied, and she was crying with her head buried in the earth. *She's alive!*

"Taimah, don't move. The bear is dead."

"*Ahpu*," she said in a faint voice. "It hurts."

"I know it hurts, Wildflower." Many Wolves took his shirt off and pressed on her wounds to stop the bleeding. She had deep scratches on her back and a bite wound between her shoulder and neck.

"I'm dizzy, *Ahpu*," she said, pushing out her words with her breath, and then she fainted.

Many Wolves felt her heartbeat with his hand on her back. It was steady. "Why did you do that, Taimah? Why did you attack it?" he said to himself as he held the shirt against her wound, turning it at times to find a drier spot. *The bear didn't want to fight us.*

Colmillo came over and sniffed Taimah, then licked her forehead. The wolf still had the bear's blood around his mouth.

"She'll be all right, Colmillo. But I need to stop the bleeding."

Noche lay next to him and the birds perched on the ground around him, watching.

"Just rest now, Wildflower." Many Wolves felt the tears welling up in his eyes. *I can't lose her. Not like this.*

She opened her eyes again. "I'm sorry, *Ahpu*."

"What are you sorry for, Wildflower?"

"That I attacked it." Her voice was very weak.

"Why did you attack it?"

"I was angry. It hurt inside," she blurted out. Tears were streaming down the sides of her face. She moved her head to try to look up at him, but he motioned for her to keep resting it on the ground. "I'm sorry."

"What hurt inside?"

"The poison, *Ahpu*. The poison in my head." she cried out with her waning strength. "Esatai's poison in my head!"

Esatai. Perhaps this was the secret she had been protecting. "What did Esatai do, Wildflower?"

"He forced himself on me, like a dog," she said, with great difficulty. "I couldn't fight him. My hands were tied, and he was too strong. I couldn't scream." Taimah was crying uncontrollably.

Many Wolves felt anger rising in his heart like boiling water. *Cold Raven said that she was not harmed.* "Did Cold Raven know about this, Taimah?"

"I don't know. He was kind to me. Esatai came to me late in the night when the others were sleeping." She stumbled with her words, trying to control her breaths.

"Take your time, Wildflower."

"Esatai said he would kill me if I told anyone." She was trying to be strong, but the blood loss and this poison had sapped her.

"Don't say any more now, Wildflower. I will take care of you. I will take care of this," said Many Wolves.

This is the end of Cold Raven's peace.

Raging Wind

Many Wolves carried his daughter to a fairly level spot on the side of the mountain and had her stand for a moment while he set up the sleeping robes. Though she was hunched over, she had the strength to stand on her own. Once the robes were ready, he helped her lie down on her stomach. The fog had not cleared yet, and now darkness was stealing what was left of the light. He started a fire while it was still light enough to find wood and grass to burn.

"I will try to find Sombre before it is too dark," he said. "Are you comfortable? Do you want me to make some tea?"

"Find Sombre, *Ahpu*. We'll have tea when you get back." Her voice was weak, hoarse, and she winced as she spoke.

"Let me start the tea." Many Wolves poured some water in a drinking-shell and set it next to the fire. Then he mounted Castano and headed back along the trail that followed the mountain. The wolves stayed behind with Taimah. He hoped he wouldn't need to go too far beyond the range of their warnings.

The black horse had been spooked by the bear, which meant it could have run in any direction. Many Wolves walked back toward the dead bear, hoping the horse was nearby. He shouted Sombre's name several times, but nothing in the stillness of the damp night answered him back.

He found the dead bear by its stench. *I should take what I need from this carcass.* He cut open the chest of the animal and removed the liver and heart. He dug out a small hole in a patch of snow with his knife and buried the heart, thanking the Great Spirit for this life. Blood was everywhere, on his hands and feet and legs. He cut off the front paws and then sliced off some of the thigh meat, packing it all in a hunting bag on his horse, along with the liver.

He shouted Sombre's name several more times, but with it was soon too dark to continue to look. Many Wolves wasn't too worried—horses could take of themselves, and Sombre would be easier to find in the morning with more light. If he was lucky, the horse might even find his own way back to them.

Many Wolves followed the trail back to camp, where he was greeted by the two wolves. Taimah was asleep. The fire had burned down low, but it was still alive and easily revived with a fresh piece of rotting wood. He took the bear meat out of his hunting bag, all except for the paws. The liver was too cold to eat for his tastes, so he placed it on a rock near the fire, not to fully cook it, but to warm it up. *I will share it with Taimah when she wakes up.* He cut the thigh meat into thin strips and also placed it around the fire on stones to dry. He saved the rest for his animals. The meat on the paws he would cook up later. He would save the claws for a necklace.

If the women were with him, they could have cut up the rest of the bear and preserved the meat, hide, sinew, and tallow. But it was just him, and it would take too long to butcher it. He didn't want to leave Taimah alone longer than was needed. He also didn't want to load down the horses.

It was strange how similar this day had been to the day he met Ten Arrows. The bear they had killed today was not as big as Gray Face, but it was as dangerous. And during the attack, Taimah had fallen from her horse, just as Ten Arrows did—and both times he was the healer. Her wounds weren't as bad as he remembered his friend's were, but she was younger and not as strong as he was.

It was comforting to Many Wolves that she was sleeping. These had been the worst days of her life—like a raging wind cutting through an unprepared village. But she had made it through, and hopefully she would be stronger for it.

I can heal your wounds, Taimah, but I can't cure Esatai's poison.

* * *

"How are you feeling, Wildflower?" asked Many Wolves the next morning. He had already started a fire, made her some tea, and fed the birds some of the bear meat. Taimah had woken long enough the previous evening to eat some of the liver, and the wolves had eaten then as well.

"It burns my back, *Ahpu*, and it stings even more when I try to move."

"You don't need to move for a while. Are you hungry?"

"No, that liver was enough," said Taimah. Though she was in pain, her spirits seemed better than they had been. "When can we go to Sky Lake?"

"When you feel well enough to ride."

"How far is it?"

"It's not far from here."

"More than a half a day's ride?"

"No. Much less than that." Many Wolves was happy to hear so many questions. He had missed them. "We will leave later in the day and arrive there by dusk." The weather was warm and clear. The sun would be good medicine for Taimah, and would also help dry the bear meat.

"You saw that Sombre is back?" Many Wolves asked.

"*Haa*. Did you find him last night?"

"It got too dark to look for him anymore, but I had a feeling he would be back this morning," said Many Wolves, smiling at her. "And here he is."

She smiled back at him. "I would go crazy without that horse, *Ahpu*."

"I know, Wildflower." Many Wolves laughed.

Sombre has returned. And so have my daughter's warm spirits.

Death on the Prairie

Three days had passed since the audition and Captain Mac had drilled the men hard throughout that time. Each day there was target practice, using rifles on foot from long range, and pistols from horseback at short range. The targets were wooden posts set up at distances chosen ahead of time by the captain. Riding practice consisted of timed riding around obstacles and picking up objects like hats or blankets off the ground in a full gallop. Captain Mac's belief was, "to kill a Comanche you gotta fight like one." Ramon's muscles were sore from riding, especially his legs and back, but it felt much less painful today than it had the previous day, and he hoped the worst of it was behind him.

He was seated around one of the camp's fires, just outside of Nacogdoches, with Cornelius, Little Sky, and a *mexicano* named Ernesto Lopez. The clear sky around them was tinted orange from the sun's rising, and the heat of the day was finally starting to arrive, following a brisk night. A soft breeze teased the green prairie grass around them.

The common language between the four men was Spanish. It wasn't the favored language of Cornelius or Little Sky, but they understood and spoke it well enough to converse. It was language that bound the various groups of men together. The group of five *vaqueros* at the fire next to them also spoke Spanish, but that was it; the rest of the camp spoke *Texian*, as Ramon thought of it, an American flavor of English. Only Cornelius often moved from one fire to the next, since he was not limited to a single language and had many acquaintances among Captain Mac's men.

"Ramon, why do you think the *capitán* only lets us shoot our *pistoles* from a *caballo*?" asked Ernesto, a man of small stature, with a voice that made him sound much younger than his early twenties. "I would shoot better if I wasn't shaking like a rattlesnake's tail."

"You can't be trampled from the back of a *caballo*, Ernesto," said Ramon.

"A *norteño* can ride faster than wind," added Little Sky, who was gnawing on a piece of jerked meat while the other three men ate portions of beans that were cooking in a small pot on the fire.

"But I haven't hit a target yet from my *caballo*," said Ernesto. "Not once in *tres días!*"

"Practice, *mi amigo*," said Cornelius. His language skills were like two sides of a coin. His Spanish was brief and to the point, while his English was elegant and elaborate.

"Ernesto, your riding skills are *muy fabuloso,* so you just need to work on your shooting," said Ramon. "Most of the men here will never ride a *caballo* as well as you." He remembered how well Ernesto had picked up hats off the ground from his horse.

Suddenly, a man rode into the camp and stopped just shy of Ramon's cooking fire. "Where is Captain McCord?" the man said in Texian with a tone of urgency.

"He's the smaller of those two men standing over there," said Cornelius, pointing to Captain Mac and Possum Jack, who were standing about fifty yards away.

The man tipped his hat and quickly rode over to the captain and dismounted. Ramon heard the words "smoke" and "Cummings," but couldn't make out anything else.

"Cummings?" Cornelius repeated. "That was the family we settled a fortnight ago. I made the acquaintance of the brothers, John and James Cummings, and their delightful family."

Possum Jack ambled over to his horse as the stranger continued talking with Captain McCord. "Saddle up!" Possum Jack yelled. "Cap'n McCord needs ya to gather up!"

Ramon grabbed his saddle and slung it over Cavador, packed his blanket and eating supplies, and mounted up. The other three men in his group were ready soon after. They rode up to where Possum Jack and Captain Mac were waiting. The stranger was with them also.

"The Cummins' place is on fire," said Possum Jack. "Most likely Comanches done it, but we needs to find out. Your guns should be loaded 'n' ready. That there's the cap'n's rule."

"Follow my lead, gentlemen, and be prepared for a skirmish. Let's go!" shouted Captain McCord, turning his horse around and riding away from the rising sun.

The hooves of thirty or more horses kicked up dust and followed the captain and his second-in-command, Possum Jack. Ramon didn't know what they would find at the end of the their ride, but for many of these men he expected it would be their first deadly encounter with *indios*. He had seen only marginal improvements in their shooting and riding skills over the past few days, but he had been impressed by their toughness and resiliency. A poor round of shooting or a fall from a horse didn't seem to dampen their spirits. And when there was personal failure, there was encouragement by the other men, often times initiated by Possum Jack or even the captain himself.

The men rode hard. Finally Ramon spotted a thread of smoke winding its way skyward. The flaming remains of the homestead, built from logs, soon came into view. There were no men or horses in sight.

Captain Jack was the first to arrive at the burning structure. He ordered the men to hang back as he and Possum Jack kept riding, looking for any signs of humanity—that is, any signs other than the stench of burning flesh. Ramon and a few of the men dismounted for a closer look at the remains of the house.

One of the men shouted, "There's a body here!" His name was Biggs, and he was one of the handful of veteran rangers in the group. "Good God, fire don't leave any portions for the buzzards. That's for damn sure."

Ramon walked over and saw a man's blackened body smoldering in the wreckage. There were several arrows sticking from his chest, and his face was badly disfigured. The smell oozing from the body assaulted Ramon's senses, making him feel nauseated, but he held himself together. Several of the other men were worse off and could not hold their meals. Ramon guessed that the body had been there at least a few hours, but not more than a day.

"John Cummings," said Cornelius from Ramon's left. "I recognize the shiny buckle on his belt."

Captain Mac and Possum Jack appeared to have found something lying in the grass. Ramon assumed it was another body.

"James Cummings," yelled Possum Jack. "Comanches."

Captain Mac rode back to the rest of the men. "Connelly, tell Little Sky I need to know how many Comanches and what direction they rode off in."

"Yes, Captain," said Ramon. He repeated the command to Little Sky, who instantly rode off looking for signs.

"Biggs, any other bodies?"

"No, sir," said Biggs, who was easily distinguished by the tall crown on his black hat.

"I presume they've taken the woman and the two little girls as captives," said the captain, his steely eyes boring into them, each in turn, like they were the targets for his pistols. "Comanches kill the men and take the women and children. Every minute we waste is a slow, painful minute for Mrs. Cummings and her two girls. Dammit! We should have had men on patrol." It was the first time Ramon had seen the captain show frustration.

"The Cummings family is as nice a folk as you're gonna meet," said Biggs. "We gotta find those little girls and their ma."

"Connelly, I want you to help Little Sky find their trail. We'll stay back and salvage what we can from the ruins and bury these two men."

"Yes, Captain," said Ramon.

Ramon spotted Little Sky's horse to the northwest. The tracker was kneeling in the grass looking at hoofprints in the earth when Ramon rode up. Little Sky looked up. "Twenty *jinetes*," he said. "Fresh prints, northwest, easy to follow. Tell *Capitán*."

Ramon rode back to the captain and relayed the information.

"Twenty," repeated the captain. "That's a sizable raiding party. Most are ten to fifteen warriors. Stay on their trail, Connelly. They'll stop at some point, and the buzzards will show us where. Those birds are like hunting dogs—they don't miss a scent. We'll catch up to you and Little Sky soon enough. We gotta save those girls."

Ramon nodded at the captain, then rode back to find Little Sky and the war party's trail.

Patient Eyes

Many Wolves decided it would be best if Taimah rested another night before riding out to Sky Lake the following morning. He attached Sombre's lead to his horse so Taimah could rest during the ride. The journey was slow, with the horses walking all the way, but that was good: a slowed pace allowed him to take in the hidden world around him—the activity of smaller animals and birds feeding their young, engaged in play, or being hunted by predators. It was the village of nature that he had grown up with.

"How is your back, Wildflower?"

"It burns like fire, *Ahpu*, and it hurts even more when the horse moves." She was leaning forward, resting on Sombre to try be as comfortable as possible. Chachara and Espera were perched on Taimah's sleeping robe, which was rolled up behind her. From time to time, Chachara chased the lower-ranking bird off the perch to claim it for herself.

"We can stop if you want."

"No. Let's keep going. Stopping doesn't help it feel any better." Taimah's voice quivered like she was walking on hot stones, or as if she was expecting a surge of pain to come with her next word.

"I remember taking this path when I was injured. It was a difficult journey, but Ten Arrows took good care of me." She was experiencing it like him, Many Wolves thought, except it had been his leg that was cut up by bear claws, not his back.

"The scars on your leg?"

"*Haa.*"

"I'll have scars too?"

"I'm afraid so, Wildflower. But you still have a lot of healing to do first."

Though Many Wolves's scars were a painful reminder of nature's wrath, they were also a reminder of his past bravery, in much the same way that scalps were a reminder of a warrior's past glory. It was not his wish for his daughter to endure this suffering, but it would make her stronger, and hopefully she had learned that nature could bite back. Besides, it wasn't these bear wounds that troubled him. They would heal in time, but he wasn't sure about the wounds from Esatai. Those would leave scars that could not be seen, and a memory that could not be forgotten.

They saw the lake at last, just as the sun was reaching its pinnacle, burying their shadows deep beneath their feet.

"It's as blue as a thousand blue jays," said Taimah.

"But much more peaceful," said Many Wolves in a loud whisper, turning briefly to look back at her. Many Wolves marveled at how the lake's surface mimicked the trees and mountains around it like a giant mirror. He once imagined dropping a rock from Chiquito's claws high in the sky and shattering the lake into a thousand pieces, then watching it reform into a different shape like a lizard reforms a lost tail.

As they descended closer to the water, Many Wolves was pleased to see many flocks of ducks. He knew that if there were ducks, then maybe the duck hawks would come—the great diving falcons from the sky world. This was the only place where he had seen one, and it was one memory that never faded. His mind slipped into the memory.

The duck hawk sailed high in the clear blue sky, higher than most hawks and vultures, just a tiny speck to Many Wolves's eyes. It was circling high over the lake, watching and waiting for the ducks floating below to leave the safety of the water. Startled by something around them, the water birds lifted themselves up on running feet and flapping wings that carried them across the water and into the air. The vigilant duck hawk tucked its wings and fell, faster than a falling star, faster than anything Many Wolves had ever seen. Toward the earth it fell in a magnificent dive; it crashed into one of the speedy flyers in a splash of feathers, knocking the much larger bird out of the air. The duck hawk circled back and killed the flopping duck instantly. And it had all happened so quickly that a blinking eye would have missed it.

Like a beautiful sunset, seeing this bird hunt was a gift from the Great Spirit.

Many Wolves wondered what it would be like to train such a powerful bird. He believed their spirits were too strong to be tamed by a man. But an even more exciting thought was: *What would it be like to mind-journey with a bird that could fall like a star?*

"What are you thinking about, *Ahpu?*" asked Taimah, pulling herself up to look at him.

"I was thinking about birds," said Many Wolves, shaken from his thoughts.

"What birds?"

"A falcon that I saw at this lake once. They hunt these ducks, so I call them duck hawks. I'm hoping I will see another one here, but they are very rare, like the white buffalo."

"Maybe I can see one too."

"Only the most patient and watchful eyes can see them, Wildflower."

"I can be patient."

"Anyone can be patient. Like practicing to ride or shoot, this too must be practiced."

The old camp overlooking Sky Lake looked the same as Many Wolves remembered it. It brought back fond memories of his friend Ten Arrows. When Many Wolves was injured, he had spent much of his time watching Ten Arrows practice his skills with the horse and bow here. Like the duck hawk and the white buffalo, Ten Arrows was a rare spirit. A gifted rider who could fire arrows from the left side. A kind and gentle two-spirit who could warm a cold winter night with his smile and laughter. His life-brother.

Ten Arrows, I know that you and Soft Cloud are happy together in the next world.

Many Wolves set up the camp with the two sleeping robes, then carefully helped his injured daughter down from her horse. She walked slowly over to a nearby pine and squatted down next to it, releasing her body-water. "That's one less pain I have to worry about," she said when she was finished.

She walked with old man steps back to her sleeping robe and gently set herself down on it, lying on her side. She took several deep breaths and exhaled, obviously still in a lot of pain. Both of the wolves lay on the ground next to her, and the three birds perched in pine trees around the camp. Chachara squawked at a blue jay, which squawked back at her.

"Do you want me to make you some tea?" asked Many Wolves.

"*Haa.* Then I will need to rest for a while. I am tired."

"The mountain air steals your breath away. Rest and sleep will give you your strength back," said Many Wolves, digging out a small hole for a fire pit. "After I make your tea, I will take these birds out and see if they remember how to hunt tree squirrels before the sun leaves us." He was half-joking.

"They will remember."

"You're right, Wildflower," he answered with a smile. "These birds forget nothing about their past hunts. If they could talk, they would tell us hunting stories in great detail." Many Wolves walked around the camp gathering pine needles, twigs, and dried branches.

"You would have no peace at all, *Ahpu,* if Chachara could talk."

Many Wolves laughed. It was good to see Taimah's sense of humor returning, like the sun bursting through the clouds.

He finished lighting the fire, set his daughter's tea next to it, and then walked over to her. He untied the lacing on the back of her deerskin shirt and inspected her wounds. The bleeding had stopped, but the lacerations were purple and white and badly swollen. He gently spread bear tallow over the wounds—the same medicine that Ten Arrows had once used for him—hoping it would soothe her pain and quicken the healing process. She flinched several times when he touched a tender spot, but did not complain.

When he was finished, Taimah rolled onto her stomach and rested her head on the buffalo robe.

"You should have seen those birds go after those rock squirrels," said Many Wolves. "Like a great war leader, they made a plan and then executed it to perfection. These wolf hawks show you something new each time you offer them a new challenge."

"What did they do, *Ahpu*?"

"Chachara and Espera waited by the rocks while Flecha flushed a squirrel toward them. Then they caught it before it could reach its home in the rocks. It was like Malone herding a buffalo to you for the kill. After each failed attempt, I could see them changing their roles and positions for the next chase until they finally made a kill. They hunt rock squirrels, tree squirrels, and rabbits all with different plans and tactics."

"Chachara was the leader?"

"*Haa*, Wildflower, as always. You watch the way she scolds the other two when they make mistakes. She is definitely the leader of their little pack."

Many Wolves stood up, put his fist-perch on, and called for Flecha. "Get some rest, Taimah. The wolves will stay with you, and I won't wander beyond the range of their barks."

Rolling and Falling

When Many Wolves arrived back at the Sky Lake camp just before dusk, he was greeted by the excited howls and wagging tails of the two wolves. Taimah had been asleep, but stirred in response to all the ruckus. *At least she got some rest.* He tried to quiet the wolves, hoping she would return to her slumber, but it was an impossible task. *They are probably more excited to see what's in my hunting bag than they are to see me.*

The three birds perched on pine trees around the camp and started up with their grooming ritual. They had eaten their share of the kill earlier, so were content for the moment.

Taimah rolled over to look at Many Wolves and in a sleepy voice said, "How did the hunt go?"

"We got five squirrels, but it took awhile."

"You aren't used to doing all the hunting work, *Ahpu*," she said with a wry smile and a touch of her mother's sarcasm.

He laughed. "*Haa*, Wildflower, I had to do all the hunting work myself, just like in moons past."

Many Wolves unstrapped his quiver and hunting bag and set them beside his sleeping robe. The wolves sniffed the hunting bag with eager anticipation. "You'll get your share soon enough, little beggars."

He walked over to Taimah and knelt down beside her. "How is your back feeling?"

"It hurts. I would like more of your medicine tea. Do you make it with bear root like *Shimaa* does?"

"*Haa*, Wildflower. Does the medicine make if feel better?"

"A little. The pain only goes away when I sleep."

"Perhaps I should put more than just my medicine herbs in your tea…" he said, dropping a stone to see if her mind would catch it.

"You mean the white flower?" Taimah's voice perked up.

"*Haa*. It is not yet dark, and the birds are still awake." Like nuts in a grinding bowl, Many Wolves had ground the idea in his head all throughout the hunt, and he didn't see any reason to wait. He was excited to share the medicine with his daughter, to see if she could mind-journey like him, and if so, what it would be like for her. No one else had ever even tried besides him. *How might it be different for her?* A part of his mind was excited, while another part was fearful. *What if she can't do it?*

He filled his drinking-shell with water and nestled it between two of the rocks in the fire pit. He added some pine needles and small sticks to revive the flames. When the fire was sufficiently heated, he walked over to his hunting bag and pulled out two of the largest squirrel carcasses. The two wolves, who were lying next to Taimah, kept their eyes on his every movement. With his hunting knife, he cut open the chest cavity of the first carcass.

"Noche, come!"

The black wolf quickly came to his master's open hand.

Many Wolves offered the carcass to the wolf, who took it gently from him. "Easy," Many Wolves said, reminding the wolf of his earlier training.

The wolf carried the meal away to a quiet spot in the camp.

Many Wolves repeated the same feeding ritual with Colmillo, who responded with the same sensitivity as her brother.

"What was it like, *Ahpu*? Your first mind-journey."

"It was very unpleasant. The peyote made me very dizzy and sick, and nothing special happened." As he spoke, he broke a few pieces of peyote, showed them to Taimah, and crumbled them into the drinking-shell. He made sure to use a fairly small amount, because in his experience that was all that was needed, and he didn't want her to get too sick, like he did the first few times. He wanted to be extra careful with this powerful mind medicine.

"So it might make me sick?"

"*Haa.* Your stomach will hurt and you will feel dizzy. You will see many different colors in your mind. It's important that you have Chachara with you and that you keep your eyes closed so that your spirit eyes will be open. Even if you feel very sick, try to keep your eyes closed and focus on the colors. Through your bird's eyes, the world will appear much sharper, and faraway things will appear much closer. When you open your eyes, the vision will end." As Many Wolves spoke, he mixed pieces of the white lion's paw flower into the heating water.

"I am a little scared, *Ahpu.*"

Many Wolves laughed. "Killing a buffalo is much scarier. Nothing bad will happen to you. I will be with you, like Ten Arrows was always with me. Don't worry if the mind-journey doesn't happen the first or second or even third time. It takes some practice, just like shooting a bow or riding a horse."

Taimah cracked a little smile, but also winced from the pain in her back.

"Also," Many Wolves added, "the peyote will make your pain go away, at least for a little while. Are you ready to try?"

Taimah nodded.

Many Wolves cut a small piece of meat from one of the last two squirrels and handed it to her, along with her fist-perch. "You'll have to sit up to do this. Call Chachara to your fist-perch and feed her a few chunks of meat so she is comfortable."

Taimah whistled for her bird and did as her father instructed.

Many Wolves pulled the tea from the fire so it could cool down, then set it next to his daughter. "When she is done eating, close your eyes and drink this down quickly. Stroke her breast feathers and talk to her gently while your mind focuses."

Taimah motioned that she understood. She fed Chachara more scraps of meat until it was all gone. Chachara cleaned the blood off of her beak by rubbing it on the fist-perch, then puffed her feathers in a relaxing pose. Taimah took the tea, closed her eyes, and drank it down.

"It's very bitter," she said, twisting her lips and contorting her face as if she were about to cry.

Many Wolves laughed. "*Haa*, it is. It will take several moments before you feel the medicine."

Taimah began whispering to the bird and stroking its chest feathers. Several times it appeared as though she was losing her balance, but each time she would plant her hand on the ground to catch herself just before she fell. Beads of sweat rolled down her face and her body was trembling, but she kept speaking and touching Chachara, just as her father had instructed. It looked to Many Wolves as though she was in even more pain than before, and it was difficult for him to see her this way.

"Try to relax and keep your eyes closed, Wildflower."

After a short while, Taimah started to groan. "My stomach is hurting now." She tilted her head to the side and vomited.

"Keep your eyes closed. Do you see the colors yet?"

"I see some colors, but everything is blurred."

Many Wolves did not say anything more; he did not want to distract her. He tried to remember how long it had taken him to jump into his bird's mind, but his memories could not paint a clear picture. Sometimes the mind-journey came quickly, and other times it did not. And his first couple of attempts were unsuccessful, but then again, he was essentially alone, without anyone to guide him through the strange, windy path. Surely Taimah would feed off his experience and knowledge and find her way quickly.

She vomited again and then screamed in displeasure. "It's not working, *Ahpu*! I can't do it!"

She opened her eyes, and Chachara flew off her fist to a nearby branch. "I don't feel well. I want to lie down." She groaned and curled up on her side.

"What did you see?"

"Spinning colors. Everything was blurry. My head was whirling as if I had just rolled down a very long hill, and I had no control of anything, like being thrown from a horse. That's how it felt."

"It was your first time. The spirit walk did not happen for me the first time either, and maybe not even the second or third. I don't remember. It was a long time ago. I remember my first few times were very unpleasant, but I did not give up. The old man, Hadakai, had said that this medicine would work, so I did not give up."

"I won't give up, *Ahpu*. I will try it again and again until I figure it out."

"I know you will, Wildflower. Do you want anything else to eat or drink?"

"No, *Ahpu*. I want the spinning to stop. I don't want to move or do anything until the spinning stops."

Many Wolves walked over to his daughter, wrapped her sleeping robe around her, and kissed her on the forehead. "You will feel better soon."

The Gathering Cloud

Taimah remained in her huddled resting position throughout the night. She didn't move or speak, but her eyes remained wide open, staring into the flames of their modest fire. The two wolves were curled up beside her, eyes closed but ears alert.

Many Wolves had cooked the remaining squirrel earlier and had eaten most of it. Taimah had refused to eat anything at all because her stomach was twisted like a hair braid, she had said, but he saved a small portion of the cooked meal just in case she wanted to eat later. The mind-journey tea had brought her dizziness and stomach pains, but at least her ailing back did not seem to bother her as much—or if it did, she didn't complain about it.

He admitted to himself that he had thought she would be successful with a mind-journey the very first time. She had always been a quick learner. Many things came easy to her, like shooting a bow from a horse and training the birds. These were skills that some people could never master, but she figured them out quickly and with a tireless attitude that would not allow her to give up easily. *Can she train her mind as easily as her body—train it to master a seemingly unpleasant task?* Both Ten Arrows and Malone had always said that spirit-walking was a gift given to Many Wolves by the Great Spirit. Many Wolves had to believe that his daughter had this gift as well. He saw how the wolves and hawks responded to her. He saw so much of himself in her. *She must have this gift too.* It might take her one or two or maybe five more attempts, but she would get it.

As Many Wolves sat, his mind drifted to a different topic—one that sat like a pebble in his moccasin. *What will I say to Cold Raven when I meet him?* Cold Raven's humbled words had been heartfelt and forgiving, but how could Many Wolves believe him after what Esatai did? How could there be any peace when there was war in his heart, and how much did Cold Raven know of Esatai's attack? The image of Esatai and Taimah violated his thoughts relentlessly, and there was no way to kill it or to tell it to go away. If anything, the image was more vivid now than it had been when he first imagined it. Like a gathering thundercloud, it was growing more and more powerful each time it appeared in his mind. He had no idea how to stop it, or even how to slow it down. But one thing he knew for sure: Esatai's attack was his fault, a father's mistake. How could he have left his daughter to hunt alone in strange, unfamiliar lands?

"What are you thinking about, *Ahpu*?"

"Nothing Wildflower," said Many Wolves, trying to conceal his thoughts.

He felt a small tear tickle his cheek, so he quickly brushed it away. He wanted to tell her he was thinking about Cold Raven, but he knew his words would eventually lead their talk to a darker place—to Esatai. He didn't want to go there now.

"Are you sad because I failed at the mind-journey?"

Many Wolves smiled, relieved that he could lead his thoughts and their conversation away from Cold Raven and Esatai. "No, I am not sad, Wildflower. It was just your first time."

"Tell me what it is like. What do you and your bird do in the mind-journey?"

"In some ways, it's like riding a horse. When you ride, does it sometimes feel like the horse knows your thoughts? It turns when you want it to turn in your mind? It stops before you give it the command to stop?"

Taimah nodded.

"The same thing happens with a mind-journey. The bird somehow knows your thoughts. You think 'climb,' and it climbs. You think 'dive,' and it dives. You think 'fly to those trees,' and it does it. You can do tricks with the bird also, like a horse does tricks."

"What tricks can you do?"

Many Wolves smiled and thought for a moment before speaking. "One of my favorite tricks I call 'rolling.' Do you remember when you were young and would roll down a hill?"

Taimah laughed. "*Haa*! And I would be so dizzy when I reached the bottom."

"Well, I tell the bird to 'roll' in my mind, and the bird rolls on its back in midair and then rolls back to its normal flying position. You don't see birds do this in nature, only when they are avoiding a flying predator or receiving food from a mate. Chiquito loved to do it, more so than Flecha."

"I will have to try that, *Ahpu*."

"Now I think you need some rest, Wildflower."

"My back is starting to hurt again."

"Let me make you more medicine tea. No peyote this time." He smiled.

"We will try that again tomorrow?"

"*Haa*, we will. But now you need to find sleep. Sleep will heal you."

If only sleep could heal the storm in my head.

The Bleeder Watch

"Mr. Connelly, Little Sky told me that you procured another antelope for us today," said Cornelius, looking at Ramon. "A bountiful hunt for two straight days. You seem more than adept with the rifle."

"Thank you kindly, Cornelius," said Ramon. "I wish you would call me Ramon."

"We are in a business, are we not? I prefer to use surnames. It's a matter of formality."

Ramon and Cornelius were waiting in the food line for their portion of the antelope meat. The line began at the front of the cook's fire pit, the same path marked by the aroma of roasting flesh. The cook, who was nicknamed "Salty" because he added salt to everything, was also serving beans.

Captain McCord's men had followed the *norteños'* trail for over two days, and the sun had just left them on the third. The captain seemed sure that there wasn't much prairie left between them and the *norteños*—at least, that's what he told the men, and Ramon believed him.

The journey had been hard and long. They rose at sunrise and spent all day on the back of a horse. Ramon would have welcomed a full night's rest, but it was never granted to him by his hard-nosed leader. Every man had a night watch to serve as part of his duty, and the captain insisted that Ramon's three-hour shift lay smack in the middle of normal sleeping hours. The men called it the "bleeder" shift because you "damn near had to cut yourself with something" to stay awake. Was it a punishment for him for being Mexican, or did the captain trust that he would stay awake during the deepest part of the night? Ramon didn't know.

Carl Biggs and his friend, Richard Chambers, appeared from out of the darkness and approached Ramon. "Connelly, ya need ta move to the back of the line with the other greenhorns. Ya should know the rules now. Veteran rangers, like Chambers and me, eat before ya."

Biggs was a gruff, broad-shouldered man, larger than most. His face was dirty and unshaven, and several teeth were missing from the bottom of his mouth, most likely from fighting. Among McCord's men, Biggs was the most prone to bullying other men, especially the "greenhorns," as he called them, the men who had just started rangering when Ramon did. Ramon was one of the few who did not back down to the larger man, and Ramon knew that conflict, like a kettle left on the fire, was soon to boil over.

"I don't recall the captain making such a rule," said Ramon, holding his ground.

"Never said he did," said Biggs, pressing his eyes against Ramon's. "Ya need ta move to the back of the line, Connelly. The back of the line is for greenhorns and Mexicans, and ya happen to be both. No god-damned Mexican is gonna eat before me!" Biggs raised his voice to a shout.

Ramon looked ahead and counted about ten men in front of him. A few of them were upstart rangers as well, but it seemed like Biggs had singled him out—perhaps because he was the first Mexican in the line.

"I'm not gonna move for you, Biggs," said Ramon calmly in his Irish-stained accent. "You should start at the back of the line like the rest of us did."

Biggs grunted and pushed Ramon, but Ramon held his footing. The larger man swung wildly with his right fist, but Ramon ducked out of the way. Ramon's reactions felt labored, slower than normal because of the sleep loss, but they were enough. And when Ramon saw an opportunity to retaliate against his flailing attacker, he held back. *I don't want this trouble.* It was easier and required less energy to stay on the defensive.

"You sumbitch, Connelly!" Biggs lunged at Ramon and grappled him to the ground, but just as he was reaching back to throw another punch, a huge arm grabbed Biggs and pulled him off Ramon and threw him aside.

"I ain't havin' no fightin'!" yelled Possum Jack, who now stood between the two men sprawled on the ground. "Now stand up, both of yous! I can't have my men hurtin' each other."

Ramon pulled himself up with some effort.

"Possum, I ain't gonna let some god-damned Mexican eat before me. That ain't right!" said Biggs in a complaining tone, brushing the dirt off his clothes with his hat as he stood.

"There ain't no rules 'bout who eats first, Biggs. The captain and I eat after all yous eat, so it just don't matter. You ain't starvin', are ya, Biggs? Ya should be thankin' this Mexican here for fillin' your plate with fresh meat. Now get to the end of the line. I don't wanna hear no more flappin'!"

"Sheeit!" said Biggs, pressing his hat on his head and glaring at Ramon. "Don't be thinkin' ya won here, Connelly, 'cause ya didn't!" Then he and Chambers walked away toward the end of the line.

Possum Jack looked at Ramon and softened his voice. "Don't ya be yankin' him, Connelly. Biggs is a good ranger. I can't have ya at each other's throats."

"Yes, sir," Ramon said. He was glad it was over.

"Now git yourself somethin' to eat—it's your turn."

Salty spooned some antelope stew and beans on Ramon's plate and squawked, "Next!"

"I take it that you are not acquainted with such foul treatment, Mr. Connelly," said Cornelius, walking beside him with his own meal. "I surmise that few Texians like Biggs reside in San Antonio."

"Not too many Texians, but it doesn't mean I didn't get into any scraps," said Ramon. "My skin is lighter than most there, and when your skin is different, you'll find some people don't take to you so kindly." To Ramon, a man like Biggs was no different than any of his childhood bullies or that son-of-a-bitch Pancho Jimenez who rustled Ramon's feathers in Saltillo. And backing down to a bully just wasn't in his blood.

"Well, you're not the first Irish bulldog I've had the pleasure of knowing, Mr. Connelly," said Cornelius, bending a smile his way. "My childhood companion, Billy O'Reilly, would certainly be the first. He made it his habit to protect all the scrawny youngsters, myself included, against any person who was in the business of bullying. You see, Mr. Connelly, Billy was a devout Protestant, and he believed that shepherding a flock of helpless sheep would bring him that much closer to heaven, even if it led to violence and bloodshed. I admired his divine aspirations, to say the least, and benefited profusely from them."

Ramon enjoyed the company of the eccentric surveyor, but at times his long-windedness was as hard to bear as the bleeder shifts. Cornelius wasn't a boring man, by any means, just talkative. And as each tiring day passed, Ramon felt a little more exhausted and a little less patient with his friend's stories, especially the late-night ones that stole his sleep.

The two men sat together around one of the "Mexican" fires, as they did most nights. Cornelius was still talking about the Irish bulldog friend of his from his childhood, using his broken Spanish, but Ramon only heard bits and pieces now and then between his rushed bites. The hot stew and beans were exactly what his body was yearning for. By the time he had finished his plate, it felt like some of his strength was returning.

Cornelius's jabbering was interrupted by Possum Jack, who stopped by their fire pit. "Connelly, I reckon the cap'n wants you on the bleedin' shift again tonight. You and Lopez. You'll be relievin' Harper this time."

Ramon was not surprised. "Will I ever get a different shift, Possum?"

"I reckon you will someday, but Cap'n Mac wants a good gun on ev'ry shift. We can't have no Comanches pokin' our ponies. It'd be the death of us out here, ya know that. I know that shift is rough. I'll bend the cap'n's ear to see if he can get ya another."

"Thank you, Possum. I'd appreciate it."

"All right then. G'night, Connelly." Possum Jack disappeared into the darkness.

To Ramon's knowledge, Cornelius never had to do a watch. Ramon believed it was because he wasn't a ranger like the rest of them. It certainly explained why he had all this energy for spewing out words.

Alone on the Prairie

"Ernesto, did you hear that noise?" said Ramon in the dead of night.

"I heard it, *amigo*. I think it's just a small animal or something."

Ramon and Ernesto were in the middle of their watch, nestled around a small fire. Most of the men's horses were picketed nearby, except for Captain Mac's, which the captain kept near himself when he slept. Ramon watched the horses carefully. He knew that the horses' ears and noses were keener than his. If any *norteños* were near, an anxious horse would be the first sign of it, especially on nights like this where everything in sight was swallowed by the hungry darkness.

Ramon heard the distant noise again. It sounded like whimpering, like a hurt animal, perhaps a wolf or a coyote, though this wasn't a typical howl or yip. He knew *norteños* used animal sounds to call each other, and this thought shot a shiver through his spine. But he didn't want to panic Ernesto until he was more sure of what he was hearing. If it *was* a *norteño* signal of some kind, there was no reply. It was just this one ongoing sound that carved its way through the grunts and snorts of the sleeping horses and the crackling fire.

"Ramon, it almost sounds like a crying *niño*," said Ernesto. Ramon could see the concern in his friend's fire-lit face.

That same thought had occurred to Ramon as well. Could a wolf or coyote make a sound like that? Was it a *norteño* trick to try to lure them away from the horses?

"Ernesto, you stay here and yell to me if you hear anything. Watch the *caballos*—they will know if a stranger is near."

"*Sí,* Ramon. Don't wander where you can't see *el fuego.*"

Ramon nodded, grabbed his rifle, and walked out toward the sound, but it had now ceased. His swishing *botas* blanketed the fading sounds of horses as he walked deeper into the prairie. He stopped, hoping to hear the sound again, but again found only silence. He glanced back to make sure Ernesto's fire was still in his sight, then crouched down and waited, his ears tuned to any stray sound.

Several minutes passed before he heard the sound again. It was farther to the left than he had originally thought, so he moved slowly, silently toward it, keeping an alert eye on the faint flames behind him. Without the fiery beacon, he would have only a rough guess at the correct direction, using the stars and the moon as his guide.

Ramon drifted closer to the whining. The improved clarity of the sound made him almost certain that it wasn't a wolf or a coyote, but a human. It sounded like a child. *Is it one of the little girls?* Realizing this possibility, he moved with more urgency.

"Hello!" he shouted in English, but there was no response. The sound subsided again, but he had a good idea now where it had come from, so he moved forward. "Hello!" he yelled again.

"Help!" a small voice uttered. "Help me!"

Ramon ran in the darkness toward the child's voice. "Hello! I'm here. Keep talking so I can find you."

"I'm here. I'm over here."

Ramon spotted the child ahead, sitting in the grass, crying and sobbing.

"Please don't hurt me. Don't hurt me anymore."

Ramon approached slowly, crawling on his knees. "I'm not going to hurt you."

When he was a couple of steps away, he saw that the child was a little girl with long blond hair. Her dress was tattered and torn in many places. "Are you hurt?" he asked.

"I'm scared, Mister, and I'm cold," said the girl. She started to cry again.

He removed his coat and wrapped it around her. "Is that better?"

She was still crying, but she nodded her head agreeably.

"Are you thirsty?"

Again she nodded.

He set his rifle down, withdrew his water flask, and offered it to her. "Drink it slowly."

She took a mouthful and swallowed. After several mouthfuls, she handed the flask back to Ramon.

"What's your name?"

"Sarah Cummings," she said, sobbing.

Ramon stood up and looked around for Ernesto's fire, but couldn't find it—just flat black prairie in every direction. Crouching back down, he found traces of his former path in the beaten grass. The moon was also his guide. *I will go this way and hope I find the firelight.*

The little girl was sniffling now, but she wasn't crying anymore.

"How old are you, Sarah Cummings?"

"Seven and a half."

"Take my hand," said Ramon. He extended his hand, and she took it. Her hand was cold, almost lifeless. He pulled her to her feet. "Can you walk all right?"

"I'm okay, Mister. I can walk. I'm hungry. My stomach hurts."

Ramon pulled out a small handful of pinole, or what the Texians call parched corn, and gave it to her. It was all that was left in his side pocket.

"Thank you, Mister." She quickly ate the offering.

The two of them then walked hand-in-hand back the way he had come, hoping to find the firelight and the camp.

Ramon was not comfortable around children. Luis's children were the only ones he had ever interacted with regularly, and even then, their parents had always been with them. He'd never had a brother or sister and had always wondered would it be like. His mother almost died trying to give birth when he was twelve, and the doctor had told him that he had a sister in heaven now. His father and then his mother soon joined her there. When his mother died of the fever, it was the moment in his life when Ramon felt the most alone. It was the moment when his family was gone.

"Your hand is warm, Mister," said the girl, glancing up at him, his coat draped around her shoulders.

Ramon just smiled back at her. She was probably alone now too. Her father and uncle were dead, and her mother and sister were captured by *norteños*—if they weren't dead already. He held back his questions about how she came to be where she was and what had become of the others. For now, he just wanted to be with her and make her feel safe.

"Mister, you never told me your name," she said in a sweet, innocent voice.

"I'm sorry, that wasn't polite of me. My name is Ramon."

"You talk sorta funny for a Mexican man."

Ramon laughed. "Part of me is Mexican and part is Irish."

"I knew an Irish boy once. His name was Seamus. He talked just like you."

Sarah seemed incredibly cheerful for a girl who had probably seen her father killed and had been a *norteño* captive just hours ago. It gave him hope that her mother and sister were still alive. As far as he could tell, she had no serious injuries, just some cuts and bruises. She also probably hadn't eaten much during her captivity.

"You see that campfire ahead, Sarah?"

"Yes."

"That's my friend Ernesto there," he said with relief. "And behind him is the ranger camp."

"What's a ranger?"

"It's a bunch of men who want to keep the land safe from *indios* and other bad men."

"You mean Indians?"

Ramon laughed. "Yes."

"I remember men helping us to build our house, but I don't remember you, Ramon. I remember a captain and a man with a funny name. 'Possum' or something like that."

"They are my superiors."

"What's a superior?" she asked, looking up at him. Ramon kept forgetting that she was just a child.

"My bosses. They are the men who tell me what to do."

They entered the firelight, and Ernesto stood up with a look of amazement. "*Dios mio!* One of the Cummings *niñas?*"

"*Sí,*" said Ramon. "I'm going to take her to the *capitán.* You stay here, Ernesto."

"*Sí,* Ramon."

Ramon walked with the girl past the horses toward the captain's camp. He was not surprised to find Captain McCord reading by his modest campfire; Possum Jack could be heard snoring a short distance away.

The captain looked up as they approached. "Good God!" He set his book down and rushed over to them, bending down to talk to the girl. "Sarah?"

"Yes, Captain. I'm Sarah." She seemed relieved to see a familiar face.

"Did they hurt you?" he said with concern.

"No, I'm okay."

"I think she's hungry, Captain," said Ramon, releasing her hand.

Captain Mac walked over to where Possum Jack was curled up in his blanket and shook his arm several times. "Wake up, Possum! Wake up!"

"What is it, Cap'n?" Possum said, still half-asleep.

"Ramon found one of the Cummings girls."

"Well, I'll be damned," said Possum. The big man lumbered to his feet and slipped his boots on. He and the captain walked back over to Ramon and Sarah. "You, little girl, are a welcome sight for these tired old eyes!"

"Possum, wake up the cook and have him heat up some stew for her."

"Yes, Cap'n," said the big man. "I knew there was a damn good reason for puttin' ya on that bleeder watch, Connelly." Possum Jack winked at Ramon, then walked away.

The captain removed Ramon's coat from the girl and handed it back to Ramon, then wrapped her up in a blanket and had her sit next to his fire. He crouched down beside her. "How did you get away, Sarah?"

"The Indian men weren't watching me. They were watching my momma and my sister, but not me. My momma said to run away when I got the chance. So I ran away when it got dark. I just kept runnin', Mister

Captain. When I heard their horses comin', I lay down real quiet-like in the grass until they was gone. Then I started runnin' again until I was too tired to run no more. Then I rested and walked some more, following the moon. I just kept walking and talking to the moon, Mister Captain, like it was my friend. I felt like I had walked forever until finally I couldn't walk no more. That's when Mister Ramon found me."

"You're a very brave little girl, Sarah," said Captain Mac. "So your momma and your sister, they're still all right?"

"When I left them they was, yes sir."

Captain Mac looked at Ramon. "They're closer than I thought. Get some sleep, Connelly. I'll find someone else to finish your watch."

The Hornets' Nest

It was a bell that woke Ramon the following morning. Not the familiar mission bells from his childhood, but a cattle bell. Possum Jack used it every morning to wake the men. "Up, sallies. Up! Let's go. Yer movin' like slugs on salt! Let's go!" he shouted.

Ramon yawned, then swung open his blanket and pulled himself to his feet. Another couple hours of rest would have been welcome; with all the excitement from finding the little girl, it had been difficult to get any sleep at all last night. But now it was time for his day to begin.

He rolled his blanket up and carried it and his saddle over to Cavador, then loaded up his mount. After relieving his bladder, he drank a few gulps of water and grabbed a piece of jerky from his saddlebag—a typical breakfast out on the range.

"Cap'n wants ta talk to y'all," yelled Possum Jack. "Mount up!"

The men did as ordered. The news about the little girl was already spreading around the camp like an untamed fire. The voices of the men buzzed like locusts through the morning dampness.

"Quiet down!" yelled the captain, once the men were gathered around him. "As you all know by now, we found one of the Cummings girls last night. It was Divine Providence that allowed her to escape unharmed. She is safe now, and I will be choosing two men to ride her back to Nacogdoches." The captain shifted around on his horse so he could look at each and every man. "Today, I believe we will come upon the savages. It is my hope to bring Mrs. Cummings and the other little girl back to

Nacogdoches alive. If this cannot be achieved, then so help me God, we will not spare a single Comanche life. Use your training, men, and we will most certainly prevail."

Captain Mac turned to Ramon and Little Sky. "Find their camp; it can't be far from here. Then report back to me."

"Yes, sir," said Ramon. Little Sky nodded. The two of them rode off.

As they trotted along, Ramon said, "Let me show you where I found the *niña*. Her trail will lead us to the *indios*."

"Find the *niña's* trail," said Little Sky, repeating the words in broken Spanish.

Ramon started at the fire pit and rode out toward the area where he thought he had found the girl. Since it had been dark and there were no real landmarks, his best guess would have to do. He hoped Little Sky's tracking abilities would pick up her trail if he could get the scout close enough to the girl's path.

They rode in circles for a while before Little Sky spotted the place where the girl had lain in the grass. He called Ramon over to it and showed Ramon a small piece of cloth from her dress that confirmed the spot; then he pointed in a direction that he believed she came from. "This way," he said. He remounted and led the way.

The Lipan tracker stopped now and again for a closer look at the girl's signs. To Ramon, it was an invisible path, just endless prairie grass, but to Little Sky, a small patch of broken grass blades here and a half footprint there marked the trail like a torch on a dark night.

While Little Sky kept his head to the ground, Ramon kept an eye out for riders and scavenger birds. "You can't hide a camp from the buzzards" was what Captain Mac had said. Ramon wondered if the *norteños* were still looking for the girl. He worried that if they were, they might find him and Little Sky first.

They kept riding, and tracking, through to the middle of the day. *How could the girl have wandered this far in one night?* Ramon was beginning to worry that they had lost her trail. The Lipan insisted that it was right, but Ramon thought he detected a tone of uncertainty in the man's voice. *Are we going in circles?* The only mark on the land that stood out in the vast, endless prairie was a lone oak tree that they had passed a while ago. If he saw that tree again, he would know that they were traveling in a circle. He felt vulnerable—at the mercy of his partner's skill and knowledge. *We can't get lost out here.*

The Lipan tracker stopped again and dismounted. After studying the ground, he pointed toward a hill to the west of them. "From there."

Ramon rode out ahead, up the rolling hill. At the top, a large valley unfolded before his eyes, and he sighted the buzzards he was looking for, circling lazily over a camp. *norteños.* Ramon could see smoke and horses in the distance, and a throng of tipis, around twenty of them. *This is a village, not a raiding camp.* Beyond the village was a stand of trees. Ramon surmised it marked a creek or a river, although from here he could not see the water.

He waved at the tracker with his arm. *Over here.* He did not want to rouse unwanted attention with a raised voice.

Little Sky rode over to him and looked over the camp. "*norteño* village."

Ramon nodded. "I think the *capitán* will be pleased. We won't have to chase them anymore."

"*Sí.* But more warriors to fight, and dogs to warn them."

Little Sky was right. This wasn't just a raiding force of twenty or so warriors on the run. The task was more difficult now. The rangers would be outnumbered and fighting on soil that was familiar to their enemy. Would the captain risk the lives of his men with the odds tilted against them?

From the direction of the camp, Ramon heard a distant scream.

"Mrs. Cummings?" he said to the Lipano.

Little Sky nodded his head in agreement.

"Perhaps they are torturing her because they believe she helped the *niña* escape. We must get back to the *capitán*."

Ramon and Little Sky turned their horses around and sprinted back toward their own camp. Ramon was both fearful and hopeful—afraid of facing such a large *norteño* force, but hopeful that it would soon be over and the woman and little girl would be safe. He had heard many stories of *indio* torture, but only now, with the woman's scream, did those stories become real to him. It was hard to imagine what that felt like. What he had endured in the Saltillo jail at the brutal hands of Roberto Jimenez was not to be compared to *norteño* torture. Colonel Tejada had once told him they found a man with only half his fingers left and his tongue cut out. The man had been beaten, scalped, and left to bleed to death. And this was only one of several stories he knew about *norteño* brutality. It was stories like this that bred fear in the minds of the people of San Antonio.

"Ramon!" shouted Little Sky, pointing to their right.

Their visit had found enemy eyes.

Two *norteño* riders were chasing them, and were already close enough for their war cries to be heard. Ramon urged Cavador to push harder, but the horse was laboring, already fatigued from the day's ride. The captain's men were nowhere in sight. *They could be leagues away from here.*

Ramon's fear grew, feeding panic. His mind was racing. *Do we try to outrun them or fight?* Fighting these warriors on the open prairie would be certain death. Even though there were only two, it would be like shooting darting jackrabbits. *I would have to dismount to shoot them.*

Ramon felt a familiar sense of helplessness—like he had felt when he was sinking in the swallowing waters of the Rio Bravo. He needed to find a rope to pull him up.

The *norteños* were closing the distance quickly. *Their horses are well rested.* Ramon scanned the land ahead, hoping to see the captain and his men, but found only an endless sea of prairie and a horizon that stretched far beyond his reach. The lone blemish on the ceaseless landscape was the oak tree, a singular landmark that reminded him he was heading back the way he came.

Instantly a thought occurred to him. *The tree could provide a shelter from the norteño arrows.*

"Little Sky! Ride to the tree!" he yelled, forcing the words out through his labored breaths. He steered Cavador toward the tree, and the Lipan followed. But the *norteños* were still gaining on them. *Soon we will be in the range of their arrows.*

The world slowed around Ramon as if the hooves of his horse were swallowed in sand. Fatigue had sucked all the strength from Cavador's legs. *Get to the tree, Cavador.*

The twang of a bowstring cut through the sounds of heaving breaths and pounding hooves. Ramon felt nothing and heard no screams from Little Sky. The Lipan was still with him. And Ramon was afraid to look back, even for a second, fearing it would impede his horse's sprint. He had no idea how far the arrow had been from hitting him, but he knew the next arrow would be closer.

The tree was close now, but so were his attackers. Two more arrows were launched, one after the other, but again he felt nothing and heard nothing from his *indio* companion. The rhythm of hoofbeats remained unbroken between Cavador and Little Sky's mount, reassuring him.

Another bowstring swished, and this time Ramon saw the arrow blur past. *They are close.*

Ramon rode under the huge tree, bending down to avoid the lowest branch, and halted Cavador. His horse stumbled and almost toppled over, but held its footing. He grabbed his rifle from the scabbard in Cavador's saddle and to the trunk of the tree. Little Sky was at his heels, bow in hand. The old oak's trunk was thick enough to cover both of them.

The two *norteño* riders pulled up their grunting ponies, perhaps fearful of the rifle's range. Still facing Ramon and Little Sky, they talked to each other. They were in Ramon's range, but he was not confident in his accuracy at this distance, and he did not want to waste the shot. Still, he was relieved to be safe for the moment.

The warriors were both shirtless, wearing only loincloths and moccasins. Each had a bow and a quiver of arrows, but no shields. One wore a single feather, while the other wore an animal skin as a headdress, a coyote or wolf skin.

"*Que haces*, Ramon?"

"We wait, *mi amigo*."

Ramon knew how close the *norteño* camp was, and he knew a gunshot would certainly reach their ears. That would awaken the *norteño* hornets' nest and surely start a race—a race they would lose if the captain didn't hear it. But would the captain hear the gunshot too? How close were the rangers? *The captain must be getting closer. We have to buy more time.*

"If they move, Little Sky, I need you to move the *caballos*. Keep the tree between the *indios* and them. I'll keep the *norteños* in my sights. *Comprendes?*"

"*Sí.*"

Then the *norteños* did something that Ramon did not expect. The one with the feather on his head started to ride away from the other, in an arc around the tree, staying out of Ramon's range. *They are surrounding us.*

"*Que haces?*" Little Sky said in a fearful voice.

"Hide the horses from the one with the animal skin," said Ramon, thinking as he spoke, watching the feathered *indio* through the sights of his rifle. "And tell me everything he does. I'll track the other one." Ramon knew that if they lost their horses, they would be at an even greater disadvantage. "Tell me if he moves."

"Not moving."

The *norteño* continued in his arc until he reached the side opposite his partner. Ramon and Little Sky were pinned squarely in the middle.

Then the two *norteños* bellowed a war cry and started to charge at them.

"He's coming!" yelled Little Sky.

"So is this one. Just stay behind the tree." Ramon held the screaming *indio* at the end of his barrel and tried desperately to calm his breathing, to keep his hands steady. The *norteño* whistled an arrow at him, but it stuck in a branch above him. His weaving target was well within range now, but it wouldn't be an easy shot.

He fired—hoping to hit the *indio* or his horse, *something*.

The rifle blast echoed through the landscape like the tortured woman's scream, certain to fall on enemy ears. Through the smoke, the *norteño* stalled for a moment and then charged again, unperturbed, invigorated.

Ramon flung his rifle to the ground and snatched the revolver from his belt. The *indio* rode at him and shot another arrow past him. He had placed the tree at his back, a barrier to protect him from the other *norteño*, but not this one. The rest of the world was blocked out except this one enraged *indio*.

He fired his revolver, but it had no effect on the charging rider. The *indio* shot at him again and Ramon fired back. This time he saw the *indio* shift his body as if hit, but perhaps not—he immediately resumed his attack. Ramon blasted another shot at his assailant—and this time the warrior screamed, clutching his shoulder.

The *norteño* yelled again, then leaped from his horse, war club in hand.

Ramon grabbed his *escopeta* from his saddle scabbard. It was loaded and ready. The *indio* was almost on him when Ramon unleashed a blast from his powerful weapon into the *norteño's* chest, knocking his attacker off his feet.

The bloodied *indio* tried to pull himself up, but he was clearly weakened from the chest wound. Ramon grabbed his revolver again and fired, close-range, into the *norteño's* head, silencing him.

Ramon spun around and saw the second *indio* veering off, perhaps out of fear of suffering the same deadly fate as his fellow rider. Little Sky shot at the retreating *norteño*, but his arrow fell short. The *indio* was yelling at them, not as a raging predator, but as an animal gripped with fear. The rider guided his mount to a gallop and rode off toward his home camp.

"Little Sky, we must go now!"

Ramon sheathed his weapons and mounted. There was no time to reload. The fresh mounts of their enemy would soon be chasing them. His greatest hope now was that the captain had heard his weapons and was racing toward them, closing the gap, pulling them to safety like the wet rope. For if not, the endless prairie would be as deafening and suffocating as the cold, dark river, and the legs of their horses would be like drowning lungs, soon to falter and lead them to a fatal end.

Little Sky rode stride for stride with him. Ramon was thankful that his partner was a skilled rider on a strong horse. Most other men would have tired by now, dragging him down like a stone.

Find the captain.

A Deep River of Prairie Grass

Ramon and Little Sky rode deeper into the prairie. There were very few landmarks, and the sun was at its peak, so it, too, provided little guidance, and there were no moon or stars to help them find their way. Thus their heading was steered purely by instinct—and Ramon relied heavily on his tracker's over his own.

"Are you sure this is the way to camp?" Ramon said through heavy breaths.

Little Sky hesitated before responding. "I think so."

The horses beneath them labored; sweat oozed from their hides, and tongues dangled with every gasping breath. They ran at half speed, as if swimming in a deep river of prairie grass, driven only by the urgency of their riders and a deep desire to please them. Ramon knew a good horse would run to the grave for his rider, but with angry *norteños* buzzing like mad hornets behind him, his horse's grave would be his own grave as well.

Of equal concern, Ramon knew most of his weapons were not fully loaded. This gnawed at his mind like a hungry tick. If they were caught, he would have little hope of prolonging the fight—of providing more time for Captain McCord's arrival.

"Ramon, small creek ahead. It is *conocido*," the *indio* said in broken Spanish.

Ramon saw it too, and it was familiar to him as well. This was a good sign—they weren't completely lost.

"Let's stop and water the horses, *pronto*," said Ramon. "I will reload while they drink."

The two men dismounted and led their horses to the creek. Both men and horses drank the cool water.

"We need the *capitán* to find us if we can't find him," said the tracker. "But we don't have time for a signal fire."

"Any signal we make would be seen by the *norteños* as well," said Ramon, loading his rifle.

"They will track us, signal or no signal…"

Ramon finished the thought. "But the captain will not find us, unless we help him."

The tracker nodded.

Ramon finished loading his rifle and *escopeta* and returned them to their scabbards. He pulled his flintlock revolver from his belt and fired one, then two shots into the air, emptying it. "That will bring them all to us."

Little Sky nodded and smiled. "We go now."

Ramon reloaded his revolver while Little Sky waited for him. When he was finished, he jumped on Cavador's back. "Let's hope the right war party finds us first."

They commanded their horses to gallop and headed off again in what Ramon hoped was the right direction.

Two gunshots cracked in the distance ahead. "Captain Mac!" he said with an excited, hopeful voice. The two riders shifted their heading toward the sound, invigorated by the prospect of a lifesaving reunion with the captain and his men.

Ramon looked back after a minute of hard riding, as was his ritual, and saw a group of *norteño* riders crossing the creek where they had rested. "There's more of them," he yelled to Little Sky, who also looked back. "But the *capitán* isn't far." Ramon tried to remain hopeful, despite the distant *indio* war cries.

"Go, Cavador! Get me to the captain!" Ramon was pushing every last breath from his horse.

"Ramon, there!" said Little Sky, pointing ahead and to their right.

The captain's men appeared on the prairie as if from some wonderful dream. Captain Mac was drilling them with orders that were barely audible to Ramon. Half of the men were dismounting while other men remained ready with their weapons. Ramon looked back to see that the *norteños* were gaining on them, but were not yet close enough to be in range.

Captain Mac motioned for the Ramon and Little Sky to ride to his right. "Fall behind the line, Connelly!" he yelled. *He wants us out of the crossfire.*

Ramon and Little Sky rode to their left and around the men, then fell in behind the barricade of unmounted rangers.

"Little Sky, stay behind Biggs and ready your weapon," barked the captain. The tracker dismounted and prepared his weapon next to Biggs, who was aiming his musket from one knee. "Connelly, ready your pistols and be ready to charge on my mark!"

Ramon positioned himself on the right side, next to Possum Jack and opposite the captain. He pulled his two pistols from his belt, checking to ensure they were properly loaded. Including the three of them, ten men were mounted, divided evenly on either side of the unmounted riflemen. In the middle of the pack of grounded men was Cornelius, who was to lead them in the captain's absence, as he had done in drills.

"Hold your fire!" yelled the captain.

The line of Comanche riders had stopped short of the range of their rifles, a tactic that Ramon had seen before—both in San Antonio and earlier that day. The *norteño* leader bellowed encouragement to his men, and they cheered in response. There were about twenty riders in all, Ramon estimated, and all had bows and shields, some with lances as well.

Captain McCord rode behind his men. "Rangers, when I signal rifle fire, I want you all to fire whether they're in range or not. I want to draw them in. After that, reload your rifles and be ready with your pistols if they charge. Riders, follow my lead! Remember, target the throats of their horses. I want them off their mounts!"

"A sound approach, Captain," replied Cornelius. "I will ensure that the men are aptly prepared for a second volley."

The captain nodded to Cornelius.

It seemed to Ramon that they would be wasting precious gunpowder, but he trusted that the captain had a plan.

"Rifles on my mark!" shouted the captain. "Fire!"

The rifles and muskets flashed and boomed, filling the air with gunsmoke.

As if called to war, the *norteño* leader screamed and charged, leading a line of riders on either side of him.

"Rifles reload!" yelled the captain, his pistol raised to the sky. "Riders, on my mark! Pistols ready!"

The wide-eyed *indio* riders rushed toward them carving out windy paths in the tall prairie grass. A flurry of arrows whirred through the air, knocking down two of the men on the ground. One screamed while the other cursed at his misfortune.

"Riders, charge!" barked the captain, and he sprinted toward the enemy.

Ramon and the other riders on his side followed their captain's lead. The cascading barrage of whispering arrows was swiftly answered by rapid bursts of gunfire.

Ramon shot twice at one of the wild-eyed *norteños* closest to him, injuring the man's horse and throwing the rider from his mount. Switching pistols, the Irish vaquero fired once more into the chest of his fallen target with his single-shot pistol as he passed, then tucked the weapon back in his belt.

He drew his *escopeta* from his shoulder scabbard and searched through dust and smoke for the next oncoming *indio*. He quickly ducked to avoid an arrow, then blasted his *escopeta* into the chest of the warrior who had loosed it at him as their horses nearly crashed headlong into each other. The force of the weapon launched the rider off his horse, and he fell to the ground bleeding and screaming.

Ramon did not see any more enemies rushing toward him. The twangs of enemy bowstrings faded into silence, but the popping gunfire continued to ring through the prairie. At that moment, Ramon knew that the skirmish was over and the *indio* force quelled. The few *indios* that had survived had retreated.

"Let them go," Ramon heard the captain shout.

* * *

Captain Mac, Possum Jack, and the other ranger riders finished off any surviving *indios* with close-up shots to the head or chest. The rest of the men on foot were cheering and waving their rifles in the air to celebrate a great victory. Cornelius was the loudest of them and had the biggest smile. Three of the captain's men were injured, including Ernesto, but none of the injuries appeared grave.

The captain gathered the men around him. "Gentlemen, you fought well. Indeed, a small victory for Tejas. But our work is not done. We must find the Cummings woman and her daughter before their lives are taken. Those survivors are most certainly on their way to warn the village. We must not dawdle." The captain shifted his mount to look at Ramon. "Connelly, did you find the village?"

"Yes, Captain."

"Take us to it. But first, Cornelius, bandage those men. No man is left behind. We cannot waste another minute."

"I will ensure their wounds are properly attended to, Captain," said Cornelius.

"Thanks, Corny," said Captain Mac with an appreciative smile.

Ramon realized at that moment that this was the finest force of fighting men he had ever been associated with, led by the greatest *indio* fighter he had ever seen, Captain James McCord.

Justified Violence

The captain's men rode at a brisk pace. Ramon's sweaty hands gripped the slippery reins of his horse as the late afternoon sun beat down on his shoulders. The brief rest had been barely enough to restore Cavador, but at least the third trip through this patch of prairie was much less feverish than the second.

Ramon and Little Sky were in the lead, spurred at times by the captain's words: "Faster, Connelly." Little Sky seemed to know the way, so Ramon trusted the tracker's instincts, even after his previous doubts. After some time, they reached the small creek where they had rested before.

"Fill your canteens and water your horses," ordered the captain. "It might be a long while before we find water again."

Ramon dismounted and let Cavador drink the creek water. He spotted Ernesto, still atop his horse, with his arm bandaged. "You need help, *amigo*?"

"*Sí*," said Ernesto. A smile erased the worry from his dusty, sweaty face.

Ramon walked over and pulled Ernesto's canteen, a large leather pouch, from his horse. He filled it at the creek before filling his own.

"*Gracias*," said Ernesto when Ramon strapped the canteen back on his horse.

"How is your arm?"

"It hurt like hell, *amigo*, when Possum yanked the arrow head out," said Ernesto, grimacing at the thought. "But it's better now. Captain Mac wants me to stay back if we get into another skirmish."

"It doesn't hurt too much to ride hard?"

"No. I can handle the riding," said Ernesto. "The other two *hombres* who were injured are having a much harder time keeping up."

"Saddle up, boys. Time's a-wastin'!" yelled Possum.

"*Adios*, Ernesto," said Ramon.

"*Adios*, Ramon."

Ramon mounted and caught up to Little Sky, who had a head start.

"You know the way, Little Sky?" Ramon trusted that he did, but he wanted confirmation.

"*Sí,*" said Little Sky with confidence.

* * *

It was almost dusk as the company arrived at the hill overlooking the *norteño* camp. Ramon signaled to Captain Mac, who ordered the rangers to stop. Ramon, Little Sky, Captain Mac, and Possum rode to the top of the hill.

From that vantage point, Ramon did not see any more tipis, but there was activity in the camp. They were too far away to spot the white woman or her daughter on the darkening prairie.

"The women have packed the tipis," said Little Sky. "They are moving."

"Good," said the captain. "Their horses will be burdened. They will have only a few mounted warriors to fight us. This is favorable. But we will need to find the woman and the girl quickly, before they kill them and before darkness sets in. Let's talk to the men."

The four of them rode back down the hill to where the rangers were waiting.

"Check and double-check that your weapons are loaded, gentlemen," said the captain. Ramon translated for the Mexicans. "The health and well-being of the Cummings woman and her daughter are of utmost importance. These savages may try to kill them before we get to them. We cannot let that happen. If it does, then my intent is to bury every last one of these *indios*. Is that clear?"

The men nodded favorably.

255

"You're damn right, Cap'n!" barked Biggs in support, and other men cheered in agreement.

The Mexican men nodded to Ramon when he had finished translating the captain's orders.

It had been a long day for them all, and the earlier fighting had taken its toll on their bodies and minds. Ramon was impressed that most still had the spirit to fight—perhaps they were invigorated by the captain's unwavering hope and confidence. It had been an especially long day for Ramon and Little Sky, and Ramon felt it in his back and legs.

"Pistol riders will lead the charge," the captain continued, "and you men with rifles will bite our dust and finish off any we miss. Understood?"

"Yes, Captain," said several of the men. Cornelius was the most cheerful of them.

The captain rode around inspecting each man to ensure that his weapons were ready. When he was finished, he rejoined Possum. "Are you ready, Possum?"

"When ain't I ready?" said Possum with a hint of a smile. "Born fer it, Captain."

"Cornelius?"

"Locked and loaded, my captain," said Cornelius.

Captain Mac looked at the other riders. They all nodded that they were ready. Then he looked at Ramon. "Ready, Connelly?"

Ramon was fearful, and fatigue was biting at his mind like vicious horseflies, but his fears were calmed knowing that Captain McCord was leading them. What he had witnessed earlier that day was an outcome he had not thought possible against such a formidable enemy. Now his fear was laced with hope—hope that this fighting would soon be over and he would live through it. He felt that the worst fighting was behind them.

"Yes, Captain," said Ramon, his heart caught in a flutter of butterfly wings.

"Riders, charge!" shouted the captain.

A torrent of pounding hooves erupted around Ramon, accented by the shouts of eager, bloodthirsty men. Ramon pushed Cavador and whispered through heavy breaths, "It will be over soon, my friend."

The company of riders raced down the hill toward the enemy. Though much of the color of the landscape was masked by sunset, the shapes of horses and men were still easily recognizable.

"Find those captives!" the captain shouted, a pistol raised in his right hand.

Ramon drew his pistol from his belt as they drew closer to the enemy. The *norteños* shouted and ran for their own weapons and horses. Five of them mounted and charged at the rangers, bows in hand, while the rest of the camp retreated away from the attackers.

As they rode closer, Ramon heard the whisper of arrows. One of the rangers screamed and feel from his mount.

"Riders, fire!" yelled the captain.

A barrage of gunfire erupted around Ramon. Three of the *norteños* fell immediately. Ramon shot the horse of one of the other *indios*, forcing it screaming to the ground with its rider, and Possum Jack's horse trampled the fallen rider as he tried to get up. The final mounted opponent was lifted from his horse by a blast from Captain Mac's pistol.

"Find the captives!" yelled the captain.

"There!" pointed Little Sky.

Ramon looked to his left and saw a lone warrior riding away with a white woman.

"Connelly, with me! The rest of you find the little girl!" said Captain Mac.

Ramon followed the captain in pursuit of the Cummings woman. Her captor's horse was in a full gallop, but it was dampened by the weight of the captive, giving Ramon and the captain a chance to catch up. Still, the chase continued for several minutes, the rangers' target getting closer and closer with every stride. Then, as if sensing his impending capture, the warrior halted his mount and turned to face his pursuers.

"*Aaa-Hey!*" he shouted, then swept the blade of his glittering knife across the screaming woman's throat. She fell to the ground, lifeless.

The captain yelled in anger.

"Take a shot, Connelly! Use your rifle!" Captain Mac ordered.

The captain and Ramon dismounted, pulled out their rifles, and aimed them at the fleeting warrior, but it was the captain who fired first. His shot knocked the rider off his horse, so Ramon pulled his weapon back.

"Lets go," said the captain, mounting once again.

The distant blasts of gunfire had now ceded to silence. Ramon surmised that the rest of the company had finished their part of the skirmish.

Ramon followed Captain Mac to where the *indio* lay on the ground, not moving. Captain Mac dismounted and pulled out his pistol, then approached cautiously. The warrior was lying on his stomach, bleeding profusely from the gunshot wound in his back. The captain rolled his body over with his foot. There was no life in the man's eyes.

"This is Black Bear of the Penetaka," said the captain. "See the bear claw tattoos on his chest? Just as Little Sky described them to me. He is one of their war leaders."

The captain fired two shots into the face of the dead *norteño*. "These savages believe that injuries carry over into their next life. I've made damn sure this one will see nothing."

Ramon was horrified by this gratuitous act of violence, but he had known this about the *norteño* beliefs as well, so he understood the captain's intent. The Cummings woman's death was equally as horrifying, so retribution by the captain seemed justified. Ramon was glad that this *norteño* was dead.

"Let's get her body and ride back, Connelly," said the captain, with some of the hate lifted from his voice. "We can only hope that her daughter is safe and unharmed."

The captain wrapped the woman's body in a blanket and hoisted it on top of his mount, then the two of them rode back.

When they returned to find Possum Jack standing next to a little girl, wrapping a blanket around her, Ramon saw a rare smile flicker across the captain's face.

"She's unharmed, Possum?" asked the captain.

"Li'l shocked, Cap'n. But she's all right. She be called Louise."

"Any more casualties?" asked the captain in a serious tone.

"None serious, Cap'n. We kilt 'em all. The women and children too. Like ya wanted. Well, 'cept for one."

"One got away?"

"Yes, Cap'n. Little Sky's gonna track him."

"We should not kill him too soon, Possum. He might lead us to another village. That is my sincere hope."

"Never thoughta that, Cap'n." Possum grinned. "Glad we didn't kill him."

"Well, I got some news for the little girl. You better let me speak with her alone," said Captain Mac in a somber voice, getting off his horse.

"All right then, Cap'n."

A Bone Without Marrow

Three more sleeps had passed, and Many Wolves was breathing life into the flames of their fire pit to bring them some warmth to quell the morning chill. Taimah's health had improved each day; quick healing was a gift of her youth.

"Are you feeling well enough to begin the journey home? I'm sure your mother misses you," said Many Wolves.

"I can ride. I want to go home."

Many Wolves was ready to leave too. His spirit was dampened by thoughts of the previous night. Taimah had tried the mind-journey medicine two more times since the first time, and again she was unsuccessful. He didn't understand why she had failed. While she was sleeping one afternoon, he had tried the medicine himself using the exact same ingredients, and Flecha's vision came quickly to him. Did she need more peyote in the mixture? He was afraid to give her too much because it was dangerous medicine, but maybe he would add a little more next time. It saddened him to think that the mind-journey medicine only worked for him. His life would have been much more difficult, perhaps not even survivable, without this special gift, and he desperately wanted to share it with her.

"Let's pack the horses. The animals ate well last night, so they won't need to hunt again until dusk." Many Wolves had made sure that the wolves and hawks ate full meals, in hopes that Taimah would be ready to travel and a hunt wouldn't be needed the following morning. He had made especially sure to feed Chachara as much as she would eat, so that he, and Noche, didn't have to endure her early morning hunger rants.

Taimah packed Sombre, moving a little more slowly than normal, then mounted carefully. Many Wolves packed Castana and buried the fire pit with dirt. He filled the water pouches with lake water, then handed Taimah's pouch to her, urging her to drink, before taking several gulps himself.

"I'll take your quiver, Wildflower, so you won't be burdened by it."

Taimah handed it to him, and he tied it tightly to his riding pad. Then he mounted Castana and commanded the chestnut horse to a brisk gait, heading southeast back toward the Rio Pecos, back toward their home.

They traveled most of the morning with Taimah in front, setting a pace that was most comfortable for her. Very few words passed between them until Taimah finally said, "I never did see a duck hawk, *Ahpu*. I was hoping to."

"Neither did I, Wildflower. Like many animals I know, they are very secretive, which makes it even more special when you see one. Many amazing things are found when not searching for them." Many Wolves smiled to himself. It reminded him of his chance meeting with the old man in the desert. "Did I ever tell you about Hadakai?"

"No, *Ahpu*. Who is Hadakai?"

Many Wolves rode up alongside his daughter. "He was an old Mescalaro I met when I spent my first summer in the wilderness. I was looking for a safe shelter along the Rio Pecos when he found us, Chiquito and me. You remember Chiquito, right?"

"*Haa*, your favorite wolf hawk."

"That's right. Hadakai shared a meal with us that night and told me many stories about grizzly bears, about Laughing Crow and his men, and about the mind-journey medicine."

"He was alone?"

"*Haa*. He left his village expecting to die, but somehow the river revived him."

"Did he show you how to mind-journey?"

"No, but he told me how to make the medicine and where to find the white lion's paw flower. I would never have known about the medicine if not for him. Somehow, this wise, visionary man found me in the wilderness, and I never saw him again after that night." And everything Hadakai had said about bears, and about the mind-journey medicine, had proven to be true. There were times when Many Wolves wondered if Hadakai had really existed—or if he was instead some form of spirit that had appeared in a dream. He and Chiquito were the only ones who had ever seen this mysterious old man.

"Cold Raven is Laughing Crow's son?"

"*Haa*, Wildflower."

"Esatai is his son also?"

"No. Esatai is Thorn Bird's son, but they share the same mother." Many Wolves dreaded having to talk about Esatai again. The hate was again boiling in his mind.

"Thorn Bird was also Laughing Crow's son?"

"*Haa*. His oldest son."

"Malone once said that he was Laughing Crow's friend, but you are Laughing Crow's enemy. It doesn't make sense to me."

"Long ago, Malone and Laughing Crow were close friends, but then he left Laughing Crow's village to live on his own. A long time after that, Malone and I became friends. Did Malone tell you why he left Laughing Crow's village?" Many Wolves didn't know how much Malone had revealed to her. Many Wolves himself had not broached these topics with her; he had decided that, like the spring sun slowly melted the snow-covered earth, these things would be revealed to her in time. But as she had grown older, she had also grown more inquisitive about their past.

"Because his family died," said Taimah, looking at him with sad eyes.

"*Haa*, and he didn't want to be in Laughing Crow's war parties any more."

"How did you and Malone become friends?"

The questions were coming in a rush now, and Many Wolves wanted to be very careful with his answers. He wanted to keep the killing and torturing in his past hidden from his daughter. Malone had agreed that this would be the best path to follow.

"We met in the wilderness, Wildflower, just like how I met Ten Arrows, though I was much younger when I met Ten Arrows—fairly close to your age." It was the truth, with some of the details removed, much like a bone with the marrow sucked out of it.

This answer seemed to satisfy Taimah's curiosity for the moment. Many Wolves knew that there would be more questions and that he would someday have to tell her everything about Laughing Crow and Thorn Bird and how he had played a part in their deaths.

"*Ahpu.* How will you make peace with Cold Raven knowing what Esatai did to me?"

How did she know this was dwelling in my mind?

"I don't know, Wildflower. I don't know."

Words, Not Arrows

Malone rode up to Many Wolves and greeted him with a forearm embrace. "Welcome home."

"It's good to be home," said Many Wolves.

The mid-afternoon spring sun pressed down on them. Many Wolves could not see a cloud in the vast blue sky, and there was no breeze to cool his skin.

Malone rode over to Taimah and hugged her, but she pulled away, wincing. "You are not well, Daughter of Thunder."

"I was attacked by a grizzly, but I am much better now. *Ahpu* has taken good care of me." Taimah smiled at her father.

"We killed it," added Many Wolves.

"I want to hear the whole story later, when the stars are out and there is smoke in my lungs."

The three of them rode side-by-side back to the village, with Malone in the middle. The tired wolves followed them with dangling tongues, and the birds flew ahead to their familiar perches.

"Did you find the spirit-walking flower?"

"*Haa.* My medicine bag is full again," said Many Wolves with satisfaction.

Malone nodded, clearly pleased.

"I tried the mind-journey medicine, but it didn't work for me," said Taimah sadly.

"That doesn't surprise me, Daughter of Thunder. Such powerful gifts are not easily received," said Malone. "It will take some practice, like I'm sure it did with your father. A medicine man does not receive his most powerful visions after one or two sleeps; it sometimes takes many moons or many summers to receive this gift. It is a gift not taken, but received."

"We will keep trying, Wildflower, and you will get it," said Many Wolves, trying to reassure her, though he harbored a lingering fear that she might never receive the gift.

When they arrived at the camp, Nina and Topusana were standing by the cooking pit watching them with joyful faces. Malone dismounted first and grabbed Sombre's lead, slowing the horse to a stop so Taimah could get down. Her hampered movements did not go unnoticed by her mother.

"Little Flower, what is wrong with you?" asked Nina, her smile turning to a look of concern. She hurried over to her daughter.

"Just some scratches," said Taimah, trying to downplay the injury.

Many Wolves was relieved that the scars from Esatai's attack were not obvious. Taimah wanted that secret to be kept between father and daughter, because they both knew how much her mother would worry.

"On your back?" asked Nina.

"*Haa*, mostly," said Taimah, slumping some.

Nina pulled her daughter's shirt up to observe the wounds. She gasped when she saw them. "How did this happen?"

"It was a grizzly attack, *nupetsu*," said Many Wolves, dropping down from his horse. "It surprised us, but we killed it."

Nina's eyes bored into Many Wolves. "She could have died out there! You both could have died!"

Many Wolves didn't know what to say, because he knew Nina was right. The attack could have been avoided, but he wasn't going to admit it, and he knew Taimah would not utter a word. More marrow stripped from the bone of truth. "We didn't die, and your daughter is stronger and wiser for it. She has learned that the world out there can bite back." *She was bitten deeply by Esatai too, but some things you must not know,* nupetsu, *until your daughter is ready to share them.*

If Taimah had been a son, Nina would have been swelling with pride, but a daughter was different. Many Wolves sensed that his wife somehow knew just how much danger they had faced. It was a communication between two minds, with no words spoken, like two ants brushing feelers. But not all of his thoughts would be revealed so easily.

"Come with me, Taimah. I will rub more medicine into your wounds," said Nina, leading Taimah away by the hand and glaring back at her husband.

There will be more talk later.

Topusana embraced Many Wolves and said, "It is nice to have you both home." After a few moments, she released him. "Are you hungry? We have some blackberries and chicory leaves that we gathered earlier."

"*Ura*, Topusana. Some food will give me strength for the hunt later on," said Many Wolves. "A little afternoon sleep would also help."

"I will join you for a meal shortly, though I am only hungry for talk," said Malone. He unpacked both horses and led them away for water and food.

Many Wolves sat down next to the cooking fire as Topusana set water to boil on the low flames. It felt good to be off the back of a horse. It had been a long, slow journey home, with frequent rests for Taimah. The long days ended with hunts with just the birds and him, leaving the wolves to guard Taimah. Most days, there was scarcely enough fresh meat to feed the animals, so he and Taimah ate pemmican and any nuts or berries he could gather from around their camp. Earlier, when Taimah had hunted with him, there had often been an abundance of fresh meat. This journey had made him realize just how much of an excellent provider she had become for their village.

"Was there any excitement here while we were away?" asked Many Wolves, watching Topusana prepare the chicory root for his tea.

"It was quiet around here without the birds and wolves." Topusana looked up at him and laughed, then continued with her work. "Malone took care of us. He killed an elk a few sleeps ago, so we have had plenty of meat. We did receive a visit from Matsokai yesterday. There has been more fighting with the *taiboos*. He spoke mostly with Malone."

"No other visits?" Many Wolves had expected a visit from Cold Raven.

"No, just Matsokai."

Many Wolves didn't want to tell her about his meeting with Cold Raven, because he wanted to talk to Malone first. He still didn't know what he would say to Cold Raven, but with Malone's advice, he would find the right words.

Topusana served him a bowl of blackberries mixed with chicory leaves and a drinking-shell filled with hot tea.

"*Ura*," he said as he took the bowl and tea.

As Malone returned from tending to the horses, Topusana said, "I will leave you two to talk. I have more gathering to do."

Malone hugged her and kissed her forehead before sitting down across the fire pit from Many Wolves. "Topusana told you that Matsokai rode in for a visit?"

"*Haa*. More trouble with the Mare-cans?"

"*Haa*," said Malone, packing his pipe with tobacco. "Matsokai says Lead Fingers is gathering more men for his war parties." He lit his pipe and sucked in some smoke.

"What does Crooked Eagle want to do?" Many Wolves set his food down.

"He wants a council with the leaders of the other Noomah and Kiowa bands to discuss this new threat." Malone's voice was firm and serious. He blew out the smoke from his lungs straight up into the sky. "Crooked Eagle wants us to be at the council also."

Many Wolves was stunned into silence. *He wants* me *to be on his council? I have no wisdom to offer.* It seemed like a very strange request. "Why does he wants us there?"

"He needs warriors… and leaders."

"I am neither of those."

"You are wrong, Many Wolves. You are both. I have seen you fight, and I have seen you lead," said Malone, exhaling more smoke.

"I can't leave this village. One of us needs to stay here."

"Crooked Eagle is only asking that you bring your words, not your arrows. We will return home soon after the council is over."

Many Wolves nodded his acceptance. "My words, not my arrows."

Malone smiled at him. "Good. I will tell Matsokai that we will be there after three sleeps."

Burdens

"Is Cold Raven one of the leaders invited to this council?"

Malone must have sensed the urgency in his friend's tone, because he offered the pipe to Many Wolves, who took it and inhaled the smoke into his body. Malone had once told him that the smoke was an offering to the Great Spirit above, who dropped down blessings to those who offered it. Untruthful smoke must never be offered.

"No, he was not invited," said Malone. "The blood spilled by Thorn Bird is not easily washed away." There was a sudden coldness in his voice that even the warmth of smoke could not hide.

"He wishes to be at this council, Malone."

"How do you know this?"

"Because he told me. He and his men found Taimah and me in the high country."

Malone was about to take another puff, but then held himself back, as if the words caught him unguarded. "What happened?"

"He wanted to talk to me. He wants peace with us and with Crooked Eagle. The Mare-cans killed the leader of his village, Half Weasel, and his mother, Valencia."

"Matsokai told me about this attack," said Malone, resuming his smoking.

"It's strange, Malone. Cold Raven looks so much like his father that it was very difficult for me to trust him at first. His father's hateful face is burned so deep into my memory. Cold Raven could have easily killed or captured us, but he didn't. Then I remembered that you and Laughing Crow were once good friends. This thought opened my mind to his words."

"What did he want with you? To make his peace with Crooked Eagle?"

"*Haa.*"

"Why doesn't he speak with the head man himself?"

"Because Crooked Eagle will not offer him a council," said Many Wolves, trying to recall Cold Raven's exact words.

"Cold Raven still bears the burden of Thorn Bird's deeds, like a weak horse who must carry a heavy pole-drag." Malone took another puff from his pipe. "Crooked Eagle has not forgotten the death of Ten Arrows—and killing a Noomah peace leader, Gray Elk, also surrounds a man with a terrible stench that is not easily lost."

"But it was Thorn Bird who killed those men, not Cold Raven."

"Thorn Bird was the leader of their village when he did those killings, so the village itself has been marked. The stench is passed from one leader to the next. And now Cold Raven must bear it."

Many Wolves found it difficult to understand why Cold Raven should be punished for deeds that happened when he was a child. He had smoked with Cold Raven and believed that his words and intentions were sincere—that he truly wanted peace. However, that was before he had heard what Esatai did to Taimah. The question kept biting at him like a hungry mosquito: *How much did Cold Raven know of Esatai's attack, and could he have prevented it?*

"Cold Raven and I spoke with smoke in our lungs, so I believe there is truth in his words. But…" Many Wolves hesitated.

"What is it?"

"There is something else that you should know," said Many Wolves in a quivering voice.

Malone pulled the pipe from his mouth and stared into Many Wolves's eyes, perhaps sensing the importance of the words that were coming.

"Before I met with Cold Raven, my back was sore from riding. I needed to rest, so Taimah went to hunt alone at dusk. I must have fallen asleep, because when I woke it was sunrise and Cold Raven was calling my name.

Taimah was not at my camp, because Cold Raven's men had captured her. Cold Raven said that she had not been harmed in any way, and he returned her to me. It was then that we spoke."

Many Wolves motioned for the pipe, and Malone handed it to him. He took a deep puff and then exhaled, blowing the smoke into the sky, hoping for a blessing of wisdom. He handed the pipe back to Malone.

"Taimah was not the same cheerful girl after that. She was quiet and withdrawn. I sensed that something was wrong, but I didn't know what it was. There was nothing different about her appearance, no bruises or cuts of any kind. However, after the grizzly attack, she told me that Esatai had forced her to couple with him. It all made sense after that."

Water glazed Malone's eyes. "I would not have guessed that such a terrible thing happened to her. The bear attack was horrible enough."

"Her spirit is better now," said Many Wolves. "I think it helped for her to talk with me about it, but we agreed that we wouldn't tell Nina until Taimah was ready. It is a scar that will never heal, Malone. I shouldn't have let her hunt alone in a strange place. I blame myself for it." Many Wolves felt heat rush to his head; regret attacked him like a poison. *I should have gone with her.* His mind was battered and bruised from this one recurring thought.

"It's a small burden that you must carry now, Many Wolves. We all have our burdens. You cannot hold her wings up when she flies from the nest; she must learn to use them. You won't always be there to catch her when she falls."

"I know. But it hurts that she fell this time and with this predator in her path. There is a hate I feel for this Esatai. It runs even deeper than the hate I felt for Laughing Crow or Thorn Bird. Because of it, I don't know if I can offer any peace to Cold Raven."

"Do you think Cold Raven knew what his brother did?"

"That is the question that burns me inside. My mind has no answer, only silence. I will see Cold Raven soon enough though. He wants to meet you and me at Three Trees Crossing. I was surprised you hadn't seen him here already, because he knows about our camp."

"That doesn't surprise me. He is clever like his father. Laughing Crow always had his scouts watching Noomah lands like an eagle."

"Thorn Bird was never this clever?"

"No—hate clouded his vision and his mind. The tracks of the coyote crossed Cold Raven's path, but not Thorn Bird's, and from what you have just told me, not Esatai's."

The Extraction

Ramon and Little Sky had tracked the lone *norteño* for a night and most of the following day. Finally, as night was falling on the second day, they spotted a small fire blazing in the distance. Neither of them had actually seen the survivor, so the tracker crawled in closer to confirm that it was just a single man, though he couldn't tell how old he was or if he was injured.

"We should tell *Capitán*," said Little Sky when he returned.

"I'll wait here. You can find your way back here in the darkness?"

"*Sí,*" said the Lipan tracker, smiling back at him.

Ramon knew the captain and his men weren't far behind, though they had lost sight of them. And if anyone could find them and find his way back, it was Little Sky. It was if the Lipan tracker had a secret set of maps that he never shared with anyone. Maps that would allow him to navigate in the dark as if it were daylight.

As the Lipan departed, Ramon removed the saddle and other supplies that were tethered to Cavador, so the horse could rest and eat in more comfort. The horse nickered at him as if knowing the work was over for the day. Ramon responded with soft words and by gently stroking the horse's mane and nose.

The *vaquero* set his blanket in the grass and positioned the saddle so his head could rest on it. There was little soreness in his body, only fatigue. In only a few short weeks, his service in Captain McCord's ranger outfit had hardened his body for riding long distances. During this time, Ramon had pushed Cavador harder than he had ever pushed his faithful mount before.

He ate a small ration of *pinero* and drank some water. It had been three nights since he'd had a cooked meal, he thought to himself as he gazed up at the dark sky. It was strange that he barely even thought about Maritza out here in the deep prairie; instead, thoughts about simple comforts like rest at the end of the day or a cooked meal were foremost in his mind. Just staying alive was comforting. Still, the memories of the day when Maritza met the little girl with the flowers still lingered in his mind like an unforgiven sin, slowly eating away at the memories of the ravishing young woman. *What will happen when I go back? Can I ever love her again? Can she change?*

Cavador stirred and grunted, and moments later Ramon heard hooves beating down on the earth. He stood up and saw Little Sky riding toward him with the captain and Possum Jack. They pulled up and dismounted.

"Connelly, where is his camp?"

"Over there, sir," said Ramon, pointing.

"I want him alive," said the captain. "I want to know where his village is and who his leader is. Do you speak Comanche, Little Sky?"

Little Sky looked confused, so Ramon translated the words into Spanish.

"*Un poco.* But if he is a warrior, he will say nothing, even with torture," said Little Sky in Spanish. "He will not let a white man pull words from his mouth." Ramon translated that for the captain.

The captain shook his head. "If we follow him, we could end up in another fight, but even bigger than the last one. I'm not sure the men are ready for that, and now we have fewer who are fit to fight. I think we have to capture him and take our chances."

"Even if he was dead, his village probably ain't too far from here," said Possum Jack. "I reckon we'd find it eventually."

"You're probably right, Possum." said Captain Mac. "If somehow he cooperates, then he might also be useful as a messenger."

"What kind of message, Captain?" asked Ramon.

"Peace talks, Connelly." The captain looked out into the distant, blackened prairie. "They know our resolve now and what we can do. It was

Austin's plan to make peace with them, and we should try to see it through."

"We didn't try to make peace with the ones who killed the Cummings family," said Ramon.

The captain turned and cast a stern look at Ramon. "Connelly, if you recall, you brought those hot-blooded Comanches into the range of our weapons, and we took action. You can't negotiate with a hot-blooded savage." Then he relented some. "And I'm glad you did. Like I said, it shows our resolve and makes our peace talks more meaningful."

Ramon was no expert in these kinds of negotiations, but he trusted Captain Mac's judgment as a man of extensive war experience. Any treaty that would keep the *indios* away from his home in San Antonio was one he was in favor of. In his lifetime, Ramon had seen the Lipans in Bexar honor a peace agreement, so perhaps there was some hope for the *norteños*.

"We'll pay this Comanche a little visit later in the night. Maybe he'll be asleep," said Captain Mac, looking around at the three of them. But we need to make damn sure the rest of the men keep quiet. I don't want to spook this fellow or his horse. You and Little Sky should join the other men and get a little shut-eye, Connelly. I'll post a couple other men here to keep an eye on him."

"Yes, Captain."

After riding back to join the others, Ramon lay back and stared at the sky, watching more and more stars pop into view. Against a backdrop of chirping crickets, he heard Captain Mac puffing on his pipe and Possum Jack singing some crazy song to himself. The words he heard most were "Kentucky," "farm," and "sweet ole Maggie." It wasn't a very cheery song, but he'd heard Possum Jack sing it before a time or two. Though Possum wasn't a very good singer, the song was soothing to Ramon, and soon he was asleep.

* * *

"Are you awake, Connelly? Up like the daisies. Let's go."

Ramon felt someone shaking his arm and he jerked from his sleep. He looked up at Possum Jack and sighed in relief. "I'll be ready soon enough," he said, then yawned.

"Wilkins says that injun's fire is still burnin', but it ain't been kindled in a while. Cap'n thinks he's probably asleep now." Possum Jack offered Ramon a hand getting up off the ground.

Little Sky was awake already. He was a light sleeper. Ramon wondered if all wild *indios* were like that.

Ramon checked his pistols before tucking them in his belt. He also checked his *escopeta* before securing it in its scabbard, then slung it over his shoulder. His mouth was dry, so he took a few sips of water.

The captain joined them. "You boys ready to go?" He turned to Little Sky. "Bring some rope. *La sopa.*"

Little Sky grabbed a coil of rope from his horse and returned to the other three men, a bow in his other hand.

"Remember, I want him alive," said the captain. "No gunshots. He'll probably try to get to his horse if he wakes up." He looked at Little Sky. "Kill the *caballo* if you have to, with your knife. Tell him, Connelly."

Ramon translated, and the tracker nodded.

Then the four men walked toward the *norteño's* camp, their chaps swishing and grass crunching underneath their boots.

"We'll surround him. One man on each side," the captain whispered in the darkness. "Tell Little Sky he needs to calm the horse. Now, spread out."

Ramon and Little Sky veered left while Captain Mac and Possum moved to the right. Little Sky approached the horse slowly and calmed it with words and stroking. Possum Jack stopped on the near side of the *norteño's* camp, while Ramon and the captain continued walking, moving around the sides of their target. Ramon could now faintly see the shape of a man lying near the popping fire pit.

On the captain's signal, the three men moved in slowly.

Suddenly, a stick snapped under Possum's boot. The *indio* awoke, and when he saw Captain Mac coming toward him, he stood and limped toward his horse. *He must be hurt.*

The *indio* jumped on his horse's back, but Little Sky was holding the horse's lead firmly, and the other three men surrounded them with pistols drawn.

The *indio* was just a boy—thirteen or fourteen years old, Ramon guessed—and his upper leg was bloodied from what looked like a gunshot wound.

"Little Sky, tell him to get down," said the captain. Ramon translated the words into Spanish for the scout.

After Little Sky spoke to the *indio*, the boy yelled at him in foreign words. Little Sky kept trying to calm him down, but it was no use. Finally the captain just grabbed the boy's arm and pulled him to the ground. He screamed and kicked several times, but the captain held him down while Little Sky tied his hands behind his back with rope.

They then walked the captive back to his fire pit, half-carrying him when he struggled. Little Sky spruced up the fire pit with dried dung he found in one of the *norteño's* bags.

"Possum, fetch Cornelius and tell him to bring his medical supplies," said the captain.

"All right, cap'n," said Possum, and he left walking as fast as his bad knees would carry him.

"*Donde pueblo?*" said the captain to Little Sky, in an American's Spanish.

Little Sky spoke to the *norteño* boy with what Ramon assumed was the *norteño* language. The captive shouted something back, and Little Sky didn't seem pleased with the response. The Lipan tracker spoke again, more forcefully. The captive spit and then shouted back defiantly.

"*Nada,*" said Little Sky to the captain.

"Dammit," said the captain. "Any ideas, Connelly? How can we get him to talk short of torturing it out of him?"

Ramon just shook his head.

"Captain McCord, I have brought the medicines," said Cornelius, walking out of the darkness.

"Good, Corny. I think he has a gunshot wound in his leg," said the captain. "I'd like to keep him alive."

"Let me inspect the subject's leg then."

Little Sky and Ramon moved the injured boy closer to the flames so that Cornelius would have more light to work with. Ramon held the *indio's* legs while their medical expert studied it carefully for several moments, looking at it from many different angles.

Cornelius then looked at the captain. "The metal ball is still lodged in the wound. I could clean it and encase it a medical wrapping, Captain, or I could extract the ball if you like. It's not too terribly deep, but it will not be pleasant for this fellow."

Captain McCord took a few moments to think, then looked at Ramon. "I think we've found our torture, Connelly. The savage won't know we're trying to help him." To Cornelius he said, "Extract it. I'll have Little Sky ask him a question or two while he's under duress."

"Yes, Captain. I'll start by cleansing the wound."

"Connelly, tell Little Sky that when the boy starts screaming, he should ask him where his village is and who his leader is."

"Yes, Captain.." Ramon translated the instructions for the Lipan.

The wound must have been very tender, because the boy gritted his teeth as if trying to hold back a scream even while Cornelius merely cleaned it. Ramon held the *indio's* legs down with the weight of his body so he wouldn't kick his surgeon. The boy had the eyes of a scared calf.

Then the ranger doctor pulled a pair of long shiny prongs from his bag. He held them where the *indio* boy could see them, then nodded at Little Sky to prepare himself.

"Don't be too hasty with that extraction, Corny, if you get my drift." The captain winked at Cornelius.

"It's against my nature, sir, but perhaps I could deliberate on this one occasion, since there is more than just a metal ball that needs to be withdrawn from this patient."

Little Sky began speaking with the captive again, and once again the boy yelled back at him. But then Cornelius inserted the medical instrument into the boy's leg, and the boy screamed. Meanwhile, Little Sky just kept on with his questions. When Cornelius retracted the prongs and then reinserted them, the boy screamed again, but this time he formed a few words.

"His *pueblo* is northwest of here," said Little Sky. "Not far."

Corny repeated the procedure several times, and Little Sky continued with his questioning until at last the boy screamed out more words.

"Crooked Eagle," said Little Sky.

The captain grinned almost from ear to ear. "He's the one, gentlemen. The most influential of the Comanche leaders. This war begins and ends with him." To Cornelius he said, "Finish the surgery and bandage him up. We need him to ride out of here."

Cornelius nodded with a smile.

"Connelly," the captain said, "give this message to Little Sky. The boy is to return home and tell Crooked Eagle that Captain McCord will meet him in the valley of the two oaks in two days' time at noon. It's about a half day's ride due north of here. Little Sky will know it, and the Comanches will certainly know it. We will start our peace talks there."

The Village Hearth

Many Wolves, Noche, and Flecha had returned to their camp as darkness was settling. The hunt had not gone as well as Many Wolves had hoped. Only a single jackrabbit was caught, and most of that he had fed to the birds and wolves soon after his returning. But he had saved one of the rear legs for Taimah, which was all that was left of the carcass. *Fresh meat will help her heal.*

"Can you cook this for Taimah, *nupetsu?*" he asked, handing the rabbit leg to Nina.

"Only one this time?"

"*Haa.* A slow day. Flecha was not as sharp as usual; perhaps I fed her too much this morning." Flecha might have been part of the problem, but Many Wolves also admitted to himself that he had been distracted by all this talk of Cold Raven and Esatai. In his mind, he had tried to imagine what Cold Raven would say to him when he asked about Esatai's attack, and how he would react to any of the possible answers.

"We still have plenty of elk meat for the rest of us to eat," said Topusana with her usual cheerfulness. "I will start cooking it."

"Can you cut a few pieces for the wolves? They probably didn't get enough of that rabbit."

Topusana smiled and nodded before walking to get the elk meat. The woman who had taught Many Wolves the landscapes of a woman's body on that dark night long ago still drew his eyes to her, like a moth is drawn to a flame. The passing winters had not diminished her looks.

As the two women cooked the meat at the fire pit, the rest of village gathered around. The birds slept in the surrounding trees, while the full-bellied wolves laid down next to their favorite keepers: Noche with Many Wolves and Colmillo with Taimah.

"What was your favorite part of the journey, Taimah?" asked Topusana, cutting meat on a piece of bark.

"Killing the grizzly," said Taimah, without much thought.

Malone laughed. "You sound like a Noomah warrior! I want to see your grizzly hunt dance when you are fully healed, Daughter of Thunder."

"I don't want to think about that hunt," said Nina. "That bear could have killed her."

"But it didn't kill her, Nina," said Malone. "It has made her stronger. We must honor the bravery of both the hunter and the bear with this dance."

"You must have been terrified, Taimah," said Topusana.

"I was scared," said Taimah. "I thought I was going to die, but *Ahpu* saved me. It is the first time I have seen *Ahpu* as a warrior. He had no fear." She shot a smile at her father.

"It was that same warrior who killed the great bear Gray Face," said Malone, looking at Many Wolves with admiration.

"Now I will be able to see that story more clearly in my mind," said Taimah. "That bear was the scariest thing I've ever seen. Its paws and head were massive. Those claws were much bigger and sharper than Colmillo's." Taimah held her hand up like a claw as she spoke.

"I was scared that I almost lost you, Wildflower," said Many Wolves. "My fear of losing you is my greatest fear. The next time we travel to the high country, I will be more careful." Many Wolves was not thinking of just the bear attack, but of leaving her alone to hunt. But of course he did not say so aloud. He and Malone had agreed that what was discussed earlier between them would not be brought before the women of their village until after they had talked with Cold Raven. And that was not his only secret; he and Taimah had decided it would be best to not admit that Taimah had attacked the bear first. Many Wolves wanted the responsibility for the bear attack to fall on himself.

"No more talk of the bear hunt," said Malone. "Save the story for the grizzly hunt dance."

"*Ahpu*, will you make a necklace from the bear's claws?"

"*Haa*. I will make you a necklace now that I have my tools. It will be ready for your dance."

Taimah's eyes lit up.

Many Wolves felt a father's pride stir inside him. He would make her a hundred necklaces if he knew it would heal her wounds. But only time could heal them, and perhaps even that would not be enough.

"Your footsteps are following your father's path, Daughter of Thunder," said Malone.

Malone was right, but there were places that Many Wolves hoped she would never go. There was too much pain and death in his life. Enough for both their lives. He wished there was a way to shelter her from the evils of the world, but he knew it was impossible. All he could do as a parent was ensure that she was prepared for it.

"So, our village hunter only brought one rabbit leg to feed all of us?" Nina said. "We are fortunate that Malone provides for us, otherwise we would all starve!"

Many Wolves, shaken from his contemplation, laughed. He knew that when Nina called him the "village hunter" or "village leader," it was her humor stalking him like a cat. Nina's hand squeezing his also reassured him.

Then the delicious aroma of roasting elk meat made his stomach rumble so loudly that all of them heard it, and everyone laughed.

"You see, even the great hunter himself would starve!" Nina added with a smile.

"*Nupetsu, nupetsu, nupetsu.* Don't you think you would have starved already if not for me?" Many Wolves put his arm around her and squeezed her body close to his. "I can always put you on a horse and send you back to Proud Toad, so you can eat the tasty scraps from around his fire pit."

"No, *ura.* I think a blind dog could provide better than Proud Toad."

Many Wolves got on his hands and feet, then closed his eyes and barked like a dog before tackling Nina to the ground.

It is good to be home.

Preyed Upon

Many Wolves awoke the next morning after a refreshing sleep in his lodge. Nina's body was curled around his like a vine, and her breaths caressed the skin on his neck. There had been talk during the night, but Many Wolves had gripped Taimah's secret deep in his mind without loosing it. And after their talk, he had enjoyed his wife's warmth and delicate touch after being without out it for many sleeps. He had welcomed the restful sleep that followed.

Chachara's squawking and a need to release his body-water finally roused him to his feet.

Nina stirred and mumbled, "Are you going to hunt?"

"*Haa*. I'll take the birds and Noche. Taimah needs her rest."

"I hope it goes better this time," she said without opening her eyes, but with a small twist in her lips.

He kissed her forehead, then crawled over to Taimah's sleeping robe. Her eyes were open. "You need to rest, Wildflower. Colmillo will stay with you," he whispered.

She nodded and closed her eyes again.

Many Wolves stood up and walked into the filtered light of sunrise. The chill raised the hairs on his arms and legs, and Chachara's crowing quickened his pulse. "Quiet, Chachara," he said, but he knew it was hopeless to stop her. He relieved his bladder, slipped on his deerskin shirt and moccasins, and grabbed his hunting bag, water pouch, and quiver. Then he whistled quietly for Noche and the birds to follow him out of the camp.

He rode out to the dry creek bed where he had hunted with Taimah many times before. There were always rabbits lurking in the sage and mesquite here, despite their frequent hunts. It seemed like every rabbit they took from this place was replaced by two others. He reached into his hunting bag and took out a piece of rabbit skin, then called Noche over and leaned down from his horse to let the wolf sniff the rabbit scent. "Find it, Noche. Find it." He returned the skin to his bag, put on his fist-perch, and called Flecha to it. Chachara and Espera were perched on mesquite branches, dividing their attention between the wolf and the surrounding landscape.

Noche's nose was pinned to the earth as he moved forward at a steady pace, frequently stopping to gather more scents, or perhaps to pick up a scent he had lost. The black wolf was very thorough and patient, much more so than Colmillo. *In a village of wolves, Noche would be the scout.* The wolf weaved through the brush, searching for animal signs and listening for any sounds that might lead him to prey. Many Wolves rode closely behind the wolf with Flecha on his fist-perch, while the other two birds followed on either side of the tracker with great anticipation, knowing that the wolf would soon find a furry prize hidden in the desert chaparral.

In an instant, the search turned into a frenzied chase as a jackrabbit bolted from a bush just ahead of Noche. Many Wolves yelled, "Go, go, go!" but the three birds were already after it.

Flecha took the lead and drew closest to the quarry, but a quick turn by the rabbit threw him off the chase. Espera was not so easily fooled, and she crashed into the dodging rabbit. Both bird and prey tumbled on the sandy desert floor, and the rabbit slipped loose—but before it could reach full speed again, Chachara bore down on its head, slamming it to the ground. The rabbit's scream pierced the morning air. Chachara held on to the much larger animal as it struggled to pull free once again.

Suddenly, the rabbit's cries were deadened by the whoosh of a speeding arrow slicing through its body—but it wasn't Many Wolves's arrow. Noche growled and assumed an attack pose, hackles drawn. Many Wolves looked behind him and saw the rabbit's killer sitting on a horse, a bow in his hand.

It was Esatai.

"Why waste your time with these animals when a good arrow is all you need?" Esatai yelled in a pretentious voice, then laughed.

Many Wolves could barely make out the warrior's white teeth as he smiled. "Noche, easy!" The wolf was still growling, stalking closer to the Northerner. "Down, Noche!"

"Call that wolf off or I'll rip an arrow through him too!"

The three birds clamored over the carcass, completely unaware of the impending danger. Many Wolves could not help them now. He turned his horse to face Esatai and rode slowly toward him. "Down, Noche!"

Finally, the wolf stopped and crouched down on the dirt, still growling. Many Wolves had not taken his bow out of his quiver. *I can't do that now. Esatai has the advantage.*

"You could have killed my bird with your arrow, Esatai!" Not many men could have killed a rabbit from that distance, Many Wolves thought, and even fewer from the back of a horse. It was an impressive kill.

"I see where the arrow goes, Many Wolves, and it goes there. If I had wanted to kill your precious bird, it would be dead." Esatai moved closer. "So, you know who I am. I wasn't sure."

"You are Thorn Bird's son and Cold Raven's brother." *And you are my daughter's torturer.* The hate was growing like a spring weed in his heart. He wasn't sure if he could control his wolf if Esatai kept moving closer to him, so he commanded Castana to stop. "I don't think you should come any closer, Esatai. The wolf will protect me if he senses I am in danger."

"Then I will kill it like my father killed your other wolf. I do not fear your animal magic. That is what the stories say it is, but it is not what I believe. The black wolf will die from my arrow, just like the rabbit died, and just like your other wolf died from my father's arrow." Esatai moved even closer, his bow still in his hand, arrows protruding from the quiver on his back. He didn't stop until he was five horse lengths away. "But I am not here to kill your wolf—or you. I promised my brother I would not harm you. That is the only reason why you still breathe." He slid his bow back into his quiver.

Like Thorn Bird, Esatai was a frightening man, despite his youth: large, muscular, and with no fear in his voice or eyes. His hair was long and straight and covered much of his face. He wore only one eagle feather in his scalp and tucked the hair back behind his ear on one side, revealing a long, dangling earring made with beads of several colors. A necklace of small bones adorned his neck and bare chest. Many Wolves wasn't sure what kind of bones they were.

"I was hoping to come closer to you, Many Wolves."

"Why? We can talk from this distance."

"I want to see if you smell like your daughter. I liked her smell." Esatai laughed again, showing the same bravado Many Wolves remembered from his father.

Many Wolves's thoughts were festering inside, eating away at his mind. *I have to control my thoughts. He will kill me if I try to kill him first. That's what he wants.* "Did your brother know what you did to my daughter, Esatai?" Many Wolves tried to remain calm, but he could feel his body shaking and his voice quivering. His heart was ready to burst like a tick.

"She told you. I'm not surprised. My brother doesn't know. It was our little secret, until she shared it with you," said Esatai with a satisfied grin. "And I have another secret for you."

"What is it?" Many Wolves was growing angrier with every word.

"I think she enjoyed it," said Esatai in a lowered tone. "Look at me, Many Wolves. Am I not pleasing to a woman's eye?" Esatai held his arms out and then pointed to his chest and body.

"Enough of your crooked tongue, Esatai!" Many Wolves yelled. "Why are you here?"

"You are not enjoying our talk? I'm disappointed!"

"Why are you here?" Many Wolves repeated in an angry voice. "Why are you following me?"

"I have a message from my brother," Esatai said at last. "He will meet you and Malone at dusk at Three Trees Crossing."

"Why didn't you just come to my village and tell me this?"

"Then we couldn't have had our talk." Esatai smiled again. "My kill is yours."

The brutish warrior commanded his painted mount to a gallop and rode off.

The Spirit of the Father

Many Wolves returned to his camp when the sun was at its highest point. Despite the unpleasant visit from Esatai, the hunt had been successful. The birds caught two more jackrabbits besides the one that had succumbed to Esatai's arrow. Many Wolves was thankful that none of his birds had been injured by the reckless Northerner. He was also thankful to be alive himself.

The hunter dismounted and led Castana to where Malone's horse was grazing. His horse nickered a greeting and rubbed noses with Castana, who snorted with excitement. Their friendship was as strong as their riders'.

Many Wolves pulled the dead rabbits from his hunting bag and walked toward the village tipis with Noche beside him. The birds were already resting in trees around the camp, content from their meal. Taimah and Malone were there to greet him.

"A better hunt than yesterday, *Ahpu!*" said Taimah.

"I have to prove myself every day for your *Shimaa,*" said Many Wolves.

"*Haa,* you do if you want to call yourself our leader," said Nina, appearing from inside their lodge. "Let me take those."

Many Wolves handed her the three rabbits, one of which was a carcass with no legs, as he had shared it with his hunting partners. "Can you cook one of these up now, *nupetsu?* Malone and I need to leave before the shadows grow too long."

"Where are you going?" asked Nina.

"We are meeting with the leader of Malone's old village."

"Nokonis?"

"*Haa*. We are meeting with Thorn Bird's sons, Cold Raven and Esatai," said Many Wolves, though Cold Raven was really Laughing Crow's son by blood.

"You never told me this!" Nina protested.

"I didn't want you to worry. Cold Raven has offered us peace and friendship. I know I will sleep better at night knowing I have one less enemy."

"How do you know you can trust him?" Nina seemed a little calmer now.

"Taimah and I met him in the high country. We were outnumbered. He could have killed us then, but he didn't."

"When were you going to tell me this? When my skin was wrinkled and my hair falling from my head?" Nina again protested.

"Because of the bear attack, I didn't want you to worry about this too. It is my burden to carry, not yours. Cold Raven wishes to discuss further peace with Malone and me at Three Trees Crossing. We must go there at dusk." Many Wolves did not make a habit of withholding knowledge from Nina, but war was discussed among men. It was the way of his people and Malone's people, and no different from any other village he had lived in.

Nina relented and smiled at him, showing that she understood. "When will you be back?" She hung the rabbits on sticks and prepared one for the cooking fire.

"If the moon shows us the path home, we will return in the dark. If not, then expect us in the morning."

Nina seemed satisfied. She quietly prepared the cooking fire for their meal.

Many Wolves walked over to the river to wash his hands and face. Malone followed him. "You saw Cold Raven while you were hunting?"

"No. It was Esatai who found me. He almost killed one of my birds with his arrow. He is reckless." Many Wolves knelt down and drank from his cupped hands.

"He wasn't trying to kill them, was he?"

"No. The birds were struggling with a rabbit and he shot it from a distance. I know I couldn't have done that with a bow, especially not from horseback." He poured water all over his face, arms, and chest to clean the dirt off.

"If he has the skills of his father, then it doesn't surprise me. The *taiboos* fear him more than any other warrior." Malone bent down for a drink as well.

"I see the same hate in him, Malone, as I saw in Thorn Bird and Laughing Crow. Hate I did not see in Cold Raven. Why is Cold Raven different?"

"You never knew Laughing Crow the way I did. There was hate in his heart because he lost his son. He fiercely protected his village and his people. There were many who wanted to take what was his, so he fought to keep it. He was a great leader, Many Wolves. He was a brilliant planner and very unselfish with the spoils of war. He cared deeply for his men. But Thorn Bird... he was none of these things. He was a ruthless warrior and a vicious torturer. I believe there is a lot of Laughing Crow in his son, Cold Raven, just as there is a lot of Thorn Bird in Esatai."

Both men stood up and Many Wolves looked into Malone's dark eyes. "But Cold Raven never knew his father. How can he be so much like him?"

"I believe the spirit of the father lives in the son, just as the spirit of Ten Arrows lives in you. And someday your spirit will live in Taimah."

Three Trees Crossing

Many Wolves and Malone rode north along the Rio Pecos toward Three Trees Crossing. Smoke from a signal fire rose into the sky ahead of them; perhaps it was Cold Raven's way of welcoming them. As they moved closer, the orange flames appeared ahead, surrounded by the three large pines that marked the location. Four horses stood next to the river, and their four riders sat around the fire. Many Wolves recognized two of them as Cold Raven and Esatai.

The Northerners stood when they saw their visitors coming. Cold Raven said some words that Many Wolves could not hear and then motioned for the two unfamiliar men to leave. They seemed young, of similar age to Cold Raven and Esatai, but they looked like children standing next to the two larger men.

Many Wolves and Malone dismounted, and Malone took the two horses and tied their leads by the river. They walked together to meet the two Northerner warriors.

Cold Raven acknowledged Many Wolves with a forearm greeting, then looked at Malone. "I am Cold Raven of the Nokonis, and this is my brother Esatai. The last time you saw us, Malone, we were small boys."

"*Haa*, I remember you both," said Malone with a warm smile, offering his forearm in return to Cold Raven. Esatai did not extend his arm to either of them. *Is it because Malone betrayed his father?* Many Wolves wondered.

Through Many Wolves's eyes, Cold Raven's smile seemed genuine, while Esatai's seemed forced. Both of their faces and bodies were painted in yellow and red—perhaps a Northerner custom, but Many Wolves wasn't sure. He remembered Ten Arrows wearing these colors for his ceremonies as well.

Cold Raven motioned for them to sit around the fire. "I am told you were good friends with my father," he said to Malone.

"*Haa.* That was a long time ago."

"Those were the days of the Blood Riders. Am I right?" Cold Raven's voice was calm and relaxed.

"*Haa.* A long time ago," Malone repeated.

"You are the last of them?"

"The Blood Riders only live in the next world. They have left this one."

"My mother told me there was no greater honor for a warrior. I would love to see the Blood Riders ride once again." Cold Raven smiled, pondering the thought. "However, my village does not have the warriors and the horses that my father's village once had."

"I'm sorry for the death of your leader and your mother," said Malone with sincerity.

"We were not there to protect them," said Cold Raven, pointing to Esatai. "We left the village exposed like a turtle on its back. We did not expect an enemy to find our village and attack us. We were fortunate not to suffer greater losses to this brazen white-skin, Lead Fingers."

"How many men attacked you?" asked Many Wolves.

"Around twenty riders. Not all of them were *taiboos*—some were *mexicanos* and some were Navoonah. The one called 'Big Yack' was also with them." Cold Raven pulled out his pipe and looked at Malone, who nodded his approval.

"Who is he?" said Many Wolves.

"He is the large *taiboo* who rides with Lead Fingers," said Esatai in a more serious voice than his brother. "He is a brave fighter. It is not the first time he has ridden in Lead Fingers' war party."

Cold Raven lit his pipe and took several puffs to ensure the tobacco was burning, then handed it to Many Wolves.

"Many Wolves tells me that you want to make peace with Crooked Eagle and his village," said Malone, who was sitting on Many Wolves's left and across the fire from the two Nokoni.

"My village needs his protection, and he needs our warriors. His greatest warrior, Spotted Dog, died of the white man's disease last winter. He needs warriors to lead his men. Warriors like you and me. Like Esatai and Many Wolves." Cold Raven looked each man straight in the eye as he spoke of them. "How many more Noomah must die to this Lead Fingers? My people have never feared a *taiboo* before. They have never seen a magic weapon that can match the speed of our arrows. He hunts us down where we live like a fox hunts a favorite prairie dog village."

"Have you tried to talk with Crooked Eagle yourself?" asked Malone, taking the pipe from Many Wolves.

"*Haa.* I have sent scouts to his village asking for a council with him. He says we are poisoned by Thorn Bird's deeds and that he doesn't want this sickness in his village. I need you to bring my words to him. He will listen to you and to Many Wolves, his friends."

Many Wolves believed that Cold Raven's words were true and that they were words from his heart. Though the tone of his voice was youthful, the young Nokoni spoke with the eloquence of a man twice his age. Cold Raven seemed ready to go to war with the Mare-Cans; there seemed to be no doubt. But the same wasn't true for Many Wolves. *Is this stranger pulling Malone and me into this war? Is it our war to fight?*

Many Wolves knew that Malone had hate in his heart for the hairy-faced hollow men and would follow Cold Raven into war. But Many Wolves wanted no part of it. He wanted to remain in the safety of his wilderness village with his family.

Many Wolves looked over at Esatai. There was the same one-sided anger in Esatai's eyes that he remembered in Laughing Crow and Thorn Bird, and in his childhood tormentor, Kicking Bull. He had never trusted any of them, and now he was being asked to fight alongside Esatai, to trust him. Yet Esatai had no remorse for what he did to Taimah; instead, he bragged about it. *How can I fight with this man? How can I sleep in the same camp as him?*

Many Wolves was now sure that Cold Raven did not know about the attack on Taimah. *Should I tell him?* He felt like he was being sucked into the swelling current of a flooding river, and he didn't have the strength or the wisdom to fight his way to the safety of solid ground.

Hoofbeats shattered his thoughts, distant and approaching. The four of them stopped their talk and stood up. A single rider came toward them in a billowing dust cloud. Esatai rushed to his horse for his weapons.

"Wait! It's Matsokai," said Malone, holding his hand up to stop Esatai. "He is my friend from Crooked Eagle's village. Cold Raven, I told him that we would be meeting you here at Three Trees Crossing."

Many Wolves was relieved, but Esatai did not stop. The warrior grabbed his bow and loaded an arrow, then walked back toward the other men. "I do not know this man," he said with snarled lips.

"Hold down your weapon, Esatai!" said Cold Raven in a stern voice, a tone that Many Wolves had not heard before.

Matsokai stopped his horse, dismounted, and ran over to them. In winded breaths, he spoke. "Lead Fingers has killed our war leader and has found Crooked Eagle's village. He has over thirty men with him. They are watching us like wolves watch a buffalo herd. You must come now. The council is now. Crooked Eagle has sent scouts to the Kiowa, the Wichita, and the Pawnee."

"If our warriors join you, who will protect our villages?" asked Cold Raven.

"Bring your people to our village. We will protect them there," said Matsokai. He turned to Malone. "Bring your wife and Nina and Taimah to our village. They will be safer with us."

"We will use the darkness to hide the dust of our pack horses," said Cold Raven, whistling for his horse.

Malone looked at Many Wolves, but said nothing.

"Taimah and the animals cannot live in a crowded village," Many Wolves said. He knew that would be difficult on the animals, and it would be hard on Taimah as well. He remembered feeling like an outsider the first time he lived in Crooked Eagle's village. "We will need to move them to a more hidden camp, and Taimah is not well enough to hunt."

"I will kill a deer for them at sunrise, then we will move them," said Malone. "I know a safe camp, and no one will be looking for them." He looked at Matsokai. "I will ride back to your village in two sleeps."

Matsokai nodded his acceptance and looked at Many Wolves.

Many Wolves hated to leave his family, especially Taimah, with danger looming like a storm cloud. *I will be living in a village that is not my home, and fighting in a war that is not my war.* Staying with his family was the safest path for him. But then he remembered how Malone had once risked his life to help him escape from Thorn Bird's village, and how Crooked Eagle had protected him. *Can I turn my back on them now when they need my help?*

A clear answer appeared to him from his hazy thoughts.

"I will ride with Malone."

River Camp

Captain McCord's men traveled north along a branch of the Rio Colorado. They had ridden several leagues already with the river at their side, and Ramon was thankful that the pace was slow.

Though trees lined the banks of the river, the captain was looking for a spot with larger trees, and more of them, for their next camp. The captain had said there was ample time to find a camp and still meet with Crooked Eagle at the appointed place. The horses, and the men, needed a rest. The last two or three days had been hell for all of them.

"That looks better up there," yelled the captain, who was riding ahead of Ramon with Possum Jack. Cornelius was on Ramon's left, and Little Sky was far ahead of them.

Ramon saw that indeed the foliage was thicker ahead. A large oak had saved his life and Little Sky's from the two *norteño* warriors, so he knew exactly why the captain coveted tree cover so much.

"Trees and water and flat ground to train the men. This place looks sufficient, Possum," said the captain. "This Texian sun will suck the life out of you, if the Comanches don't kill you first. Without a horse or knowledge of water sources, a man would quickly be a meal for the wolves and buzzards. This is the heart of Comancheria."

When they reached a clearing, the captain raised his hand and stopped. "We'll make camp here, boys," he yelled. "Water your horses and let them eat their fill."

The men waited as Captain McCord and Possum Jack picked the spots they wanted, then the rest of the company spread out to settle in. Ramon found a shady spot under a pecan tree next to the river. Ernesto and Cornelius set up next to him.

"This place has more amenities than the Hotel St. Louis in New Orleans, Mr. Connelly," said Cornelius. "Ample shade and clear running water. I'd venture to postulate that there's plenty to hunt here as well. I would measure that the captain sees it as a fortress of sorts. A keen military eye can see that there are plenty of trees to stop arrows and a deep river to slow Comanche horses. I think I will enjoy this place, much more so than any other bivouac we've set our boots on so far. Would you agree?"

Ramon half-heartedly tried to follow Cornelius's fancy talk. "At least we aren't out in the open like we have been. Though I'm not sure I can relax knowing there are *norteños* in easing riding distance of this place."

"I'll grant you that, Mr. Connelly. Better this than a june bug lying on its back." Cornelius smiled and winked.

"How is that arm, Ernesto?" Ramon asked.

"*Bien*, Ramon. Getting better *todos los días*. Señor Cornelius has taken good care of me," said Ernesto. "The *capitán* said that I won't be fighting, or even training anymore, and that he'll find work that a one-armed man can do." He laughed. "I'm not sure exactly what that is, *mi amigo*, but I'll find out soon enough."

"Well, if you need anything, let me know," said Ramon.

"You can tell Ernesto that I should redress that bandage of his at his earliest convenience," said Cornelius, removing medical supplies and books from his saddlebags.

While Ramon was unpacking some of his own supplies, the captain walked up. "Connelly, from what I know of these peace talks, only the leaders will meet. I don't know it to be true or not, but I've been told that many of these Comanches speak Spanish. I guess they've learned it from their slaves." The captain took his hat off and wiped his brow, then placed it back on his head, paying extra attention to making it straight. "I'm hoping one of their leaders will speak it, which means I'll need you to translate for us."

Ramon remembered how Little Sky was able to talk with the *norteño* boy. "Little Sky speaks Comanche."

"To be honest, Connelly, I'd rather not have information that could mean life or death for me and my men being delivered to me by a savage. Little Sky is as trustworthy as they come, but he's red-skinned, and I can't completely trust him with important matters like this. I've seen you kill these red son-of-a-bitches, so I know your blood boils for them," said the captain in a more serious voice. "But I haven't seen Little Sky kill a single damn one. Understand?"

"Yes, Captain. I'll do whatever you need me to do."

Crooked Eagle's Village

Malone and Many Wolves neared Crooked Eagle's village in the heat of a spring day. Their bare-chested bodies glistened with sweat from the long ride. Flecha and Noche had come with them, and the hawk had taken frequent rests on Many Wolves's fist-perch, but the wolf had not been offered the same respite. Now Noche's tongue hung from his mouth as he trotted through the green prairie grass.

Many Wolves hoped that the women would be safe in the secluded camp Malone had found for them, nestled in a grove of pine trees. Malone had killed a deer for them before they left, so they had plenty of meat for themselves and the animals; the surplus could easily be preserved. In addition, Taimah was feeling stronger each day and would soon be able to hunt again to provide them with fresh meat. This brought some peace to her father's mind.

Matsokai and another Penateka warrior rode out to greet Malone and Many Wolves when the village was finally in view. "Crooked Eagle is holding the war council in his lodge," Matsokai said.

"I will need to stop before we reach the village and tie Noche on a lead," said Many Wolves. "I don't know what he will do with so many strangers around him." He knew that Flecha would be fine; the bird wasn't a danger to anybody other than the small animals that tried to find an easy life around the village.

The four men moved through the horse herd, drawing stares from the boys who watched and tended to the horses. Men with bows and shields were positioned as guardians for the precious animals. Many Wolves sensed the intensity from both boys and men; none of the boys were smiling or playing, and the faces of the men were serious. He heard his name whispered, and Malone's too, so the village people knew who their visitors were.

The village dogs barked at them also, but most kept a safe distance from the strangers and especially from the strange wolf, which was easily twice their size. Only one dog came close—a reddish male that was bigger than the rest of them. He was aggressive toward Noche, snapping and growling at the larger wolf. But when Noche snapped back at him, the dog retreated.

"That dog is the bully of the dogs," said Matsokai. "He growls at me and snaps at the small children too. One day I'm going to put an arrow in him."

When the spread of tipis came near, the men dismounted and Many Wolves grabbed a horsehair rope from his riding bag. "Noche, come!"

The tired wolf approached him slowly, in an obedient pose, and Many Wolves slipped the looped rope around his neck.

Malone took the leads from Many Wolves's horse and his own horse, and the four men walked toward the bustling village. Many Wolves whistled and called Flecha to his fist, which drew even more stares and whispers from the villagers.

The smell of burning buffalo dung and cooking meat hung in the air. Threads of smoke from several cooking pits floated into the sky, mingling with the buzzards and crows that circled the village. The village was at a different location than it had been the last time Many Wolves had visited. He knew there must be a river nearby, but he hadn't seen it on their approach.

"Flecha, you should stay close to us. Those crows will want a piece of you," he whispered.

A group of three children approached them, one boy and two girls. The girls wore only breechcloths, like the men of the village, and the boy was naked. They were not older than seven winters, guessed Many Wolves.

"Are you Many Wolves, the animal man from the stories?" asked one of the girls.

Many Wolves nodded and smiled at her.

Satisfied, the three of them ran away.

"Your stories are the children's favorites," said Matsokai, looking over at Many Wolves. "You are the only one who knows which stories are true. The elders like to embellish your stories to keep the children entertained."

"I do the same thing with my daughter's stories," said Many Wolves, smiling back at Matsokai.

"Are you hungry?" asked Matsokai, looking at both Malone and Many Wolves.

Many Wolves said that he was not.

"We will eat after the council," said Malone.

"Can we take the horses for you?" asked an older boy.

"*Haa*," said Malone, handing the leads to him.

"Follow us, so we can unload them at their lodge," said Matsokai to the boys. "Then you can feed and water them."

Even more people gathered around them when they reached the lodges; the crowd now hummed like a hive of bees. Many Wolves looked over the people's faces. Some of them were vaguely familiar, but he didn't remember their names. The passing of sixteen winters had erased many of the names he once knew.

One face that was familiar was the face of Proud Toad, who glared back at him. *He remembers me too.* Many Wolves remembered what Nina had said about Proud Toad and the blind dog, and he smiled to himself. A younger woman was tending Proud Toad's fire pit. *He probably beats her too*, Many Wolves thought, though he didn't see any cuts or bruises on her.

"That large lodge over there is Crooked Eagle's," said Matsokai, pointing.

"I remember it," said Many Wolves. Crooked Eagle's lodge was the largest in the village and had many paintings on it. "It's hard to miss."

"I have a lodge set up for the both of you," said Matsokai. "It's this way. It's on the edge of the village, away from the other lodges. No one will bother you there."

Many Wolves spotted a solitary tipi at the base of a large rock formation.

Next to it was a large juniper tree. *A good resting spot for Flecha where he can hide from the crows.*

Matsokai turned to the Penataka warrior that had accompanied him to greet the new arrivals. "Crow Foot, tell Crooked Eagle that we will join him soon."

Crow Foot nodded, then took Matsokai's horse by its lead and headed off toward Crooked Eagle's lodge.

Many Wolves and Malone followed Matsokai toward the isolated tipi, with the two boys bringing their horses along behind. The villagers didn't follow, and now only the red dog-bully watched them. The ground here was patched with short grass that had been well-trampled by horses and humans. Several rock formations surrounded the area, but most of the land was flat.

"Is there water near here?" asked Malone.

"The Brazos is on the other side of the village. It's a short walk. You can fill your water pouches there or I can have one of my sisters get it for you. They can cook for you as well. We have plenty of buffalo."

Malone nodded.

At the tipi, Flecha flew to the juniper tree and Many Wolves removed the lead from Noche, who instantly found the shade of the tree and lay down.

"*Ura*, Matsokai. This will be a nice camp for us and for my animals," said Many Wolves, inspecting the camp.

Matsokai smiled. "Come to Crooked Eagle's lodge when you are ready."

Lead Dog

Matsokai greeted Malone and Many Wolves at the entrance of Crooked Eagle's lodge. The three of them entered the smoky lodge, and Matsokai directed them to where they should sit, which was across from Crooked Eagle. The Penateka warrior moved to sit beside Crooked Eagle.

"Sit down, Malone and Many Wolves," wheezed the venerable peace leader, smoke from his pipe streaking past his face. Crooked Eagle looked much older and thinner than when Many Wolves last saw him. His voice was rougher and more crackly, and much of his hair had fallen out, but his eyes were still sharp.

Malone sat on Many Wolves's right; Cold Raven and Esatai were on his left. Cold Raven nodded and smiled a greeting at them, but Esatai did not even glance their way. Another man was on Esatai's left, but Many Wolves did not know him. He didn't look like a Northerner. He was as large as Esatai and Cold Raven, and his face was less rounded than a Northerner's, more like a white man's face. Also, his hair was not parted in the middle like the Northerners, but rather, a small tuft hang down the center of his forehead, surrounded by tipi-shaped patches of bare skin on each side, and his hair hung long in the back, easily reaching the ground as he sat.

Crooked Eagle looked over at the long-haired man. "Runs With Buffalo, this is Malone of the Nokoni," he said, pointing to Malone. "And this is Many Wolves."

The man looked at Many Wolves and Malone. "I am Runs With Buffalo of the Kiowa," he said in a low, soft voice. "Your stories are known to our children—the one who commands the animals and the famous Blood Rider." He seemed to have some difficulty using Noomah words.

"We will smoke from one pipe," said Crooked Eagle, "because we are one people fighting a common enemy. The smoke we offer to the Great Spirit must be the smoke from one pipe. Smoke that is offered from each of us as leaders."

Crooked Eagle paused to refill his pipe, spilling much of the tobacco on the ground because of his old, trembling hands. The other men at the council waited patiently for the elder, who didn't appear to be in any hurry. When at last the tobacco was loaded, he grabbed a small twig that was resting in the fire and tried to light it. It took him three attempts to reach the pipe with the twig's flame, but at last he did it, and he sucked in the smoke to fire the tobacco. When he was satisfied, he passed the pipe to Matsokai.

"Our lands have been invaded by a predator," said Crooked Eagle. "A predator who has tasted our blood and now thirsts for it. A predator whose hunger for death only grows stronger. This predator is the *taiboo* called Lead Fingers. He has drawn blood from both the Nokoni and Penateka. In moons past, we could outrun our enemy's horses, hide from their trackers, and kill their men while they loaded their fire sticks. But Lead Fingers has taken this from us. He has bred horses from our horses, befriended Navoonah trackers to follow our scent, and created weapons that do not need to be loaded. Even now, he watches us from a camp less than a day's ride away."

When the pipe had circled around the council, Crooked Eagle himself took several puffs and looked into the eyes of each of the men gathered around his fire pit. Then he passed the pipe to Matsokai and began speaking again.

"We will need our bravest and most skilled warriors to defeat him. This is not a Penateka war or a Nokoni war, it is a war of all people who drink the waters of the Brazos and hunt the buffalo of the Staked Plains. Today he hunts the Penataka, tomorrow the Nokoni—and when the new moon comes, he will hunt the Kiowa and the Wichita too.

"I am pleased that we are friends once again with Cold Raven's Nokoni," he continued. "The blood drawn by Thorn Bird long ago has sunk into the earth where it no longer stains the feet that walk on it. Cold Raven has offered his friendship, and we have accepted it. Runs With Buffalo has also offered his friendship to help us fight this Lead Fingers. We have accepted his friendship also. And we are also pleased to have the company of Malone and Many Wolves.

"There are many great warriors and leaders at this council, but we must decide who will lead our war party. I am too old to ride, and the Penataka do not have another proven war leader. I will not speak again until this council has chosen a war leader from among you."

The lodge fell silent for several moments, and only the puffs from the council pipe could be heard. The pipe circled the council one more time before Runs With Buffalo broke the silence.

"Malone should lead us. He has ridden in many war parties."

Malone would be a great leader, Many Wolves thought. He remembered how well Malone had prepared them for Thorn Bird's attack.

"I am not a leader of men," said Malone.

"You have ridden in many war parties with my father," said Cold Raven.

"Not as a leader," said Malone. "I will fight, but I will not lead."

"Then who should lead us, Malone?" asked Runs With Buffalo. "I have never ridden in a Noomah war party, and I do not speak the Noomah tongue easily."

The silence returned, but soon it was broken by the sound of dogs fighting.

Noche. "I have to go. I think it's my wolf," said Many Wolves, jumping to his feet.

Crooked Eagle nodded and said, "Matsokai, go with him."

The two of them ran out of the lodge toward Many Wolves's camp, which was definitely the source of the noise. As they ran, the growls and snarls were replaced by a high-pitched yowl, which lasted for several moments before subsiding.

At Many Wolves's camp, they found a small crowd gathered. Many Wolves pushed through the crowd; at its center, the red bully-dog lay dead, blood pouring from bite wounds in its neck. "Where is the wolf?" he asked.

"Over there, in that lodge," said one of the boys, pointing at Many Wolves's tipi.

Many Wolves ran over and found Noche lying quietly inside. There was blood all over his jaws and mouth, but otherwise he seemed unharmed. The wolf looked at him as if he had done something wrong, his ears pulled back submissively.

"It's all right, Noche. You were defending yourself." He stroked the wolf's head and neck, but then the wolf began growling again.

"I hated that dog. Your wolf has done us a favor," said Matsokai, standing at the entrance. "Your wolf is the lead dog now. Come back to the council when you are ready." Matsokai left them alone.

After staying with Noche for a short while, Many Wolves stood up. "Stay, Noche. I need to return to the council. Stay!"

Many Wolves walked back to Crooked Eagle's lodge and found the council just as he had left it.

"We have come to a decision, Many Wolves," said Crooked Eagle. "But I want your approval as well. We have chosen Cold Raven as our war leader. Malone will help him command."

Many Wolves nodded his approval. *There is much Cold Raven can learn from Malone.*

"Cold Raven," said Crooked Eagle. "Lead Fingers has asked for a meeting to discuss his terms of peace. I have let too many sleeps pass without answering him. My words do not carry the power they once did. I need you to meet with him. Bring men you can trust and meet him in the Valley of Two Oaks." He tapped his pipe against a rock to clean out the tobacco. "This council has ended. I need to rest."

Guardian Wolf

Dusk was settling around Many Wolves's lodge as he and Malone sat around the fire pit. Earlier, one of Matsokai's sisters had brought some uncooked buffalo meat for them and Many Wolves had carved out a large slab of meat for Noche to enjoy underneath the juniper. He had then meticulously cut the leanest pieces for Flecha, and was now feeding the hawk from his fist-perch. Malone had sliced the remaining meat into thin strips, and it was roasting over their fire pit.

"Do you think Cold Raven will be a good leader?" asked Many Wolves.

"He is confident in his ability to lead," said Malone. "I didn't see this same confidence in the eyes of other men in the council."

"How old do you think he is?"

"He has lived through at least twenty winters," said Malone. "Laughing Crow was also young when he became the war leader of the Nokoni."

"Does he have any war plans?"

"He knows he must barter for time. More warriors are coming from the North to help us fight this war." Malone removed the meat from the cooking fire to let it cool down.

"Runs With Buffalo's people?"

"*Haa*. Runs With Buffalo's Kiowa and the Wichita. Crooked Eagle has not said if the Pawnees will help us. As of now, we have at least two warriors for every man Lead Fingers has. When the Kiowa and Wichita warriors come from the north, we will have a much greater advantage."

Many Wolves finished feeding Flecha and watched as the bird cleaned every tiny scrap of meat from its feet and beak. He stroked the bird's chest, and Flecha puffed out its feathers, a sign of contentment. *I'm pleased you are relaxed in your new home.* Matsokai had picked a perfect spot for his lodge away from home.

Many Wolves's thoughts drifted back to his family. He wondered how they were doing without the men of their village. *Is Taimah well enough to hunt yet? Will she be frightened to hunt by herself?* She hadn't hunted alone since Esatai's attack. Hopefully she would not stray too far from their hidden camp and Colmillo would always be with her. The wolf would be her protector now, just like Rojo had protected him through so many seasons.

"Malone, how can I be friends with Esatai when there is only hate for him in my heart?"

"You don't have to be his friend. Just fight with him. It is much better that his arrows will not be aimed at you, but your enemy. When this war is over, you will not have to see him again."

"*Haa*, when this war is over," repeated Many Wolves. "I don't belong in this war. I'm not a warrior like you and Esatai. The stories these people have heard about me are wrong if they say I am a warrior."

"My brother, you have shown your warrior spirit to me," said Malone, stopping what he was doing to look at his friend. "Cold Raven will not ask you to ride on the front line, but he will need you as a scout, and he will need Noche to fight for us. I will make him understand what your strengths and weaknesses are, and I trust as a good leader he will know how best to use you to aid our war party."

Many Wolves reminded himself of the danger Malone had put himself in for him. *I must be strong like Malone. If we do not stop this Lead Fingers, who will protect my family and village from this dangerous man?* The peaceful winters his family had enjoyed after Thorn Bird's death were coming to an end. Now a white cloud of death was blowing in from the east, and Many Wolves knew he had to do everything he could to help shelter the red-skinned people from it.

"Many Wolves, I have something to ask you." Malone walked over to his saddlebag and pulled something from it. It was the old *libro* with the bird pictures.

"Why did you bring that?"

"I wanted to make you a war shield." Malone flipped his fingers through the pages of the book. "I can use these *paginas* to make you a strong shield—a shield that can stop arrows and the *balas* from the white man's guns. These *paginas* have magic. They have been blessed by your white father. He can protect you in this war."

"But I have had that *libro* all my life. It's the only thing I have left from my white parents." Many Wolves had always hoped that someday the *libro* would help him find his white parents, but as the moons had passed through the seasons, that hope had become more and more distant, like the tiniest star in the sky that would eventually disappear forever. "I wanted to leave it with Taimah. The pictures will help her to train birds like it helped me, and she loves looking at them. May I see it?"

Malone handed him the *libro*, and Many Wolves looked through it like he had done a thousand times before. He flipped to one of the pages at the front of the book where there was a picture of a shield with some strange symbols next to it. "This looks like a shield, Malone, with a wolf on it. I've always wondered why it is here. It's the only picture that has colors. I wish I knew what the symbols meant. Perhaps it is something about my white-skinned parents, like their names."

"Maybe the wolf is the guardian spirit of your white-skinned father also," said Malone. "I can try to draw the guardian wolf on the outside of the shield I'll make for you, and then we can put the *paginas* inside to strengthen it—or I can make you one without the *paginas*. The one I made for you when we fought Thorn Bird also had a guardian wolf on it. It looked like Rojo."

"That shield saved my life."

Part of Many Wolves believed that the book would lose its power if it was torn apart, but another part of him agreed with Malone. It was strange that his white-skinned father had also had a wolf to protect him. *I wish I knew who he was and more about him.* He wondered how much use the *libro* would be to Taimah. She knew who her parents were, and she knew how to train birds, but he also knew that she loved to look at the pictures in the *libro*. He knew all of her favorite ones.

"I can return the *libro* to Taimah if you wish," said Malone.

"No. Let me tear out Taimah's favorite pictures, and you can use the rest of the *libro* for my shield."

"Are you sure you want to do this?" Malone asked.

"*Haa*. I will need another guardian wolf shield, but with a black wolf this time."

Malone was very pleased. "I will get started on it after we eat."

Lead Fingers

Malone and Many Wolves were making arrows when they were alerted by Noche's growling and the rumble of hooves. It was Cold Raven and Esatai.

"Noche, wait!" said Many Wolves in a commanding voice.

The two Nokoni slowed their horses and stopped about ten steps in front of them. They were dressed for war: war shields, bows, and lances. There faces were painted black and yellow. Through Many Wolves's eyes they looked very much like their fathers. It made him shiver for a moment, though the sun was hot and at its highest point in the day.

"Lead Fingers is ready to meet us. We must go," said Cold Raven. "Bring your weapons and the wolf."

"These are peace talks?" asked Malone. He started packing arrows in his quiver, and Many Wolves did the same.

"We must be prepared for peace *or* for war. We cannot trust this Lead Fingers." Cold Raven's voice was firm and serious. He seemed much older than his twenty winters.

Malone and Many Wolves packed their horses with food and water, then grabbed their shields and quivers.

"A black wolf shield?" asked Esatai, walking his horse over to where Many Wolves was mounted.

"Malone made if for me."

Noche snarled and growled as Esatai got closer to Many Wolves.

"Easy, Noche!"

"You should teach that animal that I am not your enemy," said Esatai, snarling back at the wolf and laughing.

But you are *my enemy.*

Esatai inspected the shield and nodded his approval. "Malone makes strong shields. It will protect you as well as any I have seen." Then he rode back to his brother.

"How many men are coming with us?" asked Malone.

"Just us and the warriors from my village. Eighteen men," said Cold Raven. "Runs With Buffalo will stay back with the Penataka to guard Crooked Eagle's village and my people who are here."

"How do we know this isn't a trick?" asked Many Wolves.

Cold Raven swung his horse around to face Many Wolves. "We are meeting in Two-Tree Valley. It is flat prairie land where a man can see as far as an eagle. We will know how many men are with them. Lead Fingers is also bringing twenty men, but only the leaders will meet while the others watch from a distance. Let's go!" Cold Raven commanded his horse to a gallop, and Esatai's horse ran alongside him.

Many Wolves whistled for Noche and Flecha, and they chased the dust of the two Nokoni horses.

The four of them rode hard, heading north through the rolling hills of prairie grass, until they met Cold Raven's men atop a hill overlooking a valley. Many Wolves looked down and saw the two trees that Cold Raven had spoken of. Several men were gathered near them—*Mare-Cans*—and far past these men was a group of about fifteen riders. Cold Raven was right: it would be impossible to hide men in this valley.

Cold Raven spoke to his men. "Follow us, but do not come any closer than their men. Be ready for war." Then he turned to Malone and Many Wolves. "Ride with Esatai and me. Many Wolves, you and Esatai will stay several horse lengths back while Malone and I talk with Lead Fingers."

"I will stay with Esatai," said Many Wolves.

Then Cold Raven turned to Esatai. "Brother, you know what to do if they raise their weapons. Kill Lead Fingers first."

Esatai smiled confidently.

"Follow me," shouted Cold Raven.

Cold Raven and Malone took the lead, Many Wolves and Esatai went next, and the Nokoni men brought up the rear. Many Wolves and Esatai kept some distance between them because of the wolf, but Cold Raven and Malone rode shoulder-to-shoulder. Flecha perched on Many Wolves's shield, his new fist-perch, it seemed.

Three hairy-faced men waited for them next to one of the two trees. Many Wolves didn't recognize any of them. They wore hats, and leggings that stretched all the way down to their feet. Their feet were covered with thick leather that crawled up their legs. And all three carried many weapons: *pistoles,* long guns, and knives.

Esatai looked over at Many Wolves and nodded, so they both stopped, while Cold Raven and Malone continued to walk closer to the three men. Cold Raven's horse snorted nervously, bobbing its head up and down, while Malone's remained calm. When the noses of their horses were half a length away from the Mare-Cans' horses, they stopped.

Esatai shifted his horse farther away from Many Wolves, perhaps to give himself a clear aim at the Mare-Cans.

The hairy-faced man in the middle spoke, but Many Wolves didn't understand the words. They sounded like Mexican words. Although this man seemed younger and smaller than the other two Mare-Cans, Many Wolves guessed that he must be the leader, Lead Fingers, since he had spoken first. The man on his right was much larger and had the most hair on his face. The man on his left had darker skin, but not as dark as a *mexicano,* though he was dressed like a *mexicano* and wore a *mexicano* hat.

The darker-skinned man was the one talking now, in the Mexican words. Cold Raven was talking back to him using the same language. *Cold Raven knows the Mexican words?* Many Wolves noticed that the dark-skinned man kept looking at him when he wasn't talking, more so than the other two. *Why is he looking at me?*

Why is the green-eyed man looking at me?

Familiarity

Ramon looked at the painted face of the large *indio* in front of him. The man was familiar, but he'd never seen him this close. The *indio* wore black and yellow war paint painted with quick strokes of the fingertips. His hair was greased black and parted in the middle. He wore beaded earrings and a necklace of claws and buffalo teeth. He held a large shield in one hand, elaborately decorated with pictures of black birds, and a lance in his other hand.

The *indio* next to him was older and more average in size, though his body was still very muscular for a man of his age. His face was not painted. He had never seen this man before. Behind them was the terrifying warrior, Esatai—he was sure of that. And he guessed that the white man with the hawk and wolf was the one Paco had spoken of. *Many Wolves.*

I thought this Many Wolves was an enemy of the norteños?

"Connelly, introduce us. Use your Spanish," said Captain Mac.

Malone looked at the two *indios* and spoke. "This is Captain James McCord," he said, pointing to his right, "and the *hombre* next to him is Possum Jack Akers. I am Ramon Connelly."

The younger *indio* spoke back to him in almost perfect Spanish. "You are the Green-Eyed Coyote," he said, "and you," he turned to Captain Mac, "are Lead Fingers." To Possum Jack he added, "And you are Big Yack. These are your Noomah names. This is what we will call you."

Ramon translated the names for Captain Mac and Possum Jack.

"The Green-Eyed Coyote," Captain Mac repeated, and chuckled to himself. "You are more famous, Connelly, than I would have expected."

"I am Cold Raven of the Nokoni," said the *indio*, almost stomping on Captain Mac's words, "and this is Malone of the Nokoni. The man behind me is *mi hermano* Esatai, and the white-skinned man is Many Wolves."

Malone? That was my uncle's name. A strange name for a norteño.

Cold Raven continued to speak. His tone was serious. "What peace do you offer us?"

"Translate my words, Connelly, exactly as I say them," said Captain Mac.

Ramon nodded.

"Cold Raven, it is my hope that you will listen to my words of peace. The rivers run red with the blood of the *indio* and the white man. We must stop our fighting so that the rivers will be clean again for our *niños* to drink. It is the desire of our leader from the south that we share the land with the *indios* from the north. We humbly ask that the lands that lie between the Rio Colorado and Rio Brazos be safe for the white man's villages. The lands west of the Rio Colorado and east of the Rio Brazos are safe for the *indio's* villages, as well as the lands north of the Rio Red. We will share this great land with you and there will be peace and prosperity for all the people of Tejas. If your people continue to live on the prairies between the Brazos and Colorado, we will force them to leave, killing any and all who oppose us. This is my offer of peace, but it can be war if that is what you choose."

Ramon translated as Captain Mac spoke, and Cold Raven, in turn, loudly translated the words into his native language for his companions. But throughout it all, Cold Raven stared directly into the eyes of Captain Mac; he did not alter his gaze until he was finished.

Esatai grew angry and shouted something that Ramon and the white men didn't understand.

Cold Raven then turned to Malone and spoke with him in a much calmer voice, almost a whisper. The two of them conversed for several moments, and then Cold Raven turned to face Captain Mac once more.

"You ask my *niños* not to drink from the Brazos… not to drink from the Colorado… when my *padre* and his *padre* before him drank from these *rios*. You ask us to drink only from the Rio Red and let the white *niños* take our *rios* from us. I would rather drink blood from the Brazos, white man's blood and *indio* blood, than give it to the white man. We do not want your peace."

Ramon translated for Captain Mac. The captain gave no outward reaction, remaining stoic and composed. When Ramon was finished the captain said simply, "Then it will be war. Tell him these words."

Ramon spoke in Spanish. "You have chosen war, Cold Raven. So be it. I will tell this to our white *padre* in the south. It is sad that *hombres* must die when there is plenty of land for all our villages. Plenty of *agua* to drink and buffalo to share. We will leave you now, but know that we will be watching and waiting like a coiled snake in the prairie grass for the right moment to strike. If you change your mind, bring me a peace flag and we will talk again."

Ramon looked again at his enemies. There was something familiar about the white-skinned Many Wolves, but he didn't know why. The green eyes that looked back at him could have been his own. *Why does he fight with the indios?* And then he looked at the *indio* named Malone. *Why does he have a white man's name? Why does he have my uncle's name?*

Captain Mac commanded his horse to a gallop and rode away from the *indio* leaders. Ramon and Possum Jack followed his lead, sprayed by the grass and dust from Captain Mac's mount. They rode fast and hard back to the rest of the captain's men.

"They have chosen war," said Captain Mac. "We must make our preparations."

The Sun and the Moon

"Wait, Noche," said Many Wolves. Noche was standing next to him, ears raised high. Many Wolves motioned for Flecha to fly to the nearest of the two trees, and the bird obeyed.

Many Wolves and Esatai then rode up next to Cold Raven and Malone, and the four of them watched the three white leaders ride away. Soon the Mare-Can leaders, and the men that rode with them, had disappeared into the vast prairie landscape. Many Wolves breathed a sigh of relief that no blood had been shed. His heart had been racing like a running bird since he had first laid eyes on the Mare-Cans, and now the bird in his chest needed rest.

"What did he say?" asked Many Wolves.

"He wanted our people to give our finest buffalo lands to the white man and move our villages to the north," said Cold Raven, still looking out at the grassland. His voice grew progressively angrier as he spoke. "I did not accept his terms. The white man thinks he can take our land just because his father in the south gives it to him. This leader in the south is not my leader, and this land is not their land. We will fight them."

"When will we fight them?" said Esatai.

"I do not know, my brother."

"We must keep Crooked Eagle's village safe until the Kiowa and Wichita come," said Malone. "Then we will gather a war party to find Lead Fingers. It would be wise to leave enough warriors to protect the village."

"*Haa*. We will divide our men. It is the only way," said Cold Raven in agreement.

"If I see this Lead Fingers again, I will kill him and hang his scalp on my lance for all to see," said Esatai with a bold tongue.

"It won't be easy, Esatai," said Malone. "It's not like killing *mexicanos* with their slow guns or Tonkawa who cannot shoot a bow from a horse. These *taiboos* are like rattlesnakes. They will kill you if you get too close."

"It is my wish too, my brother, to cure our lands of this disease," said Cold Raven, looking into his brother's eyes. "And when Lead Fingers is dead, the white man's villages between the Brazos and Colorado will be like open sores for us to poke our lances at. We will burn their *taiboo* lodges and bury the ashes deep in the earth, to bring new life to our buffalo lands. The Great Spirit will see this and know that this is the land of the Nokoni and the Penateka, and not the white man."

"It is a dream that we all share," added Malone.

"Finding Lead Fingers may not be so easy," said Cold Raven, his tone suddenly less confident. "His horses can match ours step for step, and he knows many of the same marks on the land. He does not lose himself in the vast prairie like the *taiboos* before him. His Navoonah tracker will surely lead him to the best hiding places. It was this Navoonah tracker that helped them find my village last fall."

"Lead Fingers will not be hard to find," said Malone, drawing their attention without raising his voice. "The sun will light his path for the eyes of the hawk, and the moon for the eyes of the wolf." He looked at Many Wolves and smiled.

"What does this mean?" asked Esatai, confused.

Cold Raven nodded, showing that he understood Malone's words. "It means that Many Wolves will find Lead Fingers for us, my brother."

An Odd Collection

When the men arrived back at the river camp, Ramon dismounted and let Cavador drink. Cornelius was right behind him, and Ernesto was already at the camp, having been ordered by the captain to stay behind.

"*Que pasó?*" asked Ernesto, rising to his feet.

Ramon spoke in Spanish when he was with Ernesto, because Ernesto didn't understand English at all. And Cornelius could understand Spanish if Ramon spoke it slowly.

"We met with four *indio* leaders," said Ramon, removing his shoulder scabbard.

"Crooked Eagle?"

"No, he wasn't there. There were three *norteños* and one *gringo*."

"A *gringo?*"

"*Sí.* His name was Many Wolves."

"That isn't a *gringo* name."

"From what I know, his parents were killed by *norteños*, but he was raised by Lipanos."

Cornelius examined the bandage on Ernesto's arm while the other two spoke. It was unusual for Cornelius to be silent, but Ramon had already had this conversation with him on the ride back.

"You would think he would hate *norteños*," said Ernesto.

"*Sí.* I think there was a time in his life when he did. He once killed two *norteño* leaders." Ramon was being careful with his words. He had held some information back from Cornelius about Many Wolves, and he

319

planned to do the same with Ernesto. There were still many unanswered questions in his mind as well.

"He must be a great fighter." Ernesto winced when Cornelius touched him in a sensitive spot.

Ramon knew that Many Wolves's wolf was a big part of that, but he chose not to say anything about it. "*Sí*. That is probably why he is one of their leaders."

"Who were the others? The *norteños*?" Ernesto seemed genuinely interested in learning everything about the meeting.

"One of them was named Malone. He was older than the other *indios*."

"Malone. A *gringo* name." Ernesto laughed. "A *gringo* with an *indio* name and an *indio* with a *gringo* name. Very strange, *mi amigo*."

Ramon did not mention that Malone was his uncle's name, nor had he mentioned it to Cornelius. He wanted to know more himself before revealing this to them. It was family business, and he wanted to keep it private.

"*Sí*, it is, Ernesto. The other two *norteños* were *hermanos*, and they were much younger, probably about as old as you. Their names were Cold Raven and Esatai. I believe Cold Raven is their leader. He did most of the talking. I've never heard an *indio* speak Spanish so well in all my life. Even the Lipanos in Bexar do not speak it as well."

Ernesto looked at him wide-eyed, but didn't ask a question this time.

Ramon continued. "I have seen them before, these two *hermanos*, down south in San Antonio. Esatai is a fierce fighter. He rides fast and shoots arrows like they are blasted from a *pistole*. He has no fear."

Cornelius finally spoke up, seemingly satisfied with Ernesto's field dressing. "It's an odd collection of leaders, Mr. Connelly. I would never have imagined their leaders would be so young—and one of them a white man. Perhaps in their culture, it is fighting skill that determines a war leader, rather than age and experience. I expect this isn't true of other tribes."

"It sounds like Crooked Eagle is the leader of their village," said Ramon in English, "but perhaps he is too old to fight."

"It is a hard life out here on the plains," said Cornelius, looking around.

"As the captain said, it will suck the life out of you. I would postulate that Crooked Eagle wasn't with them not because he cannot fight, but because they don't want to lose the venerable leader of their village."

"That would make sense too."

"They are probably reporting back to him as we speak," added Cornelius.

"So, *que pasó* in the meeting? What did they say?" asked Ernesto.

Ramon drank some water from his canteen. All this talk was making his mouth even drier. "The *capitán* offered them a peace agreement. He was very specific with his terms." He wiped his mouth with his bandanna.

"And what did they say?"

"They said no. They said there will be war."

Ernesto's bright eyes were captured by fear.

Old Friend, New Enemy

Many Wolves was sitting at his fire pit when Malone arrived on his horse.

"Are you making more arrows?" Malone asked as he dismounted.

"No. I am finishing the bear claw necklace for Taimah," said Many Wolves. All he had left to do was string the beads and claws on the sinew, though he was hoping to get some different beads from the village.

"I traded for more turkey feathers for our arrows," said Malone, bending down to show him the feathers in his hand. "Runs With Buffalo had brought many feathers with him."

"What did you trade him?"

"I had some extra arrow points," said Malone. "And he liked that weasel fur hat I made. He thought it would be good for catching women!"

The two men laughed.

"That hat will make the women laugh, but I'm not sure it will bring them to his sleeping robe," said Many Wolves.

"He thinks it's a magic hat that will tickle the hearts of women." Malone grabbed his bag of arrow-making supplies and sat down next to Many Wolves. He had several arrows that looked like they just needed tail feathers.

Many Wolves was sorting through the beads that he had, picking out the ones he thought Taimah would like the best. None of them were beads she hadn't seen before. "Can I find some beads in the village that Taimah has never seen?"

Malone nodded. "*Haa*. You will need to have something to trade though. I can show you the woman who has the best beads."

"What will this woman want in a trade?"

"She loves children. You can trade her something a child would like."

I can't make toys, Many Wolves thought to himself, *or children's clothes.* That was women's work. Nina could make something if she were here. *What would a child like that I could make?*

"I have an idea," said Malone with a glimmer in his eye. "You can make something that is unique to you. What if you make a fist-perch? I have some rabbit hides you can use."

"They will be too big for a child's hand." And Many Wolves didn't understand why a child would want a fist-perch.

"You can make a smaller one, to fit a child's hand."

"They don't have birds."

"I'm sure they can find an imaginary bird." Malone was looking more and more pleased with his idea. "Imagine the smile on a boy's face when he shows his imaginary eagle to his friend, sitting on the fist-perch made from the hands of the great bird-master Many Wolves!"

"You are brilliant, my friend," said Many Wolves, returning Malone's smile. His friend was getting wiser, and more clever, with age, Many Wolves thought. "If you can get me a rabbit hide, I'll get started on it right now. I can finish this necklace another time."

"I'll be right back," said Malone, playfully running his hands through Many Wolves's hair before walking away.

* * *

Many Wolves spent the rest of the afternoon making three fist-perches that would fit a child's hand. After cleaning the rabbit hide, he used his steel knife to cut it into three pieces, and sewed each piece into a fist-perch using deer sinew. It was restful—thinking about his work took his mind off the situation with the Mare-Cans. Cold Raven had asked him to fly his bird just before dusk to try to find where the Mare-Cans' camp was, and he was clearing his mind for this journey.

When the shadows grew, Many Wolves knew it was time to make the mind-journey tea. He had finished two of the fist-perches. Malone had been with him the whole time, working on arrows.

"Two of these are finished, but I need to fly Flecha to try to find Lead Fingers' camp," he said to Malone.

"I can trade them for you while you are on your journey," offered Malone.

"No—I want to see what she has. Wait for me to return. Now I need to start the tea." Many Wolves poured some water into his drinking-shell and placed it on the hot rocks next to the low-burning flames. He walked into his lodge, found his medicine bag, and withdrew some pieces of peyote and white lion's paw flower. *This should be enough.*

When the water was hot, but not yet boiling, Many Wolves crumbled the peyote and flower into the drinking-shell. *I should fly Flecha to Nina's camp too, but it is too far from here.*

"What should I look for if I find their camp?" he asked Malone.

"Finding the camp will be enough. It shouldn't be far from where we last saw them. A rough count of men, horses, and weapons would also be useful to Cold Raven."

Many Wolves nodded. Once the water had boiled and cooled, he called Flecha to his fist-perch, closed his eyes, and drank down the mixture quickly. Almost instantly, he saw the familiar rainbow of colors and felt the warmth of the medicine in his head. His stomach no longer hurt when he drank the mixture, and he was thankful for that.

The eyes in his mind opened with Flecha's vision. The hawk looked at Malone, who smiled back at him, as if knowing that the mind-journey had begun.

"Be safe, my friend," said Malone.

Flecha lifted himself into the sky on rapidly beating wings, then circled around the camp, letting the currents of air lift him higher and higher. Many Wolves could see the whole of the village now, like one big picture: the countless horses, the smattering of lodges, the circling scavenger birds, the winding Rio Brazos. There was a separate tipi area that he guessed was for Cold Raven's people. He saw several men on horses patrolling the outskirts of the village and horse herd. *Go north, Flecha.*

The swift bird broke out of his spiraling pattern and started gliding downward, heading north, with sporadic wing beats controlling his speed. The rush of air was exhilarating and refreshing. Flecha scoured the rolling prairie below for signs of movement. *Find the two trees, Flecha.*

The keen-eyed bird spotted a prairie dog village that Many Wolves remembered from his earlier journey on horseback. *This is the right direction. Keep going.*

They flew over a herd of antelope grazing peacefully. It hadn't been there earlier. *There are the trees ahead, Flecha. Fly to the trees.* The hawk flew to the trees and then circled them a few times, gaining more and more height. *Go east, Flecha. Away from the setting sun.* Flecha shifted his wings and tail feathers and glided eastward. *I have to find smoke or scavenger birds or any other signs of a camp.*

Flecha's head shifted and froze, staring at something.

Men on horses. Go to them, Flecha. It was two men on horses walking through the tall plains grass; one wore a black hat and the other a red bandanna on his head. One of the horses had some kind of an animal carcass tied to it. *Probably an antelope from that herd.*

As Flecha flew closer, Many Wolves recognized the man with the black hat. *The green-eyed man with the dark skin—the Green-Eyed Coyote.* Cold Raven had said that the Green-Eyed Coyote was a brave warrior from the lands to the south.

The man with the bandanna looked like a Lipan, but Many Wolves wasn't sure. He was familiar too—had he been at their earlier meeting? Many Wolves hadn't been able to see most of Lead Fingers' men up close when they met. He had thought the other men riding with Lead Fingers were white-skinned or mexicanos, but he wasn't sure. Crooked Eagle had said that Navoonah were riding with the Mare-Cans, as their trackers.

Flecha was close now. Close enough to hear them talking, but Many Wolves couldn't understand the words. Then the Lipan smiled and laughed. It was the laugh that uncovered Many Wolves's memory. It had been many seasons since he had heard that laugh, but he knew it. This was the man whose village had helped him fight Laughing Crow's men. This was a man who was his old friend, but was now his new enemy.

The Lipan was Little Sky.

Lead Fingers' Camp

Flecha followed Little Sky and the Green-Eyed Coyote for a short time, but Many Wolves was not able to understand any of their words. He didn't want his hawk to linger for too long, else the two men might grow suspicious of this strange bird watching them.

Flecha, fly in the direction they are walking. It will lead us to their camp.

The bird pulled out of its glide and pumped its wings rapidly, flying away from the two men. Endless stretches of rolling grass hills blurred past them, with very few rocks or trees to mark the land. *It would be easy to get lost here.* It made Many Wolves understand why the horse was so valuable to the Northerners. It was hard to imagine a life here without horses to take them from one water source to the next, and to carry supplies.

At last, Many Wolves spotted trees ahead. Where there were trees, there was usually a river—and perhaps men seeking the shade and water.

Many Wolves's suspicions were confirmed when he saw the scavenger birds and smoke from fire pits. Flecha joined the flock of circling birds above the camp, most of which were buzzards. There were many horses and men here, but no tipis or lodges of any kind. *No tipi poles and covers to burden their travel.* Many Wolves guessed that there were about thirty men and perhaps a few more than thirty horses. Some of the men were eating and talking around the fire pits, leaning back against the riding pads of their horses. Others were resting under trees, some sleeping, some visiting with other men.

Flecha, land in one of those trees there and rest your wings.

It was easier for Many Wolves to see greater detail without the blurred movement of flight. He listened to the men talk, but couldn't understand their words. Some of them spoke the Spanish words, while others spoke a language that was completely unknown to him. It was so strange, it was almost funny to him. *How can men understand this?*

Most of the men were white-skinned with hairy faces, though there were a few black-haired mexicanos with their unmistakable head coverings. There were no other Lipans here, or other red-skinned plains people, that Many Wolves could see. All of the men carried weapons with them. Most had one *pistole*—the Spanish word he had learned to describe them—around their belts, and some had two. He saw knives strapped to their belts or leg sheaths as well. None of them carried long guns, but many were tied to riding pads or leaning up against trees. A couple of the men were fixing or cleaning their weapons.

He looked around the camp and spotted Lead Fingers and Big Yack talking together under a cottonwood tree. Big Yack, a large man—a mountain next to Lead Fingers—was drinking something from a cup, while Lead Fingers was smoking a short pipe. Lead Fingers' *pistoles* were the shiniest. The sun reflected off them brightly when he turned his body a certain way.

Then one of the men in camp—an older-looking man with some gray hair—began looking up at Flecha and pointing. Another man was with him, and they were talking in the funny Mare-Can language, but they both kept looking up at Flecha. *Maybe this man studies birds like I do*, thought Many Wolves. Many Wolves knew that wolf hawks were not native to lands this far north—because of the cold climates, he assumed—and these men might know this too. It was making Many Wolves feel uncomfortable.

Flecha, we should leave. Fly back west toward the falling sun and you will find me.

Many Wolves opened his eyes and found himself at his lodge in Crooked Eagle's village. Malone was sitting across the fire pit from him, laughing.

"Why are you laughing?"

"Because when you mind-journey your eyes twitch and quiver and you move your arms around like some strange dance. I wish you could see yourself. You would laugh too!"

"I hope no one else saw me."

"No, we were alone the whole time," said Malone with a grin. "Did you find their camp?"

"*Haa*. It's east at the next river, hidden in the trees."

"I knew you could do it!" Malone said excitedly, clapping his hands. "Did you get a good count of their men and weapons?"

"*Haa*."

"You should share this with Cold Raven right away. We can do your bead trade after that."

"Malone, one of the men was familiar to me."

"Who was that?"

"A Lipan named Little Sky. He was from Big Sky's village and was the son of the leader. They were the ones who fought the war against Laughing Crow's men when he was on his path of vengeance for his son's death. Back then, Little Sky was my friend."

"Are you sure it was him? Many seasons have passed since you last saw him."

"I am sure. A man's laugh does not change so easily, and he looked very much the same, just a little older."

"Now he is your enemy. If he is their tracker, then we need to kill him almost as much as we need to kill Lead Fingers."

"But Lead Fingers is their leader."

"*Haa*, but without a tracker in our home lands, they will be as blind as hoot owls in the daylight."

A Back Wind

Many Wolves and Malone arrived at Cold Raven's lodge just before dusk. Cold Raven was alone and welcomed them inside to visit.

"Many Wolves found their camp," Malone said, with a note of pride in his voice.

"Tell me what you found," said Cold Raven, looking at Many Wolves.

"It's farther east from the place where we met them, next to a river. I counted around thirty men and forty horses. Almost every man had a *pistole* strapped to his waist; some, like the Green-Eyed Coyote, Big Yack, and Lead Fingers, had two. Most of them had long, steel knives. I don't know if every man had a long gun or not, but there were a lot of them lying around the camp. They didn't have any tipis or very many supplies."

"They travel light. That is wise. No pole-drags to slow them down," said Cold Raven. "You say their camp is next to a river?"

"*Haa.*"

"Probably the River of Threes. It is named that because one great river splits into three."

"They will be protected with the river at their back," said Malone.

Cold Raven nodded.

Many Wolves continued, "They had one Lipan with them. Malone believes he is their tracker. His name is Little Sky, and he was my friend long ago."

Cold Raven took several moments to think before speaking. "Crooked Eagle said they would have Navoonah trackers. Most *taiboos* lose their way in our lands. If the cold north winds don't kill them, then starvation or thirst will. My war parties have found *taiboos* like this. Men lost and barely alive, begging for us to take their lives. Not this Lead Fingers. He has the eyes of the Navoonah to lead him."

"If we kill this Little Sky or kill Lead Fingers, this war is over. And even if it doesn't end our war, we will have gained a great advantage," said Malone.

There was silence between the three of them. Then Cold Raven spoke. "We should wait for the Kiowa to arrive before we attempt any attack. I don't want to leave this village unguarded. If you could get Little Sky or Lead Fingers in the range of Esatai's arrow, then I know he could kill him. Did Lead Fingers' camp have any dogs?"

"I didn't see any."

"Their horses are their protectors," said Malone. "Dogs need to be killed silently, but horses just need to be calmed. I don't know if Esatai could get past their horses. It would be risky. I would hate to lose our greatest warrior because of one startled horse."

"Lead Fingers is smart. He probably has men watching the horses. He knows if he loses them, he loses this war," said Cold Raven.

"Many Wolves can find out who guards their camp at night." Malone looked at Many Wolves and smiled.

"Does he have an owl that flies with him that I haven't seen yet?" said Cold Raven, cracking a rare smile.

"No, but he has a wolf."

"Can your wolf do this?" asked Cold Raven with a hopeful tone.

"I don't know," said Many Wolves. "I've never taken a wolf into a big camp like this. The horses would panic if they smelled Noche. It would be too risky."

"Can you take Noche in and see how close he could get?" asked Malone. "Just knowing who is guarding their horses would be useful to us."

"I could try it, but I would need to be much closer to their camp. It's too far for Noche to run from here. If you want to kill Little Sky, you should wait until he leaves the camp. I saw him hunting with the Green-Eyed Coyote away from the camp."

"To kill those two would put the wind at our back in this war," said Cold Raven. "Many Wolves, can you do the mind-journey at Two-Tree Valley where we met Lead Fingers?"

"*Haa.*"

"Good." Cold Raven turned to Malone. "Take Many Wolves and Esatai to this place tonight. The moonlight will guide you. When the sun rises, Many Wolves can send out his bird and tell you if those two are alone. Esatai and Many Wolves will help you kill the Green-Eyed Coyote and the Navoonah. I want their scalps hanging in our village before the day is done tomorrow."

Malone nodded.

"It will leave the rest of my men to protect the village," said Cold Raven, sounding satisfied with his idea.

It seemed like a good plan to Many Wolves, but he wasn't sure how Flecha would travel in the darkness. It was her sleep time.

"Cold Raven, can we leave when there is enough light for my hawk's eyes? I don't think he will fly with me at night."

"It might be too late to catch them on the morning hunt. You might have to wait for them later when the sun falls," said Cold Raven.

"We will ride when Many Wolves is ready," said Malone. "We need the eyes of his bird."

The Splintered Bead Woman

Many Wolves and Malone walked back toward the center of Crooked Eagle's village with darkness preying on their shadows. The people of the village seemed happier than when they had first arrived, though a few women were still mourning. Perhaps the people sensed that they were in less danger now, with Cold Raven's warriors here. It seemed more like the village Many Wolves remembered from when Malone first brought him here after Thorn Bird's torture.

Many Wolves was excited about visiting the woman with the beads to see what different kinds she had. He had made a bear claw necklace before for Ten Arrows, but he wanted this necklace to not only show Taimah's bravery, but also her beauty. It was a much different kind of challenge for him to make a necklace for a girl than for a man.

"Let me warn you, Many Wolves. Kolokai is not the friendliest woman in the village. She loves children, but she has outlived all her friends and doesn't seem interested in making any new ones. Most days, she walks around the village with a splinter in her moccasin. So try not to kindle her temper."

"I'll let you do most of the talking."

"That would be wise," said Malone, smiling.

"It sounds like we will need to show her the fist-perches at just the right time. It will be like a male prairie chicken trying to mate. If he shows the female his mating feathers at the wrong time, she will chase him away."

Malone laughed. "*Haa.* You have earned your wisdom from the wild things, my friend."

They walked deeper into the village, past the children chasing each other and women tanning hides or tending to fire pits. *Many of the men must be out guarding the horses,* Many Wolves thought.

"Here is her lodge," said Malone quietly.

An old woman was hunkered next to a meager fire with a blanket wrapped around her as they approached.

"Hello, Kolakai. My name is Malone, and this is Many Wolves."

She glanced up at them briefly and then looked back down. "What do you want?" Her voice was old and coarse. Her lips smacked together when she wasn't talking, and her mouth was shriveled up; perhaps she was missing most of her teeth. "You're not from this village. Who let you in here?" she snapped.

"We are Crooked Eagle's guests," said Malone in a soft voice.

"That old man lets anybody in here," she said, then smacked her lips again. "He doesn't know if it's night or day half the time. All these strangers..." Kolakai moaned and shook her head. "They'll kill us all. You'll see." Then she repeated her question as if she'd forgotten she'd asked it: "So, what do you want?"

"We want to look at your beads," said Many Wolves, then he realized he should have let Malone talk.

"Oh, you do," she said, then shot a question back at him. "And who are you?"

"I'm Many Wolves."

"Oh, I know you. You're that crazy man who talks to animals. The children talk about you all the time. They seem to like you."

"*Haa,* I'm the crazy man who talks to animals," said Many Wolves with a sense of humor, hoping she would like him because the children did.

"I'm glad we can agree on something here," said Kolakai. She hadn't moved anything but her mouth since they arrived. "Crazy Animal Man, you can go look at the beads in my lodge. You can start the fire pit in there if you need more light. Use one of these sticks from my fire."

Many Wolves grabbed a stick and stuck it in her fire pit to light it.

Kolakai raised her gnarled hand and pointed at Malone. "You stay out here. The children don't know you. What was your name again?"

"Malone."

"Oh, that's right. What kind of name is that anyway?"

"It's a *taiboo* name," said Malone.

"Dearest Earth Mother, why would anyone have a name like that?"

Many Wolves entered the old woman's lodge and started the fire, but he could still hear their conversation.

"The white man was a brave warrior, so I took his name," said Malone.

Many Wolves could tell that Malone was treading carefully around her temper.

"That's the craziest thing I ever heard," said the old woman.

Many Wolves couldn't help but smile to himself.

With the fire lit, Many Wolves found three cups filled with beads. One cup had only round beads, each of a single color: red, black, yellow, and metal. Another cup had long-shaped beads, each again of a single color, and the last cup had long-shaped beads that had more than one color on them. He looked at the mixed-color beads first, selecting several black ones that were painted with red or yellow.

"What are these long beads made of?" asked Many Wolves, looking out toward Kolakai.

"Mostly bone. Some are made from horns. Some from stones. I painted them all myself. The only ones I didn't make are the round metal beads. Those are from *taiboo* traders."

Many Wolves selected several long beads that he liked and also several round ones, two of each color. He also picked out two metal beads to add to the necklace. Satisfied, he walked back outside and showed them to Kolakai.

She looked over the beads very carefully, talking to herself, then looked up at Many Wolves. "What do you have to trade?"

Many Wolves took the two small fist-perches out of his hunting bag and showed them to her.

"What are they?" she squawked.

"They are fist-perches. I use them to train my hawks. I made them to fit a child's hand."

"How do you use them?"

Many Wolves pulled out his own fist-perch, which he had brought to demonstrate, and slid it on his hand. "My hawk perches on this, and it protects my hand from its claws."

"I have no use for these!"

"I thought you might want to give them to children."

Kolakai was quiet for several moments in thought. Then suddenly she yelled, "Coyote Foot! Come here!"

Within moments, a boy of around six winters ran over to her. "*Haa*, Kolakai."

"Do you know who this crazy animal man is?" she said, pointing to Many Wolves.

"*Haa*, Kolakai. It's Many Wolves. All the children know who he is." Coyote Foot's innocent eyes bulged from excitement.

She grabbed one of the small fist-perches from Many Wolves and handed it to the boy. "You know what this is?"

"*Haa.* He wears it on his hand and his hawk sits on it."

"Put it on!" the old woman barked, growing impatient.

The boy put the fist-perch on his left hand, seemingly not shaken by her shouting. His eyes lit up with excitement, and a huge smile ran from one side of his face to the other.

For the first time, the old woman's gnarled mouth curled into a smile, and she cackled. Many Wolves looked at Malone, and his friend grinned back a him.

"You have a trade, Crazy Animal Man," Kolakai said at last, still cackling.

Little Wolf

"I'm uneasy doing a mind-journey with Esatai here. I should have told you this earlier," said Many Wolves, talking to Malone in a low voice so Esatai could not hear. The big Northerner was grooming his horse a short distance away.

The three of them had arrived mid-morning at the two trees where they had met the Mare-Cans. Many Wolves was preparing his mind for the journey and feeding Flecha some lean buffalo meat from his fist-perch. The hawk hadn't eaten anything this day until now, and it needed some rest before its long flight ahead. Many Wolves was careful not to overfeed the bird, because he knew that with too much food, Flecha would be tempted to spend the rest of the day in the trees.

"Why are you worried? I will be here with you until your journey is over," said Malone, trying to reassure him.

"I kept my mind-journeys a secret from Laughing Crow and Thorn Bird, and now I am sharing it with Esatai. I'd prefer to keep it a secret from him." Many Wolves could still vividly recall Laughing Crow's questions. Over and over he had shouted, "What is this magic? Tell me how to do this magic!" It was this secret that had brought Many Wolves satisfaction and comfort in those desperate moments. He hated surrendering this knowledge to Esatai, whom he still considered his bitter enemy.

"You're not sharing what's in the medicine," said Malone.

Malone was right, but Many Wolves wanted it *all* to be his secret—a secret he only shared with close friends and family, not with strangers he did not trust.

"I will have Esatai scout the area when you start your tea-drinking ritual, if that will bring some peace to your mind," said Malone. "Esatai is not one to stay still for very long anyhow." Malone laughed.

"That would be better. *Ura*, my friend," said Many Wolves, releasing Flecha to the tree after a brief meal. *Get some rest, Flecha.*

Esatai mounted and rode over to Malone and Many Wolves. "What do we do now?"

"I am letting my hawk rest before his journey," said Many Wolves.

"You will be here while the bird flies?" Esatai looked at Many Wolves, a confused look on his face.

"*Haa.*"

Esatai nodded, but still looked a little perplexed.

"Many Wolves and I will stay here while you scout the area," said Malone. "The hawk will fly east looking for any signs of Lead Fingers' men. You can scout the area south of us. That will cover much of the ground between the *taiboo's* camp and Crooked Eagle's village."

"What if the bird finds them?" asked Esatai, shifting his horse to get a better look at Malone.

"I will signal you with smoke from this fire," said Malone, pointing to the fire pit beside him. "Keep your eyes open."

"Or I will send the hawk to find you," added Many Wolves. "If you see him, he will show you the way."

Esatai nodded. "I will start my scouting now."

"You don't need to rest anymore?" asked Many Wolves.

"No. Rest is for the weak," said Esatai, slinging his quiver over his shoulder. He slid his shield onto his left arm, rode over to the tree where his lance was resting, and grabbed it as well. Then he turned his horse around and rode south.

"Your plan worked well, my friend," said Many Wolves, smiling at Malone.

"What plan?"

"Your plan to lure Esatai away from our camp."

Malone grinned with satisfaction. "Esatai is like a lone wolf. His mind does not rest. He needs to wander. His name means 'little wolf,' and he has the wandering wolf spirit. It wasn't much of a trick on my part to get him to scout for us."

Many Wolves and Malone sat around the small fire that Malone had built. They enjoyed some jerked rabbit meat together. Each man had his own supply, because Many Wolves liked his salted and Malone did not. Many Wolves ate only one piece, because he wanted to keep his mind sharp and his stomach empty, even though the peyote no longer made him vomit like it once did when he was younger.

After he felt Flecha had had enough rest, Many Wolves prepared his mind-journey medicine and set it by the fire to boil. He called Flecha over to his fist-perch. Of his three birds, Flecha reminded him most of Chiquito, his most cherished bird companion. They were both small, very smart, and well mannered. Their appearances were similar also, but Flecha had more red on his shoulders. Many Wolves stroked Flecha's dark brown chest feathers, and the bird playfully nipped at his finger with its yellow beak. Many Wolves believed that Chiquito's spirit had found its way back to this world and rested in Flecha, which explained their similarities. Though Many Wolves had enjoyed his mind-journeys most with Chiquito, Flecha was a very close second.

Many Wolves lifted his drinking-shell and drank the mind-journey medicine. Once again, he was seeing through the bird's eyes. *Head east, Flecha, toward the river.*

The hawk lifted itself into the deep blue sky, the midday sun presssing down on his back. Below was the same, familiar prairie land that he had traveled through the previous day, so his mind began to stray. Mind-journeys had become an escape for him, and Many Wolves felt that as long as he was high in the sky, the problems of the world couldn't touch him. Part of him wished he could just keep flying and leave this war far behind him. He was scared that soon the day would come when blood would be shed. He had already felt the pain of two wars, and he didn't want to feel that pain again. Both times he was lucky to have survived. He worried that his winter supply of luck had been used up, and that this next war would leave him cold, hungry, and dying. It was a dark thought that had nagged at him ever since he had left his home in the wilderness.

As his thoughts continued to roam, he watched the rolling prairie with a predator's eyes. With so much vast emptiness, it would be easy to find men on horses. And Flecha's eyes covered such a large area; it would take a horse half a day to ride from the end of her visual range to the other. The Northerners could not possibly find a better scout, Many Wolves thought to himself.

Flecha approached the River of Threes, as Cold Raven called it, without seeing any signs of men or horses. They spotted the same antelope herd as the previous day, but that was all. There was no sign of Little Sky or the Green-Eyed Coyote this time.

Many Wolves thought again of Little Sky. He hated having to hunt a man who had once been his friend. If he were to talk to Little Sky now, he knew in his heart they would still be friends. He pictured himself sitting with Little Sky on a tall mesa protected from the ugly war beneath them. But it was just a fleeting daydream—then his mind returned to his task.

The bird flew closer to the Mare-Cans' camp, and he heard the popping sounds of their weapons. Closer still and he could see the smoke from their *pistoles* and men riding on horses just outside their fire pits.

Rest in a tree beyond the camp, Flecha. Stay hidden.

The bird landed in a tree overlooking the camp, but a different tree than the previous day.

Many Wolves watched the men with heightened curiosity. About six men on horses took turns riding at a log that had several wooden slabs on it. With their *pistoles*, they tried to hit one of the wooden targets as they rode full speed on their horses. When a target was hit, it made a loud splintering sound and fell over. Once all the targets were knocked down, the riders would pause, and one of the other men would set them up again on the log. Many Wolves spotted Big Yack and Lead Fingers watching them. Big Yack was shouting at the men, but Lead Fingers said nothing.

Flecha looked around the camp, and Many Wolves spotted Little Sky sitting in the shade. He looked all over for the Green-Eyed Coyote, but couldn't find him. *Is he out hunting? Did I miss him, or is he hunting east of the river?*

Then he saw the older man who had been looking at Flecha yesterday—and once again, his eyes were fixed on the hawk. The old man walked over to the two leaders and pointed straight at Flecha. Lead Fingers yelled something, and one of his men threw a long gun to him. Lead Fingers raised the long gun and pointed it at him.

Flecha, up!

The long gun popped, but Flecha was already in the air. *Fly back to me, Flecha!* Flecha was fine—the *bala* had missed—and the little bird's wings pumped hard, sensing the urgency. When Flecha had flown a safe distance, he commanded the bird to turn around, but he didn't see any of them following. *Fly back to me!*

Flecha headed westward, the danger behind them. Many Wolves was relieved. *We can't go back there again, unless we are more careful.*

Suddenly he heard a long gun popping from ahead of him. *Another long gun?* It could not possibly be the same one. *Maybe it's the Green-Eyed Coyote. Flecha, fly to it! We have to be careful.* The bird steered southward.

Flecha's eyes quickly spotted two men shrouded by a cloud of smoke from their long guns. They were not mounted, but each held a horse by the lead. Another rider was approaching them rapidly. *Esatai.*

Flecha pumped his wings hard to get closer. The two Mare-Cans were stopped, loading their long guns onto their horses. Neither of them looked like the Green-Eyed Coyote. They mounted quickly and rode toward the screaming warrior, who was charging at them, weaving and cutting through the prairie grass at full speed. In a heartbeat, Esatai drew his bow and two arrows from his quiver. He whistled one of the arrows at the man who was closer, knocking him off his horse—and before the other man could shoot his *pistole*, Esatai struck him, too, with an arrow in the chest. This second man did not fall, and even managed to fire his *pistole*, but the *bala* did not hit his attacker.

Esatai rode straight at this man and drove his lance through the man's chest. The man fell to the ground screaming. The Nokoni warrior quickly dismounted, drew his knife from his leg sheath, and slit the man's throat. The other *taiboo,* who had been knocked off his horse, stumbled to his feet and tried to run, but Esatai ran him down, threw him to the ground, and drove his knife through the man's neck.

Esatai sliced off the man's scalp, then stood up with his arms raised to the sky, one of them still wearing the shield. Blood dripped down his left arm from the scalp, and down his right arm from the knife. "Ah-Yay!" he screamed to the sky.

Flecha circled around the bloodstained warrior. When Esatai saw the bird, he yelled, "Many Wolves! See how the white man falls at my feet!"

The victorious warrior let out a booming laugh.

Many Wolves's mind flashed back to that fateful moment when Thorn Bird took the life of his friend, Ten Arrows.

The Strange Hawk

Ramon walked back to the rangers' camp. He had found a shady spot along the river and had refreshed himself with a quick nap away from the burning hot sun. When he returned, he found several of the men practicing their riding and shooting. Captain Mac and Possum watched, offering praise to some and corrections to others.

Cornelius spotted him and walked over. "Good day, Mr. Connelly. I hope you were able to acquire a bit of shut-eye in all this ruckus."

"Indeed, Cornelius. I got a bit," said Ramon, yawning.

"Good, good."

From the curious look on his friend's face, Ramon sensed a question, or perhaps a discussion, heading his way, and his notion was quickly confirmed.

"I saw the strangest thing yesterday and again today, Mr. Connelly. A biological oddity, if you will. An ornithological misplacement of sorts," said Cornelius.

"Speak plainly, Cornelius, please, if you wouldn't mind." Ramon wasn't sure if he was awake enough for his friend's scientific vocabulary.

"Well, this species of hawk circled our encampment earlier, and it's uncommon enough to see a large bird of prey as it is…"

"I guess so, Cornelius," interrupted Ramon. "I typically don't pay much attention to birds unless I need them to find *indios*."

"Agreed, they have their uses for scouting human encampments."

Ramon hoped this wasn't leading up to a long-winded diatribe, and he wanted to move it along. "So, tell me about this bird, Cornelius."

"Well, you see, Mr. Connelly, this particular bird was a bay-winged hawk. Have you heard of them?"

"I have not. The only hawk that I know is the red-tailed hawk."

"Ah, yes, a universal bird, the red-tailed hawk, seen all over the world. They are quite hardy and can live in any climate. But you see, Mr. Connelly, the bay-winged hawk is not so universal as the red-tailed hawk, and I do believe they much prefer warmer climates. It wouldn't have surprised me if you had seen a bay-winged hawk in your native Bexar." Cornelius opened a book he had in his hand and showed Ramon a picture of a dark brown hawk with reddish shoulders. "You see, this is the bay-winged hawk. Is it familiar?"

"I think it looks a bit familiar. I remember seeing birds like it on the road back from Saltillo."

"And what kind of environment would you say you saw them in, Mr. Connelly?"

"Well, it was desert, I guess."

"Precisely!" Cornelius's eyes lit up and he smiled broadly. "And do you recall if you saw just one bird or a pair of them?"

"I remember there were more than two of them, like they were a bunch of buzzards, but I think they were hawks. I didn't think much of it at the time."

"Precisely!" Cornelius was almost jumping out of his boots.

"So, why is this important?"

"There are several oddities, Mr. Connelly. First, the bay-winged hawk is a desert species, not prone to live in the prairie. Certainly, it is possible to see one here during the migratory season, but this is not that time of year."

"And the next oddity, as you call it?" Ramon was willing to play along. He was curious where this conversation was leading, though still in a bit of stupor from his sleep.

"The bay-winged hawk is one of the only species of hawks in the world that is gregarious."

"What does that mean?"

"It means they live in packs, like wolves. In fact, they are sometimes called wolf hawks by the native peoples because of this unusual behavior."

Ramon was wondering what the point of this discussion was. "Cornelius, what does this have to do with me?"

"Well, besides the captain, you are probably the most educated man here. I thought you would find it interesting."

"I'm not really one who watches birds or nature, to be honest."

"There was one more oddity."

"What's that?" Ramon was hoping this was the end of it.

"When I spotted the bird, I asked Captain Mac to shoot it down for me. I speculated that a specimen of this sort could be used in a scientific dissertation with my ornithological colleagues to potentially re-establish the range of this species," said Cornelius matter-of-factly. "However—and here's the big finish, Mr. Connelly—when Captain Mac pointed his rifle at the bird, it instantly flew away, without a shot being fired. I've never seen such behavior in all my years of studying wild animals. It was as if the bird knew the rifle was going to kill it. How would a bird know that? You see, that's the biggest oddity! It's as if the bird was human or it was possessed by some kind of magic. Do you see my dilemma?"

"That is strange, Cornelius. I have no explanation for you." But even as he said the words, Ramon felt as if a huge mission bell had rung in his head. *Many Wolves.*

"My God, Cornelius," said Ramon, stunned.

"What's that? You look like you've seen a ghost, Mr. Connelly."

"When we met with the *indios*, a white man was there named Many Wolves. He had a black wolf with him and a hawk sitting on his shield." Ramon reached out his hand. "Let me see that picture again."

"Here you are," said Cornelius, presenting the book to him.

Ramon looked at the picture of the bird in the book. "I'm pretty sure it was the same kind of hawk, though I wasn't so close to it. I have heard stories that this Many Wolves trains hawks to hunt for him. Why was his hawk in our camp?"

"I am not well-versed in the ways of *indio* mysticism, but is it possible that a man can turn himself into a hawk? It's not something I would believe as a student of science, but it certainly would explain what I saw."

"Yes, it would." Ramon recalled something that Paco had said— something about Many Wolves and animal magic. *Could he change himself into a hawk?*

"Cornelius, I think we should bring this up with the captain."

A Spy From Above

A late afternoon breeze tickled the prairie grass around the ranger camp, bringing some relief from the heat. After another day of rigorous training, the men lounged under the shade of the river's trees, talking, sharing stories, and playing card games. It was a relaxing time of day, and Ramon, like the others, looked forward to it. He had ridden hard, off and on, for two straight hours, practicing his shooting and riding under Captain Mac's watchful eye.

On most days, toward the late afternoon, Ramon and Little Sky were sent out to find fresh game for the evening meal—usually prairie antelope. But today the captain had sent out two other men, one of them being Jake Masterson, who was good with a rifle. Ramon was pleased to have a little more free time on his hands, though his mind was preoccupied with wondering what the captain would say about the mysterious hawk.

Ramon approached Cornelius, who was reading a book under a tree. "Now would probably be a good time to talk to the captain."

Cornelius looked up at him and nodded. "I've just been biding my time, Mr. Connelly, reading about the great Greek warrior Achilles. Are you familiar with his story?"

"No, sir. I am not."

"Ah. Well, I will have to tell it to you some time. But now we have our own story to tell."

Cornelius set the book down and stood up, and together they walked the short distance toward where the captain was grooming his horse in the shade. On the way, the scholarly man grabbed another book from the saddle of his horse. It looked like the same book he had shown to Ramon earlier—the one with the hawk picture in it.

"Good afternoon, Captain," said Cornelius.

"Corny, Connelly. What can I do for you?" The captain's voice was muffled by the stem of the pipe in his mouth.

Ramon let Cornelius do the talking, as he was more practiced at this particular skill.

"Captain, do you remember that hawk we saw earlier?"

Captain Mac nodded. "The one that flew away before I could get a good shot at it?"

"Yes, sir. Well, I was telling Mr. Connelly here that this particular species of hawk is not native to prairie habitat, and I thought it strange to see one here." Cornelius flipped through the book to find the right page, then showed the picture of the hawk to the captain. "You see, Captain, it's more of a desert hawk."

The captain glanced at the book for a moment before returning to his task. "That could have been the hawk, I guess."

"In telling this story to Mr. Connelly, he relayed a tidbit of information that I was lacking. Apparently, the man named Many Wolves has a hawk that resembles this one and the one we saw earlier in our camp."

The captain exhaled smoke. "I remember seeing the hawk with him. Get to the point, Corny." The captain continued brushing his horse.

Cornelius shifted his feet nervously, as if in the presence of a judge and courtroom. "Well, do you remember when you aimed at the bird, it promptly flew away before you squeezed your trigger? In all your hunting experiences, have you ever seen quarry behave that way?"

"They usually react to the gunshot, if at all," said the captain, not looking at them.

"Precisely, Captain! The bird acted as if it knew your rifle was a danger to it." Cornelius paused. "Now, bear with me for a moment, Captain. Do you believe that the native peoples possess strange powers with animals?"

The captain stopped his work and looked over at the two men, taking the pipe out of his mouth. "I've heard stories, Corny, but I don't particularly believe them. Are you telling me that this Many Wolves has some kind of strange power with this bird?" The look on his face was one of disbelief.

"Yes, I am, sir. How else would you explain the bird's presence here and its reaction to your rifle?"

"You are more of scientific man than I am, Corny. I may have to rely on your judgment." Captain Mac pointed his pipe at Cornelius as he said this. "Do *you* believe this bird is spying on us?"

"I don't know exactly, sir, but I believe it is a possibility, as irrational as that might sound. I'll have you know I did see this same bird in our camp yesterday as well."

The captain shifted his gaze to Ramon. "What do you think, Connelly?"

"Sir, you saw this Many Wolves. He had a both a wolf and a hawk with him. That is unusual in itself, if you ask me." Ramon held back the information he had heard from Paco about Many Wolves, because he didn't know how much of it he believed himself. "I believe it's a possibility."

"I'll slip you some rope on this, Corny, but frankly I'm too much of a practical man to believe in supernatural nonsense. If it is true, then this Many Wolves knows all about this camp and how many men we have. That's valuable information for his Comanche friends." The captain returned the pipe to his mouth and puffed several times, walked a short distance away, and looked out toward the river.

Ramon sensed that the captain had more to say on the matter, and Cornelius must have felt the same, as they both waited in silence. Ramon thought back to his conversation with Paco. The wise Mexican had said that this Many Wolves had killed great *norteño* warriors—"legendary" warriors. And Ramon had seen the ferocity of Esatai firsthand. *How could Many Wolves have killed a warrior like this? What part did his wolf companion play in these killings?* Training a dog was one thing, but training a wild wolf to kill must be quite another. *And how could he train a hawk to spy for him?* A supernatural power with animals was one plausible explanation.

Ramon's thoughts were interrupted by the captain's voice. "Connelly, I need you to do something for me. It's something I've been thinking about since our meeting with the four Comanche leaders."

"What is it, sir?"

"We need more men. Reinforcements. If they know about this camp and our numbers, then they are most likely planning an attack. They may be looking for reinforcements themselves, from other Indian nations like the Kiowa, who they're on friendly terms with. I don't think they would attack us unless they knew their numbers weighed heavily in their favor. I need you to ride south and ask Austin for help—any help he can give us. Perhaps the Mexican soldiers would assist us. I know they hate the Comanches as much as we do."

"Sir, I am friends with Colonel Tejada who commands the Presidio in San Antonio. He might be willing to help," said Ramon in a hopeful tone. "You are right, sir. Colonel Tejada loathes the *norteños* as much as any of us."

The captain looked pleased to hear this. "Good. That's good news, Connelly. I need you to ride out as soon as you can and find him. There isn't a moment to spare. We have to assume this Cold Raven is gathering his own reinforcements as we speak. If you head straight south from here, you'll eventually hit the Colorado and San Antonio rivers."

"I can find my way home, sir."

"Good. We'll keep our camp here, so you'll be able to find us when you return," said the captain. "I'll add extra patrols during the day and ready the camp at night for any attack. The men might not get much sleep the next few nights, but dammit, we'll be ready." The captain's blazing blue eyes bored into him. "This damn fight won't be over until we send those four god-damned leaders to their graves."

Blood for Blood

Malone, Esatai, and Many Wolves arrived back at the village just before dusk. The two horses from the dead white men were tied to Esatai's mount. When the men dismounted, Flecha flew to his familiar tree by Many Wolves's lodge. *His wings must be very tired.*

Esatai's lance was embellished by the two *taiboo* scalps, which drew some cheers, but also much murmuring, from the villagers as they walked past. He also carried two of the white man's weapons with him. Many Wolves overheard one man say, "Did Esatai kill Lead Fingers?" and then another say, "Are we at war with the *taiboos*?"

Cold Raven was the first to greet them. "Is that the Navoonah's scalp?" he asked in a hopeful tone.

"No," said Esatai. "We didn't kill Lead Fingers, the Green-Eyed Coyote, or the Navoonah tracker."

"These two were scouts, I believe, sent by Lead Fingers to watch this village," said Malone, confidently.

"Tell me the rest of the story in my lodge," said Cold Raven, signaling for them to follow.

Two of the pony-slaves took their three horses, as well as the two spares that Esatai had won, to feed and water them. Runs With Buffalo and Matsokai were also there, and they followed the other four men to Cold Raven's lodge. Esatai left his lance outside the lodge, but brought the two *taiboo* weapons with him.

As the six of them entered the tipi, Cold Raven motioned for his wife to bring water for them.

"Are you hungry?" he asked.

"No," said Malone, and Esatai and Many Wolves nodded in agreement.

Many Wolves, Malone, and Matsokai sat on one side of the lodge, while Cold Raven, Esatai, and Runs With Buffalo sat opposite them. They sat shoulder to shoulder because Cold Raven's lodge was much smaller than Crooked Eagle's.

"Tell me what happened," said Cold Raven in a calm voice, pulling the long, black hair on his left side behind his ear, revealing a colorful earring made of turquoise and red beads.

As Many Wolves spoke, Cold Raven's wife brought cups of water for them to drink. "I flew Flecha to the River of Threes," said Many Wolves, "and didn't see any men or horses until Flecha reached Lead Fingers' camp. The men were practicing with their *pistoles*, shooting wooden targets while riding their horses. Lead Fingers and Big Yack were watching them, but I didn't see the Green-Eyed Coyote. Little Sky was in the camp also. Flecha watched them for a while until the older man with the gray hair spotted him in a tree, just like the last time we flew to their camp. He told Lead Fingers, and the *taiboo* leader tried to shoot Flecha with his long gun. We left the camp as fast as we could. On the way back to the two trees, I saw Esatai kill two of the *taiboos*. I didn't recognize either of these men."

"I have seen the gray-haired man before," said Cold Raven. "I've seen him mark the white man's land with his sticks."

"He knows that Flecha is my bird. Little Sky has told him of my animal magic," said Many Wolves, looking at Cold Raven and Runs With Buffalo. "The *taiboo* leaders also saw my bird at the peace meeting. I should not have brought him that day."

"Aren't there wild birds that look like Flecha?" asked Matsokai, looking at Many Wolves.

"Not this far north. Wolf hawks don't like cold weather. They are desert birds."

"We have to be more careful scouting with the bird," said Cold Raven firmly, directing his look at Many Wolves and Malone. "Now the *taiboos* will kill any strange bird that comes near them."

"I can still watch them at a distance," said Many Wolves, convinced that he could keep Flecha hidden from them. "A hawk's eye sees much farther than a man's."

All the other men except Esatai nodded in agreement.

"One thing is certain," said Malone. "Lead Fingers will move his camp now."

"Unless he is bold enough to lure us into attacking him there," added Matsokai.

Matsokai and Runs With Buffalo began to talk with each other, but Cold Raven interrupted them. "One man at a time speaks." The room was silent again, and Cold Raven looked at Esatai. "My brother, tell me your story."

Esatai stared at has brother through the dark strands of black hair in his eyes. "I found the two *taiboos* south of the two trees. They tried to kill me with their long guns, but my *puha* was too strong. I shot two whistling arrows through their chests and spilled their blood with my lance and knife. They were weak. I could have killed ten of them. There faces were not familiar to me."

"These are their weapons?" asked Cold Raven, looking at the long gun and *pistole* at Esatai's feet.

"*Haa,* two of them." He handed the weapons to his brother.

Cold Raven inspected them for several moments, then handed them to Runs With Buffalo. "These are weapons that the hairy-faced traders sell. One shot, then they must be reloaded with the exploding powder. Not like Lead Fingers' magic weapons that shoot once for every finger. It gives me hope that not all their men have those magic weapons."

"We know that Lead Fingers has two of them. I don't know about the others," said Malone, holding the *pistole* in his hand and looking at it. "His *pistoles* were much different than this one."

"Many Wolves, did you see any other men with weapons like Lead Fingers?"

Many Wolves shook his head. "I couldn't tell them apart. Most of their *pistoles* were hidden by their clothing." He paused for a moment trying to remember what he saw. "I do remember that Lead Fingers' *pistoles* were the shiniest. I don't think any of the men had *pistoles* quite like his."

"*Haa*, I remember them from the meeting at Two Trees," added Cold Raven.

The lodge was quiet again for several moments.

"Malone, two things are certain," said Cold Raven. "Lead Fingers will move his camp." He paused to look each man in the eye. "And Lead Fingers will want blood for blood."

Two Birds

Many Wolves's early morning sleep was shaken by a familiar bird call.

Chachara?

In his half sleep, he quickly dismissed the sound. *It's part of my dream.* Looking outside his lodge, he saw that it was still early in the morning, so he tried to fall back asleep, hoping to recapture the dream he was having. But then the sound woke him again. It wasn't Flecha—his pitch was much higher. It sounded like Chachara.

Now this bird is haunting my dreams, Many Wolves thought. "Go away, Chachara, I'm trying to sleep," he mumbled in a sleepy voice.

The bird squawked again, and this time Flecha joined in.

Many Wolves sat up and growled, "I want this dream to stop! Not you too, Flecha."

Malone, who had been asleep next to Many Wolves, stirred. "Are you all right?"

"*Haa.* Just a bad dream with Chachara squawking at me."

Malone sat up. "I heard it too."

"What?"

The bird squawked yet again.

"It did it again!" said Malone.

Many Wolves climbed out of his sleeping robe and walked outside his lodge. He looked around his camp and saw Flecha, wide awake, in his usual spot. Above him was Chachara. *What is Chachara doing here?*

"Malone, come see this. Chachara is here."

The Nokoni warrior came out of the lodge and looked. Chachara continued to squawk.

"What is she doing here?" Malone asked, yawning and stretching.

"I don't know. Did she fly here to be with her brother?"

Just as Many Wolves said that, another bird landed in the same tree next to Chachara.

"Is that Espera?" said Malone.

"*Haa.* I don't know why they are here, my friend."

Espera chased Flecha off his branch, squawking at him. Then Chachara flew straight at Many Wolves's head, forcing him to duck at the last moment. "What are you doing, crazy bird!"

Chachara climbed straight up in the air and circled around them.

"What's it doing now?" asked Malone, still as puzzled as he was.

"I don't know."

After Chachara had circled about three or four times, she dove straight down at Many Wolves. She rolled her body upside down and then right side up again.

"Great Spirit!" Many Wolves cried in astonishment.

"What is it?"

"It's Taimah!"

"Taimah? She's here?"

"Her spirit is here, Malone. Her spirit is in Chachara!"

"She's spirit-walking?" Malone was the only one confused now.

"*Haa.*"

"How do you know?"

"Because I told her about the rolling trick. There! Did you see that? She did it again!"

"*Haa.*" Malone was wide awake now.

"Hawks don't normally roll their bodies like that."

"She figured out the mind-journey trick," said Malone, smiling broadly. "I knew she would!"

Yes, she did. Many Wolves felt pride well up inside him. He had been so worried that she wouldn't have the same gift. Now he knew that she did.

He watched Chachara diving and soaring around him, and each time he waved his hand at the bird, it rolled, almost as if he was giving the command. A tear fought its way from his eye and rolled down his cheek—and then he started laughing. He couldn't help himself.

Malone started laughing with him.

"She did it, Malone! This is amazing!"

Then Espera lifted herself off her perch and joined her sister in the air. The two of them circled together for several moments, calling to each other. It was like a dance of mating birds. It was beautiful. They circled several times before Espera fell into a dive and rolled her body around like her sister had done.

"Great Spirit, Malone!" said Many Wolves. His heart felt as though it was about to leap from his chest.

"What is it, my friend?"

"Her spirit is in *both* birds."

"Did you ever do that?" Malone asked.

"I don't think I ever tried. I didn't think it was possible."

Many Wolves waved his hand at the two birds that were circling again. First Chachara rolled, then her sister. Many Wolves watched the two birds in awe. Taimah had not only figured out how to do the mind-journey, but she had mastered it beyond his own abilities. *I wonder why it didn't work for her before? Did she do something differently? Did she change the medicine?*

He knew now that she could hear him. *"*Taimah, you figured it out! You'll have to tell me what you did!*"*

Both birds rolled again.

Then he remembered how, long ago, Chiquito had carried the scalp for him. *Chachara could bring the necklace to her.* He walked into his lodge and found the necklace he had made with all the special beads from Kolakai. He wrapped it in a piece of rabbit hide and tied it tightly with sinew.

"Taimah! I have something for you!" he said as he stepped back outside. He put on his fist-perch, then placed the wrapped necklace on top of it. "Have Chachara take it." He held his wrist up.

The bird flew down, landed on the fist-perch, clutched the bundle in its talons, and flew back up again.

Many Wolves put his fist to his heart and looked up at the birds. *My heart beats for you, Taimah.*

Each bird rolled one last time and flew off.

Many Wolves sighed and smiled.

It was good to see you, Wildflower.

War Paint

Darkness always followed a beautiful sunset. For Many Wolves, Taimah was his sunset, a fleeting moment of beauty and happiness—but now the darkness of war was upon him. He was relieved to know that she was well, which meant that Nina and Topasana were also well; the darkness had not yet touched them, and he hoped it would stay that way. But he was being pulled into a war that wasn't his war, and like the darkness, he couldn't walk away from it.

A tension had fallen over Crooked Eagle's village. It had begun when Esatai marched through the village with the *taiboo* scalps. The women, the children, the elders all sensed that war was coming. The warriors sensed it too, but war was welcomed by them, a chance for glory in battle.

The Kiowa warriors were there, too; they had arrived the previous night, while Many Wolves was away. This was the fighting force that Cold Raven had been waiting for to defend the village. And now, the war leader had called all his warriors to join him at dusk—to prepare for war.

"I've never done this, Malone. What do I bring?" said Many Wolves. Many of the Northerner rituals were unknown to him.

"Bring your quiver and your shield. Only wear a breechcloth, not a shirt," said Malone.

"Why not a shirt?"

"Your body will be painted as part of the ceremony."

"Why?"

"To recognize your past bravery, so it will protect you."

"Only you know my past bravery," said Many Wolves, still unclear.

"Then I will paint you, and you will paint me. You will remember a past bravery that I have done and paint something on me to show this. When the painting is done, the warriors will dance and sing their war songs." Malone laughed. "Don't worry, my friend, you can just watch the other men dance."

* * *

The black of night dropped on the village like a blanket falling from the sky. A giant bonfire burned at the center of the village, close to Crooked Eagle's lodge. The flames popped and crackled. A crowd formed a large circle around the fire—men and women of all ages, and children too.

A buzz of excited voices filled the night air. Nighthawks flew past the fire, feeding on insects that were drawn to the brightness of the flames. Four young boys, chosen by Cold Raven, played war drums, one for each of the four directions.

One by one, a warrior was called to the fire by either Cold Raven or Runs With Buffalo, each calling the men from his own village. When a warrior entered the ceremonial circle, others who knew him came to him, one at a time, and painted lines, circles, and pictures on the man's body and face. The painters told a story of a brave deed from the warrior's past. Stories were told with song, with dance, or just in plain words. For some a brave deed was touching an enemy or pulling a fallen warrior from the battlefield. For others, it was killing an enemy or fighting against unfavorable odds. Some of the drawings were of animals or the sun or moon, while others were simply lines to count off enemies killed or friends saved.

Finally, after many of the warriors had been called, Cold Raven shouted, "Malone!"

The middle-aged Nokoni warrior walked to the center of the circle, facing Cold Raven, Runs With Buffalo, and Crooked Eagle, who were seated at the front. Several of the warriors cheered for him with war screams, but his face remained serious and stoic.

Matsokai stepped from the crowd and picked up a drinking-shell with red paint. "Malone has killed many buffalo for our village and taught our warriors to hunt. I am proud to say he is my friend and my teacher. I will draw the head of a buffalo to protect him from harm." Matsokai drew a buffalo head on Malone's chest.

As Matsokai walked away, a young warrior from Crooked Eagle's village stepped forward. His name was Turkey Walk. He took a different drinking-shell and walked over to Malone. "Long ago, Malone taught me to ride, and many of the other children too. He showed our village how to capture a wild horse and how to break its spirit. He is one of the most skilled riders I have ever seen." Turkey Walk painted a horse on Malone's chest with black war paint.

Finally, Many Wolves approached his friend. He was very nervous and didn't know exactly what to say. "Malone saved me from a slow, painful death." His voice was shaking. A hush fell over the crowd, though the drums continued. He looked out at the people around him. Many of the faces were blurred, but the one face that was clear was Esatai's, who glared at him with his hateful eyes. *He knows I am talking about his father's torture.* "Malone risked his life to save mine. He will always be my life brother. I will draw the claws of a wolf to protect him."

Two other warriors honored Malone with stories and paintings, and then it was Esatai's turn to come forward. He was welcomed with even more cheers than Malone. One after another, warriors from his village came forward to praise his heroics in battle. More men approached him than had approached any other warrior. Several men admitted that they would be dead if not for Esatai's bravery. Many of them marked lines on his arms, one for each man they had seen him kill.

Finally, after the men had finished, Cold Raven himself stood. "My brother has the strength of ten men and the bravery of a hundred. There is no man who can match him in battle that I have seen. I will draw the head of a wolf, his spirit animal, to protect him."

When Cold Raven was done painting, Esatai returned to the crowd and Cold Raven returned to his spot between Crooked Eagle and Runs With

Buffalo. Then Cold Raven shouted, "Many Wolves!"

Many Wolves stood and took his place by the fire. The drums pounded the rhythm of his heartbeats. He was nervous, standing before so many strange faces. His mind flashed back to the time he was taken prisoner by Thorn Bird's village. The faces there were angry and hateful. He was thankful that these faces were not. There were smiles on the faces of the elders and looks of admiration on the faces of the children.

Malone stood and picked up a drinking-shell. He grabbed Many Wolves's left arm and raised it up toward the leaders. "See the arm that bends the fangs of the rattlesnake. I draw this snake to strike at his enemies!" Malone drew a red, curvy line on his wrist. Then he pointed to Many Wolves's shoulder. "See the shoulder that bends the claws of the great cat! I draw these claws to remind his enemy that he has defeated the great cat." Grabbing a different drinking-shell, he painted the claws. Then he pointed at the bear claw scars on Many Wolves's leg. "See the leg that bends the powerful claws of the grizzly. I draw these claws to show his enemy that the courage of the grizzly lives within him."

When Malone was finished, he set the last drinking-shell down and walked back to his place in the gathering.

"Is there anyone else to honor Many Wolves?" yelled Cold Raven.

There were whispers in the crowd, but no one came forward.

The people here don't know me. Malone's recognition was enough.

Finally, Crooked Eagle pulled himself up with Cold Raven's help. "Help my steps, Cold Raven, and draw for me." Cold Raven stood up and offered himself as the old man's walking stick. "Bring that black paint with you." The two men took slow, old man steps toward Many Wolves. The crowd grew quiet.

Many Wolves was confused. *Crooked Eagle hasn't seen my brave deeds.*

The elder spoke, but his weakened, cracking voice was soft and not easily heard. "A long time ago, Many Wolves saved a friend of mine. He was one of the most honored warriors of this village. It was Many Wolves who rescued him from the claws of the great bear. It was Many Wolves who breathed life back into him when he was mourning the loss of a loved one.

Cold Raven, I ask you to draw ten arrows on the body of Many Wolves, so he will know that the friend he saved is with him."

When Cold Raven was finished painting, he walked the venerable peace leader back and helped him sit.

There was silence as Many Wolves left the circle. He was honored to have been the only one recognized by Crooked Eagle. Ten Arrows was still alive in his memories. He imagined his friend was with him now. *I will be with you, Wild Man.* Those were the words he heard his friend say. It gave him hope that Ten Arrows would be with him again in war.

War Talk

When the ceremony was over, Cold Raven invited Malone, Many Wolves, Esatai, Matsokai, and Runs With Buffalo to his lodge for a smoke deep into the night. Once the men had assembled around the fire pit in his lodge, Cold Raven lit his pipe and gave it to each of them in turn.

"Let us offer the smoke to the Great Spirit so that he will bless and guide our plans for war," said Cold Raven. He waited for each man to take a puff from his tobacco-filled pipe before speaking again. "Malone and I have had many talks of war. We agree that half our warriors, mostly Kiowa, should stay here to defend the village. Runs With Buffalo will lead these men. The remaining warriors will attack Lead Fingers at his camp. We will strike swiftly like wolves under a blanket of darkness. The eyes of our horses will be guided by a 'killing moon,' as my father once called it. We will ride like the Blood Riders once did, with the last of them to lead us."

Cold Raven looked at Malone and smiled.

"When the sun breaks the darkness," he continued, "Many Wolves will send his hawk into the sky to scout the *taiboos'* camp. We will wait for his report. Be prepared to leave this village when the sun falls tomorrow. We will travel with the silence of an owl's wings and attack them when the night is deep."

There was silence for some time as the men smoked and pondered Cold Raven's words. It seemed like a wise plan to Many Wolves, though his mind was untrained in the ways of war. He hoped Cold Raven's experience would be enough to lead them through this. But it was Malone's leadership that Many Wolves believed in. His friend's war plans had once saved him against Thorn Bird, despite the staggering odds against them.

Many Wolves looked over at Esatai, who shot a serious glance back at him. There was not a wisp of friendship between them, but still, he was expected to fight with this terrible man. *I will never like him. I will never trust him.*

It was impossible to look at Esatai without flashes of Thorn Bird budding in his mind. Thorn Bird had wished him dead, and Laughing Crow, yet now their sons were his protectors. It made Many Wolves feel uneasy. He wondered what would happen when this war was over and Cold Raven didn't need him anymore. *Will they turn against me?* With absolute certainty, he knew that Esatai's hate was tethered by only the thinnest sinew. *What will break it? When will it break?*

"Cold Raven and I believe this is our best chance to defeat Lead Fingers," said Malone, looking at each man there. "If we fight them in daylight on the open prairie, their weapons will tear us apart. Cold Raven's father used to say 'one man lost is one too many.' We must not take risks that will lose our warriors' lives. The darkness will be our friend, our brother in war, like it was in the days of the Blood Riders."

Many Wolves's thoughts wandered again as Malone spoke. *What if this war takes Malone from me?* When the fighting started, Malone would be at the lead with Cold Raven, and they would be the first in range of the Mare-Can's long guns and *pistoles.*

He closed his eyes and tried to shake the thought, but it was like an annoying fly buzzing around in his mind. Losing Malone would be like losing an arm or leg. He would still have Nina and Taimah, but without Malone, life would be much harder. *I would rather die than lose him.*

Malone continued to speak, to spill out his war experience to these men. "Fast your bodies to sharpen your minds. Bring only what you need for war. No extra supplies and no extra horses. We must remain unseen until the first arrow is released from our bows." Malone paused to smoke, and there was silence for a time.

It was Esatai who broke the silence. "I barely remember my father because he died when I was young." His look as he spoke was like that of a snarling wolf. "But I remember one thing he told me. See with your mind the many ways you will kill men before you kill them. See your knife cutting their throats before you cut them. See the battle before you fight it and you will taste your enemy's blood before they taste yours. This will be my dream when I leave this lodge."

The men sat in silence after that, the sound of smoke-filled breathing driving them like a drum into deeper thought. Finally, the calm was stirred by singing. It was Runs With Buffalo. Many Wolves didn't understand the words, because it was in the Kiowa leader's native tongue. But it didn't matter what the singer was saying, just how he said it; he drew words from his soul like a hand draws water from a creek.

Many Wolves was soothed by the singing. It chased all the hurtful thoughts from his mind. And so the white-skinned warrior sat with his eyes closed, inhaling smoke and sound and the friendship of the red-skinned men around him, enjoying the peace he knew would soon end.

The Path to War

The moon was full the following night, as it had nearly been in previous nights. Its glowing beams lit a path for Cold Raven's war party to follow through the engulfing prairie. The men rode in a single line, moving slowly through the tall grass and trying not to exert their horses. They knew where the *taiboo* camp was, not far from where Many Wolves had first seen it along the River of Threes. Many Wolves had scouted the camp earlier that day and had reported back to Cold Raven and Malone its location and the landmarks around it. Matsokai knew the place, so he rode out ahead to scout the camp himself.

Cold Raven led the procession of warriors, followed by Malone, Esatai, and Many Wolves. There were around forty men in the war party. Many Wolves wished there were more, but Crooked Eagle had not wanted to leave the village defenseless, and Cold Raven had honored that wish. From what Many Wolves had seen at the Mare-Cans' camp, neither side would have a weighted advantage over the other.

Noche walked besides Many Wolves and Castana, his horse. There was no talking or laughing, just a steady clopping of hooves. The air was cool, and a steady breeze brushed against Many Wolves's face and body. To him, it almost seemed like a strange dream. The world around him was still and peaceful. It seemed like these men were the only men left in this world—or that this was a different world altogether.

It made him think of the next world, the place where the Cloud Eagle took your spirit when you died. What was that place like? Were there mountains, deserts, prairies? And who would be at this other world? His family? Ten Arrows? *I would love to see them again. What about Laughing Crow and Thorn Bird? Will they be there, like in my dreams? What if there is no other world, but only this world, and your spirit returns in a new body—a person's body, or even an animal's body? Maybe I will be a fly and live only a few sleeps before my spirit moves again. Maybe a few sleeps to a human is like a lifetime to a fly.*

He laughed to himself. It was too strange to think about it. Only those who had died knew what happened after death. He wished he could talk to one of them, just for a moment, to get some glimpse of what was beyond this world.

Malone had once told him that he believed he would see his wife and daughter again, and Laughing Crow too. The next world would be a great hunting ground, he said, where animals were easy to kill and where, when they died, they would be born again instantly to replenish the world. It was a happy place where there was no sorrow, or disease, or sickness. Malone called this place "Cheenewa"—the happy hunting ground. Malone also said that if you died here, in *this* world, defending a friend or a village, you would receive even greater rewards in Cheenewa.

Malone slowed his horse down so that Many Wolves could catch up to him. "When we ride into war I want you and Noche to stay back," Malone said. His voice was serious, the voice of the leader who had once led Many Wolves against Thorn Bird. "Any *taiboos* who escape our first attack will die to your arrows and your wolf's fangs. Watch our backs. Do you understand?"

"*Haa*," said Many Wolves. It was a familiar role.

The silence was broken by the sound of approaching hooves. It was Matsokai. The line of men stopped as the Penateka scout spoke with Cold Raven and Malone.

"I have seen the camp. There are twenty or twenty-five men that I could see, perhaps a few more unseen. There are trees and the river behind them. I did not see any dogs. Several men were awake, sitting by a fire, but the rest were sleeping under their blankets. We can kill many of them before they wake."

"It almost seems too easy," said Malone.

"We know they don't have dogs," said Cold Raven. "The *taiboos* never have dogs guarding their camps."

"Are their horses guarded?" asked Malone.

"There are two or three men with them. One of them might have been sleeping. There are horses on both sides of their camp."

"If we take their horses, they will be like scabs for our warriors to pick," said Malone. He seemed more in favor of this plan.

"I am not here to steal horses. I am here to kill the *tuhkwasi taiboo*, the white devil. We have enough horses," said Esatai. His voice was more forceful than the others.

"We don't know which of the them is Lead Fingers or Big Yack or the Green-Eyed Coyote. Could you tell, Matsokai?" asked Malone.

"No. The men that were awake had blankets around them. I didn't recognize any of them, and I was afraid to get any closer."

"How far ahead is it?"

"It is not far," said Matsokai.

"Malone and I will ride with you so we can see this camp for ourselves," said Cold Raven. "Then we will decide if we are taking horses or scalps."

Dangerous Men

Cold Raven's war party lined up shoulder to shoulder on their mounts, with Cold Raven, Malone, Esatai, and Many Wolves facing them. The horses shifted nervously, snorting vapor from their nostrils into the cold night air. Esatai's brown and white painted horse seemed the most restless. Many Wolves sensed they were close to the Mare-Cans' camp, perhaps just a sprint away.

"These are dangerous men," said Cold Raven, riding in front of the war party on his prancing pony. "Their weapons are faster and more deadly than any you have seen. Only the Noomah arrow is more deadly. Many of them have weapons that do not need to reload. You must kill these men first. One of them will be Lead Fingers. He must die. Do not think you are safe after their weapons have fired. Ride swiftly and silently until you see the *taiboos'* faces. Do not slow your mounts for anything. If you are an easy target, you will die." The Nokoni leader spun his horse around to face Malone and nodded.

Malone rode forward and moved slowly past the row of men, looking into their faces and eyes and clashing his shield with each of them as he passed. Many Wolves had never seen his friend look this way. Like most of the Nokoni men, Malone's face was painted black, and his body was richly painted from the war ceremony. He was as fierce-looking as any warrior Many Wolves had seen. It was hard to believe that this was his closest friend, a man who was as close to being his brother as any man. A man who had once held his infant daughter in his arms and sung her to sleep.

"My words will be few," said Malone in a firm voice, but loud enough for all of them to hear. "These hairy-faced *taiboos* take land that isn't given. They kill buffalo and use the carcasses not to feed their children, but to feed the horseflies. None of you will die today. The sun will rise and welcome you to a new day. It will welcome you to a new world free of the white man. In this world or the next, you will be honored for your bravery."

The men crashed their lances and bows against their shields. Their horses grunted and stomped, preparing for the sprint. Cold Raven turned his horse with his bow held high, looked back at his men one last time, then dropped his bow, commanding his horse to ride hard. The line of riders charged behind the three leaders—Cold Raven, Malone, and Esatai. Many Wolves and Noche fell back behind the men as Malone had instructed. There were no shouts or war cries, only the thunder from hooves.

* * *

The first human sound that Many Wolves heard was the bellowing of a white man's voice, which was followed by a torrent of blasts from the Mare-Cans' flashing long guns, which came from all around their camp. Many Wolves saw several warriors fall, including Matsokai. He felt fear grip him, suffocating his mind like a snake. *How did the Mare-Cans know we were coming?*

Cold Raven's warriors charged, undaunted, into the face of the enemy. A whirr of bowstrings followed the white man's strike, and Many Wolves heard the screams of the men who were struck by arrows. For a short time the stream of arrows was constant, unanswered by the *taiboos'* weapons, but then another fierce barrage of popping came from the white man's weapons, and more warriors fell.

Many Wolves spotted a man with a long gun behind the riders. He quickly jumped off his horse, grabbed his bow and an arrow, and shot at the man. The arrow missed, but Noche darted toward the target, a black blur in the night, and leaped on him. The man screamed until Noche silenced him with a bite to the neck.

"Noche, come!" Many Wolves called as he looked around for another target.

But the wolf did not obey—Noche charged at another man farther away.

"Noche!" Many Wolves started running after him, but soon lost sight of him.

Many Wolves stopped to look around. The Mare-Cans' camp was a flurry of bowstrings and gunfire, of horse hooves and men screaming.

Then Many Wolves heard footsteps behind him. He turned and saw the angry, hairy face of a white man charging at him with his long gun held high. The man swung at him with the handle of the weapon. Many Wolves felt a hard object dash his head and a surge of pain crash through him, and then there was darkness…

Aftermath

Ramon rode with Colonel Tejada and his company of thirty men with urgency from San Antonio, northward along the Rio Colorado with the flowing waters to their left. They had ridden through most of the moonlit night, and now it was early morning.

The colonel had not been hard to find, since his men patrolled the outskirts of Bexar, and it had not been difficult to convince him to aid Captain McCord. Like Ramon, the colonel had a hatred for the *norteños* that had been built up over a lifetime.

"We are less than two leagues away, *coronel*," said Ramon, riding alongside the colonel.

"Are you sure it's up along the *rio*? I see smoke over there," said the colonel, pointing to his right. His voice was as big as a bear's. "Maybe they have moved the camp."

Colonel Tejada shifted his heading and waved his arm for his men to follow. "*Vamonos!*"

Why would they move the camp? Dark thoughts invaded Ramon's mind. He had been fully expecting to return to the river camp and find it just as he had left it. Now he had doubts. Something must have happened to force them to cross the river.

"We should approach carefully, *coronel*," said Ramon. "We don't know for sure that it's the *capitán*."

"My men will be ready, Connelly, for whatever waits for us there, friend or foe." Colonel Tejada spoke with confidence.

They reached the top of a knoll and saw men and horses on the other side. Colonel Tejada held his hand up to halt his men.

"It's the *capitán*." Ramon was relieved that it was the captain's men, but there seemed to be fewer of them than before.

"I thought you said there were thirty men, Connelly?"

"Around that when I left."

"*Vamanos!*"

They rode down into the small valley at a trot. Cornelius waved when he spotted Ramon, then yelled something to the men.

Where is the captain? Where is Possum?

Ramon rode up to his friend and dismounted. "What happened, Cornelius? Where's Captain Mac?"

"The Comanches besieged us in the middle of the night." Cornelius looked over to his left and pointed. "There's the captain. He was stabbed in the leg, but I was able to suture him up properly."

The captain was walking slower than usual, and with a limp. His shirt was unbuttoned and a bandage was wrapped around his leg. "Connelly," he said, "you are a sight to behold. This must be Colonel Tejada."

"Yes, captain." Ramon shifted to Spanish. "Colonel Tejada, this is *Capitán* James McCord."

The colonel dismounted. "Hello, *capitán*," he said in a mix of languages, tipping his hat.

"*Buenos días*, colonel," said the captain, shaking the colonel's hand. He looked over at Ramon. "I'll need you to translate, Connelly."

"Yes, sir."

"Colonel, tell your men to rest. We have food and water for them. The man over there with the bandage on his arm can help them. His name is Ernesto."

The colonel commanded his men to be at ease and relayed the information to them. They dismounted and walked their horses into camp.

"We can talk in the shade of my camp," said the captain.

The colonel and Ramon followed the captain as he limped to his camp beneath a giant oak. Ramon looked around. Many of the men were missing, including Biggs, Little Sky, Possum Jack, and most of the Mexicans, except for Ernesto. Some others were bandaged. The mood of the camp was somber.

"Sorry, Colonel, I only have water to offer you—no spirits," said the captain. Ramon translated.

Colonel Tejada removed a flask from the breast pocket of his uniform and offered it to them. "Mescal?"

The captain smiled and nodded, then pulled out three cups. The colonel poured a little of the mescal in each.

"*Salud!*" said the colonel, raising his cup, then both Ramon and the captain repeated the toast and clinked cups.

Ramon drank his cupful, following their lead, and set his cup back down, refreshed. The colonel filled their cups again.

As the captain spoke, Ramon repeated each sentence in Spanish for the colonel.

"The Comanches came deep in the night like I was expecting they would. There numbers were a least thirty, probably more, but it was hard to tell in the darkness. Our Lipan scout, Little Sky, gave us an early warning, which probably saved many lives. We were ready. Many of the blankets we padded with prairie grass as decoys, while our men hid behind trees. Possum Jack, myself, and a few others were ready on our mounts, staying as hidden as we could in the trees until the right moment. Before the fight, I told the men that I wanted the four leaders dead or captured. That was the first objective. The other objective was to kill as many of the sons of bitches as we could."

The captain paused to take a drink, then continued. "When the Comanches arrived at our camp, all hell broke lose. These were easily the most dangerous savages I have ever fought. They matched every bullet with arrows, and more god-damned arrows. Their bloodthirsty war cries were demonic, as if they had come through the gates of hell. With only the moon's light, it was difficult to find the leaders, but I know we killed a lot of their god-damned warriors. Anyone with a painted mount or a war scream was my target. I believe I shot the one named Malone, almost by sheer luck, because he moved like a ghost on his mount. I saw another one of the leaders, Cold Raven, fall from his horse, and soon after he came at me with his knife. He stabbed me here in the leg and it hurt like hell, but I was able to repel him with my horse, knocking him out soundly it seemed, with one blow from my horse's hoof. I wanted him alive, not dead. Then I looked up and spotted the large warrior, Esatai. His scream was the loudest and most frightening.

"He flung an arrow into Biggs's chest, knocking him off his horse, then shot two more into him as he lay on the ground. He whirled his horse around and our eyes locked for several seconds. Everything was moving around me at a snail's pace, it seemed. I charged at him, unloading what was left in my pistol, but somehow I missed him. I heard Possum firing his pistol as well.

"At this point, the savages were spooked by the ring of gunfire and the fall of their leader. They retreated, and the big warrior, Esatai, whose horse had been shot out from under him, sprinted off into the dark and disappeared like dust with the rest of them. I thought this damned thing was over, but then this god-damned black wolf came out of nowhere, snarling like a rabid dog, and leaped up at Possum, knocking him off his horse. I rode straight at it and discharged my last bullet, but missed. The damn thing ran off, perhaps spooked by the blast of powder at close range, but not after taking out a chunk of Possum's leg. I started to feel dizzy from blood loss, so I told the men to grab Possum and any other survivors, as well as the Comanche leader, because I saw that he was still alive, and then get the hell out across the river. We rode and never looked back."

He finished what was left in his cup and motioned for the colonel to pour him more. He drank that down too, without hesitation.

"Possum is alive?" said Ramon.

"He's under the tree over there," said the captain, pointing. "Corny has been attending to him."

Ramon had never seen the captain look so worn out before. Sweat and dust covered his face, and his clothes were not neat and orderly as they usually were. His pants were ripped open so Corny could wrap his leg with a bandage. It might have been the first time Ramon had ever seen him without a hat on.

"Where is the *norteño* leader?" asked Colonel Tejada.

The captain seemed to understand the question without need for translation. "He's tied up on the other side of our camp. We need to keep him guarded."

After Ramon's translation, Colonel Tejada said, "I'll post two men on him. Ask the *capitán* what else he needs from me."

"I need you to ride back to the river camp to see if any of our men are still alive there," said the captain. "Bury our dead." He pointed at Ramon. "Take Connelly and our Lipan scout with you. I want to know which of their god-damned leaders are dead. We will break camp now and head out toward Nacogdoches. The colonel can meet us there."

Ramon nodded and then translated the message.

"*Sí*, captain. We will ride out now," said Colonel Tejada. "*Vamonos*, Connelly."

A Proud Name

The warm morning sun beat down on Many Wolves. He cracked open his eyes, staring into the brightness. His head was throbbing from pain, and he didn't remember how it had happened. He felt around the back of his head and found a bump and dried blood that was painful to touch. His black wolf was lying beside him in the prairie grass, whining softly. Noche licked him and breathed hot air into his face.

"Noche. What happened?" He petted the wolf's head and lifted himself up over the tall prairie grass. Slowly the blurred world around him came into focus. *Where am I?*

The only noise came from the circling crows and ravens above him. The silent buzzards floated with them, too. *Why are they here?*

His mind was slow to react, still questioning whether this was a dream. He stumbled to his feet, then almost fell as the pain crashed inside his head, bringing even more dizziness. The nauseous feeling in his stomach was overwhelming, but he did not vomit.

The trees and the river were familiar. *I've seen them with Flecha.* A stench of death was in the air. He looked across the flat grassland toward the trees. Dead horses and men were scattered all around.

Reality crashed into him like a speeding arrow. *The war with the Mare-Cans.*

One dead man, a white man, lay only a short distance from him. He still clutched a long gun, but his lifeless eyes gazed into the sun, forever frozen. Flies feasted on a gash in his neck. *Noche must have killed him.*

The black wolf started whining and barking some distance away from him. "What is it, Noche? What did you find?" Many Wolves stumbled carefully toward his wolf, afraid to run because of the dizziness.

Noche had found a man lying on the ground. But this man wasn't dead. His arm reached up and stroked the wolf's head.

A cold wind shot through Many Wolves, numbing his senses. *Noche knows him. Malone.*

His fears were confirmed when he saw Malone's horse lying nearby, motionless.

"Malone!" He ran toward them. He fell several times, but each time he got back up onto his stiff legs.

He found his friend covered in blood from three wounds to his chest— holes from the white man's weapons. Malone looked up with lazy eyes, not the bright, intelligent eyes of the friend Many Wolves remembered.

"Many Wolves," said Malone in a soft, fading voice, cracking a smile. Blood trickled down the side of his mouth. "You're alive!" He coughed up blood and struggled with every breath.

I have to stop the bleeding. Many Wolves spotted the dead body of white man nearby, two arrows sticking out of his chest. He walked over to the body, tore off the shirt, and brought it back to Malone. He pressed the cloth against Malone's wounds.

"I was hoping this was a dream, Malone. Tell me it's a dream!"

"It seems like a dream to me too." Malone struggled with his words. "You should go home. Your village needs you. The women need you. This is Crooked Eagle's war, not yours. Let him fight it. I'm sorry I pulled you into it." He took a shaky breath, then pulled Many Wolves closer with his weakened arm. "I have something to tell you."

"I'll stop the bleeding, Malone! You need to rest. Don't talk," Many Wolves pleaded.

"I knew your father," said Malone.

"What? You knew Red Arrow?"

"No. Your white father. Your blood father."

Many Wolves was confused. How was it possible?

"His name was Malone. I took his name. Laughing Crow tortured and killed him," said Malone, gasping for breath. "He was very brave."

"How do you know it was my father?"

"When I saw your *libro*, I knew. I first saw the *libro* when we captured your father." Malone's lazy eyes strayed into the distance.

"Why didn't you tell me then?"

"I didn't want to tell you how he died. I didn't want you to know that I helped to capture him." Malone's eyes shifted back to meet Many Wolves's gaze. "I can still remember it. It was a horrible torture. But he didn't cry out. Your father didn't beg for his life."

He gulped, swallowing blood. "I am proud to have your white father's name."

Malone smiled, drew one last breath, and then his eyes gazed into the distance. He didn't look back at Many Wolves again. There was no more life in him.

The black wolf licked Malone's face as if it hoped that would revive him. Many Wolves just rested his head on his friend's chest, salting his wounds with tears.

I hope Cheenewa is a beautiful place, my friend.

A Broken Promise

Many Wolves lay with his friend for some time.

I need to take him home.

He got up and found Malone's sleeping robe on the Northerner's dead horse. He carefully wrapped his friend's body in it.

I have no horse to carry him. Where is Castana? He looked all around him, but the horse wasn't anywhere in sight, alive or dead. He hoped that his mount had survived and that someone in Cold Raven's war party had found him. *Did anyone survive?*

I can at least carry Malone to the shade, away from the rotting sun.

He pulled the wrapped body up and slung it over his shoulder, almost losing his balance. He walked, one grueling step at a time, toward the trees and the river. *I must do this.* Somehow his balance held up. It was like his body coursed with poison. Some of his strength was returning and the dizziness was fading, but his head still throbbed.

Many Wolves walked past one dead man after another. He recognized some of the faces of the red-skinned bodies, but not the whites. The white bodies were easily spotted thanks to the arrows protruding from them. He took a rough count and decided the numbers on each side were about the same. *Did anyone survive this war?*

He heard a horse coming behind him. He turned around and was relieved to see a Northerner riding toward him. *Esatai.*

Noche growled and hunched his back aggressively. "Easy, Noche! Easy!" The wolf relented. Many Wolves laid his burden down to give his body a rest and waited for the rider to come.

"Many Wolves. You are alive!" said Esatai with a surprised look, pulling up just short of Many Wolves. Esatai was not riding his usual mount, but he was still carrying his bow and shield.

Again, Noche growled.

"*Haa*," said Many Wolves, "but Malone is dead. Many of our men are dead. What happened, Esatai?"

"Too many *balas* for our shields to stop. Look at my shield. There are at least six or seven of the white man's *balas* in it. We have lost many warriors. I have come back to find survivors and to find my brother. And I will take the scalps that are mine."

"Cold Raven? Matsokai? Are they alive?"

"Matsokai is alive," said Esatai, glancing over at Noche. "My brother was injured and taken by the *taiboos*. I don't think he is still alive. If he is, then the *taiboos* will surely kill him."

"Are you going to try to help him?"

"I am the only one who wants to fight. I will find where the *taiboos* have taken him. Many of them will die. They are not as strong now."

Many Wolves heard a familiar scream in the distance and saw one of his hawks flying toward him. *Flecha?* When the bird flew closer and circled above him, he saw that it was Chachara. Then the bird rolled over in the air. *Taimah.*

Esatai looked over his shoulder at the bird and then looked back at Many Wolves. The warrior's voice turned suddenly cold and hateful. "If my brother is dead, Many Wolves, then so is my promise to him." He pulled two arrows from his quiver and loaded one of them. "I realize now that I should have killed you when I found you hunting alone. My father has haunted my dreams since that time." He raised his bow and aimed it at the wolf. "Now, you and your wolf will die."

The wolf snarled at Esatai as if sensing the immediate danger.

From the trees behind Esatai, Many Wolves heard horse hooves, the twang of a bow, and a hissing sound. The arrow crashed into Esatai's back, and its point split right through his chest, spitting blood. His body jerked, and his arrows fell from his hands into the tall prairie grass. Esatai looked at Many Wolves in shock.

Now Many Wolves saw the source of the arrow. *Taimah!* She was riding toward them in a full gallop, her bow drawn. Her second arrow again cut through the warrior's body, and this time Esatai fell from his horse, screaming in agony.

Noche reacted instantly, leaping at the big man, knocking him back, and digging his fangs into his right arm. Esatai shook the raging wolf off his arm and threw him aside, but Noche charged again and locked his powerful teeth onto the warrior's arm again. The Nokoni cried out in pain and reached for the knife in his leg sheath with his free arm, but he lacked the strength. His injuries were draining him. He tried to punch the wolf, but his attempt was feeble.

Then the snarling animal lunged for Esatai's throat and sank its fangs there.

"Back, Noche!" Many Wolves yelled when he saw the blood gushing from Esatai's neck.

The wolf backed off, but continued growling. The Nokoni warrior's blood dripped from his jowls.

Taimah stopped her horse just short of them, looked at Esatai, and jumped off. "*Ahpu!* Are you all right?" she said, throwing her arms around him.

"I'm fine," Many Wolves said, comforted by her warmth. He still watched Esatai.

"You? It was you?" growled Esatai, trying to stop the bleeding in his neck by holding it with his hands. "You shot your cowardly arrows because I could not see you!"

Taimah looked back at him, her hand still clinging to her bow.

"I can smell you," said Esatai, grinning and coughing up blood. He tried to rise to his feet, but his body was not cooperating. "I can smell you from here."

Many Wolves felt a surge of anger. "You are poison like your father," he said, gritting his teeth. He grabbed Taimah's bow, and an arrow from her quiver, and aimed it at Esatai's chest. "There is no goodness in you!"

The warrior growled, grabbed his knife at last, and staggered to his feet.

Many Wolves released the arrow into his chest.

The warrior grunted and fell. This time he did not rise again.

Many Wolves dropped the bow and hugged Taimah. "It's over, Wildflower." His voice was trembling. "I'm sorry you had to see this." He felt her tears against his bare chest. He tried to settle his racing heart, his quivering body, but it was difficult. He just wanted to hold her, knowing she was safe from Esatai, forever.

They held each other for several moments in silence.

"I'm sorry about Malone, *Ahpu*. He was my father too."

He wanted to tell her what Malone had said, but it wasn't the right time. Someday he would tell her how brave her grandfather was. But another thought came to his mind.

He pulled her away so he could look at her. "How did you figure out the mind-journey?"

"I just needed to use more of the peyote, *Ahpu*. That was all. Once I figured that out, the mind-journeys were easy." She sniffled and wiped the tears off her cheek.

Many Wolves had noticed that her eyes were redder than normal, and not just from crying. *Is it the peyote?* "How many of pieces of peyote did you use?"

She shrugged. "I don't know—two large pieces I guess. But it was more than what you used."

"It doesn't make you sick?" It seemed like a large amount to Many Wolves. He had never taken that much before.

"Sometimes it makes me sick, but only when the mind-journey is over. Then I need to sleep for a while."

"And you can control two birds at the same time?" Many Wolves asked, remembering how she had flown both Chachara and Espera to his camp at Crooked Eagle's village.

"*Haa.* I wasn't trying to. It was an accident. But then I realized I could do it. I can journey with a bird and a wolf also."

"You journeyed with Colmillo?"

"I wanted to see if I could do it." She paused, gathering her thoughts. "And I don't need to close my eyes when I do it, like you. I can walk or ride a horse. I use my thoughts to jump from one bird's eyes to the other and then back to my own eyes. It's like riding a horse. The horse can just sense what you want to do. It's the same with the birds and the wolf for me. But it makes me really tired if I do it too much."

Many Wolves was shocked. He had never even tried any of this. He wouldn't have thought it was possible. But his daughter had always had a more fearless nature than he did, and somehow, it didn't surprise him that she had taken these risks. *She is fearless and headstrong and doesn't give up easily.*

"Where is Colmillo?" he asked.

"I left her to protect *Shimaa.*"

"Let's load Malone's body on Esatai's horse and take him home," said Many Wolves.

"Yes. I want to go home," said Taimah, smiling at him. "I want my *Ahpu* home again."

Many Wolves wanted to go home too. He wanted this day to be over and to never live through another day like it again.

Four Leaders

Taimah helped Many Wolves lift his friend's body onto the brown and white painted horse that Esatai had ridden. After tying it securely, Many Wolves walked back to the spot where he had woken up and looked around. His quiver, bow, and shield were there on the ground. He placed the bow in his quiver and slung it on his shoulder. He held the shield and studied it, admiring Malone's craftsmanship. The wolf had been his white father's guardian spirit, just like it was now his. *I wish I had known him.*

"*Ahpu!* There are men coming!" yelled Taimah, pointing to the south.

About ten riders were coming toward them. Their clothing and the color of their horses told him that they were not his Northerner friends. He ran over to Taimah, who held Esatai's horse by a lead, and mounted the unfamiliar horse. The animal grunted and bucked at first, but settled down some with Taimah's calming words.

"Who are they, *Ahpu?*" she said as she leaped onto Sombre's back.

Many Wolves studied them. They were all wearing hats and dark shirts, with long guns in their hands. Then he recognized one of them—the one with the *mexicano* hat. *The Green-Eyed Coyote.* The other men looked like *mexicano* soldiers.

"They are not our friends," he said. "Taimah, go!"

Many Wolves yelled a command and squeezed his legs hard, urging his horse to sprint. The horse hesitated at first, shaking its head, but then it moved its powerful legs. Taimah was already a good distance ahead. Many Wolves looked back; the men were chasing them.

Taimah pulled away from Many Wolves even more; the burden of Malone's body was slowing down Many Wolves's horse. *This animal is already tired from Esatai's journey.* He yelled and pressed even more, but the horse did not run any faster. *It knows I'm a stranger.*

The soldiers were closing the distance quickly. One of them was shouting, but Many Wolves didn't understand the words. *Taimah can outrun them, but I can't. It's me they want, not her.*

Many Wolves looked down at Noche, who ran alongside him. "Taimah, don't stop!" he shouted. "Take Noche! Call Noche!"

Taimah circled around to face him and called for the wolf. Noche ran to her.

Many Wolves slowed his horse and stopped to face the riders. As they came closer, he saw that Little Sky was with them. *Maybe my friend will help me.* Many Wolves dismounted and placed his shield and quiver on the ground. *I do not want to fight.* The brown and white horse wandered away from him, still carrying Malone's body.

Glancing over his shoulder, he saw that Taimah had stopped as well; she refused to leave. "Stay there, Taimah. Don't come any closer!"

The soldiers pulled up in front of him. Six of them jumped off their horses and surrounded him with their long guns.

The large *mexicano*, who remained on his horse, wore a tall hat with a feather and many decorations on it, so Many Wolves assumed he was the leader. When he spoke, his voice was loud and deep, like thunder, but Many Wolves didn't understand the *mexicano* words. Little Sky, however, nodded his head as if he understood. The Green-Eyed Coyote said nothing.

"Many Wolves, you are a captive of Tejas," said Little Sky, using the Lipan words.

Many Wolves looked at Little Sky for a sign of friendship, but the Lipan's face was expressionless. "Do you remember me, Little Sky?"

"*Haa*, Many Wolves, I remember." His face softened a little. "But you are friends with my enemy now, which makes you my enemy."

"I will go with you, Little Sky, but let my daughter go. Let her return to her village with my friend's body. She is not your enemy."

Little Sky spoke to the *mexicano* leader with more foreign words, and the man answered him.

"That looks like a Northerner horse. Is that Esatai's body?" asked Little Sky.

"No. It's Malone. You will find Esatai's body back there on the ground," said Many Wolves, pointing.

"He is dead?"

"*Haa*. We killed him, Taimah and me." Many Wolves hoped that would please his captors. "Esatai was not my friend."

Little Sky translated this for the leader, who ordered the Green-Eyed Coyote to ride back toward the field of war. The leader then spoke with the other mounted *mexicano*, who rode out to Esatai's horse and brought it back by the lead.

Many Wolves saw that Taimah had not moved. Noche was next to her, watching, and Chachara was circling overhead.

Little Sky unwrapped the robe around Malone's body and looked at his face. The *mexicano* leader rode over to look at is also. The two of them conversed briefly, then Little Sky spoke again. "It is Malone, one of the four leaders. If Esatai is dead, then you are the last of the four leaders. Captain McCord will be very pleased."

"Who is he?"

"You call him Lead Fingers."

I have to protect Taimah. Nothing else matters. Many Wolves knew that she could outride these men. It was a risk asking her to take Malone's body, but he had to do this for his friend, and for Topusana. "Will you let my daughter go and take Malone's body with her?"

"*Haa*. If we know that Esatai is dead."

They waited in silence for the return of the Green-Eyed Coyote. The six *mexicano* soldiers kept their weapons pointed at Many Wolves. He could not run.

When the Green-Eyed Coyote came back, he spoke with the *mexicano* leader. Many Wolves could see that they were very pleased. *Esatai was their most dangerous enemy. They are happy he is dead.*

The soldier with Esatai's horse led the animal, carrying Malone's body, away from the men. He left the horse where he had found it and then rode back.

Little Sky spoke. "Tejada, our *mexicano* leader, says she can go and she can take the body with her. He said he doesn't believe that the girl killed Esatai, but that it was you and the wolf. He also said it doesn't matter who killed him, only that he is dead. Tell your daughter to tell Crooked Eagle to gather the bodies of his fallen warriors. Our men will not try to stop them. This is a promise from Lead Fingers."

Many Wolves looked back at Taimah and shouted this message to her.

"The black wolf will go with her?" asked Little Sky.

"*Haa.*"

Little Sky looked back at Tejada and nodded as if a question had just been answered.

Taimah rode over to Esatai's horse. She took its lead and tied it to Sombre.

"*Ahpu,*" she shouted. "Why can't you come with me? Please come with me. Tell them you will not fight them anymore!" Many Wolves could hear tears in her voice, without seeing them.

"I have to go with them," he shouted back. "Go now. Take Noche and go before they change their mind." *Go, Wildflower.*

She looked at him for a long moment. Then she whistled for Noche, turned, and rode away.

Many Wolves felt the tears well up inside, realizing that he might never see her again. He watched her until she disappeared from view. It reminded him of the time he walked away from his grandfather when he left his Lipan village as a boy.

He never saw his grandfather again.

The Stubborn Badger

A *mexicano* soldier bound Many Wolves's hands with rope and then tied him to one of their horses, facing backward. Tejada barked at his men, and they hurried up with their tasks. It appeared as though they were looking for survivors and gathering weapons from the field of war. One white man survivor was found, but Tejada ordered him shot. Perhaps there wasn't much life left in him and Tejada didn't want his travel burdened by a badly injured man.

When they had searched the field of battle and what was left of the Mare-Cans' camp, Tejada commanded the men again, and they began burying their dead. The soldiers had tools for digging up the earth, which made their job easier.

Little Sky and the Green-Eyed Coyote stayed with Many Wolves, but neither of them spoke. And the Lipan warrior, who always used to smile, was a different man now. The wrinkles around his eyes had stolen the good spirits from his face. *Riding in the white man's war parties could do that to a man*, Many Wolves thought. He wondered what was left of Big Sky's village after so many winters. *Have all of Big Sky's people surrendered to the white man?*

Many Wolves studied the Green-Eyed Coyote. His skin was so much lighter than a *mexicano's*, and his eyes were green, unlike most *mexicanos* that Many Wolves had seen. Many Wolves wondered if the man's mother or father had been white-skinned. The hair on his face was not scruffy like most of the other Mare-Cans and *mexicano* soldiers, but short and neatly combed. And he had many weapons on him, which made Many Wolves think that he had been in many war parties. His weapons were new and shiny, like those of Lead Fingers, especially compared to many of the *mexicano* soldiers who had old, dirty-looking *pistoles* and long guns.

Feeling Many Wolves's gaze, the Green-Eyed Coyote smiled at him briefly and then averted his eyes. But when a soldier picked up Many Wolves's quiver and shield, the Green-Eyed Coyote intervened, taking those items for himself and loading them onto his horse. *What does he want with my quiver and shield?*

"Do you want any water?" Little Sky asked after much silence, offering his water pouch.

Many Wolves shook his head, though he was thirsty.

"Do what you want," Little Sky said in a serious tone, drinking some for himself.

Tejada yelled again, and the soldiers worked faster to finish up the graves, leaving Cold Raven's dead warriors untouched. Soon they were packing their tools and long guns on their horses. Then Tejada and the Green-Eyed Coyote removed their hats, and the latter said some words in Spanish, finishing off with a hand gesture. Perhaps it was some kind of a prayer for the dead, Many Wolves thought.

They put their hats back on, and Tejada barked out another command. The men responded by quickly mounting their horses. Another command from the *mexicano* leader started the journey south along the River of Threes.

Many Wolves's hands were tied together in front, so he could still hold on to the back of the horse's leather riding pad. He could only see the Green-Eyed Coyote as he rode, since all of the other men were riding ahead of him. *What are they going to do me?* He tried to push this question from his mind, but like a stubborn badger, it wouldn't leave. *Are they going to torture me? To kill me?* He didn't know what the Mare-Cans did with their captives, but he had the same feeling of nausea in his stomach that he'd had when Malone captured him and took him back to Thorn Bird's village. *I can't endure more torture.* He remembered what Malone had said about his white-skinned father. "He did not cry out. He did not beg for his life." *I am not that strong.*

Perhaps in seasons past, Little Sky would have helped him, but now the Lipan scout acted as if he didn't want friendship. And what about the Green-Eyed Coyote? There was something mysterious about him. *Might he help me?*

He knew that was wishful thinking. A quick death was the most pleasant possibility. He hoped the Mare-Cans would treat a white-skinned captive more favorably. He remembered Walking Free's words from long ago: "Your white skin might help you someday." Maybe that was true.

As his horse pushed on, the trees and river were to Many Wolves's left and the endless prairie to his right. These were strange lands to him. Where was he going? To Lead Fingers' camp? To a white man's village? Wherever it was, it would be strange to him, and full of hateful faces like Thorn Bird's village.

Tejada shouted, and the horses stopped. Many Wolves twisted his head and saw they had arrived at the river. The men talked in the *mexicano* words, then one of them rode his horse across the river. *They are going to cross here.*

Little Sky got down and offered his hand to Many Wolves. "Get down."

With help from both Little Sky and one of the soldiers, Many Wolves got down from the horse.

"You will ride with me across the river," said Little Sky. He mounted his horse again, and the soldier and the Green-Eyed Coyote helped Many Wolves up onto Little Sky's mount. "Put your arms around my waist and hold on."

Many Wolves lifted his hands over Little Sky's head and then held on to his body.

The Lipan commanded his horse to ford the river. The animal was reluctant at first, but then entered the water. After several strides, the horse couldn't stand anymore and started to swim. Many Wolves was up to his neck in water, but he held on to Little Sky until the horse regained its footing again on the other side.

Little Sky then turned his horse to watch the others cross. One of the soldiers brought Many Wolves's mount on a lead. The Green-Eyed Coyote was the last to cross. His mount was restless, perhaps sensing the nervousness of the rider. It took a while for them to finally enter the water. The Green-Eyed Coyote's face looked strained as they crossed. *He's afraid of the water*, Many Wolves thought. But at last, the half-*mexicano* made it safely to the other side. He took his hat off and wiped his sweaty brow, then dismounted again to help Many Wolves off Little Sky's horse and onto the horse he was riding before.

The horses started off again. Many Wolves watched the trees and the river fade away behind them.

He felt like he was leaving his home forever.

The Human Cage

Just as dusk was settling, the party of riders arrived in a place unlike any that Many Wolves had seen before. It was a village not of tipis, but of stone lodges. He had never seen lodges like this. They had smoke-holes like tipis, but were of a different shape—a man-made shape, like a *libro*.

This is where the Mare-Cans live.

The soldiers walked their horses through the dwellings. There were men, women, and children here, white and *mexicano* mostly. They stared at Many Wolves as he passed. Many Wolves held his head low, his long, brown hair hanging down over his face. Some of the children pointed at him, but he couldn't understand their words. They weren't angry though, like the women and children of Thorn Bird's village. He felt more like an oddity to them than a hated enemy.

They stopped, and Many Wolves was helped down from his horse. With Tejada and the Green-Eyed Coyote walking ahead of them, two soldiers, one on each side of Many Wolves, led him to a large stone lodge.

When they entered, Many Wolves immediately recognized Lead Fingers. He had a bandage wrapped around his leg, and blood seeped through it. Beside him sat the older man who had recognized Many Wolves's hawk.

The soldiers forced Many Wolves to sit on a piece of wood that they used for sitting. He faced Lead Fingers, who was smoking a pipe. The Mare-Can leader spoke and laughed, then spoke again in the funny-sounding white man's language. The Green-Eyed Coyote translated the words for Tejada and the soldiers that had joined them in the lodge. The *mexicano* leader bellowed a laugh when he heard the words. It was the first time Many Wolves had seen Tejada smile, but the Green-Eyed Coyote was the only one there not laughing along with the others.

When Lead Fingers was finished talking, he put his pipe back in his mouth and waved his hand as if signaling them to leave. The soldiers prodded Many Wolves to stand, then led him out of the lodge. They took him away on a dirt path to another lodge that was some distance away from the other dwellings.

This lodge was bigger than the one Lead Fingers was in, and the inside smelled like human waste. On one side of the lodge were strange metal walls with people behind them. They reminded Many Wolves of the cages that the French traders used for animals, except these were larger and built for humans.

Cold Raven was in one of those cages. A bloody white bandage covered one of his shoulders, and another was wrapped around his head. His face was bloodied and bruised, like he had been beaten. Worst of all, his look was empty, as if his spirit was not there.

The soldiers put Many Wolves into the cage next to Cold Raven. The cage had three walls made of metal poles, and the fourth wall was stone. The ground was stone as well. A hole was cut into the stone wall, too high to reach, that allowed the waning daylight to pour through. Some symbols were carved into the wall, but he didn't know what they meant. They looked like the symbols he remembered from the *libro*.

The cage was empty except for an old wooden pot in one of the corners. It smelled like body-water and feces.

Many Wolves looked at the cage beside him, opposite Cold Raven. It held a white man. His hair was long, and he had long, scruffy hair growing from his dirty face as well. He scowled at Many Wolves and mumbled some strange white man words. *They put their own men in these cages too*, Many Wolves thought.

Then Many Wolves turned and faced the Nokoni leader. Cold Raven was singing a song to himself—it sounded like a prayer of some kind—but it was not loud enough for Many Wolves to hear clearly. "Cold Raven," he asked, "where are we?"

Cold Raven glanced at Many Wolves briefly, but said nothing. He had the same despondent eyes that Malone had before he died. *He does not want to be disturbed.*

All the soldiers had left the lodge except one. This soldier walked up to Many Wolves holding a bowl in his hand. The soldier said the Spanish word "maize," which Many Wolves had heard before. He put the bowl to his mouth and pretended to eat it, then pointed at Many Wolves. *He wants me eat it.*

The soldier placed the bowl of maize on a flat object made of stone, then slid it on the ground so Many Wolves could reach it. He then retrieved a stone cup with water in it and placed it in the cage. The soldier again put his hand to his mouth. *Eat it.*

Many Wolves wasn't hungry, but he was thirsty, so he drank the water. His hands burned and itched where the rope had been tied around them. He needed to relieve his body-water, so he flipped up his breechcloth and sprayed the stone wall.

The soldier banged on the metal poles on his cage and yelled at him, interrupting his release. Many Wolves didn't understand the *mexicano* words, but the soldier kept pointing at the wooden pot.

He wants me to spray in the wooden pot. So Many Wolves walked over to it and finished releasing his body-water in the pot.

"Bravo!" the soldier smiled and yelled, clapping his hands together. "Bravo!" He said other words too, but that was the only one Many Wolves was familiar with. The soldier walked back to the wooden thing he was sitting on.

That must be what the white men and mexicanos use the pot for.

Exhausted, Many Wolves curled up on the floor. Darkness crept in through the holes in the stone wall. He wasn't sure he could sleep, because the fear in his mind was buzzing like a beehive. *What will they do to me? What kind of torture does the white man do?* He didn't want to think about it. He had experienced torture from Thorn Bird. He had seen bodies that the Northerners had tortured and mutilated. He could see that Cold Raven had been beaten, but he didn't see any injuries worse than that. *Maybe they are waiting to torture us together?*

Cold Raven was still chanting a prayer of some kind. *Perhaps that is all that I can do too*, thought Many Wolves. *Pray that the Great Spirit will bring me the bravery of my white father.*

Shizeede

"Hey! Hey, *indio!*"

Many Wolves heard metal clanging. Startled, he jumped up. In his mind, he was hunting deer with Malone in the high country. But as he looked around, he realized that this had just been a dream, and now the reality of the human cage squeezed his mind from all sides. From the light streaming in, he guessed it was morning.

"*Indio!*" the soldier yelled again, then banged his long gun against the cage. This was a different soldier from the previous night. Two men stood next to him, both of them familiar: Little Sky and the Green-Eyed Coyote.

The soldier opened the door to let the two men inside, then closed the door behind them.

"Sit down," said Little Sky, speaking with Lipan words. He wore only a breechcloth and a bandanna around his head.

The Green-Eyed Coyote sat on a wooden seat he had brought with him. Little Sky sat cross-legged on the ground, as did Many Wolves. The light *mexicano* wore a black *mexicano* hat, a red shirt, and black pants. He also wore the hard leggings with the shiny metal circle on the back, which had sharp edges all around it.

"This man here, his name is Ramon Con-Lee," said Little Sky. "That is his name from his white father. The Northerners know him as the Green-Eyed Coyote." The Lipan talked to Many Wolves as if they were strangers. Their friendship was long ago forgotten, it seemed. "He wants to ask you some questions."

The Green-Eyed Coyote said some *mexicano* words to the Lipan, then turned to Many Wolves as Little Sky translated.

"What do you remember about your white-skinned parents?"

"Why should I answer your questions?" asked Many Wolves defiantly. "You have not shown me friendship, Little Sky. I thought we were friends. And I don't know this man. Why should I help him?"

"If you want any hope of returning to your people, you should make friends with him. Our friendship is dead, Many Wolves. You eat, you drink, you sleep with Northerners now. I cannot be your friend."

Many Wolves thought for a moment. *Is there anything I should hide from these men?* Though the Green-Eyed Coyote was his enemy, there was a softness to his voice, a kindness in his eyes. Many Wolves would trade his answers to find out more about this man. And he felt there was a friendship being offered by the light-skinned *mexicano*. Perhaps befriending this man would help him leave this cage.

"I did not know my white-skinned parents," said Many Wolves, choosing his words carefully. "They were killed by Northerners when I was very young. I saw the attack in my dreams. I found out that Laughing Crow killed them and tortured my father."

Little Sky translated for the Green-Eyed Coyote, who listened very intently, though it seemed like he was having some difficulty understanding the Lipan's words. Perhaps Little Sky did not speak the *mexicano* words very well, thought Many Wolves. Then the *mexicano* reached into his shirt and pulled out a torn page from a book. It looked like a page from Many Wolves's *libro*. He handed it to Many Wolves.

"Do you know what this is?" asked Little Sky.

"*Haa*. It's a *pagina* from the *libro*. The *libro* belonged to my white parents."

He knew the page well. It was the page with the white man's symbols and the wolf picture—the only picture in the *libro* with colors.

"The picture of the wolf. Is it the same picture that is drawn on your shield?"

"*Haa*. Malone drew this picture on my shield."

Little Sky talked with the Green-Eyed Coyote, then spoke to Many Wolves again. "That wolf picture in the *libro*. That is the Con-Lees' family picture."

Many Wolves didn't understand. "What do you mean?"

"It means that Ramon's family is also your white-skinned parents' family. Ramon wants to know why your friend's name was Malone. That is a white man's name, and your friend wasn't a white man."

Many Wolves recalled the story that Malone told him when he died. "Malone took the name of my white-skinned father. He saw my white father die. Malone told me this just before he died."

Many Wolves watched the Green-Eyed Coyote as Little Sky told him this. The *mexicano* looked at Many Wolves and smiled. It was not the smile of an enemy, but of a friend.

Little Sky spoke again. "Ramon's father had a brother named Malone, which means your fathers were brothers. Ramon and you are *shizeede*. You are cousins."

Many Wolves felt a strange warmth inside as he looked at the man who smiled back at him. His eyes were like the eyes that Many Wolves saw when he looked at his reflection in a mirror or a lake. He had spent so many winters thinking about who his white parents were—and now he knew his father's name. He had thought all of his white family was dead— but now this man was alive. He felt as though a web had been strung between them now.

"Con-Lee," Many Wolves said.

"That is your white-skinned father's family name. His white name was Malone Con-Lee."

"Con-Lee," Many Wolves repeated. "Do you know my mother's name?"

Little Sky asked Ramon the question and then translated the answer. "Her name was Mad-line. But people called her Mad-dee."

"Mad-dee," Many Wolves repeated, but he had no picture of her in his mind anymore after so many winters. That unpleasant dream had faded away from his memories. His white-skinned parents were just names to him now.

He wanted the Green-Eyed Coyote to tell him more about them, and he wanted to know more about the man who was his cousin. This strange and unlikely conversation had pulled him away from the misery of his situation, at least for the moment.

"Ramon wants me to tell you some things about your white-skinned family," said Little Sky.

The Green-Eyed Coyote smiled at Many Wolves and began speaking. The Lipan translated his words.

"Your father was a farmer," Little Sky said. "He grew plants in the earth and raised animals for food. He lived in the village south of the Great Cliffs called San Antonio. He was also a good hunter. Ramon Con-Lee doesn't know much more about him because he disappeared when Ramon was very young. Your father and Ramon's father arrived at the village of San Antonio on a large boat that came from the white man's lands across the Great Sea. Ramon's father built lodges like this out of stone. Ramon's mother was Isleño, from the Canary Islands in the Great Sea, and was dark-skinned like a *mexicano*. His father was killed by *indios* too."

Many Wolves tried to understand the words, but there were many things he didn't know. He had never been to this San Antonio village and had never seen a boat or an island, though he knew what they were. But it pleased him to hear that his white father raised animals and was a hunter like him.

"My father's *libro* had many pictures of birds in it. He must have liked birds like I do," said Many Wolves with pride. "Those pictures gave me many ideas on training hawks."

"Ramon says that there are white men across the Great Sea who train hawks to hunt like you do. It is the pastime of princes and kings, who are the rich and powerful leaders of the white man's villages across the sea."

Many Wolves wondered about the white man's villages across the sea. He knew that the Spaniards and the French traders came from these villages. Malone had once told him that there were as many white man's villages across the sea as there were stars in the sky. It was hard to imagine such a place.

More questions popped into his mind. "Why does the white man want to take our land when he has his own villages across the sea?"

The Green-Eyed Coyote listened to the question and then answered it to Little Sky.

"Many white people are unhappy with their villages and their leaders. They want to find a new village to have a new start with their life, away from these leaders. This land they call 'Tejas.' It is good land to grow food and raise animals. Some white men believe if they work hard, they can become rich men and leaders in Tejas."

"Why can't they let us have the good buffalo lands?"

"Because more and more white men are coming each day, so more and more land is needed for them."

The *mexicano* talked with Little Sky again.

"We must go now, Many Wolves, but Ramon has one more question. Was the girl we saw your daughter?"

"*Haa.* Her name is Taimah. Her mother's name is Ninakabaru. She is Lipan like you, Little Sky."

"Taimah knows how to train birds and wolves like you?"

"*Haa.* She has already mastered training in a way that I could not. Malone has taught her to ride a horse and to shoot a bow like a Northerner," said Many Wolves with great pride.

The Green-Eyed Coyote looked at Little Sky as if he had figured something out, then the Lipan spoke again. "It was her arrows we found on Esatai's body?"

"*Haa.*"

Little Sky and the Green-Eyed Coyote stood up and signaled to the soldier to let them out. As they were about to leave the lodge, Little Sky said, "Ramon will talk to Lead Fingers about freeing you, but he does not promise anything."

Then they were gone.

A Plea for Mercy

When Ramon woke up early the next morning, the first thought that came to his mind was that he had family again. It had seemed almost impossible to him that this man Many Wolves was his cousin. They were so different. Many Wolves was an *indio*, and Ramon had grown up hating *indios*. Many Wolves had spent his life living in the wilds, while Ramon had lived in the largest *villa* in Tejas. They didn't even share a common language. It seemed the only thing they had in common was the color of their eyes. But after what he had heard from Many Wolves, there was now no doubt in his mind. They were family.

After his visit with Many Wolves, he had told Little Sky that he wanted to be alone. He rode out of town and found a grassy hill to sleep on, surrounded by the full moon and the stars. Captain Mac had taught him that his camp was anywhere he dropped his saddle. He enjoyed this freedom, not being bound to the civilized world. Maybe that was another thing he shared with his wild cousin.

He thought a lot about the girl, too, as he lay under the stars. He guessed she was around sixteen years old. She sounded just as dangerous as the *norteño* warriors who had killed half of their men the previous day. It was hard to picture a young woman, or even an average man, killing a powerful warrior like Esatai, but the piercing arrow wounds in Esatai's body showed otherwise. The arrows had been shot with the strength of a warrior.

Ramon put his boots on, then his serape and hat, and slung his saddle on his horse. The hot sun had already melted the dew away and he didn't want to waste another moment. He didn't know what Captain Mac's plans were for Cold Raven and Many Wolves, but he knew the captain would not let them sit in a Nacogdoches jail for much longer.

As he rode back into town, he heard a piano playing in the town's saloon. *Cornelius. He will know where the captain is staying.* Ramon tied his horse out front and walked inside. The place was empty except for Cornelius and a man and woman who looked like the owners.

The large man behind the bar tipped his hat. "Mornin', sir."

Ramon nodded back to him.

The woman, who was sweeping up in the back, looked up briefly but didn't say anything. She seemed to be enjoying the music much more than the man was.

Cornelius smiled and raised his hand when he saw Ramon, pausing to play the piano one-handed for a time before returning his waving hand to the keyboard. "Nothing rouses a man's soul, Mr. Connelly, like a healthy serving of allegretto in the morning! Let me finish this dissertation and then I will grant you my full attention."

Ramon nodded. How anyone could have this much energy in the morning was beyond his understanding. Usually it was mescal or a good woman that put an ordinary man in this kind of a mood. But then, Cornelius Potts was no ordinary man. And his piano playing was better than any Ramon had ever heard in San Antonio, though most of the musicians there preferred the guitar.

Cornelius finished his lively song with a gentle ending, then opened his eyes to look up at Ramon. "How might I be of assistance, Mr. Connelly?"

"Do you know where Captain Mac is staying?"

"Yes, of course," said Cornelius, stroking his mustache. "He is the most distinguished guest of a Mr. John Tuttle, who is the proprietor of the town's livery and, I believe, a dear old friend of the captain. You will find his modest dwelling about a mile past the main thoroughfare on the left side."

"Thank you, Cornelius. A good day to you," said Ramon, tipping the brim of his hat.

"I am indeed tickled to have been of some assistance, Mr. Connelly," said Cornelius, removing his own hat. "A pleasant day to you as well."

Ramon rode through the town, past the blacksmith and coffin maker, who were both busily tapping away with their hammers. He wondered if the coffin was being made for Biggs or one of the other men who had died. Captain Mac had said something about a church funeral for the fallen men, but Ramon had forgotten the details. A few of the bodies had been brought back to town, per Captain Mac's request, but most had been buried where they died.

He located the Tuttle house easily enough. It was a single-room log cabin with a small porch in the back. He found Captain Mac sitting on that porch, reading a book.

"Connelly, what brings you out here?" asked the captain, his voice unusually cheerful.

Ramon dismounted and tied his horse up. "I have a matter I'd like to discuss with you, Captain."

"Well, sit down then," said Captain Mac, motioning for Ramon to sit in the chair next to him. He pulled out his pipe, packed it with tobacco, and lit it.

"Mind if I smoke with you?" Ramon asked.

"Not at all, Connelly. You have your own tobacco?"

"Yes, sir." Ramon pulled his church-warden from his side pocket and prepared the chamber.

The captain's eyes studied the pipe for several moments. "Thats a nice pipe, Connelly. If you ever run into another one like it, I'll pay handsomely for it," he said with a grin on his face.

Ramon puffed a few times to fire up the embers. "I'll keep my eyes peeled for one, sir."

The captain nodded appreciatively. "So, what is it you wanted to discuss?"

"It's about the prisoner, Many Wolves." Ramon felt suddenly nervous bringing up his request with the captain. "I've recently discovered that he's kin to me, sir."

Captain Mac took his pipe out of his mouth and puffed out all the smoke. "What? He's family?"

"Yes, sir. A cousin to be exact. Our fathers were brothers."

"How can you be certain?"

Ramon took the page from Many Wolves's book out of his pocket and handed it to Captain Mac. "This is the Connelly family crest, sir, and you see the name 'Malone Connelly' there at the bottom."

"Who is Malone Connelly?" asked Captain Mac, looking it over carefully. "It's not that *indio*, is it?"

"Malone Connelly was my uncle. Many Wolves said his *indio* friend took the name for himself."

"I admit, it's a very odd name for an *indio*, and I expect not that common for a person of Irish descent either."

"You're right, sir, not very common at all."

"So, where did you get this page?" asked Captain Mac, handing it back to Ramon.

"I found it hidden in Many Wolves's shield."

"I don't think he was hiding it, Connelly. The *indios* use pages from books to reinforce their shields."

Which explains why there were a lot of pages in the shield, thought Ramon. "Many Wolves said that he's had the book all his life. It was his only possession from his real parents. They were killed by *norteños*, or Comanches, as you call them."

"Well, you got the same damn green eyes as him, Connelly, I'll admit to that. But I don't see any other family resemblance between a civilized man such as yourself and that savage."

Ramon took offense to the term "savage" being used to describe his own cousin, but he held his tongue, not wanting to offend the captain. If Captain Mac had been at the jailhouse last night, would he have thought differently of Many Wolves? Ramon was sure of it.

"So, let's all agree for the sake of argument that you and Many Wolves are cousins. Is that all you have to discuss with me? I'd like to get back to my reading."

Ramon was feeling nervous again. The captain's tone didn't give him much hope. "Captain, sir, I'd like to ask you to release Many Wolves to my custody."

"Whoa, whoa, whoa. Connelly? Are you out of your damned mind?"

"Can I speak my mind, sir?"

"Speak it. I'm growing impatient."

"This man is my only remaining kin, sir. He and his daughter. He's not a savage or a bad egg, sir. If you heard him speak, you'd be convinced of it yourself. Let me take him back to San Antonio. From what Little Sky has told me about him, he has the skills to be a good tracker, sir. You will need more trackers in this war with the *indios*."

Captain McCord sat back in his chair for a moment, composing his thoughts. Then he set his pipe down and leaned over toward Ramon, staring squarely into his eyes. "I ask again, are you out of your god-damned mind, Connelly? That damned cousin of yours bleeds god-damned Comanche blood! How many of my men did he kill yesterday? That hellish black wolf of his killed at least five, according to Colonel Tejada. Did you see the bite wounds on Possum Jack's arm and leg? He was ripped apart by that god-damned animal! I got to hope to God that horse doctor can sew him up. And this god-damned *indio* friend with the messed-up Irish name killed several of my men too!"

Ramon had never seen Captain McCord like this. He'd gotten a glimpse of his temper when the captain met Colonel Tejada, but otherwise the captain had always been calm and collected, especially in the face of danger. It was this self-control that had earned him the respect of his men and made him a great leader.

The captain was about to smoke, but then withheld his pipe. "Sure as shit, Connelly, I was having a damned good day, and you know why?"

"No, sir."

"I was minding my own damned business, relaxing and reading my book. Trying to forget the horrifying deaths of my men yesterday. Trying to forget this god-damned knife wound in my leg, which hurts like hell now that you got me all riled up!" Captain Mac leaned in closer and lowered his tone. "I tell you this, Connelly. When the sun goes down today, the hangman is gonna send those last two *indio* sons of bitches to their graves. Then all the four *indio* leaders will be as dead as dormice and it will be the greatest god-damned celebration this little hellhole of a town has ever seen."

The Last Sunset

Soldiers came to the cage lodge as the afternoon sun was fading away. Many Wolves was hoping to see the Green-Eyed Coyote with good news from Lead Fingers, but his *shizeede* never came. The soldiers' arrival was not a promising sign.

Two of the soldiers opened his cage, and one of them made Many Wolves stand by prodding him with his long gun. The other soldier pulled his hands back and tied them together tightly with rope.

"Where are you taking me?" asked Many Wolves.

They did not reply, probably because they did not understand him.

He looked over and saw two other soldiers tying Cold Raven's hands the same way.

The four soldiers led the two captives out onto the big path in the middle of the village. A crowd of people had gathered to watch them, many more than the previous day. Some were cheering, while others were yelling at him with angry faces. It reminded him of the time Thorn Bird led him through his village before his torture. *I must prepare myself for torture.*

Cold Raven held his head up and stared straight ahead , singing softly to himself. *How is he preparing himself?* One boy threw a stone at the Nokoni leader, hitting him in the back, but Cold Raven did not cry out. He merely grimaced, then continued singing.

Many Wolves recalled that at least half of Cold Raven's men had died in the battle. How terrible it must be to know that a battle you planned had failed, and that, as a result, many of your men were now dead and most of your village was gone. Perhaps this explained Cold Raven's silence and indifference. Cold Raven didn't even know yet that his own brother was dead—or that it was Many Wolves who had killed him. It didn't matter now.

The Nokoni leader had kept his promise of friendship, while his brother Esatai had not. Cold Raven had taught Many Wolves a great lesson in forgiveness—a lesson not easily forgotten. Many Wolves knew that it would be a devastating loss to the Nokoni people if this great leader was taken from them. Cold Raven's fathers, Laughing Crow and Thorn Bird, had chosen vengeance over forgiveness and had died for it—but that had not been Cold Raven's choice. Many Wolves was convinced that Cold Raven would have been the greatest Nokoni leader of them all. But now it looked like he would never see his people again.

Up ahead stood a structure built of wood, with two looped ropes hanging from it. They reminded Many Wolves of the snares he used to make when he was younger. He understood their purpose. *Those are for us.*

He spotted Lead Fingers and Tejada sitting together on wooden seats under a large tree. They were smiling and laughing together. He also saw the Green-Eyed Coyote and Little Sky standing together watching the procession, but their faces were somber. Several other men were standing near them with white bandages on arms, legs, or shoulders. Lead Fingers' injured men, Many Wolves guessed.

The soldiers led Many Wolves and Cold Raven up some steps onto the wooden structure. One of the loops of rope was placed around Many Wolves's head and tightened behind his neck. Next to him, the same was done to Cold Raven. They faced the crowd now, almost all of them strangers. Some faces held smiles. Some angry stares. Others were solemn and emotionless. A few men and boys jeered.

Lead Fingers stood up and waved his hand, the crowd quieted. He shouted words which Many Wolves did not understand in a tone that was cheerful and celebratory. When he was finished speaking, he raised his *pistole* into the air and fired a single shot. The crowd clapped and cheered, some of the men fired their *pistoles* as well.

The Green-Eyed Coyote, or Ramon Con-Lee as the white men knew him, walked up and stood between the two captives, a *libro* in his hand. The crowd quieted as he started to read from the book in the white man's words. *Is this some kind of blessing or prayer from his world?*

(*The Lord is my shepherd; I shall not want.*
He maketh me to lie down in green pastures.)

Many Wolves believed he could have been friends with this man if circumstances had been different. There was a kindness about him that Many Wolves liked, and his eyes were trusting. He was different from all the other white men here; he was above them. Many Wolves felt honored to be his *shizeede*, his blood. But they would be family in this world only for a short time, it seemed. *I hope he will find Taimah just as he found me. She should know her white family.*

(*He leadeth me beside the still waters.*
He restoreth my soul.)

The finality of the moment fell on him suddenly, like a heavy stone in his heart. *These are my last moments in this world.* He looked out at the people again, then looked past them, toward the grassy hills and the brilliant orange sky. He wondered what Nina was doing now. *Does she know I'm not coming back?* He tried to remember what he said to her the very last time he saw her, but it was hard. Instead he reached further back into his memory, to happier times—like the first time she had given her heart to him on that rainy night long ago, and the look on her face when she saw her daughter for the first time.

(*He leadeth me in the paths of righteousness for His name's sake.*
Yea, though I walk through the valley of the shadow of death)

Crashing through his daydream came the raspy cry of a hawk. He looked up at the orange sky and saw them: three birds, circling. Three wolf hawks. Instantly his memories fell back to his childhood, and he thought of Reina, Cazador, and his favorite, Chiquito. *Are they here to welcome me to the spirit world like the Cloud Eagle?* The thought made him smile.

The birds circled closer and closer until they were just overhead. Everything was quiet now except for the Green-Eyed Coyote's prayer and the calls of the three birds.

(I will fear no evil, for thou art with me.
Thy rod and thy staff, they comfort me.)

One of the birds dipped from the sky and rolled several times. Many Wolves shook out of his daydream; he realized that these hawks were from this world and not the next. *Taimah is here.* Suddenly, all the pain and the dread of the moment floated away as if these birds had somehow lifted the burden from his shoulders. He blocked everything else from his mind except the birds, the gorgeous sunset, and the peaceful voice of his newfound friend.

(Thou preparest a table a table before me in the presence of mine enemies.
Thou annointest my head with oil; my cup runneth over.)

He thanked the Great Spirit for painting this last sunset for him and for bringing him a sanctuary in these final moments. He thanked the Great Spirit for bringing the Green-Eyed Coyote to him, and for helping him to discover his white family. He thanked the Great Spirit for his life brothers, Ten Arrows and Malone. *I hope to see you, my friends, in the next world.*

"Thank you for Nina and Taimah, Great Spirit. Keep them safe in this world," he said to himself. "And thank you, Earth Mother, for my friendships with the animals of the earth."

He saw Flecha fly past him and land in a tree close by. The bird was looking at him, his head cocked to the side. Many Wolves knew it was Taimah saying goodbye to him. *My heart is with you always, Wildflower.*

*(Surely goodness and mercy shall follow me all the days of my life,
and I will dwell in the house of the Lord forever.)*

The Green-Eyed Coyote stopped with his prayer and turned to Many Wolves. "I'm sorry I couldn't save you, my brother." He said these words perfectly in Lipan, though it wasn't his native language. Many Wolves saw the water in Ramon's eyes and the kind look on his face, and smiled back at him.

Someone covered his head, leaving him in darkness.

A loud sound followed, and Many Wolves fell into a new life.

Another Request

Ramon watched as the soldiers gathered the two bodies and placed them in coffins on a carriage. The soldier who was driving the carriage pulled at the reins and commanded the horses to move forward. Another soldier on horseback followed the carriage out of town.

Cornelius approached Ramon. "That biblical excerpt was eloquently read, Mr. Connelly. If there is a God, I'm sure he was listening."

"Thank you, Cornelius," said Ramon graciously.

"Those hawks showed up as if they were doves released at a matrimonial ceremony. One of the most unusual things I have ever witnessed at an execution."

Those were his friends, Cornelius, saying farewell to him, Ramon thought, but he chose to say nothing, not wanting to reveal what he knew about Many Wolves. He knew that Cornelius's relentless curiosity would demand to know everything.

"It would have been fascinating, Mr. Connelly, to say the least, to have discussed ornithological matters with this man. Sadly, he chose to oppose us, and the cruel hand of justice has taken him."

Ramon smiled and nodded his head in agreement, but still said nothing. *It was fascinating, Cornelius, to know him.*

"I see that your thoughts are otherwise preoccupied, Mr. Connelly. I bid you good day, sir." Cornelius tipped his hat, bowed his head, and walked away.

Ramon was curious to know where they were taking the bodies. He had a notion to claim Many Wolves's body himself and take it back to San Antonio—but for that, he needed Captain Mac's permission, and after their last encounter, Ramon believed he was not in the captain's most favorable graces. He hoped, however, that this request was a simpler one. The captain had achieved what he had sought—the deaths of the four *indio* leaders. Perhaps he would now be more cheerful.

Ramon asked a passing soldier, "Do you know where I can find Captain McCord, *por favor?*"

"*Sí,* Señor Connelly" said the soldier. "You'll find him with most of the *hombres* in the saloon. Colonel Tejada and Captain McCord will be buying the first couple of rounds. I am on my way there now."

Ramon walked with the soldier toward the center of town. The soldier was young, probably still in his teens, and he was familiar. "You are from San Antonio?"

"*Sí.* I remember you from the cattle drive to Saltillo. I was one of the men who pulled you out of the Rio Bravo."

Ramon was embarrassed that he didn't remember the soldier. "I'm sorry, I don't remember your name."

"*Me llamo* Pedro Garcia."

"Nice to meet you, Pedro."

"Well, here is the saloon, Señor Connelly. I need to find an *amigo. Buenos noches!*"

"*Buenos noches,* Pedro."

The saloon was bustling with activity—a much different scene than what he had witnessed earlier. Colonel Tejada's soldiers sat together at the bar, and most of the tables were occupied by Captain McCord's men and townspeople. A few ladies were dressed to entertain and were circling about the patrons trying to earn a few silvers for their services.

Ramon spotted the captain sitting with Colonel Tejada and another soldier. As he approached the table, it was Colonel Tejada who saw him first. "*Hola,* Ramon! Come have a drink with us and help us celebrate this great victory!"

"No, *gracias.*" In Ramon's heart he felt it was more of a day of mourning than celebration. "I wish to speak briefly with Captain McCord, *por favor*." Then he turned to face Captain Mac. "May I have a word with you in private, sir?"

"I don't think there's anything you can say to spoil my mood today." Captain McCord stood. "We'll talk outside, it's quieter."

Ramon followed the captain out. The saloon already seemed even louder than it had been when he first walked in.

"Well, what is it then?" The captain's face was close enough for Ramon to smell the liquor on his breath. Ramon had only once seen the captain drink before.

"I'd like to take Many Wolves's body with me to San Antonio and give him a proper Catholic burial. I'd like to bury him next to my parents, since he's family."

Captain Mac's face betrayed nothing, but when he spoke, he was cordial enough. "You hardly know the man, Connelly. But I can't say I'm surprised by the request. I don't know any good reason why you can't take it. One less grave for the colonel's men to dig tomorrow."

"Where did they take him?"

"It's a graveyard about a mile east of town. You can't miss the tombstones. You can ride out in the morning with the gravediggers, if you like."

"Thank you, sir."

"You're welcome. Now, you should loosen up and have a few drinks with the men. Today is a great day in Tejas. If you'll excuse me, I have a bottle waiting for me at the table." With that, the captain walked off.

After their heated exchange earlier, Ramon was relieved that this conversation went well. It seemed that the captain didn't harbor any ill feeling toward him. *Of course, whiskey in a man's stomach can make him a lot more agreeable.*

Ramon knew that Many Wolves probably had his own god, but reading Psalm 23 before he died and receiving Father Padilla's blessing was as much as Ramon could do for his cousin's soul. *Just because you aren't Catholic, doesn't mean you're going to hell.* He had always believed that. His father once told him that a man's good deeds could save him—no matter what god he believed in.

A Shadow in the Night

"It would be better to take Many Wolves back to his *casa*," said Little Sky.

It was a clear night, and the full moon was low on the horizon. Ramon and Little Sky were sitting around a small fire away from the town celebration, each smoking a pipe. In the distance Ramon could hear loud voices singing and shouting, and an occasional gunshot. The saloon had no doubt sold more whiskey and mescal today than the rest of the year combined, he thought.

"I don't think I would make it there alive," said Ramon. He had told Little Sky about his request of the captain.

"Crooked Eagle would not touch you. Respect for the dead," said Little Sky, looking at him from across the flames. "The Great Spirit's blessing is far better than any from a white man's god. Without this blessing, Many Wolves's spirit would remain here, haunting the people he loves."

Little Sky's words made Ramon think carefully. "I know if I died, I would want a padre like Father Padilla to bless my spirit. The place that you speak of for restless spirits is called *purgatorio* in my religion. It is not heaven and it is not hell; it is a waiting place in between."

"You want your cousin to go to this waiting place?"

"No. I want a better place for him."

"Then return him to his people."

Ramon thought about what to do. His father would have wanted a Catholic ceremony for a deceased family member. But Ramon wasn't his father, and he had always believed that religion was a man's own choice.

Many Wolves had chosen his own gods, and Ramon agreed with Little Sky that he should honor this choice.

"Would you take this journey with me, Little Sky?"

"I would do this with you, though he was my enemy," said Little Sky with conviction. "We should take Cold Raven's body as well. If we head west, Crooked Eagle's scouts will find us."

"We will need the captain's permission to take Cold Raven's body too. We will travel in the morning?"

"*Sí*. We must collect their weapons. They will need them in the next world. We can get the *capitán's* permission then."

"I don't know where Cold Raven's weapons are," said Ramon. "I have Many Wolves's quiver and his shield—what's left of it."

"*Capitán* Mac has Cold Raven's things at his lodge," said Little Sky. "We should get them now and journey at sunrise."

Ramon agreed. "Let's go."

The two men rode back into town toward Tuttle's place. The saloon was still loud and bustling. A couple of men walked out, one helping the other, who was too intoxicated to walk for himself. The two men stopped in the middle of the road, and the drunken one vomited all over his own boots. Ramon and Little Sky steered their horses clear of them.

Once out of town, the noise quieted, and Ramon could hear the crickets again. The two men picketed their horses next to the front door of Tuttle's house, where the captain was staying.

Ramon heard the twang of a bow coming from the back of the house, followed by a man's groans. Then another twang followed that. "Did you hear that?" he whispered to Little Sky.

"*Sí*. Other side."

They moved quietly along the side of the house. Ramon heard growling and snarling, as if from a large animal, and then a man yelled. Ramon's *pistoles* were drawn, and Little Sky held his knife in his hand as they moved slowly along the wall.

"What the hell is going on?" said a man from inside the house.

"Noche! Colmillo!" yelled a voice—a girl's voice.

"Oh, God! Jim!" said the man's voice, followed by the loud blast of a shotgun.

Then the sound of two more hissing arrows sang through the air—and a man screamed.

Ramon turned the corner of the house and saw two men bleeding on the back porch. Ramon leapt onto the porch and ran over to them. One of the men was Captain Mac. He wasn't moving.

"Get in the house!" Ramon yelled to the injured man, but the man just reeled in anguish, his blood pooling on the porch floor.

Ramon looked out into the darkness and saw a horse with a shadowy figure on it. *Many Wolves's daughter. Taimah.* Lower to the ground, two pairs of eyes reflected the back porch lantern light. *Wolves.*

Ramon did not take a shot. He held his *pistoles* up in the air.

The figure on the horse commanded, "Noche! Colmillo!" and then other words Ramon didn't understand. The growling calmed a bit, but it did not stop.

The man who was hurt crawled inside the house, still groaning in pain.

"She said, 'He is our friend,'" Little Sky said.

"Noche and Colmillo must be the wolves," said Ramon. *Noche is the black wolf Captain Mac had talked about.*

The girl yelled again, and Little Sky yelled something back at her.

"She wants to know if you are the man with the *libro*," Little Sky said quietly.

"What *libro*? Ask her what *libro*."

Little Sky spoke to her again. "She said the man holding the *libro* when her father died."

"Tell her that I am that man," said Ramon, "and that I know she is Taimah, Many Wolves's daughter."

Little Sky nodded and spoke to her again.

The injured man was still moaning behind them. The Irish *vaquero* slowly put his *pistoles* back in his belt. *She is not my enemy.*

Taimah yelled something again, Little Sky replied, and then she yelled something else.

"She wanted to know our names. I told her my name and then said your *indio* name was Green-Eyed Coyote and your white name was Ramon Connelly. She wanted to know if you tried to save her father and why you called him brother."

How does she know that? "She heard what I said to Many Wolves right before he died—but she wasn't there to hear it," said Ramon, confused. "Remember, Little Sky, you taught me to speak those words in your language?"

"*Sí,* I remember. Her spirit bird heard it," said Little Sky with certainty in his voice.

"Tell her I tried to save her father, but he is not my brother. Tell her Many Wolves's white father and my father were brothers."

"*Shizeede,*" Taimah yelled back in the tone of a question, then said something else.

"What does that mean?" asked Ramon.

"Cousin."

Little Sky listened to her words and then spoke again. "She wants you to bring her father's weapons and shield to her. She knows they are here."

Ramon walked back to his horse and pulled the quiver and remains of the shield from his saddlebag. Then he walked back to the porch. "Tell her I have his quiver and what's left of his shield."

"She says to bring them to her."

Ramon walked cautiously toward her. The wolves' growls grew louder, and the girl said their names again to calm them. As Ramon came closer, he saw that her horse was black. She was wearing a deerskin shirt and an animal-skin breechcloth, and holding a bow. The details of her face were hidden in the darkness.

He held the quiver and shield up for her, and she bent down to grab them. He saw that her hair was dark brown and her skin was lighter than that of most *indios*. Her body, legs, and arms were thin, but muscular. And in the faint light, he caught a glimpse of her eyes. *Her eyes are green.*

Taimah whistled loudly, calling the names of her wolves again, and then rode off, fading into the darkness like a ghost.

Ramon ran back to the house. The wounded man was still alive, with two arrows buried in his chest. "Are you Mr. Tuttle?" Ramon asked.

"Yes," he moaned.

"Hang on, Mr. Tuttle. I need to find something to stop the bleeding." Ramon found an old coat in the house, then rushed back to the injured man. But when he returned, Little Sky just looked at Ramon and shook his head. Mr. Tuttle was dead.

Ramon walked over to Captain Mac's body. Two arrows were sticking out of his chest, and his neck had been ripped open by the wolves. His Colt *pistoles* were still in his belt. *He didn't have a chance against her.* Ramon removed the *pistoles* and put them in his own belt for safekeeping. Then he shut the captain's eyelids.

Rest in peace, Captain McCord.

"Why didn't you kill her, Ramon?"

Because she is the last of my kin, Ramon thought. But aloud, he said, "I wouldn't have had a chance against her and those wolves."

"She will be hanged for this," said Little Sky in a defiant voice. "Like her father."

There had been so much death in these last two days, Ramon thought. All the rangers killed in the war, and now Captain Mac. And Many Wolves, who had been his friend, too.

Many Wolves's daughter, Taimah, had killed Esatai and Captain Mac. She was his family, he knew that for sure, but was she his friend? Or his enemy?

Ramon needed to go home, back to San Antonio, to sort it all out. There wasn't anything he wanted more at this moment than a relaxing evening with Don Eduardo and Doña Maria at his home in Bexar. But first, he had to deal with the mess of these killings.

The Bounty Hunters

Word of Captain McCord's killing spread like wildfire through the town of Nacogdoches. Many of the townspeople were spooked by the news, thinking it was the ghosts of the dead *indios* returning for blood and revenge. Some of them sought sanctuary in the town's only church, inherently afraid of the supernatural. And as Ramon soon learned, it wasn't just Captain McCord and Mr. Tuttle who were killed—Ramon's friend Colonel Tejada and the soldier guarding the two *indios'* bodies had been killed also. *Many Wolves will be buried with his family and his people, as it should be.*

John Chesterfield, the local lawman, heard the news and asked Ramon and Little Sky to join him at the jailhouse around midnight. Cornelius, who was a good friend of Chesterfield's, was there too, as was the soldier Pedro Garcia, who had been the one to find the body of Colonel Tejada.

"Tell me what you saw, Connelly," said Chesterfield in a deep voice, standing and leaning against the single table in the middle of the jailhouse. His face glowed in the candlelight. He was a large man with a long mustache, and he wore a large, dark brown bowler hat.

"It was one rider and two wolves. The captain was already dead when we got there, and Tuttle was injured," said Ramon. He was curt, trying not to offer too many details that would lead them to think he was friends with the killer.

"Indian woman!" said Little Sky, in broken English. "Daughter of Many Wolves!"

"I'll be damned! Is that right, Connelly?" said Chesterfield, raising his bushy eyebrows in genuine surprise.

Cornelius looked just as surprised. He shot a glance of disbelief at Ramon.

Ramon nodded. "Yes."

"So much for this malarkey about Indian ghosts," said Chesterfield. "It was a vengeance killing, plain and simple. Any more details about her, Connelly? Her age, her size, her hair? Anything distinctive?"

"It was too dark to see anything, and she was on a horse," said Ramon, which was mostly true, except for the brief instant when he had caught only a glimpse of her face.

Chesterfield looked over at Little Sky, perhaps hoping for more information from him, but the Lipan just shook his head. Ramon was glad that Little Sky did not tell them that Many Wolves was Ramon's cousin, or that the girl was therefore his family as well. He hoped the Lipan would keep that knowledge locked away.

"You got a chance to look at the bodies, Corny?"

"Yes, I did, John. The arrows in the four deceased men all had the same signature."

"What do you mean by signature?"

"Indians mark their arrows with unique symbols and colors. The markings were the same on all these arrows," said Cornelius in his usual matter-of-fact manner. He showed Chesterfield two arrow shafts. "You see how they correlate? One of these was extracted from Captain's McCord's corpse, and the other from Colonel Tejada."

"So it was one person who done all these killings?"

"Yes, it was, John. One human killer, anyway. This woman also had some assistance from *Canis lupus*—two of them to be exact."

"*Canis lupus?*"

"The gray wolf. There were canine wounds on the necks of both Captain McCord and Colonel Tejada. And I would add that the killer picked an opportune time to attack these two great military men."

"Why is that, Corny?"

"Because they were both inebriated."

"Does anyone happen to know the name of Many Wolves's daughter?"

"Taimah," blurted Little Sky.

Please don't say more, thought Ramon.

"How did you come across this information, Little Sky?"

"Many Wolves told us while he was in jail."

"Did he tell you where we could find her?" asked Chesterfield.

"Deep in Comanche lands."

"Hmm. Well, that will make things difficult," said Chesterfield, scratching his chin.

"These deaths won't be classified as casualties of war?" asked Cornelius.

"No, Corny." John Chesterfield cast a stern look at Cornelius. "They were cold-blooded killings, plain and simple. The law will see it as such."

"In that case, you won't have to find her," said Cornelius.

"You won't have to find him," said Cornelius.

"Why is that?" asked John, raising his eyebrows again.

"Because Captain McCord comes from a financially well-off family back east. His father, a high-ranking military man, will pay top dollar for the apprehension of his son's murderer, and it won't matter in the least if she's dead or alive. And I am also quite certain that the Mexican governor of Tejas will throw quite a few pesos into the kitty as well to find Colonel Tejada's killer. So you see, the greedy bounty hunters will do your bidding for you."

"Ramon, ask Garcia here if that is true about the governor," said Chesterfield.

Ramon asked the soldier this question in Spanish.

"*Los cazadores de recompensas*," said Pedro to Ramon. "They will come."

Cornelius understood the soldier's words and repeated them to Chesterfield. "The bounty hunters will rise out of the ground like locusts."

The Romero Palace

After a long ride back to San Antonio, Ramon arrived at Don Eduardo's place just before nightfall.

"You two do your *hombre* talk," said Doña Maria. "I have some chicken and beans that I can warm up for you, Ramon. We already had an early *cena*."

"If it's no trouble, Doña Maria. *Gracias*."

"It's nice to have you home," said Doña Maria with bright eyes and a big smile. She left him alone on the patio with Don Eduardo.

"I found some of that cherry tobacco that you like," said Don Eduardo, handing him a pouch. "I always save the good stuff for you." He chuckled.

"*Muchas gracias*, Don Eduardo." Ramon took the pouch and held it to his nose, letting the aroma of cherry tickle his senses.

"Sit, *por favor*, and tell me how the fight with the *indios* went."

Ramon lit his church-warden with the new tobacco and told Don Eduardo everything. He described his training with Captain McCord and Possum Jack and his friendships with Little Sky and Cornelius Potts. He talked about the peace talks with the *indios* and described Cold Raven, Esatai, and Many Wolves.

"Why was a *gringo* fighting for the *indios*?"

"The *norteños* killed his parents when he was very young. He was adopted and raised by the Lipanos. His story is *muy fascinante*."

"Do not stop on my account, Ramon," said Don Eduardo, grinning and releasing his smoke into the night air.

Ramon told him what he learned from Little Sky. How Many Wolves had learned to survive in the desert with his hawks and wolf, and how he had killed Laughing Crow and Thorn Bird.

"Laughing Crow. I have heard of him. He is known in stories as *Avispa Negra,* the Black Wasp. There has never been an *indio* as feared as him, Ramon. Many believe that he was the one responsible for killing your father and his brother's family. This Many Wolves is a brave man and great warrior to kill two *norteño* leaders, and especially this Laughing Crow."

"It was his animals that gave him the power to kill these great *hombres,*" Ramon said. "His birds were his eyes, and the wolf was his weapon in battle. It is an animal *magia* that even Little Sky doesn't understand."

"Why was he fighting with the *norteños* then?" Don Eduardo asked with a confused look on his face. He poured two cup of red wine from a clay jug and offered one to Ramon, who accepted.

"I asked Little Sky the same question." Ramon laughed. "Many Wolves made peace with Laughing Crow's son, Cold Raven. Cold Raven held back his vengeance so Many Wolves would fight against us. Captain Mac always said that Cold Raven had wisdom beyond his years."

"How old was he?"

"His early twenties."

"How old was this Many Wolves?"

"Mid-thirties, I believe."

Ramon took a sip of wine and then swirled it around his mouth. Don Eduardo's wine was always smooth to the tongue, unlike other wine he had tasted. It was nice to be home again in his good friend's company, enjoying the finer things in life.

"Don Eduardo, you remember my Uncle Malone?"

"I knew of him, Ramon, not nearly as well as I knew your father."

"What do you remember about him?"

"He was a farmer. I remember buying maize and pigs from him. He wasn't as *prospero* as your *padre,* so your *padre* helped him with *dinero.* He had a lovely wife from Ireland and a small *chico.* One day they disappeared. Your *padre* suspected they were captured and killed by *indios,* perhaps by this Laughing Crow. That's all I remember. It was a terrible day for your mother and father."

"That small *chico* was Many Wolves," said Ramon.

"What? That is amazing!" Don Eduardo set his wine cup down. "That means he is your cousin!"

"*Sí,* Don Eduardo. He *was* my cousin. I met him briefly after Colonel Tejada captured him and put him in jail. That's when I discovered he was my cousin. But he is dead now. Captain Mac had both Many Wolves and Cold Raven executed in Nacogdoches last night."

Don Eduardo moaned with disappointment. "A firing squad?"

"No, a hanging. Captain Mac declared that the war was over, and there was a big celebration in town that night. But it was far from over."

"What do you mean?"

"The *indios* got their revenge for the hangings. Or I should say, one *indio.*"

Don Eduardo was captured by Ramon's story. He held his pipe down to hear the rest of it.

"Both Captain Mac and Colonel Tejada were killed that night, and two other men as well. They were all killed by arrows." Ramon took a puff from his pipe. "And wolf bites."

"Colonel Tejada is dead?" said Don Eduardo with sadness in his voice.

"*Sí.* I'm sorry, Don Eduardo, I know he was your friend. He was my friend as well."

"It is terrible news, Ramon," said Don Eduardo. He made the sign of the cross and mumbled a prayer to himself. When he was ready, he spoke again. "Let's get back to the story. You said they died of wolf bites? It sounds like the ghost of this Many Wolves came back for revenge."

"Many of the townspeople thought it was a ghost," said Ramon, taking another sip of wine. "To me, the truth is almost as unbelievable."

"Go on. Don't leave an old man hanging."

"The killer was a señorita of fifteen or sixteen *años.* She was half *gringo* and half *indio.*"

"Many Wolves's daughter?" Don Eduardo guessed.

"*Sí*. Her name is Taimah."

"She has the same animal *magia*?"

"*Sí*. Many Wolves believes that it is even stronger in her. He also said that she learned to ride and use a bow from a *norteño* who was his closest friend."

"Ah, so she is as much of a warrior as her father."

"*Sí*. I saw her in the darkness after she killed Captain Mac. I probably should have tried to kill her, Don Eduardo, but I just couldn't lift my *pistoles*, knowing that she was the last of my family. She did not intend to harm me either, because she knew I was kind to her father."

"What did you do for him?"

"I read Psalm 23 from *La Biblia* just before he was hanged."

"She was at the hanging?"

"In a strange and almost unbelievable way, she was. Her birds were there and she saw the whole thing through them. It was surreal, Don Eduardo. Those birds flying around him during the *ejecución*."

"What will you do? She is your last *familia*."

"I don't know. It sounds like there will be a large reward on her head for killing those men. I'm sure she will hide in the wilderness. That's what her father did for so many years." Ramon paused to take a drink of wine and to clean his church-warden. "We killed their leaders, and they killed ours. Nobody really won this god-damned war."

"Ramon, your father would not like you taking the Lord's name in vain."

"I'm sorry, Don Eduardo."

Doña Maria poked her head out onto the patio. "Your *cena* is ready, Ramon. Come when you are ready."

"*Gracias*, Doña Maria. I'll be there *un momento*."

Ramon looked back at Don Eduardo, who was cleaning his pipe. "You asked me what I will do, Don Eduardo. I know one thing. I will not fight this damned war anymore. I will stay here in San Antonio for a while and work for you and the *ranchos* around here." He paused. "I have a favor to ask you."

"What is that, Ramon?"

"Taimah is my *sangre*, my blood. I would like this to be a secret between us."

"I understand. She is a fugitive of the law, and you are a protector of it. Your secret is safe with me, *mi amigo*."

"*Gracias*," said Ramon. He collected his thoughts. "This Many Wolves was a very impressive *hombre*, Don Eduardo. He had huge scars on his leg and back. They looked like claw marks from a bear or some other large animal. He also had many scars that looked like knife wounds. I suspect that his was not an easy life—and yet his manner was very peaceful, very likable. Captain McCord called them all savages, but this man was no savage. I wish I could have gotten to know him better. I think we could have been *amigos*. You know that feeling you have with certain people?"

"*Sí*. It was the same thing with your *padre*, Ramon. We were *amigos* almost immediately after I made his acquaintance."

For a while, there was a silence between them. Then Don Eduardo spoke at last. "Is going to Mexico City with Maritza still a possibility?"

It had been some time since Ramon had thought of Maritza. He recalled his last visit with her and how she had treated that poor family. It still burned him to think that she had this disrespectful quality about her. Her beauty was tantalizing, and he knew in his mind he would never find another woman like her. He wanted the events of the past few days to settle down so he could think about these things more clearly.

"I don't know, Don Eduardo. Maritza is the most beautiful girl in Bexar, but there is one thing she is missing."

"What is that, *mi amigo*?"

"Compassion."

www.ingramcontent.com/pod-product-compliance
Lightning Source LLC
Chambersburg PA
CBHW020500260626
47156CB00006B/1800